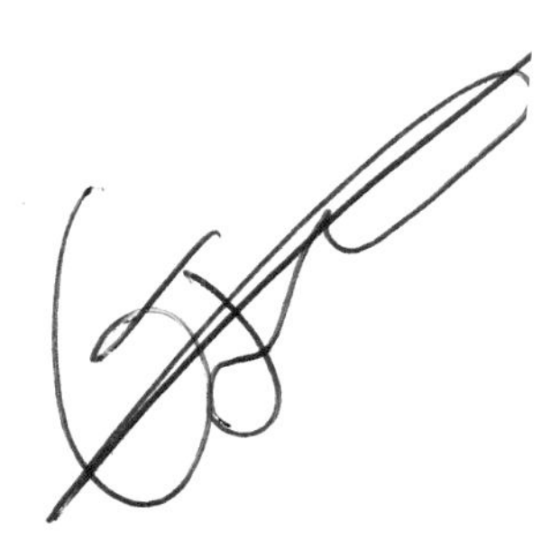

Fate's Ambition

G J Stevens

British Library Cataloguing-in-Publication Data
A catalogue record for this book is available from the British Library

Cover design by James Norbury
www.JamesNorbury.com

ISBN: 9781081692254

Other Books by GJ Stevens

Post-apocalyptic Thrillers

IN THE END (Nov 2018)
BEFORE THE END (Nov 2019)

SURVIVOR – Your Guide to Surviving the Apocalypse – Out Now

Agent Carrie Harris Series

OPERATION DAWN WOLF (Dec 2019)
Grab your free copy at www.gjstevens.com

DEDICATION

For Jayne. You make me.

ACKNOWLEDGMENTS

To my friends who inspire me every day and sometimes let me work on my passion, despite being on holiday!

Thanks to all those who helped me along the way, be it big or small, I am grateful

Prologue

I

Fisher followed behind her slender outline, their feet in step along the corridor. His survey swept in time with her dull torch beam as it cut through the darkness, bobbing from the white-washed walls and across the dust of the faded tiled floor.

Agent Harris slowed as they approached a pair of grey, windowless metal doors. In the same moment, both reached around, pulling handguns from their waists.

Fisher caught a distorted reflection, the straight line of his shoulders and the long open cut across his right cheek.

"Did you hear that?" he whispered.

Harris' tight strawberry ponytail bounced as she gave a shallow nod, her eyes pinched in concentration.

Fisher took the lead, pushing the weapon out in front before giving a light touch to the door. The smell hit as it cracked open; not strong, but recognised in an instant.

Without pause he pushed on into the darkened room. From behind, the narrow cone of Harris' torch found a metal table in the centre of the room, soon catching a pasty white ankle laid on top. Fisher watched the light slowly scan up the leg, along a sunken stomach to a faint scar between the curve of shapely breasts and on to the face of a young blonde.

She was beautiful, even in death.

Fisher swallowed as he turned, his heart pounding, looking beyond the light, nodding.

"It's her."

He felt Harris step at his side, the arch of light catching her face, bouncing along its soft angles to the index finger at her lips. In silence they stood rooted to the spot, he strained to hear anything above his breath.

A lifetime passed and Fisher moved his lips to speak, but nothing came.

In an instant, the air pulled from his lungs as he caught a metallic clatter in the distance.

The sound remained still, the pencil beam of the torch searching around the tiled room. He felt Harris' hand, her warmth on his as she pointed up, urging him to look at the ancient ventilation grill in the ceiling.

Pushing the gun into his waistband and stretching out on his toes, his fingertips touched the rough metal as it hung slack against its mounts.

The light faltered and, in the darkness, rusted metal fibres rained down as he felt his way around the edge.

With the light stuttering back, closer this time, he worked the first screw between his thumb and forefinger; the metal sagging more with each painful turn.

The noise came again, at least in his ears, and he crushed the screw harder whilst willing it to speed. Feeling it give, Fisher's eyes followed it to the floor, willing himself to catch the tiny object before it could clatter.

Harris caught it mid-air and he released a breath as the grill, with its decayed surround, fell, smashing to the tiles in a shower of ancient dust.

His hand shot to his mouth, desperate to stifle a cough. With the cloud of dust sparkling in the light, his gaze snapped toward the door.

An eternity passing, he followed the light as it drifted back upwards to the exposed shaft. Feeling a void open in his chest, all hope dashed as the beam lit the rotten, pitted metal rising above their heads.

About to lean close, he stopped when light poured in and he watched as dark figures screamed with rage, bursting through the double doors with machine guns silhouetted, their crosshair dots resting on his chest.

His eyes wide in terror, he stumbled back, only just able to snatch a look to his side. Harris's face resigned, one arm heading above her head, the other lowering the gun to the floor.

“It's over,” she said, shaking her head.

"They'll kill us," Fisher replied, watching as the dark figures marched forward, with more piling through the doorway behind.

Staring with disbelief, his heart felt as if it beat out of his chest.

"They'll kill us," he repeated.

Taking a step to his side, he clamped his hand to her wrist and, with all the force he could muster, he blurted out, "They'll kill us."

Her movement stopped.

Harris looked him in the eye, hers as wide as his.

She turned, raising her gun.

A flash lit the room and she fell backwards with each suppressed explosion.

II

Days Later

In the dimly lit corridor, Fisher drew back from the door handle, his tall, smartly-dressed escort getting there first. Instead, Fisher's upturned palm moved to shield his eyes as sunlight surged from the opening reinforced double doors.

"Sorry for the misunderstanding," the suit said, squeezing his lips in a smile.

Fisher smiled back as he walked past, spread his hand out and tipped a shallow bow. As his right leg crossed the boundary, he heard the deep voices bellow from behind.

Chancing a glimpse, he walked as two agents clad from head to foot in black body armour headed the charge through the double doors.

A light breeze blew across his face as a chorus of screams erupted from behind the advancing agent's masks. Without a second thought, Fisher pushed past his escort, ignoring the confusion written across his face and launched himself into the bleak scrubland.

The shouts grew louder as agents poured out and in blind hope he ran towards the chain-link gates. This wasn't the first time he'd been outside of the facility but he was determined to get further than the last time.

A shot rang off, echoing across the landscape as flocks of birds took to the sky. Fisher spun around and wasn't surprised to see eight dark figures gaining with alarming pace, each with an automatic killing machine aimed at his legs.

Pulling up from his flat-out sprint, the agents swarming, he lowered himself to the ground and set the stance he knew he'd be forced to perform.

He placed the side of his head on the soft mossy ground, being careful not to catch the dressing taped to his face and watched with a smile, through the forest of leather boots, the sight of his bemused escort still holding the heavy doors wide.

III

"Mr Fisher, my name is Ross. Brian Ross," the wiry man sitting opposite Fisher announced in a deep English accent, which seemed to contrast to his lean frame. Like the others before him, he couldn't quite place its origin.

Fisher didn't reply. He didn't need to. Brian Ross knew all too well who he was. Instead, after letting thoughts of the fresh air from moments before evaporate, Fisher looked around Interview Room Five with a spark of interest. He'd never been in this particular room before and apart from the numbered door, only one difference told.

It wasn't the dark wooden table or the two plastic chairs he thought were deliberately uncomfortable, or the stale air, he guessed made deliberately cold, or the lack of windows or the single solid wooden door next to his current interrogator. It wasn't that the walls were painted the same cheap magnolia or the harsh fluorescent lights sat in the yellowing suspended ceiling.

It was the long, narrow mirror, or lack of, that he'd spent so many hours staring at while avoiding their questions.

Early on he'd decided the truth was too fantastic, too unreal for anyone to believe, so he'd decided to stay quiet, to ride out the time until they gave up and let him go.

But they had more time than he did.

"The door's locked and I don't have the key," Ross said, stirring him from his thoughts.

Fisher tried his best to ignore the statement but couldn't help turning his head. This was new and he let his expression tell. He tried to let his mind drift, concentrating on Ross's deep-set eyes pronouncing his forehead, drawing out his long, angled face shadowing the surrounding skin.

Fisher smiled as he imagined thick whiskers striking out from his nose.

"It can only be opened from the outside."

Fisher's view snapped back into focus, his gaze following Ross's finger as it pointed to a discrete circle of camera lens in the corner above the doorway.

"Shall we start from the beginning?" Ross said, raising a brow.

Fisher closed his eyes and rubbed his temples.

He'd been in this facility for what he guessed had been four days. During the day he would sit in some drab room where a man in a cliché black suit would ask him questions. Sometimes they would just talk about the weather, football, even though he had no interest; sometimes they would play back his life story, or what their sparse files said.

Sometimes they wanted to discuss the dead girl. So far, he had kept pretty quiet; they hadn't asked about his ability, even though three times now he'd convinced his interrogator to let him walk out of the building. Each time he had been chased down and forced to the floor.

Now they seemed to have figured out how to stop him.

"How's Agent Harris?" Fisher said, repeating the question he'd asked so many times.

"She's fine," Ross replied, giving the same stone-faced response Fisher knew so well.

Still, he didn't believe them.

He'd seen the single bullet smash into her body. He'd watched as she lay contorted, motionless, slumped against the wall with no sign of breath.

His plan wasn't working. For the last two weeks he'd been on a rollercoaster ride, four days at least in this place, and so much happening before. Still, it wasn't time for the ride to end. He knew what they wanted and maybe the only way to get out would be to give it to them, both barrels. But he couldn't be more scared.

Since his parents died, he'd been afraid he'd end up in a room like this, but maybe he had to take the risk. Maybe they weren't going to lock him up, cutting him to shreds to find out why he could do what no one else could.

They'd had a glimpse already; that wouldn't be enough. Was it time to answer their questions? Was it time to tell them why he was in the derelict asylum next to a dead body when they found him? Was it time to tell them how he corrupted Agent Harris so easily? Was it time to tell them why eventually Ross would be so willing to let him go?

What else could he do? They held all the cards.

He was captive. He'd tried his best and he couldn't afford any more time. Fisher didn't know if there was any time left.

He drew a deep breath.

"People just believe me," he blurted out before he lost his nerve.

"Sorry?" replied Ross, raising his eyebrows.

"People just believe me," Fisher repeated, and drew another deep breath as Ross stared back, his face fixed in a frown.

"I don't," Ross said, and a grin grew on Fisher's face.

"You will."

Ross rubbed his teeth against his bottom lip. "They believe anything you say?"

"Anything plausible."

Ross screwed his eyes up, still playing his teeth against his lip.

"Example?"

Fisher looked up at the camera and pictured a room full of black-suited men leaning towards TV monitors.

"If I told you this room was fluorescent green you wouldn't believe me."

Ross nodded.

"But if I told you the corridor was on fire and we need to leave or we'd die, then it would be different."

"Why don't I believe you?"

"It was just an example."

"You can choose if you want me to believe?" Ross said after a pause, his eyes narrowing.

As Fisher nodded, he watched Ross's expression change.

"You'll understand why I'm having a hard time with this."

"Give me your hand," Fisher replied, offering his own rough palm.

Ross looked at Fisher's face, then over his shoulder. After a short pause he lay his left hand down on the table and Fisher placed his palm on top before speaking again.

"Let's say I told you I'm a doctor."

"Not a huge leap," nodded Ross.

"I'm a brain specialist and I trained alongside the best. Smith. Evans. Jones, to name a few."

"Go on."

"I noticed you have a large vein on the right-hand side of your head," said Fisher, pointing to a lump above Ross's temple.

Ross lifted his right hand to the spot. "I've always had that."

Fisher's eyes narrowed. "I noticed it when we first started talking."

"Let's talk about something else, other than me." Ross's tone elevated as he pulled his hand from under Fisher's.

Fisher jerked his hand forward and caught the escaping limb.

"You can trust me," he said, his voice calm and even, lowering his hand back to the tabletop with Ross's hand following. "It's a classic indicator of an issue with blood flow. You need to be careful when you get stressed," he said, then paused again as Ross bit at his lower lip.

"It could cause a blood clot. I've seen it happen so many times before."

Fisher watched as Ross's skin paled with each patiently delivered word.

He leant forward against the table and lowered his tone. "If you don't want a brain clot you should remain calm. Avoid stress." Fisher lifted his gaze towards the door. "I suggest you get some air."

He watched as sweat collected on Ross's hooded brow, his fingers pulling at his tight collar.

"Are you okay? It's getting hot in here, isn't it?"

Ross's eyes widened and his breath laboured. He stood, almost tripping over his own feet as he moved towards the door, his eyes blinking as he pulled, white-knuckled at the handle.

Fisher stood.

"It's locked. Who's going to open it? What if they've forgotten about you? Or popped out for coffee or fallen asleep? What if the camera's stopped working?"

Fisher watched as Ross's eyes snapped wide.

"Let me out," Ross screamed as he hammered on the door.

Fisher moved backward and out of range of the flailing fists. Quicker than he'd expected, a voice boomed from the other side.

"Stand back."

The lock clicked and the door opened. The black metal barrel of an automatic rifle appeared through the gap.

"Down on the floor," screamed the voice.

Without hesitation, Fisher went to his knees, his hands out in front, lowering his torso to the ground. As his head went down to the polished wooden floor, he saw Ross push past the armed suit, gasping for breath, his hands red raw.

Fisher smiled as he turned to the side and settled his head to the floor.

After what seemed like only a few seconds, he heard a new voice, deep and low. A sudden calm came over him.

"Mr Fisher, please take a seat."

Fisher turned his head and saw a silver-haired man, his aged face rough as tree bark, filling Ross's seat.

Lifting himself up, Fisher checked off the uniform in his head. White shirt. Black suit and tie.

The guy was older than all the other agents and wore a smile, reminding Fisher of his long-dead grandfather.

Slowly getting back to his feet Fisher dusted himself with his hands and with deliberate steps, moved back to his chair where he hesitated.

"Please sit down, Mr Fisher," the old guy said, gesturing forward.

Fisher felt like sitting; he felt like listening to this old man's voice.

"I'm Nick Dawson," said the old guy. "That was pretty impressive."

"Thank you," said Fisher, a questioning lilt to his voice as he folded his arms.

Dawson took a sip from a Styrofoam cup. "Do you mind if I call you James?" he said as he rested the cup back to the table.

Fisher shrugged.

"How's the face?"

Fisher pulled his hands up to the rectangle of dressing across his cheek. He'd forgotten about the small injury and nodded across the table.

Dawson's lip curled in a smile. "You've answered at least one of our questions," he said, then paused to take another sip. "But I need you to fill in the rest of the blanks. Please tell me what on earth is going on."

Fisher breathed in the pause. This guy was good. He made him feel safe and Fisher wanted to help. He felt like he wanted to talk. Still, something told him he shouldn't. Something told him nothing would be the same if he gave him everything.

Dawson began to fill the empty space. "We sent Agent Harris to investigate an MI6 operative who'd been acting out of character."

Fisher nodded.

"Harris missed her check-in. You can understand we were alarmed. She's one of our best. We protect our own."

Fisher nodded again.

"It took us a while to find her, and you."

Fisher kept quiet, stifling a smile.

"We knew it unlikely she'd been kidnapped. You probably know by now she's more than capable of looking after herself."

Fisher let the smile bloom.

"So she must have gone by her own free will." The deep lines around Dawson's eyes pushed together as he squinted. "But I'm not sure if I can use the term 'free will' anymore."

Fisher's smile dropped.

"So what's this all about, James?"

"Why'd they shoot her?"

"Self-defence. You'd do the same," Dawson said without pause.

Since Fisher had last saw Harris he'd gone over the moment every time he'd closed his eyes. He knew there was no escaping the reality of what he'd done. It *was* self-defence. It *was* his fault. He'd made her believe their lives were in danger. He *was* sure they were going to shoot, but maybe they weren't after all.

Fisher looked up at Dawson. "How much time have you got?"

Dawson smiled. "As much as you need."

Part One

Two Weeks Earlier

1

"She's gone," Andrew said, his eyes wide as he looked around the group of friends sat at the bench in the darkened garden, bass pouring from the door of the pub at his back.

"What do you mean gone? Gone where?" James Fisher said, stepping towards his best friend.

"She's not there," Andrew said, his palms bared at his front.

"You went in the ladies?" George said, as he moved up to James's side.

"I asked some bird cleaning the toilets. She checked for me. Nothing. I asked if there were any more toilets. There isn't. Had a little scout round, it's still busy, but I couldn't see her anywhere."

With the concern in Andrew's tone, James picked up his phone and called Susie's mobile. He stood, turning with his ear to the air, listening for the ring as he moved, scanning the darkened garden until the speaker replied with the tone of her voicemail.

"It's in her glove box," said George as James hung up. George rose from the bench, leaving the last of the friends, Alan, still sitting clutching his empty glass.

James scowled in his direction. Alan scowled back.

"She's gone off with someone, no doubt," Alan said, tipping the glass to his mouth to catch the last drop.

James's eyes widened. "Suze isn't like that. Don't be a twat and get off your arse."

Alan looked to the dark sky, then, scowling, he stood and followed the others as they headed inside. Separating, they pushed their way through the scores of merry tourists.

George and James were the first to return. As each of them met back outside, they reported finding no sign; between them they'd asked almost everyone but no one could remember seeing her.

"Where the hell is she?" James said, scratching at his forehead.

"I'm stumped," said Andrew.

Alan nodded in agreement at his side.

"She wouldn't go off with anyone," said George. "Would she?"

"No chance," James said, shooting a scornful look at Alan.

"Maybe the drink went to her head when she stood up. Maybe she wandered back to the campsite," said George.

"Possible," James replied. "Someone head back to the site and see if she's there."

"Good idea," said Alan. "We'll go slow and keep an eye out."

Alan and George trooped off through the car park, soon disappearing from view and into the darkness.

Andrew headed back inside while James waited to see if she turned up or if the others reported back. As he paced around the front garden, he stared intently at the people sat at each of the five tables as he drifted back through the last few days.

He remembered the feeling as he woke to the spritely voice of his phone warbling at his ear. Jumping from the bed as if it were on fire, he was ready in seconds, scooping up his heavy pack, smiling when reminded by the weight and swaying to balance as he negotiated the stairs.

That feeling of the night before, his Christmas Eve, the fatigue from a fitful sleep becoming just a memory as he swapped obscenities with Andrew when he found him stood by his own rucksack, tinkering with its contents.

As happened each year, they'd been planning their adventure for over three months. Their close group of friends were this time hiking in Snowdonia; three days of aching legs, dehydrated food and fidgeting for comfort on the hard floor of the tent.

A scream at his back pulled him back from his memories and he span round. It came from a group of friends, still teenagers maybe. A plump girl lay on her back, pulled down by a friend who could barely stand.

James turned as the table billowed with laughter.

He remembered back to the journey; the first hundred miles flying past the windows, lost in conversation. James and Andrew reminiscing, as they often did, about their first meeting in French class where they were forced to sit together at the age of twelve to begrudgingly find they had a surprising amount in common. It hadn't been long before they became inseparable.

Their teenage years sealed the friendship. Passing the test of ups and downs, even when neglect came with the advent of the few girlfriends, and when Andrew's future wife took so much of his time.

They'd settled into adult life together, knew everything about each other. When James left home for university and Andrew started an apprenticeship the opposite end of the country, they still kept in close touch. Sometimes months went by without seeing each other because of the distance, but every time they met it was like they'd only been together the day before.

At university, James made lots of new friends, Susie, George and Alan amongst them, but rather than Andrew feeling left out and drifting away, the friends became mutual. More recently, Andrew had been there for James when his parents had died, both murdered with the case remaining unsolved. Andrew and Susie had brought him back from the brink of doing something stupid.

He owed them his life, even though he didn't think they knew it.

His thoughts turned to Andrew. He'd been back in the pub for what seemed like an age, but checking his watch, it had only been a few minutes.

James turned back to the darkness of the car park.

He remembered Susie had called him on the way up.

"Did you manage to bring your spare sleeping bag?" she'd asked.

"Of course," he'd replied.

"You're an angel, Jim. We'll see you soon. Kisses." He heard her smack her lips together as she hung up.

"Would ya?" Andrew had said, smiling.

"Don't be ridiculous. It would be like doing it with a sister."

"You're an only child," Andrew had said, flashing his eyebrows. "I would."

"Everyone knows you would," James had said, watching the Mondeo slip off the motorway.

James recalled the rest of the journey was taken up with Andrew's favourite subject; grilling James over his lack of love life.

Andrew was often vocal about the subject. The ingredients were there. He knew women were attracted to James. He witnessed it many times. His manual job kept him in shape and gave him a weathered look that women seemed to like.

It wasn't down to lack of opportunity, either; James would be out with Andrew and together they'd flirt with girls, but a rare kiss in a club was as far as it ever went.

As always, the conversation ended with James's hands held up in surrender. He was happy and the time just wasn't right.

Later that morning they'd arrived in the tiny village of Llanberis, their notice only pricked as they caught its brightly-decorated buildings and packs of tourist climbers already congregating on the streets.

James and Andrew were the first of the friends to arrive at the campsite situated under the looming form of Snowdon.

The site was a working farm, formed of small fields no good for crops or animals and instead given over to tents and campfires.

After erecting the tent with practiced ease, it wasn't long before James caught sight of Susie's cream Nissan Micra.

James shook the memory from his mind and looked back to the pub to see Andrew coming through the door, his face falling as he saw him alone.

James's phone vibrated, his heart racing as he fumbled it from his pocket. It was Alan.

"You find her?" he snapped.

"No," came George's voice.

James conveyed the message to Andrew with a shake of his head.

"Shit," Andrew said as he took his turn to scan the faces around the garden.

James was about to speak when George came on the line to interrupt.

"Her car's gone."

2

With heavy feet, James trudged by Andrew's side at the start of the long steep driveway to the campsite. It was the same driveway he'd run to as he'd seen Susie's car approach with those stupid fluffy dice that seemed to obscure her view as they hung from the mirror.

He remembered jogging over, waving his arms as she parked next to the tent before rushing over with her arms wide and squeezing both of them in a long hug.

"Love the new look," Andrew had said, with James watching his eyes widen at the sight of her brown hair now bottle blonde.

"Thanks," she'd replied with her trademark bright-white smile beaming back. "Got a part in a play starting on Monday. Gonna see if I have more fun."

As with George, who had stayed in the car tapping at the screen of his phone, they'd been placed in the same student flat and since the very first party they'd got on like a house on fire.

James and Susie grew very close, partly because during her second year she broke her arm during a violent mugging. The break was so severe she had to have it reset under a general anaesthetic, where she soon discovered she had a rare resistance to sedation and pain medication.

Her condition meant an uncomfortable six weeks of recuperation. James stepped up, supporting her studies, helping her around the house and comforting her as she slowly dealt with the trauma. As the bone in her arm mended, they fused together as friends.

At the end of their time at university, Susie went on to act in many roles. All were minor, either obscure satellite TV or theatre. She was still waiting to hit the big time. With shoulder-length brunette hair, a clear complexion and being neither tall nor short with a slender body, you had to be blind not to find her attractive.

She didn't have a boyfriend the group knew about and she wasn't worried about being single. Andrew would regularly tell James he didn't think her best assets were her contagious smile and her willingness to have fun. Although the guys in the group started off their friendship wanting more, over the last ten years she'd made it clear it was all they were going to get. Susie had become one of the lads. No one needed to moderate their behaviour and there was no need for a separate tent, although James knew the blonde look would be a test for some.

As James saw the dark space where her car had been, he heard Alan's raised voice.

"She's fucked off," Alan said, but before George could reply, James butted in.

"No," James said, panting for breath. "She hasn't," he shouted.

"Where's her car gone then?" Alan said, pointing to the empty space lit only with the moonlight.

"What the hell?" said Andrew, equally out of breath.

"Jump in your car," Alan shouted, but George quickly blocked his path.

"No. We've all been drinking. Anyway, we don't even know where she went."

James shook his head, his breath starting to recover. "Someone must have stolen it. They must have. She wouldn't just up and leave like this."

He looked around his friends and saw their downcast expressions, George's head swaying from side to side.

"Shit," James shouted over and over into the night sky.

"What the hell is she playing at?" Alan said.

James looked up and Alan fell silent.

"Why is a better question," Andrew said.

"I don't believe it," James added, turning on the spot, squinting at all angles, searching for her car in the darkness. "Sure, she can be a little moody sometimes. Can't we all, but I didn't see any sign she was upset. Why the hell would she just up and leave?"

He didn't look up from the dark grass as he pulled out his phone and hit her number. He listened to three rings before the line went silent.

"Susie?" he said, excitement in his voice. A long tone came from the speaker. Wide-eyed, he thumbed her number again and her chirpy recorded voice came back. He turned away and stared up at the blanket of bright stars.

"You okay?" Andrew said, his voice closer than James expected.

"Yeah," he lied, blinking away a vision of her car in a ditch covered in morning dew.

"What about the police?" James said quietly as he eyed the entrance to the campsite.

George's voice came from behind him and James turned to his grey silhouette. "You want to be the one to tell them she's drink driving?"

James didn't reply.

"Maybe someone spiked her drink?" Andrew said as he followed James walking back to the main road. "Then again we'd have seen her leave with someone."

"Drugs wouldn't work," James said quietly as the streetlights of the small village grew brighter as they neared.

"Oh yeah," Andrew replied, his voice trailing off. "We know she's not in the pub."

James looked either side of the thin road, turning away from the brightness of the village and staring along the moonlit road heading out into the darkness. "Then we go this way."

Checking behind him he saw they walked alone with only their footsteps breaking through the silence. His thoughts soon drifted back to the day they'd arrived.

George had eventually pulled himself out of the Micra and strode over to Andrew, feigning a punch to his stomach. As they shadowboxed, James had jumped in, wrestling them both to the ground. Despite being the least fit of the group, George continued to prove himself capable of keeping up with their adventures.

Alan had been the last of the friends to arrive, twenty minutes after Susie and George. As he pulled off the driveway and onto the grass, sweeping his curls of shoulder-length hair away from his freckled face, he parked his Fiesta to the side of Susie's. Moments later, James had herded them towards to the Llanberis trail and the start of their climb.

A smile came to James's face as he remembered the click of the camera-phone whilst they balanced on the snowy peak several hours later. After a quick hot chocolate from the peak's cafe, they made their way down from the sub-zero heat. Heading back through the rock-filled green countryside, passing mountain lakes and ruined stone buildings, he remembered the sense of achievement felt like morphine for their pained calves and blistered feet.

Back at camp they had lifted their heavy rucksacks from their backs and one by one flopped to the floor to bask in silence.

George had been the first to rouse, the pull of the beer in his car too much even for exhaustion to challenge.

He remembered back to university where George had a long beard, smiling as he recalled how George only attended the first week of lectures and spent the next two years blagging his way through the course, going to as few classes as possible.

It had been a miracle it took so long before being kicked out, but leaving university had been the best that could have happened. Almost straight away George got a job and started making something of himself. After a few years working various roles, he got a job in the government doing something to do with roads, getting regular promotions and eventually ending up with some real responsibility.

No one could recall the details of his job; each time George tried to talk about it he read the friend's downcast faces and the subject changed. Last year he got married and a few months ago announced they were having a baby. His wife was due to give birth sometime in the new year and he would become the first of the friends to get into the serious business of having kids.

A long snort of air came from his side and James turned to Alan and chuckled. After finishing the cans of beer, each still warm from the car, they'd light-footed down the drive, floating on thin air without the weight on their backs and wearing comfortable shoes.

They'd stopped at a lonely ATM. Alan pulled out his bank card and James saw the opportunity, but Andrew got there first. As soon as the screen flashed up requesting the amount, Andrew's hand shot out to the buttons and the machine spat out a wad of ten crisp new twenties, to the chorus of howling laughter.

"You bastard," Alan had shouted as he scrambled to grab the notes.

Alan was George's best friend from school and would come over and stay in their halls many times a year. He was welcomed so often into the group, sometimes it became difficult to remember he didn't go to the same university.

Alan had been working his way up the Tesco management pyramid and although he had been assistant manager for a number of stores, he regularly bemoaned the wait to take a captaincy of his own.

Raised by his mum, when she died he'd had no choice but to move to Nottingham with a distant relative.

James felt a deep connection with Alan because of the effort he'd put in to help when James went through his own tragedy. He didn't appreciate it at the time, but Alan knew at least some of what he'd gone through.

"Drinks on you," was all Andrew could get out between panting laughter. The group eventually calmed with a disdainful look from a middle-aged woman waiting to use the machine, not hiding her contempt for the rowdy English tourists on her dark weathered face.

Eventually, as they moved away, Alan found the funny side; it was, after all, a classic trick he'd performed many times before.

Spirits were high and the thirst for lager strong as they headed to a pub just across the road.

It was at that point things had started to go wrong.

3

The Prince of Wales had a small bar to the left of the entrance, occupied by a skinny old lady who looked back at them with disinterest as they came through the door. With their feet sticking to the floor, they peered past the bar to a worn pool table and a broken dartboard propped at an angle on the windowsill.

With the background odour of the toilets on the opposite side of the room, their eyes were drawn to a large TV pouring out the Welsh commentary of a rugby match.

It wasn't what they were used to in London.

Andrew stepped up to the bar and after having to repeat the order three times, he carried pints to a table the furthest from the incomprehensible shouting from the TV. With drinks in hand, the friends recounted the day's tales of adventure and their surroundings faded to insignificance.

Halfway to an empty pint glass, Andrew noticed Susie sitting opposite him had stopped joining in, her arms folded across her chest while staring intently behind him.

"What's up with you?" he asked.

Susie spoke quietly without moving her eyes. "Don't look but there's a guy in the corner who won't stop staring at me."

James and Andrew twisted in their seats to see a young man staring in their direction. His prop forward build and age were the only positive things going for him. With a face covered in acne scarring and a thick white line from a repaired hair-lip, his eyes sat close together and black, unkempt eyebrows seemed to cover the top half of his face.

"I said don't look," Susie snapped. "He's freaking me out," she added, screwing up her eyes and pulling her sleeves over her hands.

George and Alan joined in the stare but still the stranger didn't flinch his look elsewhere.

"You want to swap with me?" James said, tipping his head to the side.

"So he can stare at my arse instead? No thanks," she said, then pushed her hand onto James's forearm. "Sorry. Don't worry, I'll be fine."

The trio changed the subject but Susie wouldn't join in as her eyes continued to flit back to the corner of the room.

"Let's go somewhere else," she said. They all agreed without question and set about downing the remains of their pints.

With the drinks almost empty, James turned to see Susie's eyes widen. Following her gaze, he watched the man swaggering towards them.

"Orright boys and girls?" came his thick North Wales accent.

"We're leaving," Alan announced as he stood.

"Won't you stay for another drink?"

"You're the reason we're leaving," Susie insisted.

"But we haven't had a chance to get to know each other," the stranger replied, pausing to look her up and down. "I really want to get to know you."

Susie pushed past her friends in the direction of the door, but before she got past Alan, a leg the thickness of a tree trunk blocked her way.

"Hey there," erupted James. "Let her pass."

He didn't react. Andrew jumped up from his seat and pushed his hands out but a giant arm shoved him back into his chair with such a force it took the air out of his lungs.

The stranger's gaze never left Susie's face.

James shot a look over to the bar, searching the room for assistance. The barmaid had vanished. Instead, he turned to George and Alan as they sat back down.

It was then James knew they'd already laid their hopes on him. With a sigh, he turned to Susie.

"Why don't you sit back down and we'll have a little chat with our new friend."

She couldn't conceal her concern at his suggestion, but nonetheless she moved back over to her seat.

Showing off his yellow teeth, the guy smiled and sat himself in a spare chair as James downed the last of his pint. Closing his eyes, he drew a deep breath.

"So, my friend, what's your name?" James said as he opened his eyes.

"Gwynn," the guy said, with his gaze still fixed on Susie as she cowered.

"It's nice to meet you, Gwynn." James thrust his hand out to the stranger, but he didn't react.

"Do you know who I am?" James added.

"No. You're not from round here and I haven't seen you on the telly."

"Okay. In that case I'll forgive you."

"Huh," came the startled response as Gwynn moved his attention from Susie for the first time.

"I'm a club promoter from Caernarfon. Just opened a new place in the centre of town. Mention my name on the door and you'll jump the queue."

Gwynn's expression didn't change. "I ain't seen no new clubs. I was in town wiv the lads last night."

"Well it's there."

"Where?" Gwynn asked.

James drew a deep breath. It was all he could come up with. Looking to Andrew and then at Susie, a smile hung limp on his face. Andrew grinned back.

It was easy for them. They thought it was a good way to solve problems. They thought James could just use his party trick and everything would be all right.

The first part was true; he could do it whenever he wanted but the second part was far from it. Something always went wrong and in ways he couldn't predict. It cost him one way or another, some of which he'd have to live with for the rest of his life.

"Right, fuck off you lot," Gwynn's voice boomed. "Me and the lady are going to get to know each other."

Susie turned to James wide-eyed, her hands gripping at the seat.

"James?"

4

"I'll arm wrestle you," James said, and Gwynn's face twisted in what James could only read as shock, but as Gwynn's squinting eyes looked over James's upper body, his mouth curled in the corner and began a deep, slow laugh.

"No problem," Gwynn said slowly as the laughter eased. "If you win you can all go on your way, but when I win," he paused and stretched the fabric of his shirt with his biceps, "she stays." He turned to look back at Susie. "Alone."

Despite avoiding her stare, James knew Susie's eyes were boring a hole in the side of his face.

"No problem," James replied, pushing cheer to his voice.

Susie let go of a whimper as Gwynn rolled up the sleeve on his right arm.

James didn't bother adjusting his clothes; instead, he positioned his elbow on the table, waiting and watching as Gwynn placed his hand in James's open palm.

As Gwynn squeezed, James did his best to ignore the pain, fixing his concentration straight in his heavy-hooded eyes.

"Right, Gwynn, I'm a mean motherfucker. I'm a champion arm wrestler. When I win, which I will, I'm going to crush your hand so you're going to have to get all your love from your left." James twitched the grip on Gwynn's hand and watched as a look of panic shot across his face before Gwynn jumped to his feet, pushing James's hand away as if he couldn't let go fast enough.

"You win, you win."

The friends watched as his bulk disappeared out of the back of the pub.

With Gwynn barely out of the door, Susie jumped out of her chair and rushed for the exit. The guys followed and caught up with her bent double outside the door to a shop opposite, her hands clasped between her legs and breathing rapid. Alan rushed over and she greeted him with a tight embrace; as she squeezed his upper body, she looked at James and mouthed 'Thank you.'

Saying nothing more, they walked along the road, their only aim to get further from that place. Andrew was the first to notice a pub called The Peak Inn.

Set away from the road and behind a spacious car park with wooden benches and parasols in a beer garden at the front, the two-storey building was nestled in a small copse of trees. With stone walls, a slate roof and a large, smart burgundy sign with bold white lettering announcing its name; all set in the shadow of the towering grey Dinorwic slate quarry rising in the distance.

Alan and George headed straight to the bar while the others got comfortable at a bench in the garden. It didn't take long for them to come back with the drinks and a shot of whiskey.

"In one, Susie," Alan ordered as he placed the short glass in front of her. With barely enough time to blink, the empty glass sat upside down in the middle of the table.

"Fucking weirdos," Andrew proclaimed after he chugged down the top quarter of his pint. "Everywhere we go. Dartmoor. The Broads. Snowdon. The locals are fucking weirdos."

"Yeah, it's bloody hot in that bar," Alan replied, putting his fleece back on. Everyone looked at him as he swept his hair out of his eyes.

"No, you lost me," James said, with the rest of the friends smiling in agreement as they waited for the punchline.

"It'll be the furnace in the basement where they get rid of all of the dead bodies," Alan replied.

Everyone but Andrew laughed.

With Gwynn all but forgotten, the conversation turned to work. Alan described his increasing frustration at being passed over for promotion again, with James joking that if he had a supermarket then he would let Alan run it. The others furiously nodded in agreement.

George talked about working in another government department. A sideways move with a slight incline was how he described it.

Andrew told them about being flat-out busy, driving all over the country, but with his job as a medical equipment service engineer, that's all he seemed to do.

Susie talked about her new role in an art house play. It had something to do with murder and incest, set in Scotland. She'd be playing a key supporting role and had been learning her lines for two weeks now. Not for the first time, she told them it would be *the* big one. In turn, they each duly promised to go and see her.

Their gazes then collectively fell on James.

He had excelled at school, college and university and was set for a prestigious placement with Google, but everything changed when both his parents were murdered. James never forgave himself for not saving them from their fate. He never joined the training programme and spent the next few years hidden away from all but his closest friends. Even though Andrew and Susie had dragged him back from the brink, he could never summon the motivation to join the highflying world he'd been told was his destiny.

Instead, James took a job as a tree surgeon. Although intelligent enough to run the company, he preferred to stay as a labourer. It had been five years and the friends made no secret they didn't believe he was content.

His friends patiently waited for his update.

Giving only a shrug of his shoulders in reply, Susie broke the silence.

"We graduated years ago now. When are you going to sort yourself out and get back some of that ambition we used to see?"

"I'm happy," James replied, sipping on his pint.

"You earn minimum wage, you don't use your brain and half the time you're drenched through," Andrew chipped in.

"Yeah, but I go home at night and don't have to think about the job. I work outside and I get to chop down trees."

"He has a point about the trees," added Alan with a wry smile as an unfamiliar silence settled in.

Susie broke in again. "We all know the real reason, don't we? You don't want to get involved with the world. You're going to let life pass you by."

James sighed and looked up to the shadow of the mountain. "I leave it alone and it'll leave me be," he said, clutching at his drink.

"Woah, we're getting a bit deep now," George said as he stood. "Leave the lad alone and get some more beers in."

James turned back to the table and thanked George with a raise of his eyebrows.

Andrew and Alan shared a look, taking the cue and headed to the bar. George following behind.

Susie laid her hands on the wooden bench and stretched across with a sullen expression.

"Sorry," she said. "I shouldn't have said that."

James took her hand in his. "I know what I'm doing."

Susie smiled softly across the table. "But don't you ever think about what could have been?"

James raised his eyebrows. "All the time. That's what keeps me where I am."

Susie stood and walked around the bench. James got up and they wrapped their arms around each other and held on, squeezing tight as George returned from the bar.

"Ah, ain't that sweet," he said. "That deserves a photo," and pulled out his phone. As he pressed the power button, the screen flashed for an instant then went blank.

"Pass me yours," he said, holding his hand out.

James reached in his pocket and chucked over his iPhone while Susie straightened her clothes.

"Get the pub in the background," she said, and pulled James round to the other side of the bench so they were standing in front of the building.

George followed her direction and with a quick call for cheese, the flash blinked and they huddled to see the picture.

"Nice," was all James said, sitting back down.

As if nothing had happened, Susie started suggesting locations in Cornwall for their next adventure, stopping as she noticed a young man striding towards them from the direction of the pub door. In jeans, an Arran jumper and blond quiffed hair, he'd caught her full attention.

Susie looked behind her but already knew there was no one else there. The guy was heading over to talk to her. James had barely seen that look in her eyes before.

"Good evening," the sculpted young man said, smiling to Susie, his accent sounding more like Kensington than Snowdonia. "I saw you earlier. Thought I recognised you. I just had to come over to offer you a drink." He paused as Susie tried to remain composed. "So what would you like? Sorry, I didn't catch your name," he said, not waiting for her answer.

"Um, Susie," she said finally.

He swapped a phone between his long, thin hands. "My name's Tristan. Would you like to join me inside for a drink?"

Susie shook his hand, but as George coughed, she looked in their direction to see her friends looking back with wide smiles and raised eyebrows. She returned her gaze to the admirer.

"Sorry, I'd love to, but I'm out with my friends."

Tristan tilted his head to the side and shrugged; his smile didn't leave his face as he lifted his hand and a flash burst from his phone.

"A memento," he said as the bright light broke her trance. He turned and walked back towards the door of the pub.

Susie shook her head as she looked back at James. "What a stuck-up twit. But I suppose I'd better get used to that."

Laughter burst out across the bench.

A few minutes later, George reminded them the others hadn't returned from the bar. He was about to go and make sure they weren't grabbing a sly swift one when they appeared empty handed.

"You get thirsty?" shouted George across the garden.

"Some problem with the pumps," said Andrew when they arrived at the table.

"They've taken the order and they'll bring it out," added Alan.

Before Andrew sat down, he reached into his trouser pocket, pulled out two red napkins, dropping them in front of James.

James looked down and then up at Andrew with his eyebrows raised and head tilted to one side.

"Turn them over," Andrew said. James turned the napkins over one by one to see, on each, what looked like mobile phone numbers. Two names, Clare and Fay, were scribbled above in Andrew's handwriting.

"You're married," James replied.

"They're not for me, you ejit," Andrew said, smiling.

James pushed the napkins to the centre of the table.

Andrew snapped them up and shoved them back in his pocket. "Waste not, want not." He then turned his attention to a short barmaid dressed in the black and white uniform of bar staff across the country as she carried a tray of drinks, heading in their direction. Andrew reached for his wallet.

"It's already been taken care of," the barmaid said in an Australian accent.

"Was it a Toff in a cream jumper?" asked James.

She burst out laughing.

"He owns the place," she said and turned around, still chuckling as she went back through the door.

"Looks like you made an impression," George said to Susie.

The banter continued, with subject again turning to where they'd set next year's adventure. After settling on canoeing along the River Wye and after finishing the free drinks, yawns spread around the table. They soon decided to call it a night. Dragging themselves up the steep driveway, they returned to the quiet campsite and were soon sound asleep.

***

James woke with an insistent but gentle pressure tugging at his arm. Struggling to rouse, his head felt stuffed with cotton wool as nausea rippled upwards from his belly. Thankful to the darkness, he eventually peeled open his eyelids.

"Did you hear that?" Susie said in a whisper, her breath at his ear.

As his brain deciphered her words, James strained to hear, but could only make out the rhythmic breath of his friends and a gentle breeze through the trees. He ached for sleep.

"What did you hear?" he croaked as he pushed his voice to speak.

"Footsteps outside the tent," she whispered, an edge of fear in her voice.

"It'll be someone going for a wee."

"And they were playing with the zip."

James couldn't miss the concern in her voice and despite his muscles screaming to relax, he dragged himself onto his front. Still inside the sleeping bag, he felt for the zipper of the inner doorway. With his vision slowly adjusting, he found the thin metal tag and pulled it up enough to squint out through the open flap.

Losing the fight with his heavy eyelids and barely able to take in the darkness of the porch, a wave of nausea stopped him before he could take in the first sight.

James closed his eyes and felt for the zip to draw the canvas back into place. Turning back, he faced Susie with his eyes still shut.

"It's fine. Must have been a dream. Come here," he whispered as he put his arm out.

Without protest, Susie lifted her head and his arm went under. Feeling her body envelop him in a warm glow, the tension bled from his muscles. As the first ebbs of unconsciousness lapped, he heard the outer zipper move just as sleep overwhelmed him.

***

James woke to a cacophony of birdsong, a shrill assault to his ears as a flock welcomed the new sun. With his head still clouded, his vision blurred to the bright morning.

He had no idea of the time but from the spluttering and snoring of his friends he guessed it was still early. Searching for his phone he realised his arm was still around Susie and eased himself from under her, thinking it best to save any confusion or comments from the others.

Moving, he felt the urgency to pee and pulled himself from the sleeping bag, attempting and failing to open the first zipper quietly.

Once through the porch, James watched the low sun chasing away the morning mist from the quiet campsite and, turning to his left, he congratulated himself on the choice of pitch.

Ignoring the stiffness in his legs, he jogged the few paces to a copse of trees.

With his urge relieved, he shook his groggy head and wandered through the dew-laden grass.

His attention caught on debris scattered around their tent. At first, he thought rubbish had blown across from other pitches; then he recognised his backpack and saw his clothes spilt out in a pile.

Alan surged from the tent and sprang to the copse, holding his stomach. His retching startled the birds from the trees.

"What the fuck happened here?" said Alan, appearing from the tree line, his face pallid and squinting as he wiped his mouth with the back of his hand.

"Susie heard something in the night. She woke me, but shit, I thought she was dreaming."

Susie emerged from the tent and scanned the scene with surprise. George and Andrew followed bleary-eyed.

"Is anything missing?" she said.

"My stuff seems all there, but it's soaking wet from dew," said James as he sealed his pack.

"Mine's okay," Alan came back as he picked up a couple of t-shirts by his feet and stuffed them back in his bag.

Andrew and George nodded as they picked up their untouched packs.

"Looks like yours took a direct hit," Andrew said, looking at Susie whilst he pointed to her small camping sack sitting empty on top of its former contents.

She rushed over to her bag and poured through the pile. James headed over to help but she shook her head as he neared.

Her lips pursed and her brow furrowed as she scooped up the contents, shaking off the dew. James crouched next to her.

"I'm sorry, Suze. I should have gone out and checked." He looked to the others dotted around the tent. "Shall we call the police?" he said, and watched as Alan shook his head.

"It was probably just kids," he said, colour returning to his face.

"Or drunks," George added, turning to look around the site.

"I must have disturbed them when I unzipped the inner door," James said.

"Anything missing?" asked Andrew as he came over and rubbed Susie's shoulder.

"Don't think so," she said with a solemn look down to her pile of belongings.

"Police won't do shit then," Alan replied.

George stood. "There's no harm done. Let's just get it tidied up, have some breakfast and get on with our day."

They soon each agreed they didn't fancy wasting their time waiting for the police when nothing had been stolen.

With the mess cleared, the friends gathered around Andrew's stove and drank welcome hot tea.

James turned to Alan, noticing his skin had paled again.

"How much did we drink last night?" he said, shaking his head.

"Five or six pints?" Susie replied, furrowing her brow as she tried to remember.

"Well it's bloody strong up here," Alan said before running off into the copse.

"Probably the altitude," Andrew said with a chuckle. "Feel a bit poor myself."

Topping up their liquid breakfast with cereal bars and after a quick change into fresh clothes for Susie, they packed up the gear for the hike, locking the rest of their belongings into the cars.

With the rest of the site stirring, they set off past the farmhouse and into the western side of the national park.

***

The day turned out as they'd planned and before they knew it the friends saw the camp ahead on the new horizon. Each agreed it had been a thoroughly enjoyable day, but with sore feet and legs they were ready for food and the evening's entertainment.

After confirming the tents and the cars hadn't been abused, they renewed their strength with hot pasta and once again headed down the steep driveway to find the car park of The Peak Inn full of brightly-coloured VW camper vans, four by fours and estate cars, the insides stacked past the windows with bedding, bags and outdoor gear.

Each of the garden benches were full, so together they piled through the door where the humidity and heat had intensified from the day before. The Peak Inn seemed to be a tourist favourite.

With the others heading back outside to wait for an empty table, James and Alan squeezed through the throng of revellers and joined the long queue for the bar.

After a short wait listening to a rabble of accents, none they recognised as native, and with a tray full of drinks, they joined their friends who stood on the edge of the car park. Huddled together, they watched a steady stream of new arrivals, while keeping a watchful eye on the prized benches.

After half an hour and with fresh drinks, none of the bench's occupants had made any sign of moving.

George paid particular attention to an older man sat alone reading a newspaper at a bench a few metres away.

Susie sipped her drink. "Let's go to the shop, buy some beers and take them back to the tent."

Alan nodded, rubbing his calves.

"My legs are killing me. We need to do something," he said.

Andrew shook his head. "Nah, there's much nicer scenery here," he said with a grin turned in James's direction.

George nodded towards the middle-aged man he'd been watching. "That guy hasn't drunk a single drop since we got here," he said.

Alan's eyes widened. "Why don't you do your 'spooky' on him? Get him to piss off," he said.

James glared in his direction. Then, looking to each in the group, he watched them smiling back doe-eyed. When he got to Susie, he watched as she rubbed the length of her legs. Andrew raised his eyebrows and beamed an exaggerated smile.

"Yeah, come on. It's not like they're losing a customer, is it? The old git hasn't touched his drink in hours."

"You have to admit he'd be much more comfortable in that crap hole down the road," piped in George.

"For God's sake," James snapped and handed his pint to Andrew.

The friends watched as he walked over to the occupied bench and spoke a few words. They almost let up a cheer as the guy picked up his drink, gulped down the remains and stood up, heading away a little unsteady across the car park.

James sat down, looked at his friends with open hands and lifted his eyebrows.

"Nice one," said Andrew, as he sat down and placed James's beer in front of him. "So what did you say?"

"I just asked him politely if he was going to be long. He said he was just about to leave." James waved his hand out in front of him. "And I didn't need any special powers."

George laughed but Andrew and Alan stayed silent.

"Would have been funny if you said there was free booze in the Prince, or the landlord would be out in a minute to kick him out."

"Or your wife's at home being shagged senseless by your best mate," Alan said, butting in whilst laughing.

Susie shot him a dirty look.

James sighed. "No, it wouldn't."

"Why?" Andrew said, shaking his head.

"There are always consequences," James said to the four blank expressions staring his way. "It took me years to understand."

He sat in silence, but their looks urged him to explain. "When I make people believe, they have no reason to doubt. If I told him there was free beer in the other pub, then he's going to think they're giving away free booze, right?"

Each nodded.

"So he goes to the boozer, orders a beer and expects it to be free. I don't know this guy, I don't know how he's going to react to finding out he has to pay. He knows for sure they were giving it away for free, so maybe he thinks the barmaid's lying, doesn't want to give him the free beer. He gets into an argument and he's kicked out, maybe even barred or gets into a fight."

George was the only one still nodding.

"Let's say I tell him his wife is having an affair. Arriving at home he finds her sitting on the sofa or in bed, but no best friend. He wholeheartedly believes me, so he accuses her and maybe, best case scenario, they split up because he doesn't trust her anymore. Worst case scenario, he goes to his best mate's house and tops him."

As James finished his sentence, he formed a gun with his hand and fired it at Alan's head.

"I'd be responsible for that. I would have killed him." He paused and stood up. "If I had to say something then I would have said that his wife misses him and would be grateful for some company. My way, what's the worst that could happen? She may actually be missing him and I've just put a little love into a tired relationship. If she's not missing him, who's going to get upset with their other half going home early to spend some time together?"

James got up from the table and headed into the pub.

When he came back from the bathroom the subject had changed, with George trying to tell a story about work, but Andrew soon changed the conversation.

A few minutes later, as Andrew told Alan about a new car he was looking to buy, with Susie and James only half listening, Andrew jumped up from the bench with his phone ringing in his pocket. As he wandered off into the car park, George and Alan headed off to the bar.

Susie looked behind her and then checked across to Andrew. When she saw he was out of earshot, she leant across the bench toward James.

"I wanted to talk to you about something. While we're alone, I mean."

James leant forward, squinting as she moved closer.

"What is it?"

"I met this guy. Well, I've been seeing this guy, right," she said, causing James to tilt his head to the side as she fumbled for her words. "Not for a long time," she paused and pushed straggles of blonde hair behind her ears. "Well," she paused again and pushed at hairs that weren't there, "a couple of days ago, in the morning, he, uh, asked me to take part in an experiment."

"What sort of experiment?" James asked, leaning closer still, a playful smile rising.

"A social experiment, with, um," she pushed more stray hair behind her ears, "you guys."

James's eyes narrowed and the smile slipped as Susie rubbed the back of her neck.

"I said no," she quickly added. "But..." She stopped talking as she caught sight of Andrew bounding back over.

"Just wifey checking up on me. What you guys conspiring about?"

"Oh, nothing." Susie turned back to James and mouthed 'later' as Andrew's attention went back to his phone.

In quick succession, George and Alan were back with drinks and the night continued.

After a couple more rounds they started to think about calling it a night.

"I'm just going for a piss," said George, as he rose unsteady on his feet.

Susie stood at the same time. "Me, too," she said, and they both disappeared into the pub.

A few minutes later, George returned lifting his jumper over his head.

"It's still a flipping furnace in there," he said as he sat back down. "Must be a busy night in the basement."

James raised a smile as Andrew lifted his hands above his head to stretch.

"It's actually all right here. Probably because everyone's a tourist," he said.

James looked at his watch. "Shall we piss off when Susie's back? Long drive in the morning."

Looking around, he saw his friends nodding with empty glasses in front of each of them.

James looked at his watch again. "She's been a while."

"Probably all this crap we've been eating," said Andrew, rubbing his stomach through his fleece. "I'm going for a piss."

Five minutes later, Andrew returned with narrowed eyes and looking like he was searching for a lost memory.

5

James was first to wake. Despite having barely slept, he bolted upright as last night's images flashed through his mind like the pages of a flip book. He'd walked with Andrew in the dark for what seemed like hundreds of miles, arriving back at the tent at the first signs of light to find the others fast asleep.

Scanning around the tent, a spark of hope hinted it had all been a dream, but his shoulders soon sank with Andrew in the space where she'd slept the night before and his spare sleeping bag lightly scented with her perfume pushed to a pile at his feet.

A dull ache grew in the pit of his stomach with the building regret he hadn't done more last night.

James raked open the inner tent and scrambled to the outer door. Jabbing his feet into his hiking boots, he pulled the flap open, his breath catching at the sight of the field empty of her car. He scanned the grey skyline; mist hung close to the ground, hiding the great mountain they'd climbed the day before.

Bundling back into the tent, he jabbed at Andrew's shoulder. "Get up, we're going to find her."

Andrew's eyes opened, his stare blank and sleep wary before the memory hit.

Together they stood around shallow tyre tracks in the mud where her car had been.

"She got stuck," George said, stretching out a yawn.

Alan rubbed his eyes as he joined them. "Makes sense. She was pissed, gave the pedal abuse," he said.

James turned and walked away; George followed behind.

"I had a thought," George said, calling softly after him. "Why would they be cleaning the toilets at that time of night?"

James stopped and turned. "Someone made a mess I guess."

He turned away, pulling out his phone, listening to her voicemail as he walked. This time he left a message.

"It's James. I don't know what's going on and I don't care. Just call me. Call someone. Call anyone and let them know you're okay. Please." He clicked off the call and flicked to the number for Susie's flat in London. It rang until eventually her flatmate's recorded voice came on the line. He didn't leave a message.

George and Alan jumped in the Fiesta and James joined Andrew in the Mondeo. They'd agreed to each search twenty miles out, Alan east and Andrew west.

Andrew prodded the trip timer and at the bottom of the driveway they headed right towards Capel Curig. Within a minute they were outside of the limits of the tiny village and after another ten had covered five miles of sparse road, dotted with the occasional row of isolated houses, their silent heads sweeping side to side.

At ten miles, a short row of houses on the left and a shabby petrol station on the right broke up the craggy landscape; the weathered antique pumps rusted with names of oil companies long forgotten. A paint-peeling sign hung on a tall wooden workshop, displaying a faded list of services.

About to move out of sight, James saw a beige Micra parked at the rear in his peripheral vision.

"Turn around," he blurted, slamming his hand on the dashboard. "Susie's car."

He kept his head pivoted towards the shed as Andrew sped up before wheeling the car around at a break in the stone wall.

"You're kidding?" exclaimed Andrew as they pulled alongside one of the pumps.

In front of them sat a Nissan Micra with its nose in the green workshop and its rear sticking out to the tarmac. The bonnet stood raised at an angle, but there was no one around working on it.

Only taking his eyes from the car for a split-second, James tapped at Alan's number.

"What's her reg number?" James shouted.

"It's a 56 and it ends L E G, pretty memorable," came George's voice from the phone's loudspeaker.

James hung up and let out a deep breath. It wasn't her car.

He turned to Andrew and they pulled back to the road, winding their way between the dry-stone walls. It wasn't long before the dial clicked over to twenty-two miles.

Andrew slowed and sluggishly turned the car at a deserted crossroads.

Arriving back at the campsite James tried to swallow down his dismay at seeing George and Alan already had the tent flattened.

They climbed out, Andrew meandering in their direction while James stayed back with the phone in Susie's flat ringing in his ear.

"Susie?" James said, excitement in his voice as he recognised her words.

"No, Kate." Susie's flatmate.

"Hi, Kate, it's James," he said, his voice flattened.

"Hiya," she said. "Everything all right?"

He instantly knew Susie wasn't there. "Yeah, not bad," he said, unsure of what to say.

"What's happened?"

"Um," he paused and drew a deep breath. "Susie's driven off and I wanted to see if she'd gone home."

"Oh," she said, not sounding too concerned. "Do you know why?"

"No."

"You know how she can be sometimes," Kate said back.

James frowned. "No."

"Look, she's probably just... I don't know, hooked up with someone."

"She's not like that."

There was a pause on the line.

"No, she's not," Kate's voice came back, quieter than before. "Look, I'll let you know if I hear from her. And you let me know, too."

James nodded as he said goodbye. He called Susie's mobile, listening as it went straight to answerphone then looked up at all that remained of their weekend; a rectangle of flattened grass.

As the group set off walking back down the drive, the village appeared drab and worn in the flat grey light, like Vegas in the daytime. Without the brilliance of the sun, even the colourfully-painted shops failed to brighten the street. The cafe sat empty and the village centre bare, save from a grey-haired old lady shuffling, her back bent at an extraordinary angle, wheeling a tartan shopping trolley across closed shop fronts.

Stepping into the bright red cafe, its windows steamed, the four turned towards The Peak Inn opposite and a flurry of glass smashed as a lone cleaner emptied large black bins at the side of the pub.

They sat by the windows, James watching as the others exchanged concerned looks.

"Stay or go?" James said, putting words to everyone's question.

"Go," said Alan immediately. "There's nothing we can do here. She'll turn up at her house or at some friends. Could even have gone to Cardiff. All the while we're hanging around here getting old."

"I think I agree with Alan," added Andrew, not moving his eyes from the menu. "The more time goes on, the more pissed off I'm getting."

"She's fucked this weekend completely," Alan chipped in, shuffling in his seat.

James knew they were all looking at him, waiting for his reaction as he stared in the direction of the pub. He left them waiting until the teenage waitress broke the silence to ask for their order. When James stayed quiet, Andrew ordered for him.

Out of the corner of his eye, he saw Alan prodding Andrew in the ribs.

"Mate?" Andrew said, looking towards James.

James turned in his seat and met Andrew's widening eyes.

"What happens if she's lying in some ditch somewhere? We've all seen these roads. It could be weeks before she's found," James said.

"We've looked. Let's take it slow on the way out, use the route she would have taken home," Andrew replied, his voice unusually soft.

Silence fell again until the same waitress brought plates piled high with fried food with his friends setting upon them like wild beasts as he turned back to the pub.

James's stomach churned as he looked down at his own carnivore's feast and ran his fingers through his short hair. Rotating his phone in his left hand, he prodded the food with a fork in his right.

He wanted to be close to her, close to where they'd last seen her. He wanted to stay until he knew she was safe.

Pushing the plate away, he saw George look up from his meal, his eyes bright with an idea.

"Why don't we take advice from the professionals?"

James tilted his head to the side, raising his eyebrows, a pang of hope shooting through his chest at George's words.

"Let's see what the police say?"

The group swapped glances, nodding in turn with full mouths.

James sat staring whilst George headed outside to make the call, coming back within a minute.

"Someone's going to call me back."

"What now?" said Alan.

They ordered more coffee.

George's phone rang within a couple of minutes and he rushed back out the door.

Five minutes later, he sat back down at the table. James tried to read his expression.

"Spoke to the duty Sergeant in CID and there's nothing official they can do. He's going to check the national computer and see if her name has been logged, or if there were any Jane Doe's reported along the route to her home address. The procedure should be to check with the hospitals but there are at least forty between here and London, so he said it would be best just to let him check." He paused, looking around the group before turning to James. "I'm not sure it was helpful or not," he paused again, and James gave a slight nod, "but he said people go missing all the time. Most of them are found within a day or two. He's going to call me if he gets any news."

"What did he say *we* should do?" asked Alan as he drained his mug.

George threw him a look before he turned back to James.

"There isn't much we can do, other than to check with friends."

"So we go home, yeah?" Alan nodded with enthusiasm.

"I guess so," replied George, looking at James's blank expression.

"Then what?" James said, speaking for the first time.

"If we don't hear anything within twenty-four hours, we need to call the police and report her as a missing person."

Everyone's eyes were on James. He cast his gaze to the table and slowly nodded.

"We should tell her parents," George said.

James slunk back in his chair and rubbed his temples. "Maybe she's there. I'll do it," he replied, his voice low as he stood from the table and headed out the door.

As he walked to the car, he tried to summon the words. He rang Kate and could hear her concern. He didn't need to ask; he knew Suzie still hadn't turned up.

With her parents' number in the phone, he took a deep breath and made the call, relieved when her dad answered.

"Hello, Mr Whitmarsh, it's James. Susie's friend from university."

"Oh. Hello, James." James heard the surprise in his voice. "Aren't you away with Susie?"

For a second time his question didn't need to be asked. "Yes, we were, Mr Whitmarsh, but Susie left early."

"Oh, okay," the deep voice replied, leaving James hanging in silence for a moment. "Was everything all right?"

James took a deep breath. "She didn't tell us she was going," he paused as he chose the words. "And she drove off in the middle of the night."

"I see," was all Mr Whitmarsh said before James relayed all of what they had done so far and the advice the police had given. "I can see what Susie sees in you."

They agreed to keep in touch and said goodbye.

James stood in the street, replaying the conversation over in his head, the last phrase catching in his mind; I can see what Susie sees in you.

He turned back to the cafe and saw his friends walking towards him. At the cars, James told them how the call had gone and saw tension relax from their faces.

"I'm staying," he said.

"Don't be silly," Andrew said, patting him on the back. "Get in the car."

James looked around the street, his gaze stopping on The Peak Inn nestled at the bottom of the grey background. He turned to Andrew, holding open the passenger door with George already in the back seat. Alan smacked him on the back and jumped in his car, speeding off barely before the door shut.

James took a deep breath and walked up to the car door held open by Andrew but couldn't help feeling he was making the wrong decision.

***

Her eyes opened to pitch black, the throb at her temples easing as she sealed them back shut. She'd have to get up for painkillers soon, but for now the comfort of her bed still held her tight.

She could feel the makeup smeared to her face and knew her mum would be pissed.

More washing, she could almost hear her say at the sight of her pillow shadowed in black and brown. *You'll learn when you have a family of your own.* Just one phrase she was tired of hearing. But she'd get away with it today. Her mum wouldn't stay upset for long; after all, it was her only daughter's eighteenth birthday.

Tomorrow would be another thing. Tomorrow her mum would have her world ripped apart. Tomorrow she'd tell her mum that she'd been offered a place at the Academy of Art in San Francisco.

It was easy to predict how upset she'd get.

Your heart condition? Your medicine?

She'd tell her mum the scholarship included medical insurance which covered her condition and all the drugs. There was even talk of taking part in a trial; a chance she'd not have to take those foul-tasting pills every day for the rest of her life.

Her mum would still get angry because they hadn't talked it through.

She'd tell her mum she would come home every Christmas and some of the summer. It was, after all, only a three-year course.

Her mum would say she wanted her near to keep her safe.

It would be fine, she would reply; there was as much chance of trouble in America as there was in their sleepy backwater.

The throb had grown and it was time for water and pills. She didn't remember drinking that much last night but when the girls got together anything could happen.

Her body felt heavy as she sat up; a memory flittered back from the recovery ward. She swung her legs around, stubbing the heel of her foot on the cold floor a couple of inches below the mattress. Her hand dropped over the edge of the bed.

Why was her mattress on the floor?

Distracted by her pain she struggled up, swinging herself in two attempts, rocking on her backside; the pounding pain in her head sending the question of the missing carpet quickly away.

She walked with stiff legs in the pitch black in the direction of her door, arms outstretched, feeling for the texture of her flower-papered walls.

Sooner than expected, her fingers stubbed against a surface much rougher than she remembered.

Pain clouded her head and her hand brushed her bare leg. She touched her top, realising she wore the short outfit from last night.

Her chest throbbed. She knew the procedure and stopped moving, her hand instinctively reaching to the faint scar over her faulty muscle.

"Deep, slow breaths. Deep, slow breaths," she said out loud, her voice low and hoarse.

Dragging herself along the wall, guided by her hand across the rough surface, her throat rasped for water and head pinched with pain. Her hand caught familiar sharp contours and she felt herself relax with the realisation she was at her friend Pippa's, at least by the feel of the square light switch.

She closed her eyes as her head still pounded with each furious beat. Her fingers pushed the long switch.

The light seared through her eyelids before she could flash her arm across her face.

She stood and waited for the wave of pain to subside, concentrating on the drum in her chest. She slowly moved her arm and, squinting hard, opened one eye for less than a second before it jammed closed.

As her brain caught up with the patterns in the brightness, she knew something was wrong.

Curiosity and fear triumphed over the pain and she opened both her eyes to a slit. She pushed her temples in an attempt to null the agony of light coursing to the back of her eye, but when her focus fixed, her hands dropped to her side as she took in the alien view.

The boarded-up window.

The yellow-stained mattress.

The lonely bucket in the corner.

"Where the fuck am I?" she screamed.

6

At home, James lay awake, the monotonous pitch of a dustbin lorry growing in his ears. He imagined harried men in fluorescent jackets ferrying the bright red bins back and forth, dumping the rubbish, pushing them back disorderly to the curb, before collecting the next load. Repeating ad infinitum.

They were doing their job, getting on with their lives. He didn't know if he could do the same.

James rolled on to his shoulder to check his phone but saw no messages.

Pulling off the covers, he began to prepare himself for his working day. A quick flick through the TV channels confirmed the news hadn't yet made the headlines; no police hunt, no public appeal. A Google search revealed the same.

He made a disappointing call to George, then left for the tube station and his depot a few stops down the Metropolitan line.

He was home by eleven.

A voicemail from a tearful Kate looking for non-existent news amplified his distraction, which had been seen by his supervisor as the onset of illness and he was ushered home.

James stared out of his first-floor window. There were still no messages. Nothing from George, her parents nor any of her other friends he'd repeatedly called. Kate didn't have a number for the guy Susie mentioned in their last conversation.

One by one, he rang all of the hospitals within ten miles of what he guessed would have been her route home; frustration increased with each of the replies, confirming they had no record of her admittance.

He started on a twenty-mile radius when a message from George confirmed the North Wales police sergeant had also come up empty-handed.

They obviously weren't trying hard enough, he thought, but of course he knew that wasn't fair.

James remembered what George had said. *People go missing all the time.*

They would be looking for hundreds of people and dealing with thousands of crimes a day. How much attention could they pay to a single case? The answer was obvious. Little or none.

There were other people who could search for Susie, professionals that could give a hundred percent to finding her. All you had to do was pay.

Tapping at his laptop, he soon found there were ten companies in London on the first page alone.

Punching the first number into his phone, after a few minutes on hold one of the lead investigators came on the line.

In five minutes, James had put over the finer points of Susie's disappearance and was told everything he wanted to hear.

Everyone leaves a trail. To find her you just had to get into her life and chase down every lead. Given time and money, they would find her.

The sales patter began.

The investigator talked about hours sifting through information. Days taking statements. Weeks chasing down leads, but James wasn't listening as his heart beat hard in his chest with the excitement of finding a solution.

Then he heard a number.

James asked him to repeat it twice to make sure. He wrote it on a scrap of paper and hung up the phone. The number in front of him was too big. He didn't have fifteen grand; he didn't have anywhere near fifteen grand.

He turned to the window; but maybe her parents did?

He grabbed his coat and shot out the door; this wasn't the kind of thing you talked about over the phone.

After the thirty-minute journey he found out they didn't have it either. He'd sat in front of Susie's parents excitedly explaining the idea. Her mum burst into tears when

Mr Whitmarsh explained all their money was tied up in a pension scheme not due to mature until next year.

Stepping out of her parent's terraced house, the weather had changed and the wind blew cold rain in his face.

Without a jacket, he ran towards the tube station. Seconds later, his pocket vibrated. Slowing to a walk, he pulled out his iPhone and his heart jumped as Susie's face stared back.

His eyes bulged and his legs froze as drops of rain gathered on her face.

A bright light shone to his left with a slow, deep rumble he recognised.

Turning his head, the Transit hit him.

7

Gasping awake, pain pounded at James's temples as dull light poured from the room. Transfixed on the discoloured ceiling, a soft call came into focus.

Head throbbing, James shuffled up in the bed, feeling a hand to his side and the pillows rearranged behind him.

Bathed in shadow, the tall figure stepped back. Andrew stood, red-eyed but with a smile stretching the width of his face.

"How's the noggin?"

James turned his stiff neck to take in the room, the white walls and the Get Well Soon balloons sagging on their strings as Andrew dragged his chair closer to the bed.

"Feels like someone's trying to get out," James croaked through a dry throat, an unease gripping him as Andrew seemed to laugh a little too hard.

James touched at his forehead, surprised not to find a rough bandage wrapping around.

"Do you remember what happened?" Andrew said as he poured water into a clear plastic cup.

"I think it was van shaped," he replied, taking the drink.

Andrew nodded.

James drained the water and, putting the cup down, wiggled his toes, lifted his legs, arched his back, then cupped his genitals.

"No physical injuries, mate."

"Just had a little sleep then?"

"Little? No, it's Thursday."

"Shit. I've been out for two days?" James said, feeling a surge of panic racing through him.

"It's Thursday 5th August. You've been in a coma for nine days."

James fell silent, his heart sinking at the thought of nine lost days. Too fast for his pounding head, he twitched towards Andrew, wide-eyed.

"Where's my phone?" James said, raising his voice as he remembered the last few moments before it all went black.

Andrew pulled open the bedside drawer and grabbed a black iPhone, James near snatching it from his hand.

A spider's web of split glass covered the screen as he jabbed at the power button. "Susie called me. Where was she found?"

Andrew frowned back, his words slow. "Sorry, mate. There's been no news."

James flung the unresponsive phone onto the blanket. "She called me, just before a van hit me in the face."

Andrew stared back, his eyes wide for a second. "Mobile or landline?"

James drew in a sharp breath and slumped back. It hadn't occurred to him. Both her numbers were just one contact in his phone. Her photo would show up if it was the phone in her flat or her mobile calling. It must have been Kate.

"I'm sorry," Andrew said, and they sat in silence.

After a couple of minutes James spoke. "So what has happened?"

"Well," Andrew leaned forward in his chair, "the police have been to see everyone and taken statements. Susie's parents have been in touch with some missing persons charities. We've setup a Facebook page, we've got about a hundred 'likes' so far. We tried getting the papers to do a story. They say they may do it next month," he announced, the pride clear on his face.

James didn't respond. It wasn't the news he wanted to hear.

"We need fifteen grand."

"Susie's parents told me," Andrew replied, looking down at the ground. He lifted his head as the door opened and in streamed three people in white coats and a nurse in a pale-blue tunic.

With short grey hair, the oldest doctor nodded a greeting to Andrew and introduced the quartet of medical professionals.

Doctor Rogers, consultant medic, explained the others were his registrar, Doctor Newman, SHO, Doctor Moore, and the young nurse Fields. Each nodded and smiled in turn as they were introduced.

"Mr Fisher, we were expecting you to wake soon. How are you feeling?" Doctor Rogers asked.

James squinted towards them. "Apart from a splitting headache I feel fine."

"We'll get you something for the pain," he said and looked to Nurse Fields, who had already turned to leave. "You suffered a nasty bang to the head. We scanned your brain. You'll be pleased to know there was a little swelling, but no damage." He turned to his colleagues and began to stroke his hand down the length of his beard. "We did, however, find something interesting."

James looked thoughtful in their direction.

"We'd like to do some further scans. It's likely nothing to do with the accident but we want to investigate further. I've booked the MRI for the morning. Are there any questions?"

"Can I go home?" he replied as Nurse Fields came back through the door with a tiny paper container. From the bedside table she pulled up the jug of water, refilled the plastic cup and he gulped down the pills.

"Physically you seem to be fine and now you're awake there is no apparent damage we didn't spot. However, the area I mentioned in your brain is of great interest. I have a colleague from the university coming over for the scan tomorrow. He is very keen to get more detail. So I will see you tomorrow morning," said Doctor Rogers. He turned and left. The nurse and the registrar followed their boss whilst the youngest doctor stayed behind.

"You've got a good friend there, Mr Fisher," she said as she nodded in Andrew's direction. She turned to leave.

"He's been here every day since you arrived," she added, closing the door behind her.

"Thanks," James said, looking at Andrew.

"Don't go all weird on me," he replied. "Just wanted to make sure you were good for that twenty quid you owe me."

Andrew turned away from the window, then without looking back he stood, told James he had to go and headed out of the door.

Thankful the pills were already doing their job, James looked around the room before settling his gaze on the space where the doctors had stood. He couldn't help wondering what they'd found, whilst knowing he didn't want them investigating his brain. Too much time had been lost already and he knew it could only be bad news.

Everyone else had begun to cope with the loss, begun to grieve even though Susie wasn't dead. For him, she'd gone missing only yesterday and too much time had already been wasted. He had to act. He just needed to figure out what he was going to do.

His last idea had been good but too pedestrian and with no money for a private investigator he'd have to do it another way. He had to get back out there but he couldn't search the entire country on his own.

His thoughts turned to his parent's disappearance, images of their life and death percolated from their deep resting place. He didn't act then and paid the price with their lives.

If he couldn't get a professional, then maybe he could do it himself.

He wasn't going to let history repeat itself. He was no PI but he wasn't helpless. He'd spent the last few years hiding the fact, but now he had to face up to it, face up to himself. He wasn't normal. He could help where most couldn't. He'd use what he'd learnt from his parent's deaths.

He didn't believe in a higher being, but he knew he had something other people didn't, and for whatever reason, be it a leap of evolution or some ordained gift, he shouldn't waste it. He couldn’t waste it. He couldn't live with himself if he didn't at least try again.

James didn't know what he was going to do, but he knew he wouldn’t be hanging around for the scan in the morning.

8

Within an hour he'd discharged himself from the hospital; the nurse had called the consultant who had fruitlessly pleaded for his stay. It wasn't long before he knew he'd made the right decision.

"Any news?" James blurted down his home phone as he picked up George's call.

"No news," George replied, his tone flat and calm. "But I've found someone I think can help."

"Who is it?"

"Let's meet and we'll talk."

Within an hour, James arrived at a bustling Victoria station in the centre of London and spotted George through the crowd, checking his watch as he stood by the ticket barriers, his head darting from side to side to scour the sea of faces.

Locking eyes, George turned and headed to the exit, forcing James to double his pace to catch up and come side by side along the busy Buckingham Palace Road.

"Should we go somewhere quieter?" James shouted, as he weaved in and out of the packs of foreign tourists noisily ambling to and from the station.

Striding along the street, George showed no sign of hearing him as he cut a path through the melee.

With James in tow, he headed down Eccleston Street before they stopped and George moved his head in close.

"Chris Smith. He's an investigator at my office."

"Missing persons?" James said with a frown.

George shook his head. "But he can help."

James watched as George's eyes flitted back and forth, scanning behind him.

"Great. Where is he?"

"You'll need to make contact."

James nodded. "What have you told him so far?"

George shook his head for the second time. "We haven't spoken. You're going to have to convince him."

James pursed his lips, a frown rising as George continued.

"It's not that he won't care, it's just that you won't be on his radar. He's a busy man doing a serious job, but I'm sure you can get him to help." George turned, twisting to check behind him.

As he looked back, he raised his eyebrows at James's disappointment. "What's the problem?"

"Consequences. Don't you remember what I told you in Snowdon?"

"James, there's a lot at stake. Just keep it simple. I can't think of any other way."

James took a deep breath, trying to conceal his irritation. Then, as he stared at George's red, tired eyes, his gaze flitting around the crowds of faces, he saw the sleepless nights and the worry. Perhaps he did care after all.

He had to give it his best shot.

James nodded, but George's solemn expression didn't change whilst he continued to scan the crowd.

"He'll get the tube from Vauxhall to Seven Sisters. It's about an hour-long journey and your best time to catch him alone. He's not a nine to five so you'll have to figure out how to find him. He normally uses the entrance on Vauxhall Bridge."

"Just tell me where his office is and I'll find him."

George shook his head, his eyes stern as he made eye contact for the first time since they'd been talking. "No."

Pulling out his phone he showed James a photo of a man with short, tidy brown hair and medium everything. With his arm around an attractive young blonde woman, both seemed relaxed, happily posing for the camera.

"Taken about a month or so ago." George dropped the camera into his pocket.

James had already forgot what he looked like. "Can you text me the picture?"

George shook his head. "Take a picture," he said, placing the phone on a nearby green plastic bin, the photo on the screen.

Grabbing his phone, James snapped the shot, the face just visible through his cracked screen and watched as George snatched it back, deleting the photo and turning the phone off. He moved to James and brought his mouth up to his ear, his hands gripping at the arms of his jacket as he pulled in close.

"Whatever happens, this can't come back to me," he whispered.

Without another word, George turned and crossed the road, disappearing behind a string of double decker buses.

James stood for a moment, lost in thought, the bustle of the crowd, the fumes from the road and the rev of engines slowly coming back into focus.

He checked his watch. It was coming up to three and the streets would soon begin to fill with commuters. A quick check on Google maps through the cracks and he headed towards the bridge.

***

With practiced American efficiency, a tall barista took his order within seconds of arriving at the wooden counter. Ignoring the familiar clutter and the background chatter, James stared through the long plate glass windows, smiling at the perfect view of the station entrance just outside.

The wide front of the coffee house took up the rest of the space before funnelling down the side wall, the long counter sweeping around to the back and the rest of the seating.

Each of the front tables were occupied. To the left sat a group of late teens, their arms swirling in animated gestures; students in deep discussion, James guessed.

Their neighbours were an elderly couple sat in silence, taking the occasional sip from cups whose size could support a small family of goldfish.

To the right were a smartly dressed man and a woman. Not a couple; he could tell from their straight demeanour. Both in their late thirties talking quietly from opposite sides of the table, an expensive looking camera rested next to a notebook.

At the fourth table sat a lone forty-something man in jeans and a t-shirt, his attention occasionally swapping between The Guardian and the view out of the window.

Still standing, James followed his gaze and for the first time noticed the building on the opposite side of the wide road. It looked fake and out of place, bulky and made from Lego, looking as if it would be more at home in ancient Babylon than central London.

Breaking his stare, the barista called his order and he moved to a free table past the counter, towards the back where the view shrank to just a sliver of glass, but at least he could see the four tables clear enough.

Grabbing an abandoned day-old edition of The Times, James sat down and made himself comfortable for the wait.

Glancing at yesterday's news, he watched the four tables whilst scanning the paper.

A tortuous thirty minutes passed, where no one made any move to leave.

Time continued its march forward and just as he'd made his mind up to intervene, the old guy stood. With their table still laid out and his companion immersed in her People's Friend, James knew he couldn't waste the opportunity.

In brown cords and a grey cardigan the same shade as his hair, the guy wobbled side to side, leaning heavily on a dark wooden stick, pushing one slow foot after another in the direction of the washroom.

James stood with plenty of time to spare and headed in the same direction.

The washroom had two cubicles, a single urinal and two sinks. Looking around the small room, he tried in vain to piece together a plan. The outer door signalled with a creak and he ducked into one of the empty stalls, George's words ringing in his ears.

Keep it simple.

Standing in the enclosing stall, he heard the inner door open, the air swishing back as it closed. Holding his breath, he listened as the adjacent stall door opened and banged closed, the lock sliding across a moment later. An ice-age came and went before he heard the faltering stream of urine in the bowl, then paused to repeat once more.

Willing the end of the lifetime, the lock slid, the door creaked and he counted five seconds before he saw the opportunity presented.

The old guy stood at the far sink, his cane leant against the counter outside of the cubicles. With his concentration on his hands under the water, James walked out of the stall, his left leg clattering the cane to the floor with a swift kick.

"Oh, I'm really sorry," James said, his tone soft as he leant down to pick up the stick.

The guy looked up with sagging eyelids.

James smiled, watching as the gesture returned. With the cane in his left hand, his fist balled over its head, James pushed it out in front of him, leaving the guy no choice but to put his wrinkled hand out.

As he did so, James moved the cane to the side and replaced it with his right hand, taking a gentle grip on his wrinkled hand.

"Keep it simple," he said under his breath, then raised his voice. "It's going to rain."

James released his grip, rested the stick back against the counter and left the room.

As the man passed by, James buried his head in yesterday's news. Looking over the top of the paper, he watched the confused companion disagree with the forecast, waving her hands to the windows. The old man ignored her protests, grabbed his coat and shuffled out of the front door. Shaking her head, she cleared away their things and limped after him.

James made himself comfortable, shuffling the seat around to the window and setting his concentration on the wide, grey scene.

With the entrance to the underground station much closer than he could have hoped and a second large cappuccino on the table, he pulled out his phone. Staring at the image, he tried to sear the unremarkable face into his memory.

Maybe it was the second cup of coffee, maybe the nerves, but either way James felt something he hadn't in a long time. He felt alive. He had a purpose. A goal. Perhaps he'd been lying to himself and his friends all this time. Could Susie have been right all along? Had he been hiding?

No sooner had a smile crept across his face when thoughts of Susie began to bleed in from the edges. With his face devoid of joy, he picked up the phone and listened to the high note of her voice, his eyes flitting across the faces of tourists passing by the window.

With each passing moment, the empty space between faces shrank; tired and humourless businessmen and women joining the ranks as offices began to empty. He sat forward in his seat, unable to take his eye from the view, the traffic a constant, unending flow. He spotted a face that could have been, but as he glanced from his phone and back up, the face had been replaced by ten others.

Huffing a great puff of air from his chest, he pushed back in his seat at the impossible task, the realisation undeniable that he could have missed his target ten times over by now.

He stood and turned, for the first time hearing the great chatter of voices, the first time seeing the long queue snaked around from the entrance.

Almost leaping his hand into the air, he saw George standing in line, but stopped himself as he caught George's mouth moving in a stone-face expression as he talked to someone James recognised in an instant. The guy he'd been looking out for all this time.

9

James didn't check the phone, instead joining the back of the long queue with a newspaper swiped from close by and pushed across his face as he peered down. Glancing up, he watched as they ordered and were served; a shoulder slapped and they separated at the door.

James pushed through the clamour, view fixed to the brown hair in the sea of heads and hats bobbing up and down.

Slamming his Oyster card against the ticket barrier, pausing as the flow stopped and started, he stood transfixed, the head disappearing, then back again, metal clunking beneath his feet as he descended further into the claustrophobia.

Hanging back from the platform, James held his ground against the swathes joining in from behind. The wind picked up; the crowd took a step forward as the rails rang out their song.

With a mechanical squeal the train rattled from its hole; all the while his stare remained transfixed and he joined the surge towards the open doors.

"Shit," he said, as he watched George's colleague, Chris, step on the train while he was pushed to the right with the masses and onto the adjacent carriage. The door alarm wailed, the station disappearing out of view.

James stood at the door between carriages, his gaze flitting between faces until he caught his man with a hand in the air, gripping onto the bright yellow bar, swaying side to side with the tide of the train.

Had it been any other train he could open the door and walk between the carriages, but not on the tube. Instead, James edged forward as metal wheels ground over metal rails, moving slowly closer to the double doors.

Their momentum began to bleed sooner than he'd expected and by the time they'd stopped at the next station, he'd made little progress. The doors would have whined before he'd stepped onto the concrete, so he let Pimlico leave while he struggled to hold his ground against the surge of new passengers. The doors sealed shut and they were off at speed once more.

He resolved to wait for a quieter station.

Victoria came next; but he found armies of people joining from the surface. Next came Green Park, quieter, but the doors caught him out as they opened on the other side. He looked at the thin map above his head, next station was Oxford Circus, which he didn't even try to attempt; Warren Street a repeat.

"Shit," he said again, mostly ignored by those around him as he shook his head. The map showed some of the busiest stations to come, Euston and Kings Cross. He had no choice; he couldn't wait with only five left until the destination.

Euston came and went; no one else could fit in the carriage. Then Kings Cross.

Without conscious decision, as the doors separated, he surged forward, pushing through the crowd to finally land on the platform.

As his feet hit the concrete he shot to his right and along the outside of the train, barging his way past the crowds of people and up to the next door.

Wide-eyed, he looked through the windows only to see it jammed full. He raced to the next door, his foot close to the edge. Again, the packed interior stared back and the alarm insisted the doors were about to close.

He pushed inside, letting the doors pinch at his coat.

Settling himself into the press, he scanned heads side by side. No one said a word as he pushed himself away from the door.

James reached up on his toes, but even standing taller he still couldn't see the target. He knew being in the same carriage meant nothing if he couldn't touch. Despair seeped through his veins and his shoulders slouched. The train jolted, the lights flickered and he stood up tall; he wasn't going to give up so easy.

Penned in with his hands jammed by his sides, he looked to his left to see a tall Rastafarian with dreadlocks covered by a hat of Jamaican pride.

James moved his hand, felt skin; the guy turned to him with narrowed eyes.

James spoke. "The train stops here. Everyone needs to know."

"Huh," came the bemused reply, but James had already turned to his neighbour in a blue pinstripe suit.

"The train stops here. We need to get off," he said, as he touched the man's finger. "Everyone needs to know."

The man squinted but turned to his right and passed the message on. James swivelled to his front and gave the same message twice more.

By the time the train jolted to a stop, the carriage buzzed with chatter and he had to push past passengers to stop himself streaming out through the open doors with the crowd.

As the train moved off, he stood in a space occupied only by those wearing earphones and found himself looking on at the other half of the packed carriage where the message hadn't had time to propagate.

The target sat among the remaining passengers, their faces eager as they spread out to take up the space.

James darted just in time to fill the empty seat at his side. Settling himself down, he watched Chris' face buried intently on the words on his phone.

Although James couldn't see what was on the screen, the black phone itself looked similar to any other modern Apple product, but with a difference, being much thicker than his or any iPhone James had seen before.

The target stopped moving his fingers and James realised he was looking over his shoulder in his direction.

"Is that you, Chris?" James said with maximum excitement.

Chris Smith looked back, his average features set in a guarded expression.

James smiled and held out his hand.

Take the hand, he said in his head, willing the stranger on.

Chris gingerly shook the hand to a growing smile on James's face.

"I was on my way to see you at home. How lucky I bumped into you," James said in a quieter tone, still shaking the hand. "Your boss told me to give you a message."

Chris leaned in.

"You're to drop your current cases. Someone else will be taking over. You have to help me with my investigation."

The train stopped and Chris looked at the sign beyond the windows for Finsbury Park station.

"But the hearing?" Chris said, an anxious look on his face.

James couldn't imagine a few held-up tax disc investigations making a difference to the world. He was dealing with something so much more important.

"It's been taken care of," he said, nodding and watching the expression on Chris's face. He could almost see the neurones firing backwards and forwards as a battle raged to process the information, trying to override what he had known to be the truth.

Finally, as the train clattered to Seven Sisters, Chris' expression relaxed.

"So what's the job?"

Chris led James to a coffee shop around the corner from the station and they took a darkened table towards the back.

"Sorry, I didn't catch your name?" Chris said, as he sipped his coffee.

James flinched at the question, realising he should have thought ahead.

Should he give his real name? What happens if they find the connection to George? But he had to give Susie's name or how else would he find her?

"James Fisher."

Chris nodded. "So what's the assignment?"

"Susie Whitmarsh went missing. It's been thirteen days and there's no sign of her," James said and gave Chris a summary of the days since Susie disappeared.

Chris listened with intent, nodding at all of the appropriate points.

"So, you see, the police won't do anything and it's really important we find her."

"Sounds like an interesting assignment. I've got a very high-profile case on at the moment, but I will start looking into this next week for you," Chris replied.

"What? That's no good. Who knows what could have happened by that time?" Anger built inside James at the thought that anything could be more important than finding his friend.

"I'll speak to my boss, but my case load is too important to shelve," Chris said as he stood.

James stood and offered a handshake.

As Chris squeezed the offered hand, James stared intently and spoke.

"Your orders are simple. Give me one hundred percent or you're out." James felt himself shaking as the words fell from his lips.

Without surprise or reaction, Chris replied, "I'll get started straight away."

They sat back down, James taking deep breaths to calm and spent the next hour going over the rest of the details.

Chris agreed to come back to him in the morning and after swapping mobile phone numbers they parted.

***

Powerless to stop himself, despite knowing the dream so well, James opened the dark wooden door. Not his, his parent's.

As it swung towards him, he saw no one standing, just an unlabelled brown box sat on the coconut-hair mat at his feet.

The next moment, without moving his legs, he stood a couple of paces down the drive. The street quiet with just the smell of two-stroke oil hanging in the air.

Within a blink, he sat next to Andrew on his parent's sofa. England drew Portugal on the deep TV. It would end in penalties, he knew.

Looking down at the box open on the table, he pulled out the bubble wrap and dropped it to the floor. Tears rolled down his cheeks, but he made no noise as Andrew swore at the TV.

James watched his hands slowly pull out a burgundy jewellery box, his fingers snapping the lid wide and it fell from his grasp. His gaze followed the box as it hit the table. Blood dripped on the cardboard as his mum's wedding ring rolled out, still attached to her finger.

10

James woke with a sharp intake of breath. Bolting up at the waist, he peered around with his mouth hung wide, unsure of his surroundings despite recognising his room.

It had been a long time since he'd had the dream. Wiping his eyes with the back of his hand, he watched as the sun streamed through the window, the light catching on the sharp lines spidering his phone. He ran his finger over the uneven face, hovering over Chris's number, then dropped it to the covers before heading to the shower.

Refreshed, he checked the phone's screen again, his heart leaping to see a missed call from Chris.

After rubbing his hands dry on the towel around his waist, he fingered redial.

It was a short conversation, with no news of a breakthrough; Chris just needed some more background information. The voice on the other end reminded him it was still early days.

James was about to hang up when Chris mentioned he was walking into his office in order to use databases that he didn't have access to from his home. Unable to convey his unease over the phone and powerless to convince him without touch, the call ended with a growing hollow deep in James's chest.

Startling him as he stared at his plain wall, the phone chirped in his hand and he saw Andrew's face smiling back.

Starting the conversation like a worried parent, Andrew delivered a brief telling off for his early discharge with no word to the guy who'd watched over him for so many days.

James apologised and Andrew's tone settled, pitching higher with excitement as he told him he'd taken a callout at a clinic just outside Cardiff.

The job would only take a few hours so he planned to visit a friend of Susie's. He'd tried calling her but couldn't get the number, so pulled a favour to swap his assignment on the off chance she knew something that could help. The call ended with a promise of news.

James spent most of the day with growing frustration, the hours passing by as his internet research yielded nothing but passive and pedestrian advice. No silver bullet. No solution leaping from the screen.

The call from Andrew came all too soon, confirming the dead end. He'd met the friend but they hadn't spoken for months.

Still he made a mental note to let Chris know he could tick that avenue off the list.

His thoughts of Chris reminded him they hadn't spoken since the morning and looked outside to the sky beginning to darken. Chris's mobile went to a generic answer phone message. He tried George and got the same.

They'll be on the tube, James thought to himself.

A grumble from his stomach caught his attention and already knowing the cupboards were bare, he left the flat for the short walk to the high street.

In a window seat, his fingers slowly picking at an order of fried chicken, James stared out across the pedestrian precinct, watching as humanity criss-crossed in front of him.

Across the random flow, his gaze settled on a bank of televisions of all conceivable colours and sizes in a brightly framed electronics shop window. They were all set on Sky News; he couldn't quite make out the story, but he caught the words *Terrorist* and *Court Case* in big letters rolling across a home cinema-sized screen.

Eating slowly down to the bones, he watched a correspondent talk to a camera outside The Old Bailey in London. The scene changed to another reporter, an attractive young woman, outside a different building which looked familiar but he couldn't quite place its name.

With half the chicken in the bin, he left the restaurant and meandered across the street towards the shop. The same story remained on the screens with the security editor in a wheelchair and a thin, boyish woman from Amnesty International in the studio.

He couldn't help but look for clues as to where he remembered the building from.

Ten minutes later, James arrived along his road, the darkness nearly complete. A single pair of headlights pulled into a space a few car lengths away and he knew it wouldn't be long before commuters would arrive back from their long days at work, filling the streets with Smart Cars and miniature Fiat 500s.

James unlocked his front door, threw his keys on the table and switched on the TV to BBC News, grabbing his laptop and opening the same channel's website where a smaller headline leapt off the screen.

MI6 blamed for Iranian terrorist case collapse this morning.

A picture of the building whose name had so far escaped him accompanied the headline. Clicking the link, the page changed to show a video player. A caption hung beneath the video.

Our security correspondent reports outside the Secret Intelligence Service, MI6, headquarters in Vauxhall, London.

James's eyes bulged as he read the line, his hand slapping at his forehead as he remembered he'd stared at the building for three hours yesterday. His relief at solving the puzzle fell away to be replaced with ice cold dread.

Chris was a spy.

11

"I'm fucked," James shouted, running his hands through his hair, pulling the skin on his forehead tight.

George worked with spies.

No wonder he was acting weird when they met. Another thought crashed into his head.

Was George a spy?

Oh shit. Maybe it was time he started listening when George talked about his work.

James drew a deep breath, his skin prickling as his room came back into focus.

Grabbing his phone, he called George's mobile. No answer. He tried the house. No answer.

"It's treason," he said out loud. "I'm going to hang."

James racked his brain, replaying the last couple of days. Meeting Chris. Their conversation in the coffee shop. Their conversation this morning as Chris stood outside his office.

As he stood outside his office.

James hadn't spoken to him since then and he dropped the phone to the floor as if it were suddenly boiling hot.

He took a deep breath, forcing himself to calm, but only succeeded in feeling the overwhelming need to leave the flat.

The phone lit up on the floor and his eyes shot wide as he stared at Alan's face. With another deep breath, he overcame the hesitation and despite his every fibre telling him not to answer, he picked up the phone.

"Hi, mate," James said, trying to calm his voice.

"How's it going?" Alan replied, a sleepiness to his tone.

"Yeah, ok, but I'm just off out."

He was sure Alan would be able to hear his heart thumping.

"Anywhere nice?"

"Uh, no."

"You ok? You sound stressed?" Alan said, the enquiry clear in his tone.

"I'm fine. Just in a hurry."

"Oh, sorry. Is there any news on Susie?"

"No," James snapped. "Sorry, I gotta go. I'll call you soon." Without saying goodbye, he clicked off the call, holding down the power button and dropping it to the table in his bedroom before snatching up his wallet.

As he shut the front door, James looked into the orange street-lit darkness, scanned left and right, then stepped out in the direction of the town centre.

The shops were closed up and after a moment's hesitation at the cashpoint, he withdrew three hundred pounds and headed into the tube station.

Occasionally checking behind him, he walked out of the other end and jumped on a bus just as it was about to leave.

James sat at the back, leaving his hometown behind.

Willing himself deep into the crease of the rough fabric of the seat, his gaze flitted to two teenage girls still in uniform, their cheeks rolling with gum, staring into white lights out in front.

Unclenching his fists, he turned to three middle-aged women, bags of shopping surrounding their feet, their voices busy with gossip.

Lastly, he eyed a builder dressed in paint-caked clothes, his head bobbing with the motion as if he were asleep.

James let out a slow deep breath and sank further into the seat.

As the miles rolled past the window, a wave of guilt caught him as his thoughts turned to the phone call. A grip of panic tightened as he recalled the urgency to leave the flat.

Why did Alan choose that time to call?

It was the first time he'd spoken to Alan since Snowdon, the words lingering in his head. He'd asked about Susie with a rare concerned edge to his voice and he'd brushed him off.

Nausea began to well in his stomach but the scream of a 747 dragging itself into the air pulled him back.

Looking out into the night and the bustling orange-lit city, signs everywhere highlighted Heathrow airport, a smile growing as the bus's airbrakes slowed them to a stop.

James jumped to his feet on impulse, stepping out into the cool air of the night. Reaching for his inside jacket pocket, he found it empty, his passport still at home in his bedside drawer. The realisation came that he'd left so much behind, not knowing if he could ever go back.

Turning on the spot, he caught the blue and white of a police car stopped in traffic. Flinching away after momentarily locking eyes with a shadowed driver, his heart leapt his legs into motion. Willpower alone kept his pace calm towards the golden letters of the Ambassador Hotel.

Maybe it wasn't such a bad idea that he'd left his passport behind.

Attempting a casual glance behind, he saw the police car already off in the distance as he grabbed the brass handle of the glass revolving door.

The wide foyer portrayed a different world; a scene of luxury alien to James and he guessed to most. With heavy legs, he stepped across the marble floor, marvelling at the shine of the wood-panelled walls and breathing in the pumped subtle air of decadence.

With a timid sideward glance, he took in the grand space, the neat collection of dark leather armchairs and overstuffed seats huddled around glass tables.

His gaze caught on a marble staircase splitting the grand reception in two as it rose to the first-floor balcony covering the wood-panelled reception running the full length of the wall.

Catching movement to his left, he saw three guests in shirts with ties hanging loose around their necks, their faces barely visible in the gentle warmth of the lounge bar.

With timid steps he moved to the reception desk and the radiating smile of the meticulously polished female receptionist.

Dressed in a black and purple suit jacket, she introduced herself as Cathy.

A bolt of panic shot through his chest. Barely raising his voice, he asked for the cheapest room. With no change to her tone, no curl of her lips into a sneer, she said a figure James could cover with the cash in his pocket, despite the large deposit to cover damages.

He slid the folded notes across the desk and received a plain white plastic card and an A5 sheet of paper in return. His heart rate tripped at the sight of the wide space for his name and address. Conscious a delay would cause suspicion, he scribbled a mixture of his friend's names on the page, pausing as Susie's address began to stain the sheet. As the pen stopped, he took a deep breath. Too late now.

The prim receptionist pointed him in the direction of the marble stairs, her few words masked by the pound of his heart.

The fine woven carpet took him from the stone steps and through a short walk along a sweeping corridor until he saw the numbers of his room. The lock chirped as the key card slid in and he pressed his hand on the polished wood, peering around as the door eased open.

Taking tentative steps, he squinted into the room.

The perimeter lamps glowed as he fingered the light switch, hurrying the locking bar into place before leaning heavily against the wood. After a few deep breaths he looked around again, the luxurious fittings barely registering as he moved to the bathroom, turning on the spot, double checking for any hiding place. Moving to the tall wardrobe and finding it empty, he let out a deep breath.

From the tall windows an orange light disappeared as James rushed around the edge of the room to draw the curtains. Just as the heavy material slid across, he watched the buzz of cars on the road before glancing around the car park.

Dropping to the bed, he closed his eyes with relief.

Bursting up with heavy footsteps from the corridor, he cowered behind the door, his eye to the embedded viewer but he found no one in the distorted image.

James turned and took in the room again. He couldn't help think the place as a cage, holding him from escape.

He couldn't concentrate behind the enclosing walls and pulled open the door.

***

Watching the quiet lounge, James took deliberate steps. He scanned the deep leather seats, the dotted booths and the empty stools peppering the curve of the long high-gloss bar.

Conditions were perfect. He could disappear into his pick of the low-lit seats and keep one eye on the wall of windows, the other on the quiet reception. If anything looked out of place, his escape options were plentiful.

The barman followed him to a booth by the window, a blinding smile shining in his direction.

"Master P, please," James replied to the unasked question, switching his focus to a young porter as he lazily pushed a tall brass-handled trolley across the foyer.

He watched the receptionist who had served him being replaced with a male colleague who looked like a clone of the barman. He glanced to the guy behind the bar, then back to the receptionist stood pulling off pages flowing from a hidden printer, their hair the only difference; the barman's highlighted brunette parted to the side.

James's mind drifted as he imagined shrink-wrapped copies of the barman and receptionist, mouths fixed in a smile, stood lined up in a storeroom ready to be unwrapped for their shift.

Movement from the entrance brought him back from his daydream, his eyebrows raised towards a young beautiful woman drifting through the revolving doors. With striking strawberry blonde hair gathered in a ponytail flowing over a light grey suit jacket, he couldn't help lingering on the matching skirt tightly peaching her buttocks as she arrived at the reception desk.

His gaze drifted down her long-toned legs to black two-inch heels. A shiver ran down his spine.

She finished at the desk and glided to the lift, effortlessly carrying a small holdall. He heard a voice beside him and turned to see his drink had arrived. Turning back, his shoulders slouched when he couldn't see her in the view.

The revolving doors turned again and James took a sip from the cool glass, nodding to the barman then fixed on a guy in a leather jacket walking to the reception. He watched him turn as he strode across the marble, drawing in the full view. James couldn't have been surer he was searching for something.

James ushered away the barman as he came to light table candles, his eyes wide to the guy now hunched forward over the reception.

James edged forward on his seat, a quick glance left and right. The left exit was closer but gave more chance to be seen. He turned back; the guy's hands were waving by his sides, then he spun around and walked away, the receptionist's smile not altering as the guy disappeared out through the gently spinning door.

James moved in his seat, following with his gaze as the man climbed into a long black Mercedes.

With the car out of sight, James pushed himself to relax into the crease, his thoughts turning to the reason he sat in the hotel lounge. He conjured images of Susie somewhere nice. An elegant hotel like where he sat. The drink would be her favourite Mojito.

James smiled. Had it all been a mistake?

Had she just forgotten to tell them she was leaving? Something had come up, a holiday she'd remembered at the last minute. His mind rebelled at the ridiculousness of the fantasy and it crumbled, the sunny images replaced with the sight of her contorted body dumped in the woods. Her once glowing face now grey and lifeless staring back at him, eyes fixed with terror.

He shook the thought away as soft piano notes began drifting across the room and he turned to the direction of the pianist playing in the opposite corner of the lounge.

Bringing the glass to his lips, James found it empty and stood, drifting with the gentle tune as he weaved left and right between the empty tables and chairs.

Taking a casual glance, his left foot missed a step, cracking his shin against the sturdy leg of a chair. Rubbing his shin, he took a second look to check the beauty he'd watched at reception now sat on a barstool, chatting to the barman.

Instead of the jacket, a blouse gripped across her ample chest with her hair loose around her shoulders. She still wore the grey skirt, pulled slightly up as she sat, exposing the lower part of her toned thighs.

Recovering from the pain and shaking off the stare, James approached the bar a few stools to her left. As the barman placed a glass of wine at her front, she turned, a shiver of pleasure running up his spine as she shone a smile in his direction.

"Refill?" the barman said, catching James entranced.

Blinking, he turned and nodded, fixing his gaze along the array of bottles whilst fighting the urge not to turn back toward her. His will soon relented and he watched in the reflection of a cupboard window as she glanced to the barman filling a clean tumbler, adding ice and dark rum as he went.

Her head tipped slowly to the side with the pour of orange juice and her delicately made-up face turned his way when the barman selected the cranberry juice carton.

"Unusual drink," she said, her voice scented with a husk which reverberated through his body.

James threw her a glance, smiling nervously back. "Master P," he said in a deep reply, alien to his ears. He coughed into his fist and watched her slowly follow the drink as it was set down in front of him. "You're… you're welcome to try it," he stuttered, lifting the bright red drink in her direction, hoping she wouldn't see his tremble.

Her smile widened. "Why not," she replied.

Without pause, James stood, placing the tumbler in her open grasp and watched as she plucked a short black straw from a dispenser on the counter, hovering it in the drink. His vision zoomed as she pursed her pastel pink lips, pulling at the colourful liquid.

He furiously blinked as she took out the straw and gave a gratified nod. "Ooh, that's nice, thank you," she said, but instead of handing it back she placed the drink in the centre of a square napkin to her side.

James stood with an awkward pause, unsure of the invitation until her slender fingers tapped at the stool. He sat and rubbed the back of his neck, eventually taking a sip of his drink.

"So what brings you to Heathrow tonight?" she said.

James froze with the glass at his lips. For the second time in two days, he hadn't prepared to be questioned. He smiled and took another sip, stalling for time but knew any longer and he would look even more like an idiot.

"I'm an Arborist. I had a meeting in London and I'm flying back to Edinburgh soon. You?"

Edinburgh, he shouted silently to himself. He knew nothing about the place and hoped neither did she.

"Oh, just a boring meeting."

James didn't think anything would be boring with her around.

"What do you do?" he said, asking the first thing which came into his head, already guessing her to be a model or lawyer, or a highflyer in some glamorous profession.

"I work for the government," she came back.

James didn't have to hide his surprise as another male clone in a purple waistcoat dropped a plate and cloche in the centre of the foyer. As the echo subsided, more clones, men and women, came and quickly mopped up the broken crockery.

“Pension service,” she said, looking back. “It's not the most exciting of jobs but you'll thank me when you're seventy.”

When both their laughter subsided, she stuck out her hand.

“I'm Trinity,” she said as he shook her delicate grip.

“James,” he replied.

Shit, he shouted in his head while somehow managing to hide his self-aimed anger.

The alcohol and Trinity's calming demeanour helped the conversation flow. He avoided anything personal and she didn’t probe, but to his growing surprise, she appeared to be interested in what he had to say.

With an accidental glance at a brass-framed clock he realised the past three hours had vanished into thin air. Trinity looked at her small watch.

“I'm going to have to go to bed soon. I think I may have a sore head in the morning.” She ran a finger around the rim of her wine glass on the bar. “I don't think there's much chance of sleep though.”

James glanced up from his half full drink.

“I don't sleep very well in hotel beds,” she added, raising her eyebrows.

Trinity stood and excused herself to powder her nose. As she walked across the reception, he watched her behind sway gently until she disappeared from view.

Alone, the lounge now empty aside from the barman, James took a deep breath and felt himself shaking. Never before had he felt like this about a woman. Sure, he'd been attracted to plenty before but this was insane, and it was obvious she liked him and wanted to take it further.

He'd never had sex on a first night and it wasn’t even a date. He'd never just met someone and slept with them.

A car horn called from somewhere outside and James spun after to search for the source. Through the giant glass windows, he saw a brunette middle-aged woman in a cream-coloured Micra impatiently waiting beside a pile of luggage.

The car caught him by surprise.

What was he doing?

Anything could be happening to Susie right now. He was here to protect himself so he could carry on and find her, but instead he'd been drinking and considering bedding a beautiful lady he'd only just met.

An alarm bell rang somewhere in his head. George's voice calmly explained this kind of thing doesn't happen to James.

When Trinity returned, he noticed she'd undone another button of her blouse and he could see the lace edging of her bra.

She walked straight up to him, leant in and feeling her breath on his ear, she whispered, "I don't normally do this…"

James's breath became shallow as her sweet perfume washed over him.

"But I really like you. Would you like to join me upstairs?" Trinity stood up straight and wet her lips, running her tongue along their length.

The tinny sound of the alarm rang far away in the depths of his head, but he still had enough control to want to be sure. Her gaze followed his as he stood, taking a deep breath.

"I want to. I really want to," he said, as he conjured Susie's image in his mind, "but I've got an early start tomorrow."

Trinity bit her lip and he added, "But are you around tomorrow? We could have dinner. I'd love to get to know you better." The words sounded so lame and he knew he would never see her again. He could already hear Andrew's laughter, knowing that despite his embarrassment he would recount this night at their next drunken meeting.

"That would be nice," she replied as she glanced to the floor.

A pang of guilt shot through him as she leant in and pecked him on the cheek. She turned and walked across the lounge. With each step he ached to call after her, but instead he sat and took in the last moments, as without a backward look, she disappeared out of view.

He sat alone, sipping the last remains of his drink, regretting his choice with every passing second. Still he tried to reason; if Trinity wasn't a femme fatale then all he'd lost was a once in a lifetime night with a stunningly attractive woman. There would be no second chance.

James chuckled out loud, but even though he knew he'd blown it, he still had to know if there was anything but his charms motivating her.

Since he'd been sitting there alone the lights had dimmed in the quiet reception. A lone attendant, this time not a clone, sat behind the long counter.

James read from his name badge as Graeme greeted him.

"Hello, sir. How can I help?"

"Hi. Nice to meet you," James replied, holding out his hand.

Clearly a little taken aback, Graeme stood and shook the offered hand as James spoke.

"I'm the new owner of the hotel and I'm a very important man, so I'm travelling incognito," James said as he applied light pressure with his grip.

"Ok," Graeme replied, his smile fixed.

"Did you see the lady who just went to the lifts?" he said, releasing the grip and pointing.

"The lady you were sitting with?"

"Yes. She's a travel writer and I want to make sure she's looked after. Can you tell me which room she's staying in?"

James saw the receptionist's expression lift. "Ah, that makes sense now," he said, nodding as he spoke. "Judy booked her into two rooms," he said, tapping at a hidden keyboard. "Trinity Smith, rooms 318 and 416."

James felt his heart sink and his legs give a tremor.

"Are you okay, sir?" Graeme asked with wide eyes.

"Ah, yes." Even though he felt anything but when he realised that not only had she taken two rooms, but one of them was next to his and the other sounded as if it was directly above.

12

Adrenaline coursing, he climbed the stairs, the void of lust overflowing with rage. How dare she trick him, taking him in so wholly.

Clenching his fists, the anger turned inwards as he thought about the blaring warning he'd been so keen to push to the back of his head. Soon realising he neared his room, with each step a plan began to form.

Summiting the steps and thankful for the empty corridor, James stepped light-footed and leant to the door next to his. Silence percolated through the solid wood and to his surprise his knuckles tapped gently.

A scurry of movement came from inside and an alarming thought struck him.

What if she wasn't alone?

What if she had a weapon, a gun even?

James chided himself, knowing he really had to start thinking things through.

The lock clicked and his pulse continued to build. The door opened inward, his eyes popped wide and he felt as if he were going to explode

Trinity stood at the door in a blood-red silk nightdress, its length shimmering high above the knee with curls of white lace chasing across the top of her plump, lightly freckled breasts.

The anger had gone. Anxiety dissipated along with his fear and defences; the startling discovery now as if a light year ago.

"Hello, James," she said, her voice quiet and sweet like honey. "Did you change your mind?" As she spoke, she tilted her head to the side and inwards towards the room.

"Can I come in?" he said, surprising himself with a voice quiet and unsure.

Her silky smile widened as she fully opened the door and stepped to the side. Without hesitation, he headed in and casually glanced around the room, but barely took in the view.

Swinging around, his gaze snagged on a black box on the bedside table; the same bulky phone he'd seen in Chris Smith's hands. Reasoning flashed across his mind.

Ignoring her smile as she stood at the closed door, he peered into the empty bathroom as she walked towards him. Even as he locked eyes, he felt a nagging hypnosis from her hazel gaze, a hint he'd made a mistake as his body craved for him to be wrong.

His head knew different and the anger began to build as he stepped forward, opening his arms to take her embrace.

"I haven't been entirely honest with you," he said softly as his hands touched at her bare upper arms. "My name is James Fisher, Agent James Fisher," he paused. "Extraordinary Investigations Branch."

Staring at her for a reaction as his mind raced at what would happen next, he watched as her expression neutralised. Releasing his grip, he let her arms drop to her side.

"Come with me and I'll explain everything."

James moved to the door, glancing back as Trinity followed, watching as she passed the open wardrobe to grab and wrap herself in a white dressing gown before snatching the key card from the dresser.

Silently, she let him lead her down the corridor and followed to the staircase where they travelled up three flights to the top floor and found an unlocked storeroom.

Packed with rows of high-stacked chairs and shelves for spare linen, James's gaze flitted around the stale, windowless room. He pulled two chairs from the nearest stack, pushing aside a litter of cardboard boxes before arranging the two chairs to face each other. Nodding for Trinity to sit, he watched her hands bind the gown together as she did what he asked without question.

James closed the door, sat down and, leaning forward, began to spin his tale as it raced from the top of his head.

"You're a government investigator."

She looked up and nodded at the statement with her arms wrapping around her stomach.

"You were sent to find me."

She nodded again.

"Because of Chris Smith."

She continued to nod.

"I set you up."

Trinity stopped moving her head, her eyes squinting.

"A girl has gone missing. Someone in your organisation's gone rogue. I'm here to find out who and to get the girl back."

Her eyes further tightened as James spoke. He looked back in awe at the change in the woman sat before him. She'd seduced him with confidence and smouldering presence; now she sat child-like and submissive as she took in each of his words.

"Do you understand?" James said after a long pause.

She replied immediately with a quiet voice. "Yes."

James nodded. "Have you had any dealings with our department before?"

"No," she said, her voice still quiet. "To be honest, I didn't know it even existed."

"Operating under the radar is how we get things done. I've confirmed you're clean so from now on you're under secondment. You'll provide assistance to my investigation, reporting only to me. You need to consider your section as hostile and report counterintelligence to your handler."

Trinity nodded as James continued. "Now tell me what you know so far." His voice was stiff and brisk, buoyed by confidence.

"My name's Carrie Harris. I'm lead investigator for Section Three. I was despatched to investigate the disappearance of Agent Chris Smith of Six Southwest Asia. He went AWOL this morning, being due to give evidence at the High Court and deliver a briefing to JSOC."

James made a mental note to look at the list of abbreviations.

"He turned up in Vauxhall after the meeting should have taken place, acting as though nothing was wrong. Noting his behaviour as suspicious, they reported it as a possible breakdown. Somehow it found my team.

"After reviewing his console log, we found the recording of your meeting. We couldn't understand why he agreed to help you, so they despatched me to investigate and take the necessary action."

"Necessary action?" James said, pulling up straight in his seat.

"Detention, monitoring or intervention," she replied with a blank expression. "I found you too easily. I should have realised it was a trap."

Harris looked James in the eye and smiled.

"You were so natural. I was outside the flat from about four o'clock. I saw you leaving and followed you on foot where I observed you get on the bus and I followed you by car."

"What were you planning?"

"Get to know you and go from there."

"Did your plan involve sleeping with me?" James surprised himself with the directness of the question.

"Not specifically," Harris replied smiling, then checked the bathrobe covered her legs.

James stood.

"Good work, Agent Harris. When did you last check in?"

"When I arrived at your flat. My next is due tomorrow morning."

"Let's get on with it," James said.

"What should I call you?" Harris asked as they stood.

"Fisher," he replied and they walked back to her room in silence.

Fisher sat on the bed and Harris grabbed her phone. Seeing him eye her with suspicion, she explained she was disabling the automatic monitoring and erasing the recording from the bar. Her head switched to professional in a matter of moments as they sat together, going over the details of the investigation. Gone were those silky stares, the wanting look and the promise as they talked into the early hours of the morning until exhaustion forced Fisher back to his room.

***

The phone woke him with an unfamiliar tone and he opened his eyes to see the receiver on the nightstand. Rubbing his hand down his face, he answered the call, watching as the surroundings became more familiar.

"I've made some progress," came a woman's business-like voice, the tone of which he vaguely recognised before the line went dead.

A smile crept across his face as he climbed out of bed, his head full of visions of her standing at the door in her scarlet nightdress. After a cold shower and dressed in yesterday's clothes, he left his room to find her door open a crack.

Pushing it all the way open and with a tinge of disappointment, he saw her dressed in yesterday's suit, hair tight in a ponytail with her left leg over the right as she sat on the bed, tapping at the keys of a laptop open by her side.

Harris looked up from the computer, greeting him with a smile radiating with enthusiasm. He walked in and closed the door, taking in her perfume and the sight of her refreshed look with the feelings from the lounge hanging heavy at the back of his head.

Don't get distracted, he repeated under his breath.

"Good morning. There's coffee on the side," she said, pointing to a tray with a tall stainless-steel pot and two plates of cold breakfast.

Walking over to the pot, he poured a cup. "What's the news?"

Harris beamed back and raised her eyebrows as she spoke. "I've gone over Agent Smith's work this morning. Not too much progress but he did get hold of her mobile phone records."

Fisher followed her finger to the small screen and a spreadsheet lined with a forest of numbers and codes. He looked closely, recognising the first columns as telephone numbers, the second as a time and date, the rest filled with number sequences he couldn't immediately decipher what they meant.

"So what does all this mean?" he said, looking up as he crouched to the screen.

Harris replied with her eyes narrowed. "It's a comms statement? Standard format. I must have reviewed thousands in my career." Her look of confusion didn't waver as he stared back wide-eyed, before being jolted by the realisation.

"Um, I've been abroad for quite a few years. On my last assignment…" he paused and took a gulp of air, "I used the Asian reports. This one seems quite different."

Harris turned slowly back to the screen. Her gaze lingered on his face before switching as she pointed to each of the columns in turn.

"Phone number. Date and time of the call. IMEI and SIM."

Fisher nodded, biting at his lip.

"Then the location codes." She looked back as she finished.

"I see now," he said, leaning closer to the screen, searching the detail for meaning. "The last call was on Saturday morning, the day she disappeared. Does that help?"

Her finger appeared at the screen. "The location codes are for North West Wales."

"And?" he replied.

"Watch," she said, as using the trackpad Harris clicked the second tab on the spreadsheet, revealing another sea of numbers.

Fisher squinted at the screen. Everything looked the same, other than the list was much longer. The calls up to Saturday morning were identical until the dates skipped before starting once more.

Fisher checked the date on his watch; the last call was only yesterday morning.

"What are these?" he said, pointing to the bottom of the list, his finger tracking along the far-right column.

"The IMEI number stayed the same, but the SIM number is different."

"A different SIM card is being used in her phone?"

"Bingo. Someone's changed the SIM."

"So where's it being used?" he said, scrambling through the data to try and figure out the information for himself.

"Same place, or thereabouts."

"Someone else is using the phone," Fisher said and turned to the window, staring out at the fresh morning.

"Or she's still using it herself. Is there a chance she could be responsible for her own disappearance?"

Fisher turned sharply to face her. "No chance."

Harris drew back. "Either way it's a lead. We need to find out who is using the phone," she said.

"How do we do that?"

"We go find it."

Fisher nodded as his smile grew.

***

Within ten minutes they had checked out of the hotel, Harris's simple plan in full swing with a short message to her handler, confirming eyes on the target at a distance with no chance yet to intervene.

After a short ride together in her Series One BMW to the local town, Hounslow, Fisher withdrew cash over the counter and stocked up on supplies for the trip. The next step in her plan was to ditch the car because of its built in GPS tracker she'd casually revealed as if he already knew.

Parking at a superstore on the outskirts of the airport, Fisher walked the short distance to the Avis check-in desk, paying with cash for the lowest model available.

Parking the Fiesta next to Harris's car, he stood beside her, watching as she popped the boot before swapping her small suitcase and Fisher's bags between the two. Despite the BMW's boot being empty, Fisher looked on with surprise as she pulled up the thin floor panel to reveal a grey checker plate-edged hatch sitting next to the car battery.

With her fingers blurring, she tapped a long code into a small keypad set into the corner. With the press of the last number it emitted a quiet click, the hatch flipping open to reveal a deep, rectangular aluminium flight case.

Muscles straining with the weight, she pulled it from the boot and into the rear of the Fiesta before placing her thick phone at the centre of the hidden compartment and pushing the hatch closed.

Without a word, she jumped in her car and drove out into the flow of traffic.

Back in the rental, Fisher busied himself registering four mobile phones he'd picked up and unwrapped the packaging from a new iPad.

With the task complete, he looked around, watching distracted people and traffic bustling around the airport perimeter.

A deep breath took him by surprise. It was the first moment since the lounge where he'd had time to think. To contemplate the enormity of the situation.

When he'd left the flat yesterday, he'd thought he was in deep, but since meeting Harris as Trinity the situation had taken such a steep dive.

Fisher couldn't help but smile as he remembered his golden rule.

Involving a second British Secret Service Agent was anything but simple. Prison could be a real prospect, but it would be worth it if he could find Susie. Perhaps then he could explain everything. Well, almost everything.

Deep in reflection, Fisher caught sight of a police car, watching as it drove across his view when a sudden thought flashed across his mind.

Were they looking for him?

With another deep breath, he told himself they couldn't be because he'd convinced Harris she was working for him.

He felt a sudden doubt; she could just be playing along.

What if she was reporting him to her masters right now to arrange for his capture?

Fisher fidgeted in his seat.

How much time could he give her before he should leave alone? He had the telephone number, the lead. Could he do this on his own? His heart rate rose as reason after reason shouted at him to flee.

He took a deep breath, reassuring himself he was being silly and watched the traffic on the busy road, catching a glimpse of what looked like Harris's car.

"It's a popular model," he said out loud as his attention caught a huge British Airways 777 launching slowly into the air. He thought of the passengers setting out on their own adventure.

As it banked out of sight, he saw a black BMW X5.

Had he seen it before only moments earlier?

Another popular model, but all of the windows were tinted, which was unusual and probably illegal.

Fisher started the engine with a turn of the key, his hand moving to hover over the gear stick.

"Five more minutes," he said out loud.

A siren's call pulled him from his thoughts and he watched wide-eyed as a huge police Range Rover raced into view from his right, his gaze following as it weaved in and out of the traffic.

"Time's up," he shouted and jammed the car into first gear, jerking the Fiesta out of the space.

13

Tyres squealing, the compact car sped around the car park's narrow lanes. With the siren long gone, he pressed his foot hard, spine jarring with each thump of the tyres against the speed bumps as he bounced across the front of the superstore panelled in glass.

With his stare set firm on the exit ahead, a Hackney cab cut across from his peripheral vision, quickly coming to a stop outside the long shop entrance. About to jab the wheel to the right, a coach pulled up against the opposite raised curb with a hiss of air lines, blocking the road.

His foot jammed to the brake, hands gripping the steering wheel as the tyres squealed, stopping a hair's width from the taxi.

With a deep breath, he feathered the throttle, frustration drumming his fingers at the wheel as he stared through the windscreen, watching the oblivious cabby complete a transaction. The kerbside door angled open and a slender leg appeared. Harris stepped out with her strawberry blonde hair glinting from the low sun.

Before he could blink, she'd disappeared into the store with the cab moving away from the curb. The Fiesta rolled forward before his foot, seemingly acting alone, brought him to a stop outside the automatic doors.

Peering out of the windscreen, the passenger door opened and the car filled with her delicate perfume. Without words, he pulled slowly away, the last ten minutes barely a memory.

With only the briefest of words, they took the M40 motorway and the long silence continued, only punctuated with her occasional narration of the route, correcting their heading to Birmingham Airport.

"We'll have two or three days," she said after confirming the address on the iPad.

Fisher nodded, the hum of the road surrounding him once more.

Minutes later, he thumbed the radio, relaxing into his seat as cheerful pop poured from the speakers.

"So what sort of music are you in to?" he said as one of Coldplay's melancholy hits played in the background.

Harris surprised him with silence and glancing away from the road he saw her raised eyebrow.

"Sorry. I'm no good at small talk."

"I'm the same. I was trying to guess what you were finally going to say," Harris said.

He glanced over to see a thin smile on her lips.

"I'd have settled on the weather."

"That was my second choice," he said, raising his eyebrows and peering up through the top half of the windscreen.

Harris gave a chuckle and he watched her cheeks form a shallow dimple.

"We seemed to be talking all right last night," she said, her face beaming as she straightened her expression.

Fisher stared hard at the road.

"Quiet music," Harris said soon after.

"Quiet?" Fisher said, turning back again.

"Rocking out on stakeout is frowned upon," she said, running her hand down her hair hanging over her shoulder.

"What about downtime?"

"Work. Sleep. That's the cycle," she said, her voice still enthusiastic. "I barely get a moment to myself." Her tone turned defensive and her eyes lit wide. "I like it that way." She paused but he couldn't settle on what to say. "Don't you find that too?"

"I can't talk about my job." The words came out harder than he'd intended, but she was quick to respond.

"Of course not. I'm sorry," she said, turning her head to the window.

"It's okay. Do you have family?"

"I've got a sister that I don't see very often. My parents died when I was young," she said, her tone levelling.

"My parents died, too," he said, surprising himself. "Four years ago now."

"I read that," her voice replied, uncertain. "I thought it was part of your cover."

"What else did the file say?" he said with his eyes fixed forward.

"They were murdered." Harris paused and he felt her turn his way. "Is that true?"

He nodded.

"I'm sorry," she said.

Fisher gave a weak smile.

There was a long silence before she spoke again. "What I didn't understand is why they asked for a ransom of a million pounds when there was no chance of raising that kind of cash."

Fisher turned to his window without reply.

"Shit," she said, catching herself. "I'm sorry."

"No need," he said, staring back at the road ahead.

They didn't speak again until the turn off for Birmingham International Airport and then only to confirm directions. Fisher stopped the car outside the terminal, unloading the bags and leaving Harris behind before taking the car to the Avis car park. Without fuss he took the courtesy bus back to the terminal and the first waiting cab already loaded with Harris and the bags.

The lunchtime rush-hour traffic in the city centre meant another hour passed before they arrived at the Hertz branch. After stopping the cab a few hundred yards up the road and after waiting for it to disappear from sight, Harris strode off to pick up a new car.

Within half an hour they'd joined the M5 in a Vauxhall Vectra and after another two and a half hours of mostly silence, Fisher took over the driving.

As he wound the car around the A roads, Harris turned the radio down.

"I'm sorry if I overstepped a bit earlier, with your parent's..." she hesitated, "case."

"It's okay."

"It's just when I put myself in one of my characters, I spend less and less time as me and it makes me a bit..." she paused as she searched for the right words, "Analytical. Hopefully not cold, but analytical."

"It's okay, really. It's quite refreshing. No-one really talks about it." He paused. "I don't talk about it."

"Well you know for the next time I put my foot in it," she said with a smile as she picked up the iPad from down the side of the seat and began tapping at the screen.

"I've got the details of the telephone masts. There aren't too many up there so the call locations are pretty approximate. Still, it looks like they centre around a little village called Llanrug."

Fisher watched out of the corner of his eye as she opened Google maps and tapped in the name of the town.

"It's only four miles from Llanberis," Harris added.

He glanced across again and saw the excited grin on her face, her fingers still tapping at the screen. He turned back to the road as she picked up one of the new phones from her pocket and dialled a number. It wasn't long before she hung up for the third time after being turned away again.

Four calls later and he heard an excited suck of air, then the words. "I'll take it for two nights, doesn't matter." Names and addresses he didn't recognise were given just before she hung up. "Double room I'm afraid," she said, turning his way. "Better than sleeping in this." Her hand tapped on the plastic dashboard.

His heart rate jumped. Had he heard right? Before he could replay the moment in his head, he corrected the steering from his veer to the curb and watched her update the Sat Nav, the arrival time increasing by only a couple of minutes.

"So why don't you talk to your sister much?" Fisher asked to get his mind from where it had wandered.

"We used to be close, but I live in a different world. It's difficult keeping normal relationships. Nothing in common anymore."

"There must be something you can talk about other than work? Hobbies?"

"I am the job and it is me. Pretty sad, I know."

"What does she think you do?"

"Trade envoy for the government."

He nodded and stared out at the road before speaking. "I'm an only child. I always wanted a sister. I've kind of got that in one of my friends," he said, then turned the radio up to try and kill the conversation he knew it wouldn't be wise to start.

They made good time through the familiar mountain roads, passing the same villages and hamlets dotted along the route, after ninety minutes catching first sight of the dark slate mountain towering over Llanberis and he could feel his pulse rise with every mile.

Another five minutes and with no traffic behind, he slowed the car to a crawl and pointed across Harris.

"The campsite's up there," he said, motioning up the steep drive. "Where she was staying," he added as the car crept along. "It leads to a farm."

Harris nodded as they rolled past stone houses, their doors butted to the pavement.

Fisher tried to hide the deep pull of breath as he turned to the right. "The last place she was seen," he said as he stared at The Peak Inn. "By her friends," he added, trying to lower his tone as the words caught. "She was here on the Friday night, then on the Saturday, the night she vanished."

Harris nodded as Fisher cleared his throat.

Passing The Prince of Wales, he spoke again. "There was an encounter here on the Friday with some creepy idiot. It'll be worth investigating."

"Who was with her?"

"Her four best friends."

"What are their names?"

Fisher didn't answer for a moment. "I'd have to check," he finally said.

"I don't think you do," she replied, and he could feel her looking straight at him as he tried his best to stare at the road ahead. "You were with her, weren't you?"

His heart sank and his muscles relaxed into the seat. He knew there was little point in lying.

"Yes," he said and turned to the disappointment in her glare.

They sat in silence for what seemed like a long minute as Fisher sped up and carried on through the village.

"So you think there's a link between the job and her disappearance," she finally said, looking straight at him with narrowed eyes. "And that's why you suspect our involvement?"

Fisher's muscles tightened as he pulled himself up straight. "Yes," he said, trying to give confidence in his words.

"So what were you working on?"

"You know I can't answer that," he said, volume returning to his tone.

"It might be relevant."

"Let's work the leads," he said, trying to suppress his smile as they passed the last squat house marking the boundary of Llanberis. Refocusing, he ignored the directions of the Sat Nav and passed the turning for the hotel, carrying on towards Llanrug.

The first sign of the next small village was the Black Boy Pub. They travelled on, passing battered old houses scattered along the road and a mix of modern and dilapidated buildings, each looking as if they'd been left for centuries to decay and crumble.

They passed a housing estate that seemed to rise from nowhere, its box-fresh red brick and tightly packed houses shined, the lines between recently turfed perfect grass still visible. The rough scrub was back as the development abruptly ended, dotting the curb with gnarled shrubbery, trees and a scattering of stone buildings crumbling to the mountain climate.

Finding only a church, a small primary school and few other buildings essential for even the smallest of villages, they soon arrived at its border, having only noticed the one pub.

Fisher turned the car in a wide dirt track and headed back the way they'd come.

Taking the turn for the hotel, they arrived at an old stone farmhouse sided with long stables converted into chalets. He pulled the car into the only remaining space in the small car park and as Harris stretched her legs, he headed toward the reception, a tiny sectioned corner of the vast old barn to find a middle-aged woman, her hair tied high with a rainbow scarf, behind the desk.

"Mr and Mrs Partridge," he said, and saw the recognition in her warm smile. With the reservation found and paid in cash for the two nights, and after almost signing the register in his own name, he left with a reservation in the restaurant and the key to Stable Fifteen, a long thin key chained to a heavy horseshoe the size of a child's fist.

Fisher walked back to the car to find Harris talking to a man who looked to be in his sixties and wore a wax jacket and a flat cap far back on his head.

As Fisher neared, the conversation finished and the man continued towards the reception, nodding and tapping his peak as he passed by.

14

Harris stood by the car, the aluminium flight case by her feet. Fisher stared into her eyes as he approached and saw what he thought were the first signs of a grin. A shiver of unease ran down his spine, but the dread soon vanished with the twinkle in her eyes, her smile beaming in his direction as she bent to pick up the heavy case.

Plucking the rest of the bags from the boot, they followed the directions on crisp new wooden signs, the range of room numbers browned into their centres.

Finding their chalet, Fisher flung the heavy door wide.

A king size bed dominated the dark room, its white cotton covers pulled tight with aged furniture lining the walls and a wide wooden-framed mirror hanging opposite the bed. Fisher scanned for a couch, but couldn't find one; instead, two wooden chairs stood around a small, dark corner table.

"Ever slept in a bath before?" Harris said, standing in the bathroom to his right.

He raised his eyebrows and dropped the bags at the foot of the bed.

"There's always a first time," he replied.

After closing the door, he eyed the flight case.

"What you thinking?" she said and he looked up to see her head turned sideways, the question hanging on her features.

"I've been dying to know what's in the metal case."

Screwing up her face, she tilted back her head. "It's a V32," she replied, her eyebrows still low as she tried to read Fisher's blank expression. "Surely you use them in your department? What was it again?"

"Extraordinary Investigations," he said, shaking his head.

"Well, it's standard issue for everyone else." For a few seconds, Harris stood still and squinted back.

Fisher felt his unease grow, realising he should have kept quiet, but eventually her expression relaxed and she pulled the case on to the bed before motioning to the large window with her right hand.

"Get the curtains, please."

Fisher turned and pulled across the rough lined fabric, flicking up the light switch. As he turned back, her fingers pulled up the central metal clasp to reveal a gloss square pad the size of her thumb. She held her forefinger against the slick finish and a low tone emitted from somewhere deep in the box. Sliding combination switches either side of the central handle, she pulled tiny metal switches outwards and the clasps flipped up in unison with a satisfying clunk.

Fisher leant forward with his mouth wide open, barely stifling a gasp as he saw the two handguns nested in black moulded foam. Like a child at Christmas, he peered over her shoulder, the synthetic smell of gun oil filling his nostrils as he watched her slender fingers locate and retract black plastic handles either side of the case. Grabbing both, she pulled out the tray.

He didn't know where to look first as it came to rest on the bed.

His eyes bulged at the two pistols, one much smaller than the other, its short barrel shining with a silvered metallic grey. He half expected the stamp of a toy company on the stumpy grip rather than the word Beretta. Fisher swapped his look to the contrast of its neighbour; matt black with a sleek profile he recognised from the movies.

Packed around the edges between slices of dark foam were two sizes of magazine. Each glinted with brass, their matt-black length sandwiching rectangular green boxes and two rows of orangey-brown cylinders just visible through the thin plastic.

Fisher turned to his side as she placed a second tray next to the first, the inside of which was crammed with metal and plastic boxes ranging in size from no bigger than his fingertip to that of a compact mobile phone. Each shape varied in colour, from black, grey, green and earthy brown, but all had a spider thread of wire coiling from one side and a set of bulleted black letters printed bold on a tiny, white label on the adjacent slice of foam.

The third layer remained in the case and he stepped into the gap left as she moved to the side. Squinting into the box, he saw a wide spectrum of what looked to be weird and wonderful items, only some of which he thought he recognised. Distress flares, smoke grenades, rolls of gaffer tape in black and earthy colours peered back and small plastic bottles with no markings, each differently coloured, a pen torch and a fierce-looking multi-tool.

"Time to come clean," Harris said, her voice knocking him out of his stare.

"Huh?" Fisher replied, blinking, forcing down the childlike grin as he realised, she'd been watching him the whole time.

"You're not a field agent, are you?"

The question came as a surprise but despite his best efforts his grin sprung back.

"What gave it away?" he said with a cheer.

"Let me think," she said, one arm folded at her waist, a finger tapping at her lips. "The phone file." As she spoke, she began to count on her fingers. "The tracker on the car." Another finger lifted. "You've clearly never seen a field kit before." Her eyes squinted tightly as she paused. "What do you do in Extraordinary Investigations? Not a field agent, that's for sure."

His smile dropped as she spoke, his face turning towards the floor then back to the bed.

Harris took a step toward him, his body tensing as she spoke in a lowered voice. "What am I dealing with here?"

15

Fisher stood in front of her as he felt himself sinking into the silence, turning his head from the guns on the bed then back towards her. About to speak, about to give it all up, he saw a minute relaxing of her expression as she spoke again.

"You've got the authority to get me reassigned, but I need to know what I'm dealing with."

He let out a breath and let his shoulders relax. She still believed.

"I'm a manager," he replied with renewed confidence, but her eyes narrowed once more.

"Oh shit," her face tensed. "We're done for." Harris turned her head sideways and spoke again, her voice slow and considered. "What sort of manager?"

A smile bloomed on Fisher's face. "IT."

"That explains a lot," she said, her head shaking from side to side. "And this is the first time you've been out in the field?"

He nodded.

"Did you even go through selection?"

Fisher shrugged.

"Basic?" she added.

He shrugged again.

"Have you ever discharged a firearm?"

Fisher shook his head and she buried her face in her hands. It was a long time before she spoke.

"Is there anything else I need to know?"

He shook his head and she let out a sigh.

"So do you want a lesson?"

Fisher nodded eagerly with eyes wide, the corner of his mouth lifting.

Still shaking her head, she stepped to the trays and pointed at the larger of the handguns.

"Glock 17. Fourth generation semi-automatic pistol." She turned back and checked he was following. "Only developed this year and I'm one of the first to get my hands on it." As she spoke, she ran her finger gently along the top of the barrel. "It's an amazing weapon, very light with a high fire rate, seventeen round capacity and unrivalled accuracy." Her hand moved over to the ammunition clips.

"Four clips of 9mm standard NATO parabellums plus two boxes of fifty rounds." Her finger moved across the foam to the smaller pistol. "Beretta .22 and two clip loaders. Ideal for concealing because of its size." She stopped for breath, raising her eyebrows as she turned back to him. "Both evaluated and chosen by me," she said with a tinge of pride in her voice as her hand moved to a small black rectangular box in the right-hand corner of the tray.

"Emergency transponder. Slide the cover up, press the button underneath. Sends a signal through multiple pathways. Wi-Fi. Mobile GPRS, or if nothing else is available then it uses military frequency to SkyNet5. The signal will be received at HQ and given a priority two attendance, anywhere in the world. Same unit hard-wired to the case, connected to tamper sensors."

"What happens if you're indoors?" Fisher asked.

"Good question," she replied. "It connects to any Wi-Fi network."

"Any network?" he said. "Even secure networks?"

"Yeah," she said, but turned back to him abruptly. "All military and commercial Wi-Fi hardware has hidden network layers allowing pass-through of the transmission. It can't be turned off." Her voice trailed to silence as she spoke, her eyes narrowing. "But you should know that."

Fisher nodded towards the next tray and she turned back.

"Various transmitters, trackers and listening devices. Most are used with the communications platform." She raised her eyebrows. "Which is in my car at Heathrow." Her hand moved to the tray still in the bottom of the aluminium case. "In here are flares, smoke canisters, distress beacon, torch, multi-tool, field medical kit, latex gloves, pepper spray, evidence management systems, various fast fixings, alcohol-based cleaning cloths, gun oil and kit to maintain the weapon systems."

As if she had done it many times before, she placed the two trays back in the case and in a fluid motion closed the lid, snapping the clasps together. "I'm going for a shower," she said, and picked up her suitcase before heading to the bathroom and closing the door. The sound of the shower started almost immediately.

Fisher staggered backwards to the bed, the excitement of the moment turning to panic, his appreciation of how deep he was in trouble growing exponentially.

For the third time since he'd met her, his appreciation of how much of a dangerous woman he'd gotten involved with grew in volume.

He drew a deep breath. At least she was on his side. For now, at least, a quiet voice whispered inside his head.

The flurry of the shower stopped and Harris soon emerged, a white bathrobe wrapped around her and her hair glistening with water. She glared at him with narrowed eyes.

"I've been thinking."

Fisher stood from the bed and pushed his hands into his pockets. "Me, too," he said, looking at the carpet.

"If you want my help then there's one way I can do this. One way."

Fisher nodded.

"Forget rank. I'm in charge."

"Okay," he replied, still nodding.

"I've got ten years of field experience, and you, with respect, know about computers. If this is going to work," she said, opening her hands out in front of her, "if we're going to have the best chance to find your friend, I need to lead the way."

"I said okay. I agree with you. This is about Susie, nothing else."

"Yes," she said, and her face relaxed. "I'll get dressed and we'll get some dinner."

"Yes, boss."

She looked back at him, her head tilted forward as she turned back to the bathroom.

***

The receptionist doubled as the waitress, the pair muting their conversation as she filled their glasses with Chardonnay.

"So what were you before you were a..." he stopped as she raised an eyebrow. "Before your current career?" he finished, raising his glass.

"A school kid."

He turned his head to the side. "Recruited out of school? Does that actually happen?"

"Did to me. I was a bit of a gymnast in my teens. I attended a few events but blew my knee. Got me two operations and a year out of training."

Fisher contorted his face as she spoke.

"It ballooned to the size of a melon."

"But it got better?"

Harris nodded slowly as she sipped the last of her wine. "A year is a lifetime out of the circuit. Everyone my age, my category, had shot out in front. I had to do something. I was piling on the weight. My coach suggested I gave the Army Cadets a try to get back to fitness. It turns out I had a talent for that, too, and I got spotted at sixteen. They put me through college, skipped university, then I passed out from Sandhurst."

"You joined the Army?"

"No. They tried but our employer insisted. After Sandhurst I went through field training and that's me really." She topped up their glasses. "What's your story?"

"Not here," he said, nodding to the waitress as she approached the table with their food.

As they ate, Fisher deflected her probing, fascinating himself with the contrasts of this night and the last, marvelling at the stark differences between Harris, her quiet conversation and the glaring confidence of Trinity, all the while his mind spamming pictures of that nightdress.

For the second night, their time together slipped through his fingers. They'd outstayed the other guests, theirs the lone occupied table with just the waitress in the corner glaring in their direction.

Taking to the night, warmth still hung in the air and they peeled from the soft glow of the car park along a gravel path heading towards the moon-shadowed mountain with their eyes slowly adjusting to the sparkling sky.

As if by the flick of a switch they were back on the case, the plan for tomorrow laid out step by step, filling Fisher with optimism as they turned around.

Arriving at their door, his mood drained at the realisation of an uncomfortable night ahead.

Closing the bare wardrobe door, he turned to Harris as she chuckled. He squinted, wondering who was she now? Someone new, or Trinity?

Hope flashed through him. Or the Harris he'd sat with so effortlessly at dinner, or the spy with the guns and menacing paraphernalia?

"I think I can control myself," she said, a playful smile on her face as she cocked her head towards the bed. "Can you?"

Fisher lost focus of the room for a moment, but it snapped back just as quickly.

"My self-control is legendary," he replied, raising his eyebrows as Harris picked up her case and shut herself in the bathroom.

He sat on the edge of the bed where his mind wandered back to last night, that frequent vision of Trinity, the silk nightdress hanging delicate from her body. Running water gushed from the other side of the door and a sudden guilty tightness contorted his chest, his mind jumping to Susie. A vision of her strapped to a bed. Her body battered and bruised. Face dull and lifeless.

The door opened and he flinched the vision away as Harris walked from the bathroom in a delicate floral shirt and trousers, her body covered from ankle to shoulders.

As he left the bathroom, he saw her curled in the bed, the covers wrapped over her. Settling himself down, he watched the back of her head illuminated by the soft lamplight and a smile spread across his face.

Andrew's never going to believe this!

16

Fisher opened his eyes to the vaguely familiar room. Still he caught sight of her stood in front of the bed. Glowing strawberry locks trailed to one side, flowing down, down, down to that nightdress. The neckline hung lower than he'd remembered, the deep pinks of her areola more than hinting against the white lace. Her ruby red lips set in a mischievous smile. Her eyes enticing as her voice rolled with gentle gravel.

"Have you changed your mind, James?"

He felt himself nodding as her hands moved to the hem. Paralysed, he watched her pull the silk upwards, the motion so slow he began to ache. All he could do was concentrate on his deep breathing while the dress rose, revealing perfect pink flesh, his body impatient for her touch. He looked up from the space between her thighs as she spoke again; this time her lips were unmoving.

"Wake up, Agent Fisher."

Bright light filled the room and he pushed his arm across his face, hovering for a second before letting it relax at the sun pouring in through the open curtains.

Harris stood in the same spot, the nightdress now an edge-straight grey suit.

"Good morning, Agent Fisher."

He didn't reply, all energy focused on clinging to the vision, even if just for a few seconds more, but the images were already too vague.

He sat up with a sigh and rubbed at his eyes as she spoke.

"Sorry to wake you, but it's almost eight."

"It's fine. How long have you been awake?" he asked, hoping he hadn't given away any hint of the visions.

"About an hour or so," she replied and he saw the edges of a smile.

"Oh."

"You seemed restless, moaning like you were having a bad dream," she said, busying herself packing clothes into her suitcase. He couldn't see her face but he wouldn't have been surprised to see it lit with a grin.

"I don't remember a dream," he said and jumped out of the bed, letting out a yelp as he stepped into the freezing cold shower.

***

With hardly a word, they ate breakfast in the room, setting off moments later to find a local payphone, repeating the short journey from yesterday and passing the pub with its black paint-cracked signs, the squat school buildings shut up for the summer, out of the other side of the village and into the middle of nowhere.

Another four miles towards Caernarfon passed by before they came across a faded red box stood in a gravel lay-by, the only man-made feature on the horizon aside from the road.

Huddled around the plastic handset, stale cigarette smoke hanging in the air, Fisher fed a flurry of coins into the metal slot one handed as Harris held out a mobile phone and rattled the payphone's volume up with the other. Twenty rings later, the coins dropped to the metal tray.

"Of course, we're screwed if no one answers the bloody phone," he said, as they pulled apart for air only to squeeze back together five minutes later.

"Hullo," came a gruff, guttural welsh tone after five rings. Neither of them spoke, each trying not to breath into the microphone. "Hullo," the voice insisted. "There's no one there," the voice said, tailing off into the distance before the line snapped off.

Sat in the car, they leant into the mobile phone between them, the words repeating for the fourth time in a row.

"What do you think?" Fisher prompted as the voice disappeared to nothing again.

"Male," she said, tipping her head to the side.

Fisher forced a smile.

"Lived close by all his life. Between twenty and forty years old."

Fisher was about to say he guessed the same when she continued.

"He has a dog. Doesn't live alone. Smokes and had eggs for breakfast."

"Huh," Fisher said, looking back, his eyes wide.

She scrolled the slider on the recording app; the quiet snap of a dog's bark came and went in the background.

"Medium size breed, possibly a Labrador," she continued.

Fisher raised his eyebrows but she hadn't finished.

"He had a submissive tone when he spoke to the other person, likely a wife or a long-term girlfriend. The smoker's rattle was obvious."

Squinting, Fisher replayed the tape from the beginning whilst shaking his head.

"The eggs?"

"A joke," she said with a sly smile.

A smirk grew on his face then dropped almost as quickly. "Where would a local, married, smoking man aged twenty to forty with a medium size dog buy a knocked off phone?" He paused before answering his own question. "The pub."

Harris nodded back. "There's only one local. I checked with the old guy in the car park yesterday."

"The Black Boy," Fisher said, nodding. "Let's go."

"And do what, even if it was open?"

"Wait for him to come to us."

"How will we know?" she said, raising her eyebrows.

For a moment Fisher pictured her as a stern primary teacher trying to draw out an answer obvious to everyone but him.

"The phone," he replied, pointing at his own handset.

She shook her head. "We can't call every time someone matching the profile walks in."

"And we don't know he'll even go today," he replied, his tone flattening.

"I can't see there's much else to do round here," she replied, looking around the bleak landscape.

They sat in silence until Fisher raised a finger in the air. "Let's invite him," he said, sitting up straight.

Harris raised an eyebrow.

"Let's call him back, tell him he needs to come to the pub."

"Why would he?"

"Tell him he's won a prize."

"What prize?"

"Who cares about the prize. We tell him he's won a raffle and he needs to collect," he said.

Harris looked back raising her brow. "When did he enter the draw? We'll need to tell him it can only be collected today."

"Sounds complicated. We keep it simple," Fisher said and stared out of the window, turning back as Harris spoke.

"He'll smell a rat when he hears our voices. Not exactly North Wales."

Fisher shook his head. "I can't do Welsh without sounding like a cartoon dragon."

She laughed and he watched as her cheeks dimpled. "Send him a text," she said. "Tell him it's automated and not to reply. Say he's won a prize and has to collect it tonight."

Fisher's eyes brightened. "We have to hope he doesn't call the pub."

"It's not perfect but we've nothing to lose."

Back in the car, Fisher took one of the two remaining spare phones and composed the message. They agreed to say they were only available at lunchtime today. With time key, if they couldn't get him to come then they would have to look at a more direct strategy. With the message sent and a couple of hours to kill, they headed to Caernarfon to get supplies so they could blend in as tourists.

The short journey should have taken ten minutes but turned into an age of start-stop traffic. Finally, they rolled past a field packed with cars and crowds of people weaving in between and a sign announcing the largest weekly car boot sale.

Back up to the speed limit, Fisher turned to Harris. "I don't understand."

"Car boot sales?" Harris said, an eyebrow raised.

"Have they not heard of eBay?"

"I know, it's weird," she said, her voice exaggerated with enthusiasm. "Some people actually like interacting and talking to each other."

He frowned, but a smirk hung on his face as he turned back to the road.

An hour later than planned, they'd parked just off the high street and split up, Fisher in search of hiking gear and Harris disposing of the text message phone piece by piece.

With his bags bulging from the first shop, he headed back towards the car park, but halfway down the street he stopped dead, his eyes drawn to a black and white poster taped to a lamppost. A picture of a young woman dominated the page and bold letters stamped underneath.

MISSING.

His bags fell to the floor as Susie stared back at him from the page.

17

Stumbling forward, he steadied himself on the cold steel pole, his eyes fixed on the curve of the grey lips radiating a familiar smile. Squinting, he drew himself up tall. Slowing his breath, he stepped back and studied the image. His guts hollowed out and his lungs stopped expanding.

It wasn't her. He snapped a picture of the poster with his phone. Dragging his bags and hanging his head, he rushed to Harris waiting in the car.

"Is it?" she said, before he'd closed the door.

Fisher was already shaking his head. "Close. Very close."

"She's beautiful."

He nodded. "Coincidence?" he finally said, pinching the image larger on the screen.

"No," Harris said, her voice firm. "Nothing is ever a coincidence. And this..." her words tailed off as she shook her head. "Two beautiful young blondes missing days apart. No." Her fingers began tapping numbers from the poster into her phone. A shrill woman's voice answered after barely a full ring.

"Rihanna?"

Harris looked up as she spoke. "No. I've seen the poster in town," she replied with hesitation, as if afraid to let the woman down.

"Have you seen her?" The voice almost leapt from the handset.

"No, but we want to help." Harris stared through the windscreen as she listened to the silence. "Are you still there? Can we come and see you?"

A flat voice recited an address and hung up the call.

After a ten-minute drive they arrived at a stout bungalow in a quiet cul-de-sac, its collection of well-kept buildings a picture postcard of quaint suburbia.

Dread added weight to Fisher's legs as he walked at Harris's side along the concrete driveway. He knew his own feelings of loss well but couldn't begin to understand the helpless pain and despair of losing a child.

Harris's fingers found the doorbell, which gave an uncomfortable shrill to pierce the sombre mood. After a few moments, a squat middle-aged woman answered. With her hand covering her mouth, red, puffy eyes stared back, full of expectation and dread at the same time. She wore a sweat top and tracksuit bottoms, her shoulders slouching. Without a word, she turned and walked back down the corridor. They gave each other a quick glance and stepped forward.

They followed her through the stale air of the corridor and into a lounge with thick curtains blocking each of the windows, the room instead lit by a series of tall, shaded lamps around the perimeter.

They found her sitting on the edge of a straight-back overstuffed armchair facing a long couch with a matching bold floral fabric, her hands messily folding and unfolding a crumpled tissue. She motioned for them to sit opposite.

The woman looked up, her eyes deep in her sockets.

Harris spoke as they sat. "Chloe and Toby Partridge. We talked on the phone."

Fisher saw the faint nod of recognition.

"As I said, Mrs Summers," Harris began.

"Call me Andrea," she interrupted in a pitiful tone.

"We help find missing people. My husband saw the poster in town and we'd like to help if we can."

Mrs Summers nodded, her eyes widening as she turned to Fisher.

"Thank you," she replied and seemed to perk up, raising her shoulders with a weak smile growing. "I've got some more photos somewhere and there's a list of all the places we've put up posters."

Harris bunched up her face in a smile and moved to the edge of her seat as she interrupted.

"Shall we start at the beginning?"

"Yes. Sorry, yes," Andrea said, her fingers working at the worn tissue.

"When did she disappear? Who was the last person to see her? That sort of thing."

Andrea drew a deep breath and rested her elbows on her knees. "Sorry," she said, taking a deep breath. "I've told this story so many times. I expect the whole world should know by now."

"It's okay, just take your time. Do you mind if I record this so I don't miss anything?"

Andrea gave a momentary weak smile and Harris took out a phone, pressed a few buttons then placed it amongst the soiled coffee cups on the short table between them.

"When you're ready," Harris said, moving back in her seat.

Andrea took a deep breath and began to talk, her words slow and considered.

"Rihanna's a student at Caernarfon Art College, studying graphic design. She's very good," she nodded, her eyebrows raising as she spoke. "She dreams of being a set designer and I've no doubt she can do it. She turned eighteen twelve days ago and was out with her friends in town."

There was a pause as her voice caught. Fisher looked at Harris, who looked on patiently as Andrea collected herself.

"She never came home. It wasn't unusual but she always, always lets us know." She picked up an old-style grey mobile phone from the table. "I checked my mobile and the home phone." As she talked, she pressed at buttons, her eyes scrolling the small screen. "But nothing." Her head shook; her eyes flitted between the pair opposite.

"I called her friend, her best friend, Charlie. She was asleep. Said she'd been put in a cab with one of the other girls. She hadn't heard from her since. Charlie called the rest of the group but they hadn't heard either." Andrea lost the battle with her tears. "We haven't seen her since," she said, dabbing her eyes with the tissue.

Harris left the sofa and crouched in front of the chair, her hands resting on Andrea's.

Fisher watched on, a huge cavity growing in his chest, until the flow of tears slowly dried.

"Thank you," Andrea said with a crack in her voice.

Harris sat back opposite. "We'll try and help," she finally said.

Andrea nodded, blinking at fresh tears.

"Can I have a recent photo of your daughter, Mrs Summers?"

"Call me Andrea, please," she replied and walked to a dark wooden sideboard. Out of the top drawer she pulled out a glossy six by nine, her gaze pausing as she caught sight of her daughter.

Fisher watched as she forced herself to hand it over.

"Cowes in the Isle of Wight. A camping trip, Easter this year."

Fisher blinked at the image, the resemblance to Susie still strong. It showed Rihanna leant against a three-slatted fence wearing a blue summer dress flowing from her shoulders to just above the grass, her hand reaching out to a horse. A great picture; he could see why a parent would want it framed. He passed it to Harris.

"Do you mind if we ask you some sensitive questions?" Harris said.

Mrs Summers nodded and let out a deep breath. "They've asked them all, the Police, the press," she said and sat up. "My daughter is a good girl. She isn't promiscuous. She isn't a drug addict. She wasn't even drunk and she hasn't run away." Andrea looked at them each in turn. "She's been kidnapped."

"How can you be so sure?" Fisher said, his voice timid.

"She has a rare heart disorder and needs tablets every day. The medication is tightly controlled and expensive. We get them delivered directly by the NHS and they have to be ordered from a central facility. The police have notified the NHS and if they get a new order then we would know about it."

"Are any of her drugs missing?" said Harris.

Andrea shook her head. “It was the second thing I checked.”

Fisher looked around the room and edged forward in his seat. “I'm sorry, but I have to ask,” he said, his voice quiet. “What happens if she doesn't take the medication?”

Andrea opened her tissue, ready for the flood they each knew would come.

“She dies.”

“I’m really sorry, Andrea,” Harris said, holding out her hands. “How long can she last?”

“Two weeks.”

18

On the edge of composure, Angela gave the friend's phone number and the name of the medication, Trimansuline, saying goodbye in a voice near begging to keep in touch before finally sobbing into her sleeve as they let themselves out.

Fisher sat, relieved to drag the bags into their stable after a voiceless journey. Harris heaved the aluminium case to rest on the floor and Fisher held up the clothes he'd picked out for her.

"You live on the edge, Mr Fisher," she said, her head tilted to one side.

Fisher looked back, his face blank aside for a raised eyebrow.

"Guessing a woman's sizes. A dangerous game."

His face dropped. "Did I get it wrong?" he said, a quiver in his voice, eyeing her nervously as she pulled black hiking trousers from the bag and peered at the labels.

"Not bad," she replied and disappeared into the bathroom, emerging moments later with a smile on her face, wearing trousers and a fleece which seemed to hug her in all the right places.

"We match," she said, her smile growing larger as he breathed a sigh of relief. "You were lucky. This time," she added, then looked at her watch. "We should get going."

Fisher nodded, watching as Harris opened the aluminium case, pulling out the tiny Beretta and with cool efficiency, loaded a clip and slid back the barrel to chamber a round. A shiver ran across his shoulders as he watched her pocket the tiny weapon before picking up the metal case and heading outside. He joined her as she slammed the car boot closed and together they set off in the car down the gravel path towards Llanrug.

The pub had only been open for ten minutes when Fisher held the heavy wooden door aside for Harris, following her into the aged decor of overpainted wood-chip, tar stained from when it wasn't a crime to smoke indoors, the walls lined with weak watercolours and faded images of the tall tourist attraction to their backs.

He counted ten men already scattered around, most propping up one length of the long dark bar, the rest around a pool table in a side room with wide-open double doors.

Half of them broadly matched the profile. Harris shook her head as she saw him reach for the phone.

Behind the bar, a plump twenty-something woman nodded as she stood from a stool. With brunette hair cut in a mess around her eyes, she wore a black vest top, her arms decorated with faded flowers and the rich red of a writhing dragon.

Harris ordered a tonic and lime and he immediately regretted his choice of a Guinness, another mark on his pretence of professionalism.

Sat at a table by the window selected for its full view, they half talked, her gaze natural and with a smile unforced. Fisher fidgeted, his gaze falling on each of the occupiers whilst trying not to squint as he looked for some tell.

It wasn't long before the doors of the pub swung open and in walked a tall middle-aged man with a skinny frame and bright ginger hair.

Fisher flicked a look to Harris and swallowed a deep breath as she pulled out the phone, placing it on the table. He sat upright, but even stretching out he couldn't hear the words spoken to the barmaid. As they shared laughter, the guy moved to a table and Fisher relaxed back into his seat.

Moments later, the door opened a second time. Fisher twitched forward, shooting Harris a glance as he felt the warm squeeze of her hand on his knee, her mouth silently telling him to relax.

Enjoying her heat as the hand lingered, he pulled at his pint and watched the newcomer, another middle-aged man, his head devoid of any hair, his body covered in yellow skin-tight Lycra.

Watching Harris's exaggerated smile out of the corner of his eye, her brows rose as she gave just a single shake of her head. Still he watched the guy give a long order, the tattooed woman pulling glasses from high shelves. With his mind only half on the view, the other on her hand still on his knee, she pulled away and he caught movement in his peripheral vision.

The door closed behind a tall man with long, dark hair. With a weekend of stubble, his heavy-set frame carried a rounded stomach pushing out from a faded Metallica t-shirt. They watched him wait, his fingers squeezing at his lower lip as he stood beside the cyclist still at the bar.

The barmaid smiled back at the new guy as his head bobbed to catch her attention and the pair watched on from their table.

Fisher stared at her face fixing in concentration as the rocker took the cyclist's place. He spoke and pushed his hand in his pocket. As he drew out a phone, a jolt of recognition shot through Fisher.

Right size.

Right colour.

The barmaid gave an indiscernible reply, her brow furrowing as she shook her head. The guy pushed the phone closer and she leant in, her face still screwed up and shaking. She turned and left through a door behind the bar, leaving the guy alone tapping at the floor with his right foot.

Fisher's gaze left the guy for the first time as he fidgeted his attention back and forth to his watch. Turning to Harris, he didn't need to ask; the curl in the corner of her mouth said it all.

He turned back to the bar as a rounded man in chef's whites came through its door, the girl's gestures mirrored at the phone's screen before he stepped back, shaking his head and pulled the guy a pint of beer. They chatted for a moment as the pint changed hands and the chef disappeared, leaving him to sip alone. His shoulders slumped as he leant heavily on the bar top.

Fisher watched Harris, unable to gauge the plan. They'd only discussed how to find the guy with the phone, not what to do next.

Fisher picked at the nail on his thumb and stared at her in expectation. As he watched on, her expression changed, a slight raise of the eyebrow and he turned to see the empty spot where he'd leant.

Alarmed, Fisher turned back and Harris spoke in a quiet voice. “Toilet.”

Without thought or glance, Fisher stood and headed towards the washroom.

***

There was nothing unique about the small washroom or even the guy Fisher knew he would find standing at the furthest urinal. Except, of course, he had profited from Susie's disappearance, or perhaps was even involved.

With anger surging, Fisher felt his legs carry him forward, watching on as with a lunge his hand locked around the back of the guy’s wide neck. The force knocked him forward, cracking the tile as his head smashed against the wall.

“Where is she?” Fisher said, his voice remarkably controlled.

The guy snapped his hands up either side in surrender, his head shaking, too stunned to form words.

“Where is she?” Fisher repeated, raising his voice. He felt his hand trembling, not sure if it was him or the flesh beneath.

The beginnings of a muffled sob joined tears rolling down the guy’s stubble.

As Fisher looked on, a regret picked at the anger. This pitiful creature didn’t look capable. He felt his hand relax around the warmth of the neck and calmed his breathing to a whisper.

“You wanna live, then you do as I say.”

The guy nodded as Fisher slowly released his hand, his fingers shining with sweat.

Slowly turning around with his head cowering, the guy looked up to meet Fisher’s eyes with clear reluctance.

Fisher spotted a round lump on his forehead, its mass already purpling with blood.

"Do your flies up."

The guy looked down and pulled his trousers closed.

"Meet me at the table by the window." Fisher waited until he saw him nod.

***

Sat beside Harris back at the table, Fisher stared at the bruise before speaking.

"What's your name?" he said to the guy sitting opposite.

"Umm, Darren," he replied with a quiver in his voice.

"Meet Darren," Fisher said, turning to Harris to see her smiling in fascination. "Ok, Darren," he said, leaning forward in his chair. "We have a few questions."

Darren nodded, his body quaking as he did.

"How long have you had that phone?"

Darren looked around the room and then at the tabletop between them, then back at Fisher, blinking as if he had no idea what he was referring to.

"The phone in your pocket," Fisher replied nodding down to the table.

Realisation glinted in Darren's face and he leant back, pulling the phone from his pocket and placing it on the table.

"This phone?" he replied.

Fisher nodded slowly.

"Got it for my birthday last week."

"Who gave it to you?"

"My girlfriend," he said without hesitation, a smile widening his mouth.

A short pang of guilt ran up Fisher's spine. "Did she give it to you in a box?" he said.

Darren's eyes narrowed, then relaxed again. "Oh no, it's second hand. She bought it from a mate of hers."

"It's stolen," Fisher said.

Darren simply shrugged his shoulders.

"You need to tell me who she got it from, Darren." Fisher leant forward and lowered his voice. "Do you understand?"

After fixing his gaze to Fisher for a moment, Darren's smile dropped and he picked up the handset, tapped at the screen and put the phone to his ear.

"Hello, baby," he said, switching cheer into his voice. "Yeah, I'm still down the pub… No, I haven't heard yet… Won't be long… Uh, baby, let me speak… Sorry." He listened on, his eyes rolling as he stared back at Fisher. All of a sudden, he cut in. "Who'd you buy my phone from?" Darren blurted out. "No, there's nothing wrong," he said, then changed his tone. "Um. Oh yeah, it's stopped… Yeah, yeah, I can still make calls… I know there's no warranty, least I can see… Baby, it's really important." The last words almost pleading.

Fisher stared back, lowering his eyebrows.

"Tell me who you bought the bloody phone from, woman." Darren listened, his eyes going wide. "Thank you and I'll see you soon." He hung up the call and placed the phone on the table.

Fisher raised his eyebrows. "Well?"

"Do you know Jattick Murray?"

"No," Fisher replied.

"One of the Murray brothers?"

Fisher shook his head.

"They're a couple of…" Darren paused. "Entrepreneurs," he soon said, as his eyes un-bunched from a squint. "Useful for getting most things, uh, cheap like. Get you anything you need less than half price of new."

"Where do we find them?" Harris said, and Darren turned in her direction as if seeing her for the first time.

"I wouldn't. But if you had to, you'd find them either in the cop shop or in the alley a few doors down. What ya gonna do?"

"We just want to ask some questions," Fisher replied.

"Do me a favour. Don't tell him it was me or the missus, please?" Darren said, near pleading.

Fisher reached out and shook Darren's hand. "You're safe now. Don't worry," he said in a low voice, then turned and headed for the door.

***

Like a neon sign topping the mountain, pungent weed and thumping bass guided them the short walk to Murray Enterprises HQ. Its co-founder, Jattick, found in residence, the faded tattoo across the loose skin of his forehead better than a photo ID.

He stood in the middle of the alley, bounded either side by un-weathered brown fence panels, the stink of creosote coming only second to the penetrating smoke. Wearing skin-tight jeans and a long parka coat, the furred hood framed his bald, wrinkled head. A Doc Martin rested on a battered boom box, his foot juddering to the electronic bass.

"You cops?" he slurred, his voice a guttural North Welsh tone as his head flicked around to the alley behind.

"No," Fisher replied.

"Cos' ya gotta tell me if I ask, don't ya?" he said, shooting his wide-eyed glare back in their direction.

"Not cops, customers," Harris replied, slowly stepping forward, holding her hands down by her side.

His face turned to an ugly wrinkled grin of browning teeth rotted to stumps. "What's a pretty lady want from me?" He eyed her up and down, his lip curled in a lecherous sneer as Harris carried on toward him.

"Benzos?" she said with confidence, her face close to his while Fisher tried to hide his concern.

Jattick twisted to see behind his back and seeing no trap he turned around, reached inside the long coat and pulled out a small zip lock bag of pink tablets.

"You like to chill?" he said, squinting as his head bobbed in time with hers. "How many?"

"All of them," she snapped.

Before Fisher could react, the bag fell to the floor.

In one fluid movement, Harris grabbed the tattooed hand, spun him around, collapsing his knees with her foot and he lay on the floor with her boot on his back and his arm angled high in the air.

Wide-eyed, Fisher watched Jattick's mouth open in the shape of a scream but nothing came out as his body went limp.

"Shit," Harris said, as she shoved his frame into the recovery position and pulled up the lid of his right eye. "Fucking druggies." She huffed in frustration and patted at his jacket, then gingerly pulled out a wooden-handled flick knife and pushed it in her pocket. "Didn't even get to ask," she said, then stopped abruptly as she turned back to Fisher, her focus behind him.

"Ask him what?"

Fisher span around to the rough new voice at his back and saw a mirror of Jattick standing. As he read the different name across his loose forehead, it took him a moment to see the long-bladed combat knife held out like a tiny sword.

Harris stepped past Fisher. "Does your mother forget your names?" she said, laughing.

Fisher forced a laugh.

"Pa, actually," the twin replied. "You're gonna pay for what you done."

"Oh, that," she said, turning and kicking the slumped body. "What a waste of skin," she said.

The twin's head twitched before turning on his heels and running back down the alley like a whippet chasing a rabbit.

Fisher hesitated but Harris sprang off without delay. He turned down at Jattick, grabbed the bag of pills and launched himself into their dust trail.

With the pair already out of sight, Fisher raced through the wooden-slatted labyrinth, only able to use the roofs and the grey mountain far in the background as his guide. Side-stepping wheelie bins, he clattered to a junction.

With a gut-decision he sped to the right and came out into a quiet street. Spotting the black of Harris's jacket disappearing around a corner ahead, he bounded across the road, back into the maze. Darting left, then right, then right again, he dashed between the fences. Ahead, a shrill scream called out. He smiled when he realised it wasn't hers.

A shadow caught his attention to the left before disappearing out of view and Fisher followed the flow of the fence; turning another corner, he saw Harris on her backside, the Jattick clone looking back with a sly smile as he turned, bounding over the wooden barrier.

"You okay?" Fisher panted as he arrived by her side.

"I'm fine," she replied, taking his outstretched hand.

"We'll find him," Fisher said, not understanding how she could have lost the fight.

"Guaranteed," she said, and to his surprise a broad smile spread across her face.

***

Back at the pub, they jumped in the car and without words Harris busied her fingers at the radio, tuning to AM and pushing the selector until the green display read six eight zero. As static poured from the speakers, her eyes narrowed as if hearing something Fisher couldn't.

"This would be a whole lot easier if I had my communicator," she said, breaking through the crackle of the radio.

Fisher shuffled with discomfort in the driver's seat, waiting for instruction.

"Drive," she said, and pointed to the car park's exit. Still staring at the radio, she spoke again. "I dropped a tracker in his pocket. He thinks he put me down but I knew he wouldn't talk, not if he has the pain threshold of his brother. We're going to have to do this the old-fashioned way."

Fisher shook his head as they turned left on to the village road.

"The old fa…" he said, stopping himself as Harris raised her hand and leant closer to the speaker.

"It's a low-power AM transmitter. Gives us about five hundred feet of range. It's World War Two technology, but it works when you leave the proper tools behind in an airport car park." She turned and glared at him for a short moment.

"We have to get closer," Fisher said, as static poured from the speakers.

"You got it," she replied, pointing her thumb in the opposite direction. "Turn around. There's nothing this way."

Within a minute of retracing their route, Fisher heard an intermittent beep buried deep behind the static.

"Faster," Harris said, pointing forward.

He pushed the accelerator hard, the engine screaming as their speed built. A minute later he caught sight of a twenty-year-old rusting silver Mercedes spitting smoke on the road in front.

With the ping now clear above the hiss, he eased off the accelerator.

Harris turned the volume low and they watched as the Mercedes wallowed around the stone-walled road.

Settling back in her seat, she turned to Fisher. "What did you say to Darren as we left?"

He looked at her, but not able to hide his surprise, he turned back to the road.

"I just made a little threat about his safety."

"He's a big man. I think he would have come off better." She turned her head back to the road, the Mercedes' right brake light barely shimmering as they reached an isolated row of houses.

"Pull in," she said, pointing to a short driveway outside a house to the left.

Fisher slammed on the brakes, just managing to stop as the front bumper met the bricks. "What if someone's home?"

"Shhh," she hissed past her finger while looking across him.

He turned back to the stationary Mercedes in the distance, the smoke no longer billowing, but the man hadn't got out. Movement at the net curtain where he'd parked pulled him back, but he turned away as the rusting silver door opened and Jattick's brother pulled himself out to the curb.

With his phone to his ear, he struggled one-handed with an iron gate before hurrying up to the house and knocking on the door.

Fisher's attention snapped back to the house at his front as the door opened.

"Deal with that," Harris said, her concentration still on the house in the distance.

He turned to her but she moved to look around him.

Movement turned him back to the front door again and to a woman standing in a mismatched tracksuit and a red-eyed toddler sat on her hip.

Fisher gave a weak wave in her direction whilst flicking his eyes back to the right and the twin looking the other way. With care, he opened the door and, keeping his back to the target, he held out his hand in greeting before speaking in a quiet voice. "We're the Police. Please step inside."

The woman was about to ask a question when their hands met and Fisher repeated the instruction.

With the door closed, he peered around the edge of the building, watching the brother with his phone to his ear walking to the car, but instead of taking a seat, he moved past it before stopping in the middle of the road.

Fisher glanced back at Harris, then turned again to see black smoke pouring from the Mercedes, the brother back in the car, bumping down the curb and heading in their direction.

Harris slunk down in her seat. Fisher turned back to face the door, listening to the thud of the engine.

"Follow him?" he said, turning the key in the ignition.

After a few seconds pause she pointed to the right, shaking her head. "No. I want to know who he ran to."

***

Fisher's attention fixed ahead as they pulled to the curb.

"What?" said Harris, but he didn't respond, his focus firm on the view, the vibrant green hill to his left looming over the four houses, their faded brick walls smoothed from years of abuse. As his head travelled right, his eyes lit up with the vague familiarity of the rundown petrol station, its off-white canopy towering over a mechanic's shed. A smile formed as he spoke, almost laughing.

"I remember searching here when she first disappeared."

Harris raised her eyebrows.

"I thought I'd seen her car parked by that green shed."

She leant forward as he spoke, her survey following his finger to linger across the road.

"It wasn't hers," he said, and Harris left the car without saying a word.

The houses were set back from the road, each behind a large front garden with trimmed grass and crisp bright white fences. The last flowers of the year sprayed vibrant colour out from the edges. All except for one.

The house they stood in front of.

Chaos began at the gate.

The once ornate sculpture in iron hung on one hinge, a tangle of thinning browned metal flaked paint with each slight breath of wind.

Lifting the gate to one side, they walked past the decaying curves of a Volkswagen Beetle, half buried in black bags, its windows and doors long gone, cubes of glass glinting in the browning surround. Weeds as high as their knees grew all around, mottled with debris and split rubbish sacks, their contents strewn.

Old furniture with laminate peeling from ballooning board, their surfaces rippling with nature potted the view. A doorless fridge lay on its back next to a mattress with browned metal coils puncturing through the surface.

Reaching the end of the path, they both stopped and looked at each other, eyebrows raised as they stood at the untarnished bright white plastic of the front door.

Harris rattled the round metal knocker with two sharp taps and stood back to wait. There was no answer, even from the second, more insistent knock.

Harris crouched, pulled up the stiff letterbox and peered in. Lingering only for a moment, she shook her head, moving aside for Fisher to take his turn to view the immaculate hallway with plush carpet and neat surfaces, crisp paintwork and bright flowered walls.

Walking back to the car, Fisher watched her scan the view, following her gaze whilst trying to guess her thoughts.

"We need to get around the back," she said.

At her words, he bounded back to the car and plucked the iPad from between the seats, his fingers soon on a Google Map, tapping at buttons and links almost before they appeared.

A rich, rendered map appeared on the screen, the white line of the road under their feet soon disappeared to be replaced with the green of the surrounding hills. Pinching his fingers, they saw the house, easy to spot from the same debris littering the view even from tens of thousands of miles above.

"There's a track around the back," he said, his head bobbing in the direction further down the road.

Harris leant in, looked up, then cocked her head along the row of the short terrace.

With a quick pace their feet found the dirt, a compacted track bounded by a coarse hedge snaking towards the hill before it took them through a sharp left turn. Thick bracken grew to the right, a long row of six-foot fences stood to the left. Their heads turned towards the road and the blur of a car rushing past their view leaving a tumble of air in its wake.

Fisher turned back to see Harris already heading down the track towards the only garden whose complete fence, otherwise featureless, hinged at the sides, a thin gap sagging in the middle and a pool of darkness leeching to the ground from inside.

As Harris angled herself to peer in through the gap, Fisher picked up a clod of matted earth and rolled it between his thumb and forefinger. An oily slick stained his fingers.

Harris nodded as she watched, then shook her head, pointing to the insignificant gap in the fence. She turned, scanning the alley. Her lowered brow soon told him she hadn't found what she'd been looking for.

Fisher reached out with his palms up, fingers interlinked as he lowered to his knee.

"Don't drop me," she said with a flick of her eyebrows, raising a boot to his hands and pulling herself up on the edge of the fence as he tensed. He watched Harris's head tentatively rise over the boundary where she immediately motioned to be lowered.

"There's a canopy. A tarpaulin, I think. I can't see a thing." She moved to the boundary with the house on the left and waited, arms outstretched for Fisher to join her and resume the position.

Raising up, she fished in her pockets and brought out a multi-tool, flicking open two inches of serrated blade. With her free hand, she worked it on something behind the wooden panel.

"Higher," she whispered, and Fisher strained her up, the muscles in his arms burning with the effort.

"Got it," she finally exhaled. Pushing the multi-tool back in her pocket, she swapped it with a phone and balanced against the fence, snapping shots one-handed.

"Hurry up," he whispered as his screaming muscles shook.

She nodded urgently, which only served to worsen the pain.

"A few seconds," she said quietly, shifting her weight to one side.

Still looking up, he watched as her head twitched, snapping up in the direction of the first floor.

A dull thud came from the other side of the fence.
"Shit," was all he heard as he lowered her to the ground.

19

Harris jumped from Fisher's hands, dust rolling into the air as she dropped to a crouch with a hand on his shoulder, pulling him down with her. As the dust settled, he watched her eyes narrow, fixing somewhere in the distance with her head cocked to the side. She was listening for something.

"I dropped the phone," she finally said with a whisper.

"I guessed that," he said, stretching out his aching arms to his side.

"I saw someone in the house. I'm pretty sure the net curtains moved."

Fisher rose from his crouch, lifting so his eyes rose just above the fence line and lingered for a couple of seconds before crouching back at her side.

"Couldn't see anything," he said, shaking his head. "A trick of the light?"

Harris shrugged. "I need that phone, the photos."

"What did you see?"

"I'm not sure."

Fisher nodded. Still crouching, he ran his fingers over the surface of the fence, pulling and probing at the wooden slats.

"What are we going to do?" she asked.

Fisher felt his chest puff out, proud to have the answer. "I know wood," he replied, mocking himself and put his hand out for the multi-tool.

Dragging out the knife, he snapped the blade into place. With the tool in his left hand, he ran the tip of his forefinger along the fence. As the digit skimmed across the dry wood, he moved his head closer to the board.

Finding what he'd searched for on the third panel, he took the knife in his right hand and with one swift movement, jabbed the blade into the edge of a weakness just off the ground. The knife pushed through the knot to the other side and with all of the effort he could force out of his aching arms, he pushed the blade down in the direction of the grain until it came out at the dirt floor.

With both hands empty, he pulled the split wood in opposite directions and with his face contorting, the wood gave way with a satisfying crack. Forcing himself to still, he listened, but hearing no response he stood back to his feet, raising slowly over the fence line.

The curtains moved and he ducked back down.

"A trick of the light," he said to himself in a whisper.

"Again?" Harris asked, eyebrows raised.

He didn't respond. Instead, with his shoulder at the dirt, he reached his arm through the gap, groping around edges of cold metal, their surfaces slick with grease. A bark echoed in the distance as his hand touched something warm and plastic. He clenched his hand around the rectangle and pulled out the phone.

Pride welled as he saw a glint of something in Harris's eyes which meant so much more than her mouthed word of thanks. The moment of warmth broke with the hairs on the back of his neck standing proud as he heard the dog close. Harris heard it too and turned, standing but staying tight to the fence as she headed back the way they'd come.

Fisher followed and, rounding the corner, they spotted the dog walker turning towards them as he joined the start of the track, his eyes narrow. As his gaze fell on Harris's, his face relaxed as if coming under a spell.

With a quick nod to the guy as he passed, they were out on the road, but Fisher's blood felt as if it froze when he spotted a middle-aged guy dressed in oil-stained overalls crossing from the other side.

"We should have moved the car," Harris said under her breath as Fisher came alongside.

The mechanic had thick black hair with brown oil plastering his hairy forearms. His eyes where fixed in their direction, then turned, lingering on the open gate as he approached.

Controlling their pace, they walked past him as he headed up the garden path with his head sweeping up to the first floor, then turned back to the click of the Vectra's central locking.

Fisher chanced a look as their car left the curb and saw the front door of the house close behind the mechanic's back. He wasn't sure if the curtains moved again.

They were a good mile down the road before Harris pulled over into a wide stone-walled parking area, parking between two coaches whose passengers dotted around, huddled by the burger van or staring up the heights of the impossibly beautiful mountains.

Ignoring the scenery, she pulled out the phone, wiping away grease and dirt on her trousers before scrolling through the photographs.

Fisher watched from beside her. A blur of a tarpaulin, the nearest corner hanging down to reveal nothing but blackness.

The next few came from below the tarp, a darker image lit only by the weak flash, showing crowds of dark machinery and oily mechanical parts. Some were stacked together in blue barrels, others strewn, haphazard, around the stained dirt floor.

The third shot angled lower. A flash of bright reflection came from inside an empty barrel near the bottom of the frame. The fourth showed a zoomed in version of the last.

At the centre of the image were cubes of blurred plastic. Fisher grabbed the iPad and held out his hand for the phone, which she passed over with a raised brow.

Tapping at the screens of both, Fisher soon had the pictures on the iPad's larger screen, pinching his fingers on the glass, the bottom of the barrel enlarging. He lingered on the images, then snapped around to Harris.

"Number plates. They're fragments of number plates."

"How can you tell?" she said, and he swiped forward to the fourth photo and explained, unable to hide his enthusiasm.

"This one shows the light reflecting from the flash. You can just about make out the top of a black character." He swiped back to the third and zoomed back in. "These are fragments of plastic, most are white but down here," he said, zooming in further, "this one is definitely orange. Front and rear number plates."

Harris nodded slowly as Fisher grinned.

"The car parts, the oil and the gate in the fence. He's no scrap dealer. He's breaking up whole cars."

"Who says he's not just a scrap dealer?" Harris said, her eyes narrowed.

"Why would you destroy the number plates? It can't be legit." He looked at her as she turned and stared out of the windscreen in silence.

"What is it?" he said, not hiding his impatience.

She turned back and looked him in the eye, her expression chilling as she spoke.

"Why did you decide it wasn't Susie's car?"

20

Arriving back at the hotel, Harris parked around the corner from their chalet with Fisher barely able to concentrate on pulling open the passenger door.

With shallow breath, he kept thinking over the moment Andrew's Mondeo pulled back on to the road, having dismissed the car they'd found in the garage as a coincidence. He'd been right there only hours after she'd gone missing. Why didn't he check? Those stupid dice were probably still hanging from the mirror.

Harris's door slammed shut and pulled him from his thoughts. About to return to his self-punishment, he caught the sight of a scruffy, short black guy wearing a puffer jacket and fatigue trousers, skulking from around the corner in the direction of their room. His spaced-out stare kept Fisher's attention, the guy's head jolting around as they locked eyes for a fleeting moment.

Something wasn't right, Fisher could tell, but ignoring his first instinct he pulled open the door as the boot closed. Harris tucked in beside him and they walked towards the chalet.

"We should get a better look. See if we can find any trace of her car," she said, her voice pulling him back to his guilt.

"We'd have to watch them first," he paused. "That place doesn't sit right. There was someone in that house, I'm…" He stopped mid-sentence at the sight of their door ajar. Any thought of a cleaner or housemaid at their work vanished as they saw the split door jamb and the splinters of wood sprayed over the floor.

Fisher quickened forward, pushing the door open, exposing the chaos. Their bags lay ripped apart, clothes strewn around the room and the mattress angled on the floor.

"The mirror," Harris said, her voice calm and a finger pointing to the words scribbled in black marker across the silvered glass.

We are watching you!

The image of the man he'd just seen flashed into his head. His legs sprung to life and he was back out of the door, running up the path, but the man had vanished.

With nowhere else the guy could have gone, Fisher pushed himself to a sprint, climbing as the dirt path rose.

Adrenaline soon began to fade, his muscles complaining at the effort. He caught sight of a jogger over the brow of a tall hill. The clothes could be a match, at least from the distance.

The sighting spurred Fisher on and he doubled his effort. Concentrating on the speck ahead, he thought he saw the figure slow. Panic gripped around his chest, concerned he could glance backwards any moment.

Ducking into the treeline, his clothes catching on sharp branches, he struggled to calm his breathing.

A second wave of panic tightened as Fisher thought of Susie. This man could be connected, but he was escaping. With a new determination, he jumped from the trees and pushed through his panting breath, slowing only when he couldn't catch sight of the figure again. His lungs gave him no choice but to stop and bend over to catch his breath.

Standing tall as the race of his chest slowed, he spotted a figure over the brow of the hill; his pace casual this time.

A new excitement flooded through Fisher's veins as he realised he hadn't been seen.

Jumping sideways to the edge of the trees, he peered around a branch, watching as the figure disappeared down the side of a hill.

Fisher came back out onto the path and sprinted forward, preparing his body to pounce as a third and fourth wave of adrenaline pushed him to the extreme.

Cresting the hill and quickly down the other side, he followed the snaking bend in the path and took in the long clear view. Once again, the guy was nowhere to be seen.

Blinking sweat from his eyes, he walked the path as it wound upward to disappear over the skyline, then jogged up the slope and expectantly crested the hill but found the horizon clear for miles.

Bending at the waist, he drew a deep breath. Fighting his aching legs, he rose tall and climbed the path up to the highest point.

Fisher turned, scanning a complete circle. The view was empty of all souls.

Plodding down into the valley, the defeat weighing heavy, he scanned around the hollow, tracing either side of the path blanketed by a dense gathering of fir trees. The guy had vanished and Fisher stopped at the lowest part of the valley.

Footsteps in the slate path behind caused him to turn back. He'd expected to see Harris but instead saw down the barrel of a handgun pointed at him.

21

"Who the fuck a'you?" came a booming Caribbean accent from somewhere deep inside the man he'd been chasing.

Fisher shot his hands up in the air; his wide eyes wouldn't stop blinking as he stood in shock. The stupidity of the chase bore down on him.

"Said' who the fuck a'you? What you snoopin?" the guy insisted, his voice loud as he waved the gun out in front.

Fisher gulped air, realising he'd been holding his breath.

"I'm uh, um, uh," was all he managed.

"Don't tink I won't use is. Tell ma who the fuck you is?"

"We're searching," he said, stumbling over the words. "We're searching for two girls."

"Oh, shit," he replied, then looked down and kicked the stony ground. "Who d'you work for? Tell me now." As he spoke, he jumped from one foot to the other, his eyes flitting between Fisher and the ground.

Frozen to the spot, Fisher didn't know what to say. He didn't know what to do, despite racking his brain. His eyes stopped blinking with a desperate idea taking hold.

Drawing a deep breath, he held his hand out, but the guy's eyes widened further and his words echoed out.

"You stupid? I'm gonna fucking use this 'ting."

Fisher took a step forward and a single round exploded around the valley. His eyes slammed closed and his body jolted as if hit by electricity.

But he felt no pain.

22

The echo hung as he stood with his eyes closed, waiting for the inevitable. When after a moment he felt no foreign change in his body, no searing pain, he opened his lids, expecting to see bright white or a deep suffocating darkness. Instead, the valley stood before him just as lush and green as before.

Fisher looked down. Everything the same. No holes where holes had not been before. No warm patches of blood leeching through his clothes. No cold chilling him to the core.

Startled, he looked up at a slumped figure, the attacker awkward on the gravel and a hue of strawberry rising over the hill.

Fisher watched on as he saw her face set stern, her stare fixed on the lump of flesh with her child-size gun stretched out in front.

"Are you okay?" she shouted, her voice distant. "Fisher? Are you okay?" she insisted when he didn't reply.

"Yeah, I think so." His voice was soft and breathing shallow.

"He was going to shoot you."

"Yeah," was all he managed.

"Come help me," she called, her voice nearing normal.

He tried to move but felt his feet frozen to the spot.

"Pull yourself together and come help me," Harris shouted. "Now."

Her tone snapped his daze and his legs began to move through the stiffness.

Standing over the body, Fisher tried his best to avoid the grim view, instead watching as Harris pulled on surgical gloves. He followed her hands with a strained curiosity as her fingers pushed against the brown flesh of the neck.

He gave a nervous chuckle. Even he knew the man was dead, the bullet having smashed a ragged trail from the back to the front of his head, spewing out a bloody grey mess across the crushed slate.

Harris looked up, plucking a pair of surgical gloves from her jacket and flinging them in his direction.

"Put them on." Her tone gave him no option.

Fisher did as she asked, watching her uncurl black fingers from around the grip of the gun, a weapon similar to the one in her case but metallic grey and with busy lines along the barrel.

Holding the gun in clear view, she removed the clip, pulled back the slide and exposed the round glinting in the chamber.

"He was going to shoot you," she said as she pointed to the red dot above the grip. "The safety was off."

He nodded slowly as she removed the chambered round, put it back in the clip and pushed it deep into her pocket.

Like a practiced procedure, she twisted on her feet, scanning the horizon. With no one in view, she pulled out her knife with one hand and with the other hoisted up the body's sweaty t-shirt.

Giving two quick, controlled slashes, two sections of t-shirt fell away and ripped down the middle.

Kicking the feet together, she crouched down, lifting the legs on to her knees and tied them together with a strip of shirt. Moving to the head, she tied the arms stretched out to his front.

Harris stood and looked around, searching for what, he didn't know, but seemed to find what she was looking for a few paces back the way they'd come. She walked over to a bin Fisher hadn't noticed before and pulled out the liner, keeping the rubbish in the green plastic container. Putting her hand in the bin, she pulled out an empty crisp packet. As she walked back, she stooped and picked up a long thin stick the size of a school-child's ruler.

Gripping the bloody head by short afro curls, Fisher helped her pull the bag around the face then laid it softly on the ground. Wincing, he drew back, a wave of nausea washed over as she plunged the stick into the gaping hole in the dead man's head and swirled it in circles, pushing aside fragments of shattered bone.

With a flick of her wrist, a deformed, blood-ridden pellet of metal popped out, splattering to the dirt. She turned the crisp packet inside out and using it as a second glove, picked up the deformed metal and folded the bag neatly around.

Fisher's nausea began to pass and with the bag stuffed into her pocket, elation began to surge as he came to the realisation the beauty kneeling in front of him had saved his skin. The price of his stupidity lay crumpled, tied and bound at his feet and he bore witness to his beautiful saviour retrieving the evidence. Glancing back, he saw the process was far from over.

Harris pushed the stick alongside his open head, pulling the rest of the sack over the wound before tying it where it met his neck. With the body bound, she grabbed him under the legs and nodded Fisher to the arms. Together they lifted, then stopped mid-air as a loud bark echoed at their backs.

"Oh great," Harris said, pulling the weight higher whilst shuffling into the tree line. "Wait here," she said, her voice insistent as she lowered the legs to the soft forest floor.

Fisher stood, his arms aching as he watched her jump back through the undergrowth and out to the path. Watching as she kicked dust and gravel, he lay the body down gently with intrigue as Harris pulled out a small yellow bottle and covered the path with a fine spray.

The kick of pepper followed her back in the trees as they heaved the body deeper into hiding. Stopping every few paces, she gave a generous spray around their feet; each time irritation built in the back of his throat.

Manhandling the dead weight across browned fern and years of shed leaves, they made slow progress into the darkness.

After five minutes of struggle, Fisher followed her gaze as she looked back through the undergrowth. Surrounded by darkness at each side and with only limited light penetrating through the canopy above, they dropped the body to the springy forest floor.

Harris examined the ground, lifting dead layers of undergrowth like pulling up an old carpet. With Fisher's help, they soon made a body-sized hole and heaved the weight into the shallow grave.

"Pull off the bag," Harris said, her voice coarse and tense as she took off her right glove and pushed her hand inside her jacket.

Fisher's hand hovered over the bag, the blood having leaked around the knot. He looked up, saw impatience in her face then reached around the lifeless head and untied the matted ends.

"Stand back," she ordered, unscrewing the cap from another small bottle.

Fisher edged back into the darkness, nearly tripping over a branch. Steadying himself, he watched as she emptied the bottle's clear contents over the dead man's hands and face. Vapour rose and a tang of vinegar added to the irritation in his nose.

Harris motioned him forward to replace the layers of undergrowth and he couldn't help but stare at the red-stained bone and sinew where fingers and face had been.

Standing back they appraised the scene. A nod from Harris confirmed her approval. Other than a slight hump, there was little sign of disturbance.

Gloves off, they headed back, retracing their steps to the path. With each step, pepper flew into the air and Fisher let out a spectacular sneeze. Birds flapped from the trees and Harris turned round, her expression blank, but kept quiet, quickly turning and carried their trek forward.

Not long had passed before she raised her hand as she stopped in her tracks. Fisher held his position and searched out for what she'd heard.

Looking up from the ground, he saw the first signs of light breaking through the tree line but couldn't see or hear anything out of place.

About to break the silence with a question, he heard the disturbance for the first time. A rustling of leaves ahead and movement low to the ground on the edge of his vision ahead. The movement grew closer as he copied her stillness but breathed a sigh of relief as a cone of light from above illuminated a dark Spaniel's face, his snout rummaging in the undergrowth as he nudged along towards them.

Fisher leant to Harris and opened his mouth to speak, but without turning she raised her finger to her lips. The mutt locked eyes with Fisher for a moment and bounded closer, his hairy head raising and his tail a blur of excitement.

Harris flicked her head back, repeating her gesture and the dog shot towards her, jumping to lick at her hands. Without a noise she shushed it away but they both knew the hound wasn't going to leave without a prize.

The dog gave an excited bark and Harris's calm demeanour shifted. In one swift movement she crouched on her feet with her arm around the dog's neck, the same hand clamping its mouth shut with his bushy tail still flicking in a frantic dance.

Using her free hand, she reached around the dog's neck to feel for a collar, but found nothing buried under the mass of hair. Still it didn't struggle as her grip held firm and her other hand pulled out the multi-tool.

She looked up at Fisher; her wide eyes relayed her instruction.

He hesitated, not wanting to believe what she was asking, but soon relented and pulled out the blade.

"Look away," she whispered, but he kept on staring at the dog locked in one hand, the knife poised in the other.

"Look away," she quietly repeated, her voice insistent. "You won't want to see this."

23

As Fisher looked away, a high-pitched shout cut through the shadows.

"Ru-fus."

The dog erupted with excitement, the swish of his tail redoubling its speed from side to side.

Fisher turned back to see Harris holding herself still for a moment, her eyes narrowed and she released her grip. The dog galloped back through the undergrowth without a backward glance.

Still crouched to the ground, Fisher stared at Harris through the dim, eerie light casting shadows across her face.

She would have done it. He couldn't have been any more convinced.

Standing in silence for what seemed like an hour but in reality was much less, eventually they walked with tentative steps back out into the sunlight to find no one around.

As they headed in the direction of the hotel, Harris bent to her knees and picked up a small golden object on the grass verge.

"What's that?" Fisher said, his voice rough and mouth dry.

She turned the metal in her fingers.

"Shell casing. Lose the bullet or the casing, then you lose the gun." She turned to him and with an earnest look said, "I love this gun," as she pushed the brass into her pocket.

They were back at the hotel within thirty minutes; only then did Fisher realise how far he'd run on his doomed pursuit. Their door seemed secure until it gave way with a light touch, exposing the splintered doorjamb and the chaos of the inside.

"We must be on the right track," Fisher said as he collected up the sharp slivers of wood scattered around the door. "Nothing's missing. He must be a messenger."

"Or we've bumbled into something else," Harris replied as she stared at the words still on the mirror.

"He asked why we were here. He didn't like it when I told him."

Harris raised her eyebrows as she focused on the black writing.

"Who sent him? We've kept a low profile. How did they even know about us? Mrs Summers?" Fisher added after a pause.

"That would be an interesting twist," she said.

Fisher thought he saw a smile just as she turned her head away. "Darren then?"

But Harris just shook her head.

"Someone in the house?"

She nodded, not taking her eyes from the bold words.

"How'd they know where we were? How'd they get here before us?" he said, shaking his head.

"This place is tiny. It would be easy to find any stranger and we were by the roadside long enough."

"I knew I saw someone," he paused. "In the house."

"So did I."

"What about the dead guy? He seemed professional, the way he ambushed me."

"A monkey could have ambushed you the amount of noise you were making." Harris turned to him and saw his lowered brow. "Sorry, I just meant he's no professional. You described an enthusiastic amateur, high on drugs at best." She didn't wait for him to speak. "We need to move. They know where we are and we need distance between us and that body."

Fisher agreed and they quickly tidied their belongings back into their bags.

Harris headed to reception, leaving him sat on the edge of the bed.

As he relaxed into the springs of the mattress, his mind flashed back to the barrel of the gun. His right hand began to shake first and soon the rest of his body followed. He couldn't stop thinking how lucky he'd been.

It could have so easily been him Harris buried in the woods. But it wasn't him, thanks to the cold-blooded killer he'd shared a room with; the true professional who'd killed to defend him. Who'd have killed the dog to stop it drawing attention. The lethal, efficient killer.

His shivers grew and he felt himself losing control until a voice sprang into his head.

"Dick," said Andrew's taunting tone.

A smile bloomed through Fisher's tremors. He could almost see Andrew sat beside him, shaking his head, pouring scorn in his direction.

He felt his body calm and clasped his hands together just as the door opened and Harris stood with the manager, inspecting the damage.

She turned towards him, brow lowering.

"Are you all right?" she mouthed.

Fisher replied with a shallow nod.

***

"It's okay, you know," Harris said, as they drove towards Caernarfon.

"Do you get used to it?" Fisher said quietly.

"No," she said as she pushed buttons on her phone.

Moments later, they pulled into the town centre car park, finding the chain hotel easily enough. With an hour before they were to meet the second missing girl's friend, Fisher started to breathe easy as they walked in the anonymity of the bustling town.

In the anonymous chain hotel, the newly-booked twin room was nothing like the converted stable, but he didn't care. They weren't here for a holiday. They were here to find two missing girls.

Sat on the edge of the furthest bed, his bags dropped to the floor as the kettle quietly worked away by the small TV and he watched as Harris took off her coat, pulling out the dead man's grey handgun. She snapped open the aluminium case and grabbed items from the bottom shelf.

With the volume of the kettle building, he watched her sit, the gun already in pieces on her lap, disassembled in a flash as she dragged an oil-stained cloth through the barrel, inspecting each of the components, cleaning and lubricating as she went.

The kettle reached its peak as she snapped the pieces back together.

"Thank you," she said, taking the offered cup of tea, his eyes on the metal in her hands. "Browning L9A1," she said, pushing in the clip and pulling back the slide. "Standard service issue for our boys since World War II." Fisher nodded as he looked on. "This is the updated version with improved grip and safety. Been in service since the eighties. Heavy but solid weapon."

Fisher nodded again and she caught the raise of his brow.

"Sorry, I'm a bit of a gun geek." Her cheeks flushed red with the words.

"So he could be ex-British forces?" he replied.

Harris's coy demeanour melted and she shook her head. "Or bought on the black market from any one of fifty other countries it's been in service," she said, turning the gun over in her hands. "It's been well looked after and not seen much action." She laid the killing machine on the bed beside her and took a sip of tea.

Ten minutes later, they were on their way to meet with the friend of Rihanna Summers at a pub on the other side of the town centre. The five-minute trip took them fifteen more, time well spent disposing of gloves, the slug and casing out of sight of CCTV.

By the time they arrived at The Crown they were five minutes late. Harris made a call as they stepped into the bar and a young brown-haired woman in her early twenties soon met their attention. She stood in a dark corner, one arm hugging around her chest, the other holding a short glass of dark liquid. Tiredness hung loosely on her heavily made-up face.

"Charlie?" Fisher said and she replied with a smile he thought seemed genuine enough.

Harris pushed out her hand, taking Charlie's and giving a gentle shake. "Chloe and Toby Partridge." With a nod, Charlie moved with them to Harris's choice of table away from the windows.

"Andrea said you want to help?" Charlie said, her voice quiet as she took the seat opposite the pair.

Harris nodded.

"I'll do anything it takes to help find her. We're all so worried," Charlie said as she placed her hand on her breastbone. "If only we'd made sure she'd got home," her voice quivered as she spoke.

Harris lay her palm on the table. "Can you tell us what happened?" she said in a soft voice. "As much as you can remember. The smallest detail could help."

Charlie moved her hand back around her chest and took a deep breath. "It was Rihanna's birthday and we all met up at her house at seven o'clock."

"Whose we?" Harris interrupted.

"Sorry, it was me, Rihanna and three of our friends. Julie, Pippa and Ruth."

"How long have you known them?" Fisher said.

"We all went to school together, since infants."

He tried to give a reassuring smile.

"We had a few drinks, ordered pizza while we finished getting ready, grabbed a cab and headed into town. We went to the Wetherspoons. The one just down the road from here, next to McDonalds."

Harris and Fisher looked back at her.

"We had a few drinks, maybe three rounds. Then we moved to…"

Harris interrupted and Charlie took the chance to grab a breath. "Sorry, Charlie. Can I just ask, did anyone pay any special interest to any of you, Rihanna in particular, while you were in Wetherspoons?"

Charlie smiled. "You're joking right? We're always getting interest. Be a pretty crap night if they left us alone."

Harris replied with a smile.

Charlie took a sip of her drink. "So after Wetherspoons we went to Time. Oh, we had to go back to Wethers. Ri had forgotten her bag." She gave a small laugh as she remembered. "Found it in the toilet of all places. Anyway, I'd got us on the guest list and we were straight in. Pippa surprised us with tickets to the VIP lounge." She looked off in the distance. "It was a great evening." Her tone changed. "We got drunk pretty quickly. Some of us had had enough, me and Pippa anyway. We decided to head for food. Well, we had to convince Ri and Ruth. They still wanted to party.

"In the end we found McDonalds closed. It must have been later than we thought, so moved on to the kebab shop. We ate doners and headed home. That was the last time…" she stopped mid-sentence, her head snapping back towards them. "You asked about special interest?" she said.

Harris nodded.

"While we were waiting for food these two boys were chatting. They were talking to Rihanna and Pippa mostly, but I guessed that's because we were talking to the guys cooking the food." She smiled again and gazed ahead. "We were winding them up about having to work while everyone else was having a good time. They were proper lush and made the most amazing kebabs."

"Rihanna?"

"Sorry," Charlie said, refocusing. "We got the food and then Ri said she was going to go to another bar with those boys. We pointed out what a bad idea that would be and told the lads to bugger off." Her eyebrows pinched down. "They took it badly. The boys started having a go. Anyway, Rihanna changed her mind and agreed to call it a night. We finished our food and went home."

"How did you get home? Where did you all sleep?" asked Fisher.

"Um, we all went to our own places. I got a cab with Pippa and Ruth, then Rihanna got in with Julie."

"Where'd you get the cabs from?" Fisher said.

Charlie looked off into the distance again as her arms tightened around her chest. "They found us."

"What do you mean?" he said, skewing his head at an angle.

"We were walking and they pulled up. Pretty lucky, eh?"

Harris and Fisher shared a look before Fisher spoke again.

"Who got dropped off first, in the other cab?"

"Rihanna then Julie, I guess."

"But you don't know?" Harris said.

"Makes sense that way, but I can check if you want?"

"Please," Harris answered.

Charlie pulled out a pink phone, tapped the screen a couple of times and put it to her ear. With the call answered within a few rings, the pair listened to the one-sided conversation.

"She doesn't know why, but they went to her house first. Both of them were too out of it to notice at the time." Charlie bit at her bottom lip, running her finger down the length of the phone before eventually laying it flat on the table, the screen still lit with her list of contacts. "She was supposed to message me when she got home, but I fell asleep." Charlie half-heartedly flicked through her text messages. "In the morning there were messages from all the girls." Her arms went around and she hugged herself tight. "But not Ri."

Fisher watched a tear running down her cheek.

"I should have stayed awake."

"It wasn't your fault," Harris said. "Are you okay to carry on?"

Charlie nodded.

"Can you describe the time at the kebab shop again?"

“I think that’s everything. Those boys were talking to Ri and Pip. I didn't notice anything else 'cos we were talking in the kebab shop. We were giving them our full attention.” She smiled, but it soon faded as if she realised how stupid the words sounded. A tear fell to the table.

“Can you find out what Pippa remembers?” Harris said, pointing at the pink phone.

Charlie smiled, wiping her eyes then picked up her handset, returning it as the call went unanswered.

“One last question,” Harris said as Charlie nodded. “What was she wearing?”

Charlie gave a lopsided smile, then scrolled through her pictures before turning the phone toward them. The screen showed a picture of the group of girls, Rihanna only just recognisable as the sweet young girl in the field. The innocence had gone and so had the full-length summer dress, replaced with a strapless top and a strip of material barely covering her underwear.

With her face plastered with colour, she draped her arms loose around two other girls, both black-haired and dressed in the same loose uniform.

“Thank you. Let me give you a number. If Pippa calls you back, then please can you let me know what she says?”

Charlie nodded as Harris handed her a beer mat, digits scrawled along the white border.

Leaving Charlie in the pub, the pair walked slowly along the high street with the light beginning to fade, finding themselves outside the McDonalds. A small black and white sign stuck to the glass door read, CLOSED FOR REFURBISHMENT and it wasn't due to reopen for another two weeks.

24

Stood outside the fast food restaurant, Fisher's stomach began to complain. He prompted Harris as they walked towards the hotel, their heads turning in the same direction as a lazy melody of strings drifted, flickering candles inviting them inside a small side street bistro.

Fisher took a deep breath and shook his head. "There must be somewhere quicker," he said, turning his head around the street, but she was already walking swiftly towards the restaurant and he had to jog to catch her up.

"We need to think, unless you've got the next move figured out?" she replied. Watching as he shook his head, they passed into the twilight room.

Soon seated to the back, the waiter returned, filling her choice of wine to the brim.

"What do you think?" Fisher asked as he took a sip.

"The wine?" Harris said, curling her lips.

"Charlie," he replied, resting his glass to the table.

Her smile melted. "It looks premeditated. I doubt they were Hackneys. I had a quick look at the route. The cab would have driven straight past Rihanna's address to get to Julie's."

Fisher sat up straight. "Hackneys?"

"Mini-cabs can't tout for fares. They have to be pre-booked."

He gave a wide-eyed nod. "So it was the taxi driver?"

"Involved, but he might just have been paid off. With the McDonalds closed, we've got no idea when they came out of the club. Sounds like they were pretty drunk, maybe too drunk. If there wasn't four of them, I would have said someone slipped something in their drinks."

"So we find the taxi driver?"

"There's no time. She's been gone almost two weeks already."

Fisher's shoulders slumped and he ran his hand over his short stubble. "They'll have records of who was on shift," he said.

Harris put her drink on the table and leant forward. "Sure, but we'd need to find which company they used, which isn't impossible, then we'd need to go through each of the drivers, and if they took a payoff or were involved, they'd be hostile. We'd have to corroborate where each of the drivers were. Take statements. Cross check records. We can't just take their word for it. I don't need to tell you we don't have time."

"If only there was a way we could be sure they were telling the truth," Fisher said, almost under his breath.

"That would change my job, that's for sure, but until we get that magic device, it'll take good old-fashioned hard work."

Fisher nodded, sipping his wine. "Do you think they're linked?"

Harris pinched her lips together. "I'm working on that assumption. Timing, location, their striking resemblance. It's enough for me."

Fisher stared at the pictures on the wall, his mind running over the night of Susie's disappearance. "I didn't see any taxis when Susie went missing."

"But you were at a pub. No reason to notice."

Fisher nodded. "What else have we got?" he said.

"The phone," Harris said. "It never left Snowdon."

"The phone gave us the house."

"And the garage."

"They took her at the pub, grabbed her car, sold it."

"And quickly," Harris interrupted. "You saw it the next day."

Fisher let his gaze linger on her as she looked back.

"I should have done something."

"What could you have done?"

He shook his head. "Maybe they just wanted the car?" he replied, his tone rising with a moment of hope.

"Easier ways to steal cars and it means there'd be no link to Rihanna."

"The gunman."

"It's organised," she said, nodding.

"And why these two?" asked Fisher.

"That we know of," she said, emptying her glass. "That's the question." She grabbed the bottle, poured herself another glass and topped up Fisher's.

"So what's next?" he asked.

"You mentioned a run in with one of the locals."

"The Prince of Wales. We should take a look," Fisher replied, eagerly nodding.

Harris motioned to her mouth as their food arrived. In silence she finished first, and with her wine glass in hand he caught her watching him.

He looked up as he took his last mouthful of steak to see a broad smile on her lips. Looking away, he contended with his mouthful of meat. Turning back, her expression had changed; her eyes had narrowed and her head shook gently side to side.

"What's wrong?" he asked, picking up his glass.

"I'm putting you in danger."

Fisher tipped his head to the side and gently shook it.

"I'm making mistakes. We should have been more careful at the house. I'm distracted. Dropping the phone. Leaving the car where we did. Letting you run off." Her head movement intensified. "And this won't help," she said, looking around the candle lit surroundings.

"Your idea," Fisher replied.

"Another mistake." As she finished speaking, her hand shot up and the waiter came over with the bill. Pushing cash into the leather wallet, she headed in the direction of the bathroom.

Fisher picked up his phone and tapped in the number for a directory service and scribbled on the back of a napkin as the series of numbers were read out.

With Harris back, they headed into the night and the direction of the hotel.

"Only two cab firms in Caernarfon. A1 Cars and Dragon Cabs, and another in Llanberis, Sherpa Cars," he said, walking to her side.

"Waste of time," she said, shaking her head. "We'll follow up the guy from the pub tomorrow and see what the morning brings."

Fisher pushed the napkin back in his pocket.

She's the professional. She knows what she's doing, he reassured himself.

***

Fisher woke in the dark and quiet of the hotel room. It was either late or early, depending on your point of view. He felt like he hadn't slept for long and could still feel the numbing effects of the wine diluting his sleep, the images of the two women flowing in and out of his dreams.

Two young lives. Two to find. Two to save.

His thought's drifted to Susie's mum and the tears flowing down her face at their last meeting. Mrs Summers, her face a mirror image of pain. Two frantic families in constant fear.

Were they safe? Were they in pain? Were they ever going to see them again?

Fisher turned over, his eyes settling on Harris's figure silhouetted in the opposite bed. The thin cover draped over her perfect curves. Calm and peaceful, glowing with beauty in the half-light as she slept an arm's reach away.

Looking on, his body responded, his stomach flipped and the space in his underwear got smaller. She was the most attractive woman he'd ever spoken to, and the most capable, he added in his head. But capable of what?

He tried to force himself to imagine the things she must have done and the things she was yet to do. A shiver cascaded through him at the thought.

At least she was helping him. At least she was on his side, even though she hadn't chosen to be.

Still watching her slow breath, he remembered the words she'd spoken over dinner. Her distraction. As he tried to think of anything else, sleep slowly came.

25

Fisher woke to find sun pouring through the open curtains to his left and Harris to his right, dressed and sat up on top of the covers. Her fingers tapped at the iPad. Despite the TV being on, the sound faded into the background.

"Morning," she said, looking up from the screen.

"Morning," he replied. "Couldn't sleep?"

"No, just used to early starts. You were restless again, like you were dreaming."

Fisher raised himself up as the vague memory of a dream, Trinity in her silk, faded from his thoughts.

"Did you know you talk in your sleep?" she said, the smile obvious even though his eyes were forced towards the TV.

"What did I say?"

"Don't worry, it didn't make any sense," she said, and her tone hardened. "They've started looking for me. I've had a tip off. I told them I'm okay, but they're still coming looking."

Fisher turned his head to her.

"Protocol," she said. "I managed to get some interesting information before they shut my access down. After we found out about Rihanna, I requested the stats on missing persons in the last three years."

"That'll be a lot of people," he replied.

Harris nodded slowly. "A few hundred?" he asked.

"Try twenty-six thousand, and that's only in the last three months."

He pushed himself further up the bed as he turned to her, his eyes wide. "Holy shit."

"It's less than a quarter percent of the population," she said, shrugging.

Fisher looked back at the TV. "And we're only looking for two. A drop in the ocean."

"That's what I thought until I looked into the detail."

Fisher turned back to her.

"The information is listed by police authority, so I've sorted the data and I think I've found something interesting. Listen to these numbers." She swiped her finger across the screen as Fisher swung his legs around the bed and perched on the edge, leaning his shoulders forward. "The average number of missing persons in the UK is five-point three people per thousand population each year, that gives us the twenty-six thousand per quarter." She looked at Fisher and he nodded in agreement. "North Wales Police reported four per thousand last month."

"That's a lot smaller."

"But it used to be even lower." She met his gaze. "It used to be about three people per thousand and it's been pretty steady for the last three years."

Fisher narrowed his eyes.

"It went from 500 per quarter to 590 in each of the last two quarters. That's thirty people more per month going missing."

Fisher looked at the ceiling, the numbers running through his mind as he turned back to Harris. "That's a sixty percent increase," he said.

She nodded.

"Is it just this force or everywhere?"

"I checked and there was no real increase in any other force. The data they gave me was very detailed, so I looked to see if there was anything noticeable about who was going missing. I looked at age. The increase was in the eighteen to twenty-five range. Then sex. The increase was female only, ethnicity white British or mixed raced British. There were other factors that didn't show any increase or trend, like religion, hometown, education level or employment."

"Does it show the place they were last seen?"

"It shows the place of report."

"Is there is any correlation between their hometown and where they went missing?"

"Give me a few minutes," she replied and then set about tapping and moving her fingers around on the iPad screen.

Fisher stood. Filling the kettle, he grabbed his clothes and dressed in the bathroom.

As the kettle clicked, Harris announced the answer. "There's no link between hometowns. They went missing all around North Wales, but if you compare those that went missing in their hometown, there's a slight increase. Most were away from home."

"Tourists?"

"Or just living away, like students, yes."

Fisher stared out of the window, running through the figures in his head as he looked for a flaw, some reason not to believe the data.

"Why has no one else spotted it?" he said, spinning his head back towards her.

"Bureaucracy," she said as Fisher raised his eyebrows. "ONS collates the data, then publishes once a year."

"ONS?" he interrupted.

She hesitated before she replied in a low voice. "Office for National Statistics."

"Yeah, sorry," he said. "Of course."

"Charities, government and other NGOs analyse it, but we don't have to wait for each police authority to send the data to the ONS. We just read it live from their databases. We know before they do."

Fisher turned towards the TV; his train of thought vanished as a reporter stood with Snowdon in the background. He got to his feet and turned the volume high, watching as she talked to the camera and a rolling banner scrolled from the right of the screen.

Body found in Snowdon woods.

He turned to Harris and she stared back, wide-eyed. "That was quick!" she exclaimed and she set about gathering their belongings.

A photo of a man appeared on the screen; a face they recognised immediately, but it wasn't the man they were expecting.

26

Sat on the edge of their beds, they stared, soaking up the reporter's words.

"The body of Darren Michaels was found late last night by a group of tourists walking on the Waen-oer Ridge trail, one of the more difficult routes to summit Snowdon. Police are treating his death as suspicious and have appealed for any information about the investigation, urgently calling for any witnesses to come forward that were in the area or saw Mr Michaels yesterday."

Harris turned the volume down as her gaze fell on Fisher.

"Consequences," he said under his breath.

"Why would they kill him?" she said, frowning.

"They?" he paused, his eyes springing wide. "You think those two psychos killed him? He wouldn't have gone to see them, surely? Would he?"

Harris kept silent.

"He was scare…" He stopped himself and looked down at the floor. Harris still didn't speak and he looked up, her hand raising towards the TV.

"Put that to one side for a moment," she said, closing her eyes. "We've got one hundred and eighty missing girls in the last six months. That isn't some amateur operation. This is big, it's serious. I'd like to get this data worked over by my team."

Fisher shook his head. "Well that's not an option," he said.

Harris raised an eyebrow as if only just remembering. "We need to see if Charlie's friend got back to her and I need food. Can you get us some breakfast while I call?"

Fisher nodded. Within a few minutes he was out of the door and into the street below. As he walked the high street, the figures rolled around in his head. One hundred and eighty missing British girls. Too big to be real. A mistake. No national outcry. No evidence. Tonnes of no evidence. No trace, no bodies. One hundred and eighty people vanished. It can't be.

Back at the room, he found Harris tapping away at the iPad. She looked up, putting the tablet to one side and reached out.

"Did you speak to Charlie?" Fisher said, pulling two cups from a cardboard tray, handing one over with a small paper bag.

"Yes, but it was a no go."

"What do you mean?"

"I got a description, but it was too broad. Could have been so many people."

"Nothing unusual at all?"

"Well, they asked for a photo, but just of Rihanna. She refused. He took it anyway and left."

Fisher's grip relaxed, hot coffee exploding as it hit the floor.

Harris stood from the bed, searching around the room for a towel.

"What were the descriptions?" he said, his eyes wide, still holding his hand as if the cup was still there.

She turned and saw his heavy expression, watched as he took long slow breaths. She looked back down to the tablet.

"One IC3, short hair, smart short sleeve shirt, average build, average height."

Fisher raised his eyebrows, his mouth widening slowly.

"Afro Caribbean," Harris added. "The other guy was IC1, Caucasian, tall, described as handsome, distinctive Southern English accent."

"Quiffed hair?" Fisher interrupted.

"Yes," she replied, raising her eyebrows.

"White iPhone?"

"Same with Susie?" she replied, her eyebrows high on her head.

His heavy expression had lifted, the corners of his mouth had raised in an excited smile. "Exactly."

27

"It's him. The owner, Tristan. He took her under our noses, right there at that pub in Llanberis," he said, almost panting for breath.

His smile had dropped and a chasm of emptiness opened in his gut. Steadying himself on the corner of the bed, he watched Harris, barely taking anything in as she eagerly packed up the remains of her bag, quickly pushing his own into his hands. Leading him through the foyer, she checked out as they passed the small reception desk.

Climbing into the car, Fisher spoke. "Are we going there now?" he said, his voice unsure. He watched the shake of her head, her fingers tapping at the navigation system. He turned and stared out of the window.

As she drove at the foot of the mountain, memories flooded back. Tristan's stride as he sauntered over, with purpose and intent in his confident swagger. She'd been singled out so quickly.

Fisher held his breath.

That bastard had tried to get her on the first night, but she'd resisted. He'd not shown himself the second day, the day she disappeared. He thought of his smug face as he hid, waiting with patience for the timing to be right, the time to pounce. And then he did.

A shiver ran down his spine and he came back from the nightmare, the car rolling down a gravel track, stopping when the ruts were bigger than the wheels.

He followed as she pulled the metal case from the boot, trailing behind without conversation as they trekked for what seemed like hours through valleys dense with fern and thickets, all whilst being battered by the wind. Climbing hills of discarded slate, his feet slipped against the carpet of moss and grassy, isolated mounds.

Only harried-looking sheep crossed their path. The pair stopped in a long and narrow valley, the air stilled by a thick border of evergreens vanishing miles ahead on the horizon.

Harris rested the case on the ground. Turning to meet his gaze, she spoke. "You done?"

He gave a slow nod, surprising himself when his head had indeed cleared, the sudden mourning pushed back by the effort of the trek.

"I'm going to show you how to look after yourself," she said.

Fisher looked up, concentrating on her words.

"Two people are dead. I need to know you're not a liability."

A nervous smile sprung on his face as he watched her flip up the clasps. He spun around the valley as a worrying thought ran across his mind.

"Won't someone hear us?" he said, turning back to see the two menacing pistols nestled in the black foam.

"It's the countryside. Farmers shoot all the time. Anyway, we're miles from anywhere," she said, brushing off his concern. "How much do you know about guns?"

Fisher stared at the weapons. All he could think of were the countless cop shows and spy movies he'd watched sat alone in his flat with the curtains closed, trying to take his mind away from thoughts of his parents.

"Point and shoot?" he finally said as he made his hand into the shape of a gun and pretended to fire in the air.

Harris lowered her head, pulled the dead man's Browning from a pocket and jumped headlong into a lecture, an abridged version of the training course all field operatives receive on their first day, so she said.

Fisher listened with nervous fascination as she rattled through the basics of how guns worked and the finer points of regular cleaning and maintenance, before slowing to detail rules on safety and his rules of engagement, summing up in a final sentence. "Shoot only if you're about to get shot."

After fifteen minutes, she confirmed the gun to be unloaded and gestured for him to take it.

With a moment's hesitation he took the pistol, its metal warm from her handling. He wrapped his right hand around the grip, swapping it to the left and back again. It felt as he thought it should. Heavy. Substantial. Full of purpose.

Handing it back, he watched as she slid the full clip into the base of the grip, palming it home with a click before giving it back. Swapping the gun between his hands, Harris moved to his back and out of the arc of fire, her hands guiding his shoulders and turning him towards the far end of the valley.

For a moment he forgot about the weapon in his hands, her touch sparking electricity as she turned his body.

With a soft voice she spoke slowly. "Try it."

He wished he could, then he realised she was talking about the gun.

Taking a deep breath, he turned his attention back to the metal. The full clip added a noticeable weight and had altered the balance, but the biggest difference was how delicate it now felt. He could feel the potential, the power the weapon could unleash.

Nerves tingled in his stomach as he began to imagine unleashing the destructive force.

To his side, Harris pointed down the valley to a prominent, silvered Beech sat out in front of its companions. She softly reminded him how to chamber a round, her breath brushing across his face as she watched close to his shoulder as he pulled back the slide.

It had more resistance than he'd expected, like pulling back on a powerful spring. At her close word, he clicked off the safety, pointed the weapon down the natural range and settled his body at an angle. His left side towards the target. The right in the opposite direction.

Tensing the muscles in his shoulder, her hands softly corrected his stance. He felt her move away and he looked down the sight, centring a break in the simmering bark, his finger slowly squeezing.

Fisher took a deep breath, slowing the out breath, trying to relax and not picturing the recoil flinging him to his butt.

The trigger came back, his hands jolting up, the kick less than he feared but the explosive noise took him by surprise. With his ears ringing, the noise faded from the valley and he turned his attention to the tree. His face dropped. He'd expected a giant hole or the trunk split in two, but instead he stood shocked when the explosive forced hadn't wreaked havoc on the wood. It appeared unscathed.

With his voice heavy with disappointment he turned to Harris. "I missed."

Soon behind him, moving out of the arc of the barrel as he pivoted, her hands already back on his shoulders, pressing him down the range.

He clicked the safety with his thumb and looked behind to see a wide, surprised smile on her face.

"But I missed," he said, his voice still sullen.

"Look again," she said, pointing at the target.

He slowly turned back and squinted, moving closer a few paces and then a few more until he saw it; a glint of metal embedded at the centre of the bark exactly where he'd aimed.

Beaming as he returned to the same spot, he clicked the safety off and set the stance again.

Another round reeled from the chamber. The noise seemed less and he briefly worried he'd damaged his hearing, but the thought disappeared as he eyed the glint right next to its brother. He fired again, then eleven more propelled from the barrel until the final click echoed in the empty chamber.

Remembering the training, he checked the chamber, his hands soaking up the heat of the barrel.

Fisher took a deep breath, stretched out his aching fingers and rolled his shoulders as he tried to control his smile. The euphoria soon subsided, his thoughts turning to those tiny brass projectiles exploding into something living.

It felt nothing like the movies or a computer game; she'd shown him for a reason and he didn't know if he could do it.

"Okay. Point and shoot," she said, laughing as she arrived at his shoulder. "We should leave. I've got what I need," she added, leaning down to the case to pull out a box of nine-millimetre rounds, her fingers working the shine of the brass into its holder. "No point if it's not ready," she said as she closed the lid on the case.

Fisher checked the safety twice. "No point in having it if you're not going to use it," he repeated quietly, holding out the weapon.

"Keep it. Just in case."

Fisher sucked in a deep breath and checked the safety again before pushing the gun into his jacket pocket.

Standing together at the makeshift target, each counted thirteen holes spattered across the bark.

Harris turned to him with her eyebrows raised. "You're a natural." As she patted him on the back, he felt like a little boy being congratulated by his babysitter.

Leaving the rounds embedded in the tree but collecting up the thirteen shell casings, they retraced their steps back to the car and he realised it had only been an hour's walk.

With Fisher driving, they re-joined the main road and the high-pitched trill of a phone sprung from Harris's pocket.

"Missed call," she said as she pulled out the phone.

"Who's got that number?"

"Just the Summers and Rihanna's friends," she replied as she pushed the phone to her ear.

"Hello..." Her tone changed as she realised who was on the other end of the line. "Oh. Hi, Mrs Summers... Andrea, sorry. Are you okay?"

As Harris listened, she turned to Fisher doe-eyed, her head shaking. "No, no news yet. You'll be the first to know. Bye for now," and she hung up. "She wants to know if we'd got anywhere. Sounds pretty desperate." Harris looked out of the window, her head still shaking.

A few miles down the road, Fisher realised he had no idea where they were heading, but his stomach reminded him he'd barely eaten breakfast and they needed another hotel for tonight.

"How about The Peak Inn?" Harris asked before he had a chance to speak.

"Uh?" he said, blinking rapidly as he looked between her and the road.

"An ideal opportunity to get a look around," she said, her fingers already tapping on the iPad.

A few minutes of frustration and sucking on her bottom lip, she turned off the screen. "Looks like it's just a pub now. There are no references to rooms on any of the hotel search sites."

"That's a big place just to be a pub. Seems a waste of a prime location."

"Guess he's got a big family," she said, back browsing over the screen, then within a few minutes she'd found a vacancy in Bangor and made the booking online.

Fisher set the course on the GPS.

After an hour, they arrived in Bangor, during which Fisher relived the feeling of the gun in his hand, the ache in his upper body reminding him of the power.

Harris kept quiet, with the occasional suck of her lip, absorbing herself into the tablet.

Checking into the twin room, they were soon out of the door on the hunt for somewhere to eat. With no discussion they ended up through the doors of a greasy spoon where their feet planted to the spot and they fixed on the giant wall-hung television, reading the headline scrolling across the bottom.

Police seek young couple in Snowdon murder hunt.

28

Fisher tossed the sandwich wrap into a kerbside bin and started the engine. Harris swallowed hard with the phone in her lap, the ringing tone announcing from its speaker.

"Peak Inn. Llanberis," came a crisp male English accent.

"Hello. Can I speak to the owner please?"

"Sorry, he's not in today. I'm Tony, the manager. Can I help at all?"

"Yes, you're just the person. I'm calling from the North Wales Chronicle. We're working with the West Cheshire and North Wales Chamber of Commerce, profiling local businesses for this year's young entrepreneur award. The owner has been nominated," she paused, as if reaching for a name. "Sorry, I only have the name Tristan."

"It's Tristan Tomkin-Smythe," the manager cut in.

Fisher thought he heard a catch in her voice. A pause. About to question her with a sideways look, she spoke again.

"Oh yes, thank you. We would like to come and run up a profile. Is he around at any time today?"

"No, sorry. He won't be back until tomorrow."

Harris turned to Fisher with a beaming smile. "Okay, no problem. I'll call back tomorrow and see if I can speak to him again," and she hung up the phone before he could reply. "Change of plan," she said with raised eyebrows, just as Fisher pulled into the road.

Pulling up at a junction, the fading sign displayed their options. Llanrug to the left, a mile down the road, or right at a cost of thirty miles to avoid retracing where they knew they were being hunted by the police.

"Which way?" he said, holding his hands off the steering wheel as he checked the mirror.

"You think they might spot us?" Harris said, smiling.

"It's your call."

"Left. I don't think we're quite worthy of an ambush. Yet," she added with a laugh.

Fisher turned the car left, taking them through the familiar village. He slowed as they passed The Black Boy, his heart jumping as he saw a police panda car in the car park.

With no pounce of uniformed officers, they passed The Peak Inn, turning down a side street to park out of the way, hoping they still had time before the hotel manager called their details into the police after the television appeal.

From the boot they pulled heavy rucksacks bulked out with whatever weight they could fill from their room, slung them on their backs and headed down the main road.

Fisher felt his breath steal for a moment as he saw the packed car park, the benches full of hikers and cyclists drinking and making merry.

Leading Harris inside, they found the rest of the bar quiet and sparsely populated with pleasure walkers, judging by their gear, small packs huddled around table legs.

To his surprise, even though so much had happened and it had only been a little under two weeks since they'd been the ones resting their bones, the room hadn't changed.

At the bar, Harris announced she was heading to the toilet and he watched as she walked in the opposite direction to the sign. The barman ignored her as he greeted Fisher, his chin manicured with stubble, teeth beaming through a rounded smile.

Fisher nodded in return and leant forward towards the rows of bottles, taking his time to look over the pumps.

"Do you recommend any of the ales?" he finally said.

"Certainly. The Mount Snowdon Pale Ale is worth a try. It's brewed just down the road," the barman said without dropping the smile.

"Great, I'll have a half please, and a lemonade."

The barman stepped a couple of paces to the side, selected a half-pint glass before pumping brown frothy liquid.

Fisher picked up a crisp, laminated menu and turned it over in his hands.

"Do you have rooms?" he said, looking up to see the barman's eyebrows raised as if he hadn't heard him right. "We looked at staying here but couldn't find how to book."

"We used to have ten rooms. Owner lives up there now," he replied as the ale came to the top of the glass.

"Can't get away from him now," Fisher said with an energetic smile.

The barman glanced up, his own smile tiring.

"He must have a big family."

The barman gave an awkward smile and placed the ale on the bar and grabbed another glass. "That'll be £5.12," he said, as the second glass rested on the countertop.

Fisher paid, letting him keep the change, taking the drinks as he saw Harris heading from the opposite direction.

"Found it, finally," she said, leading them to a table in the far corner.

Fisher watched her take a sip as she peered past him into the empty lounge.

She spoke, her voice slow and dripping in a husky whisper. "I can't see how to get upstairs. It must be that door," she said, tipping her head towards a plain white door at the far end of the bar; italic black writing across a silvered plaque marked it as private.

"He lives there. Closed the hotel down when he bought the place. It had ten bedrooms and presumably a staff flat. I think it's just him up there but I didn't want to push any further."

"How long's he owned it?"

"No idea," Fisher replied.

Sitting in silence, Harris looked around the room with a distracted look as he watched the scene to his back.

"We've got to see what he's doing with all that space," he said as their eyes locked.

"We'll have to come back at night. Hopefully he won't be around."

"I've got an idea, leave it with me," Fisher said, and she raised an eyebrow as if waiting for him to allude, but he only gave a thin smile. "I'm going to the bathroom," he announced and followed the signs.

Standing at the urinal, he couldn't go. He didn't need to. He needed to calm himself down because he stood in the building where Susie had last been seen. Excitement and dread coursed in equal measures through his veins. Upstairs would be the key; he couldn't be surer. He didn't know what would be up there, but he knew it must be the start of the end.

Splashing his face with water, he felt a quake in his hands.

"Dick," he said out loud, imitating his friend and took a deep breath, his head leaning back as he looked above. "I'm close."

Stepping in the bar, his gaze shot to the car park and the fluorescent Battenberg of a white car. His heart rate climbed and he took a deep breath, walking to the table, surprised to see Harris still there, finishing her drink.

"There's fuzz in the car park." As he heard his own words, he knew his mistake, her cheeks dimpling as a smile blossomed across her face.

"The fuzz?" she said, still smiling. "Is there a time machine in the toilets?"

Fisher tipped his head forward, his face stretching as she stood.

"I'm going. You wait a few minutes then join me in the Capri," she said, her cheeks dimpling a second time.

He drew a deep breath, his eyes fixed on her behind, heart pounding with each gentle sway as she crossed the car park. He couldn't believe they'd only met a few days ago and how strongly he felt for her. How consumed he'd been by her beauty, but most of all because, unless he was reading it so wrong, there was a chance she liked him back.

A dreadful thought sprung to mind. It would all come to an end when she found he was lying to her. It would all change when she found out the truth.

Her brains matched her beauty, but both paled in comparison to her ruthlessness and drive.

He took a breath, the fluorescence of a jacket coming into view as he stared out at the policeman checking each of the parked cars, speaking into his radio as he stood. It was time to go, but he had a small job to do first.

Walking up to the bar, the lone barman stood and nodded for his order.

Fisher breathed a deep breath and held out his hand.

"Tony?"

***

Harris picked him up at the main road. Throwing his bag in the back, they headed out of the village, taking the long, sparsely-featured way around Llanrug.

"All set. We need to be back by eight. We'll have the place to ourselves."

She turned away from the road, her eyebrows narrowing as she spoke.

"Are you going to tell me or do I have to guess?"

"That copper was checking all the cars."

"Yeah, I saw it too. We'll have to swap. Nearest place is Holyhead."

"Floor it, Makepeace," he said, flicking his finger out in front. She gave him a dirty look and he lowered his hand.

Sitting in silence, they wound around the narrow roads. It wasn't until reaching the North Wales Expressway that she spoke.

"You don't talk much, do you?"

"I have my moments," he said, nervously looking at her out of the corner of his eye.

"So what's Susie like?"

The question shocked him but he wasn't sure why. It was a reasonable thing to ask and it wasn't like they hadn't talked about her before, even though he'd just relayed the facts.

"She's amazing."

"Wow. Amazing," Harris said, adjusting her posture.

"Like a sister, of course."

"Of course, like a sister."

"She's sweet. She's good to me, really helped, you know when my parents…"

Harris nodded gently as Fisher stopped mid-sentence.

"There was a time when I thought I was in love with her," he paused. "But it was obvious we wouldn't be right that way."

Harris gave a gentle laugh. "She sounds lovely."

Fisher nodded, turning his attention out in front and a long line of traffic cones narrowing the road as they stretched out into the distance. He watched as a group of four identical lorries laboured from a side road, each hauling a brown shipping container.

Harris let the car slow and joined the end of the monotonous convoy. Each time they came across a junction, Fisher hoped the convoy would divert off. Instead, they followed all the way to the port, turning as they arrived at the dock's freight entrance, peeling one by one to a small unladen ship waiting for its load.

Harris pulled the car up at the next junction and Fisher jumped out, heading to the green and white Enterprise porta-cabin. After twenty minutes, they were back in a Fiesta, crawling the opposite way as the road filled with commuters.

At well past seven they arrived back in Llanberis, less mindful of the numerous police cars, anonymous again in their grey Fiesta. Leaving the car down a different side street, they stepped into the quiet car park and saw a white rectangle of paper pinned to the wooden frame.

Closing at 8pm today. Private Function.

Fisher stifled his smile as Harris turned in his direction with a thin eyebrow raised. Still ignoring the unvoiced question, he pulled at the door, meeting with Tony's eyes, wide and optimistic, from behind the bar.

Fisher replied with a nod and watched a grin bloom as he whispered in a nearby barmaid's ear.

Taking a seat, they drank and ate at Tony's favour, but Fisher could only pick at the plate. His mind swept across the corridors upstairs, opening a door to a vision of his friend, her hands bound and mouth gagged, then safe and well. Freed by his hand. He'd hold her close and tell her it was all okay. They'd travel home, all three together. They'd stay with her until she felt safe again, then he'd start his life anew. His life with Carrie.

Fisher turned back to the present and saw Harris's lips move, the trail of her voice sweeping into focus.

"I'm okay," he replied and kicked himself for his cruel imagination. She would remember soon. She'd find out and the bubble would burst. He wouldn't be able to start life again; he would have to pay for his crimes and she would make him. He would argue he'd done it all to help a friend, to fight a cruel injustice. A crime to stop a crime. A crime to save a life. But would it be enough?

He knew it wouldn't.

The bell rang last orders. Ten minutes to go. Doing his best to control his breath, he watched the bar empty, the staff ushering drinks, hands waving away stragglers until the last left.

"All but the front doors are locked," Tony said as he handed over the keys. "Do you have keys for upstairs, because I don't?" he said.

Fisher tapped his pocket and lifted his full pint.

"We'll head up in a bit."

Almost ignoring the response in his eagerness to leave, Tony nodded and walked to the entrance. Closing the door, they saw shoulders slump in the twilight as he turned away a group of hikers walking across the empty car park.

With the last sight, Harris snapped to her feet, rushing to the door, pushing up bolts, pulling them into near darkness as she yanked at the blinds, just leaving the private entrance bathed in a soft glow of orange light.

Standing at the plain white door and already gloved in white, he watched as she peered down at the two locks, a standard latch and the other a mortice deadlock. He turned to his side, his breath catching as he saw her, a vision of beauty, her hair glowing bright. He watched her brow lower, her eyes narrow as he realised he was staring.

Her words snapped him out of his trance. "You got the keys, right?" she said, leaning in close.

Fisher stood high and smiled, walking slowly backward, stopping only as he reached the front door with his hands ushering her to the side.

"No," he said, screwing up his face, his feet pounding the floor as he ran towards the door with his right shoulder out in front. As he hurtled forward, he caught Harris shaking her head. The door held firm.

To his right, she watched as he rubbed his shoulder, her eyebrows raised and head still shaking.

To the near side of the latch, she gave a slight push before walking behind the bar.

Fisher watched, stretching out the pain in his arm as she opened a fridge, pulled out a half-full bottle of lemonade and undid the cap. The contents fizzed as it bubbled down the drain, filling the room with the scent of sugared lemons.

Grabbing a knife from a rear counter, she sliced through the top of the bottle and around the complete circumference. Repeating the action near the base and discarding the top and bottom section, she flattened out the middle, pushing down at both edges with the flat of the knife.

He watched as she came back to the door, pushed the plastic between the jamb and where the latch went hidden into the frame. While alternating pressure against the door with her palm, she worked the plastic further and further into the gap, finally slipping past the unseen catch. She turned and smiled in triumph, her hands motioning him back.

"This time no run up. You don't know what's on the other side."

Fisher nodded and moved in front of the door. Lifting his leg up high and bending at the knee, he hoofed at the last remaining lock. His sole hit square against the wood, its movement encouraging two more kicks before the plastic fell and the door sprung wide, blanketing them with incense-thick air.

29

Blinking away the stinging aroma, they stood before a hallway where a once-beige carpet tracked a grimed pathway to a set of stairs rising into darkness. To their right, a shallow cabinet clung on the wall, its light, unpainted wood hung battered and bruised. To the left, an over-painted light switch merged into the wood chip, the surrounding paint dark with grime.

Fisher peered in, his eyes watering, but looking up all he could see were dark walls as the shroud of scent blanketed his breathing. He turned to the grubby light switch, then back at Harris.

She nodded and he took a step in. The lamp lit as it dangled above their heads but still the upstairs remained obscured, new shadows deepening the darkness.

Turning, he saw Harris working on the cabinet and a tarnished lock he'd noticed for the first time. Splintering the wood, the blade of her multi-tool levered it open, wafting welcome fresh air as it sprung.

Their eyes met, lingering momentarily before they took in the contents; three small glass bottles with tiny black writing tracking across each surface. Two were full of a clear liquid, the last with a line halfway up.

"Flunitrazepam?" she said, squinting at the writing before the bottle slid into her jacket pocket.

He had no idea what the word meant and shook his head. The first step protested under his feet as he turned and began edging up. Behind him he heard Harris unzip a pocket and a bright beam shone from his side and he caught his first glimpse of a long corridor over the summit.

With the harsh, synthesised smell intensifying, he arrived at the top. Scanning left and right, all he could see was the end of the corridor lit by Harris's beam and a window, its pane shrouded with a thick, dark curtain blocking the last wisps of the day's light.

He took a step to his left and as Harris moved to his side the torch beam ballooned, for the first time giving the full scene a veil of light.

Regretting a lung full of thick air, he counted three doors on either side, before the corridor split unseen left and right. The beam focused on each of the doors and a tarnished brass number from one through to six. Odd numbers left. Even right.

The centre of the beam scanned the carpet, in several places splashed with dark, earthy stains climbing the walls, before settling on a light switch.

Stepping forward, he pushed it home. Two shade-less lamps glowed as they hung from the ceiling. Again, regretting a deep breath, he stared at the scene in its putrid glory, the dark, multi-coloured patterns revealing their sickening black, brown, yellow and scarlet hues. For the first time, he could see the source of the dense air causing his nostrils to rebel and counted twelve fragrance plugs jammed two at a time into double sockets low to the floor.

A spike of horror rushed across his chest as his survey caught the bottom of the door to room four and the thick black deadbolt running across its bottom edge. He turned to see each door in turn, finding them adorned twice the same across the bottom and top edges.

His gaze rested on the closest. Room one. The bolts were open and he leant in, resting his ear against the wood.

He wasn't sure if he should be thankful for the quiet the other side as he wrapped his fist around the handle and slowly turned. The cold metal twisted and he glanced to Harris at his back, his eyes conveying surprise as it opened. His chest pounding, he pushed the door wide and his lungs spasmed from the stench of decay and bile escaping the darkness.

With his right hand over his mouth, his left fumbled at the wall and found the edge of a light switch. The room burst into brightness from a lamp, its cable covered in cobwebs as it hung from the ceiling.

He closed his eyes, pausing to adjust and let his stomach settle. The cramps soon gave way to emptiness as he stumbled forward, looking on at the desperate scene of a hotel room no longer fit for paying guests.

Rough-cut chipboard covered the only window, its surface splashed with paint and wide, putrid marks matching what they'd already seen. A thin single mattress lay along the far wall. More stains mottled the faded fabric. A red bucket sat lonely in the opposite corner, the floor covered in a loose layer of cream Lino ill-fitting over the carpeted floor.

Harris moved at his side. Peering into the bucket, she pulled back with her hand grabbing at her nose. With a glance back, a single eyebrow raised to tighten Fisher's muscles, she stepped forward, her gloved hand reaching inside to pull out a sodden white piece of lacework. Thick liquid dripped as it raised, the smell of bile refreshed in Fisher's nostrils. With her other hand she opened it out. A blouse. Sliced open. A neat line each side from sleeve to neck

Fisher's shoulders relaxed. He didn't recognise the top.

"It's fresh," she mumbled, letting the rag slop back into the bucket.

Welcoming the heady incense, they stepped into the corridor, pushing the door firmly behind to trap the stench. They found no respite in the room opposite, a near mirror image, the hue and pattern of spray a difference, and the colour of the bucket. Green not red. With a deep breath of heavy air, he pulled open door three.

Clean in comparison and stain-free, only stale body odour and sweat hung in the air of the third room. Already in a rhythm, he pulled at handle four; the metal twisted but the door wouldn't budge. He looked to the bottom and back to Harris, her wide eyes agreeing with his pounding heart.

Slapping the bolt across, he flung open the door, his fingers jabbing the light on in a second.

He found himself in the centre of emptiness. A rectangle of clean Lino where the mattress had been, a smear of red where it had been dragged through the doorway.

Pushing his hand to his mouth, he gagged, just managing to reach the bucket, adding to its contents before rushing out.

Ignoring a look to his back, he grasped the handle of five and hesitated with a vision of terror on his friend's face, her body writhing in pain as she lay on a putrid mattress on the other side of the door.

The warmth of a hand fell on his and together they turned and pushed.

Breath sucked from his lungs and his already racing heart sped to a frantic beat.

The door stuck fast and no matter how much he rattled the handle it wouldn't move. Glancing up, he pushed the bolt to the side, the bottom metal already across. The door flung wide, his hand slammed the switch and her name breathlessly screamed from his lips.

It had been a cruel trick; the room empty of life. Fisher bent double, trying to catch his breath. Behind, he heard Harris move and another door open.

She called his name with interest in her voice. "Take a look at this."

Fisher took his place beside her and peered into the room, his eyes widening and hand grabbing at the door jamb at the sight of the missing square of floor. Leaning closer, he saw the wooden boards strewn to the opposite wall, leaving the jutting rails of a paint-splattered wooden ladder rising through the hole.

Steadying himself, he took a tentative step forward, confidence gaining as the floor remained firm. A step closer and he saw a rough hole in the plaster had been hacked between the dark wooden joists before the hole disappeared into darkness.

With a rustle at his side, he turned to see Harris with her torch back in hand. He lingered at the sight of her wide eyes and what seemed to be a grin trying to be stifled. She offered out the torch.

Ignoring the movement of the ladder loose against the ceiling, he stepped to the first rung with his attention following the bright beam as it bounced against a tiled floor of a claustrophobic room. Shadows danced as he grasped the torch, the musk of damp air and sharp sense of disinfectant rising with each alternation of his grip.

As his eyes levelled with the jagged edge of the plaster, he caught sight of a dome of white plastic fixed to the remains of the ceiling, a pull cord dropping down from its centre.

With a tight grip of the rail with one hand, he pulled the cord with the other. A satisfying click accompanied the bare, bright lamp, blinding him momentarily as it came level with his eyes. Glad of the solid floor, his feet touched down and turned in the tight space, his gaze resting on the deep bowl of a thick porcelain sink, beside a mop and bucket and the stacked rotund caustic-labelled drums.

His jacket caught at his back and as he turned, a clang of metal pinged at his feet, his survey darting to a key settling to the floor, knocked from a lock at a door he turned to see for the first time.

He looked up to Harris peering down, the tail of her hair hanging at her face and she spoke.

"Locked from inside."

Both nodded and as he picked up the key, he heard Harris speak.

"The shelf," she said, and he followed her pointed finger to the wall and an unpainted wooden shelf with a familiar clear glass bottle and stack of crisp white folded cotton squares resting on top.

Biting his lip, he pushed his ear to the door and stood listening to the silence, broken only by his breathing.

The key's edges were sharp and crisp and slipped into the lock with ease. The handle turned in silence, the hinges angling the door away without complaint.

A tampon machine hung to a tiled wall. Stepping out into the washroom and with the rattle of the ladder behind him, he walked back out to the familiar bar, Harris joining him shortly after.

The bar hadn't changed since they'd left it moments ago, but that time felt like a different era, the private door still open and lemonade plastic resting on the floor. He turned to face Harris. She did the same and he watched the smile of intrigue pluming on her face.

He took the staircase two steps at a time, desperate to talk, to roll it all over in hurried conversation. He wanted her to convince him their findings didn't mean what he feared, but he had to race on; there was still a chance he could find her alive. How much time he had left he didn't know. One call made by Tony and it could all be over.

With heavy breath, he stood outside room six, his head turning either side of the corridor at a right angle to where they had made their discoveries. To the right were two numbered doors before disappearing to stairs down to somewhere unknown. To the left were three more rooms, each without numbers, then a door which ended the passage. A small sign read *Staff Only*. He took a deep breath. Six more. Still hope.

"I'll take the flat," Harris said at his shoulder.

Fisher nodded and turned to the right, walking to the furthest. He glanced down the stairs into the darkness and nodded to himself at the outline of a wooden outside door. Looking back, he realised the corridor was cleaner than the last, the stains on the walls and carpet fewer.

He followed the floor and turned; the stains flowed from the cells around to the rooms on the left. Swallowing down a lump in his throat, he heard Harris pull the door closed behind her.

These doors were unmarked with bolts, but still a sudden apprehension tensed in his muscles. He took a deep breath; the thick air had either thinned or his lungs were getting used to the heavy atmosphere.

Fisher moved his hand towards the handle and it knocked against the weight in his pocket. He stopped still and pulled out the gun, feeling it solid in his hand. Leaning into the door, he listened, the latch clicking as he turned the round of the handle.

Pushing the pistol in the room first, his gaze darted around jumbled piles, his nose checking for a second opinion.

Pushing the gun back in his pocket, he saw no danger from the piles of clothes and no foul smells rising to his nostrils. He stepped into the room and began taking note of the disorder.

Across the back of the room were black rubbish sacks piled on top of each other. Stacks of fabric, clothes in blacks and whites and all colours of a bright rainbow. He swiped at a pile by his feet.

Cuts, folds and seams told him he was looking at clothes all right. Tops and trousers, skirts, knickers of all shapes, bras with lace and a plethora of cups sizes.

As he moved, his feet kicked at a bag and he saw others tumble underneath. Handbags, piled in a jumble, all empty, to the side. Piles of what would have been their contents. Mobile phones, bright colours, some studded with crystals, some in cases, each with a cracked screen, or a back missing or a spider's web radiating across the glass. He swiped at the pile, stopping himself as he remembered, hers wouldn't be among them.

Fisher thought of her jacket and dropped to his knees, his hands in a hill of coats, sifting. Perfume blended with stale sweat and old smoke as it rose to his nostrils. Still searching, he spotted neatly stacked packets of cigarettes of all brands, the clear plastic pulled from each, next to small and dainty lighters, lipsticks, makeup compacts and handbag-sized bottles of perfume.

He moved to a mound of purses, but all were empty. Photographs and money, cards and coins missing.

A black sack caught his eye, its contents spilling from a long split in its side. A deep scarlet stain on a white top sent a shiver down his spine. On his knees he shuffled up to the sack and pulled the black at each side.

The smells emerging were different. Coppery and the musk of being unwell. He closed his eyes and fruitlessly tried to remember what she'd been wearing that night.

At first glance, the clothes at his knees seemed the same as the other piles, but as he picked through, he soon realised the difference. These were damaged, torn, cut, soiled and stained beyond saving. He moved a white cardigan, its underside thick with dried vomit and threw it to the side. A pastel-pink Regatta polo shirt lay in front and her image flashed through his mind. He knew he'd regret turning it over.

Picking the material at the edges, he turned it, his stomach clamping tight as he saw the front, stiff with dry blood, cuts running up each arm and straight down the front.

He closed his eyes and dropped the drenched shirt; an involuntary whimper spilt from his lips and pushed the back of his gloved hand to his open mouth. Memories of that night flooded his mind. Susie sat opposite on the bench, the shirt undamaged but her smile wasn't there.

He tried to remember why her smile had gone. Was it a true memory or could he not think of her happy? They'd been speaking and she wanted to speak more, but someone had come back from the bar and they were no longer alone. They hadn't spoken since. Tears welled as he thought they never would again.

A distant noise from somewhere in the building reminded him they weren't invited guests. He took a deep breath and tried to concentrate.

Susie wanted to tell him something, the one-sided conversation now vivid in his mind. She'd said about a social experiment. He didn't know what she'd meant.

Why was he only remembering this now? He'd spent most of his time since she'd disappeared racking his brain for this kind of information. She'd been concerned and timid, the opposite of how she'd always come across. Except, of course, in those dark days after she'd been mugged and struggled with the relentless pain and feelings of helplessness.

Fisher stood and turned away from her top, his foot catching on a small rectangular box and it toppled from a mountain of others the same. He pulled out a blister of pills with a long medical name, Microgynon. Grabbing a handful, he pushed them into his pocket.

Standing out in the corridor, he listened. Hearing movement in the flat, but that's where Harris had gone. He moved to the next room.

Stale air caught him in the back of his throat as the door hit against something hard. With just enough space, he pushed his head through the door and saw the room stacked from floor to ceiling with furniture that had once populated the rooms now standing ruined and empty.

Hope began to wane as he moved to the next, but his interest pricked when he saw no number stuck to the door. In its place, an oval of un-weathered white paint caught him at eye level.

He pushed the door handle and opened it into a windowless bathroom, except there was no bath; the entire floor and all four walls were tiled in white. The floor sloped to the middle, meeting at a black iron grate.

On the far wall, a garden hose snaked up to a single tap and a mildew-mottled inflatable bath pillow sat lonely in the corner. As he turned to leave, his gaze caught on a ring of metal; a hoop as big as his fist fixed halfway up the wall.

Taking a deep breath, he thought of the hope in the two remaining rooms, but it shrank as he pushed open to find a bedroom strewn with the debris of recent occupation. Metal takeaway containers and pizza boxes lay across the mattress and untidy covers on a box bed.

A sound caught him. He turned and heard the metallic ring of a phone coming from below, the trill fixing him in place until the final echo died down a few moments later.

Fisher drew a deep breath, his hopes at an all-time low with the realisation settling in that it was too late to find her, in this place at least. Still his disappointment sunk further as he opened the final door to a storeroom stacked high with brown boxes. He felt the weight of his body pressing down as he looked on at the bulky square cartons.

There were eight in total, the count automatic. Some were unopened. Some barely filled with their original contents.

With a glimmer of interest, his hand robotically dived into each, his attention perking up as his dread seemed to peek. He wasn't altogether sure why coveralls, smocks, trousers and shirts would fill him with such foreboding.

With the boxes of plain women's underwear, thin socks and sanitary towels, it looked like a good employer's store. An employer who considered their welfare.

Circling the room, a further thought came. They were keeping them alive, but for what purpose?

Heading to the door, eager to speak to Harris, he almost missed the last carton. As he kicked the small box, a clink of glass brought his hand down to open the cardboard full of small bottles, medical vials of a clear liquid.

A phone rang as he pocketed a bottle, but with a different tone to the last. The sound came from the flat.

Fisher closed the door behind him and headed towards the noise.

Harris stood over the handset, staring down, the alert stopping as he entered the room.

Taking in the view with a glance, it struck him how normal, how homely the apartment felt. With minimal clutter besides a few smiling photographs, the clean, wide space dominated by a fifty-inch plasma screen on the far wall. He barely noticed the empty bottles of beer dotted around the surfaces.

"She's been here," he blurted.

Harris nodded. "They were all here."

She nodded again and was about to speak when they froze in silence at the sound of glass smashing somewhere below.

30

Harris's sharpened expression meant he didn't have to ask if he'd imagined the noise. Fisher light-footed to the nearby window and the view overlooking the back of the building.

Outside, through grime-hazed windows and competing for height amongst tall weeds, were a faded plastic slide and a swing set, a reminder of the family home that had been turned to its new dark purpose.

Nearer the building, he saw two parking spaces. A Ford pickup rocked to the side as the driver's door opened and the bulk of a man dressed in a black faded over-stuffed puffer jacket and jeans laboured out with a phone to his ear as he glanced in Fisher's general direction.

He backed away as the guy pushed the phone in his pocket, his eyes darting to where he'd stood before disappearing out of view, heading towards the building.

Fisher held a finger out in the air, pointing along the corridor and to the stairs leading outside. As he turned, he caught sight of the tiny gun in her hand, the other ushering him towards her.

The unmistakable rattle of keys rang from below and Fisher turned his back to Harris and moved behind the door he'd just come through. As he turned back, he watched her frantic hand urging him to go to her, a stern eyebrow raised.

He shook his head and signalled her back through the open door of the bedroom.

With a creak of dry wood from the corridor, Fisher watched Harris edge backward, her hands open and shaking her head.

A door slammed from somewhere behind, then another and she was gone. He counted to six as the cracks of wood against jamb grew closer. Floorboards creaked in the corridor, two more slams and he felt the air pressure change. A presence in the doorway with just a short thickness of wood between them.

For a moment he thought he saw the top of Harris's head from the bedroom as he held his breath.

The floorboards below his feet moved and he caught his first glimpse of a leather coat, just as another door slammed, this time below. The giant standing with his back to him wasn't the guy from the car who'd held the phone.

This guy was miles taller, with a wide build that even from the back made him seem meaner.

Fisher could feel his heart labouring in his chest, adrenaline urging him to do something, not just wait until it was too late.

Still he waited until he could see the guy's entire back and the short leather jacket and jeans. Both articles were well worn, the leather faded at the elbows. The jeans thinning on the seat.

The guy's arm moved as his head rotated around the view.

Fisher knew this was the best chance he would get, before the brass loaded in the gun would embed in his bones.

As the guy began to twist in what seemed like slow motion, Fisher pulled the gun from his pocket. The slide clicked back and the guy stopped in his tracks, familiar with the noise.

"I've got a Browning nine millimetre pointed at your head. Put your gun on the floor and stand still or I'll blow your fucking brains out."

The guy stood still, pausing as if weighing up the risks.

"Now mother fucker."

He bent at the knees, lowering through the long distance to the floor, settling the gun to the carpet.

Fisher stepped behind him as a call came from the bar.

"Ignore it," Fisher whispered at the guy's back. "I'm going to touch your hand. Don't freak out or you'll be a dead wise guy. You understand?"

The folds at the back of his thick neck expanded and contracted as he gave a single nod, then, with his left-hand, Fisher grabbed a thick wrist.

"I'm here to help. You've been set up. Tonight, either you're going to die or your 'so called' friends downstairs will." Fisher let go of the wrist and backed away behind the door. "You have to make your choice."

With no pause, the guy crouched to the gun, Fisher flinching with the speed, but fighting his urge to react and hoping Harris couldn't see, he watched as with only the quickest of backwards glances the guy lumbered back the way he'd come.

"We gotta go," Fisher shouted in a stage whisper to Harris, who stood at the bedroom door, her jaw nearly to the floor.

Without a pause, he turned and headed down the corridor. From the sound of heavy steps, the giant was already down the stairs and into the bar.

Fisher rushed down the adjacent stairs and came out through the outside door and into the half-light of the evening.

Glancing backwards, he saw Harris pulling off gloves as she ran a few paces behind with something pinned under her arm.

The sun had dipped low, haloing the great rock as they came around into the car park, deserted save a rusty Mercedes.

With his gloves stuffed in his pocket, they turned the corner on to the quiet main road and a single gunshot broke the calm.

Fisher quickened his pace. Harris slowed him, taking his hand in hers as two more cracked through the quiet.

As their car pulled from the side road, they saw no commotion. No people streaming from houses. No panic, just a single white BMW heading in the opposite direction.

31

With Llanberis fading on the horizon, they hadn't spoken. The gunshots still rang in Fisher's ears as the adrenaline faded to fatigue. He looked at Harris out of the corner of his eye, watching as she stared to her left, her thoughts elsewhere.

She knows.

Despite his urge, he broke the silence, the sickening excitement of what they'd found too much to hold in any longer.

He told of the jumble. The women's clothes. The piles of belongings, his voice cracking at the mention of Susie's top and the edges sliced cleanly through the blood. He told of the wet room, the loop for the chains. Hands tied above their heads as they were cleaned of their mess before being dressed in uniforms from the next. He told of the opening hacked in the ceiling and the ladder climbing into the cupboard as if Harris hadn't been there.

She didn't remind him. She let him talk, knowing there would be no stopping him.

When he'd said all he could, he stared off to the stone-bound road, the evening sun nearly gone.

Almost making Harris jump, he shot a look in her direction.

"They hid in the cleaning cupboard." The palm of his hand banged on the steering wheel. "The last time I saw her, she was heading to the bathroom." Fisher took a deep breath, forcing his mind to slow. "They hid in the cupboard and waited. Waited until she was ready. But how?"

"You missed the spy glass in the door," Harris added.

Fisher turned, watching as she nodded.

"They waited until the right moment. Then pounced. Crushing her arms by her side for the drugs to take effect."

"There would have been more than one person."

Fisher nodded and spoke. "One at the door. One with a hand round her face, the other clamping her with a bear hug, waiting until she went limp."

"Chloroform," Harris said, reading from the bottle in her hand.

"Then dragged them up the ladder to their prison."

Harris nodded.

"But Susie would have put up a struggle," Fisher added.

"That's what the drugs are for."

"No," he said, shaking his head. "She's resistant. Anaesthetics don't work. She'd have fought back. Hence the blood," he paused, his head still shaking. "They'd have to give her so much medication just for the smallest effect. She'd be throwing up and making their lives hell. If they up the dose, they could kill her by accident."

He held his breath when he realised he might be losing control. "They had to clean the toilets afterwards. George guessed it all."

He drove in silence, his knuckles white around the steering wheel. "She was there all along and I dismissed him." Fisher's voice cracked on the last syllable and he coughed into his fist.

Harris laid her hand on top of his as it rested on the gear stick. "You didn't know. Nobody could have known. They were clever. It looked like she'd driven away. They had me convinced for a while."

Fisher doubted that was true but was thankful for what she was trying to do.

"You couldn't just go around accusing everyone."

"I should have done something."

She squeezed his hand and felt energy surge in his body. "You're doing something now."

They drove on in silence.

Half a mile down the road, she jerked her hand away and turned in her seat to face him.

"So are you going to tell?" she said, her brows raised in anticipation.

"What?" Fisher replied, glancing back, then turned to the road as he realised the change of subject.

Before she could reply, he double took at the halo of blue flashing lights as they cut through the ever-darkening orange horizon.

Tapping his thumbs on the steering wheel, he felt his body readying for action. The distance closed quicker than he'd expected, the siren soon heard, the low profile of the police car sharpening as it raced towards them.

He glanced at Harris and back at the road; the limited options rushed through his mind. To turn around or stop? Accelerate faster, ram the car and get in the first strike?

He shot another look to Harris. She should have been the one driving.

With the police car only a few lengths in front, he turned back and before he could think, it screamed straight past, the two occupants clad in black not taking their eyes off the road.

Harris turned in her seat. "You don't get away with it that easily," she said.

Fisher sucked in a breath, the adrenaline still high as he felt her eyes boring into the side of his face. She'd seen too much, the situation unravelling with every moment.

She'd seen the truth. She'd seen him exerting his influence. He had to make another choice. Influence her again and be damned to repeat it over and over, multiplying the consequences on an exponential scale. Or risk everything and tell her the truth, putting his fate in her hands.

Drawing a deep breath, he smiled as he glanced towards her.

"People believe me."

Wide-eyed, he watched her with intent, searching for any change in her expression. Confused when he couldn't see any surprise, any shock at his words, he listened as she spoke.

"I thought so," she said.

His mouth dropped as he looked towards her, then back at the road, then to her again.

She pointed forward and he snapped his attention back through the windscreen.

"Is that it?"

For a few seconds, all she gave was a smile. "I know you did something to me when we first met."

"You did something to me when we first met. It's the same thing," he said, but regretted honesty in the words.

Her smile grew wider and she spoke again. "The things you said. The things you say," she corrected herself with a chuckle, "didn't add up. The comms file, the Ops Portfolio, your lack of training, your hair. IT. I mean, really? And what I just saw."

Fisher turned to see her looking back at him, her face flat of expression as he touched his hair.

"I'm kidding about the hair."

Fisher put his hand back to the wheel.

"And maybe you should have thought about the name a bit more. I mean 'Extraordinary Investigations'. It didn't help."

He let out a reflexive laugh and felt the muscles in his shoulders relax. "So why are you still here?"

"Two reasons," she said. "There's a case. It's not an inter-agency conspiracy," her eyebrows raised, "but there's still something that needs investigating and I don't see anyone else doing it."

"And the other?"

"You," she said without a pause, her gaze never leaving the road. "Don't get all overexcited. You're interesting. What you do," she paused, "is interesting."

He tried to stifle his smile as he drove.

Another mile and the moon had claimed the night. Harris pushed on the reading light above her head, illuminating her lap; for the first time Fisher noticed a stack of envelopes as she pulled them from the footwell.

"His mail," she said, laying them out on her lap as she flicked through the pile. "It's his place all right and there's another name." She spoke slowly as she skipped across the writing on the front of the envelopes. "TSS Holdings. Shit," she said, as she came to a large brown envelope, her fingers tearing at the paper. "Shit," she repeated. "Tristan owns Sherpa Cars."

Fisher looked sharply at the letter as she unfolded out the pages.

"I'm sorry. I should have listened. It was a lead." She scanned the statement. "He owns it."

Fisher kept quiet as she opened the rest of the envelopes, sorting them into two piles on her lap.

"He might well be entrepreneur of the year. It looks like he's got fingers in most pies in Llanberis."

Fisher glanced over.

"There's The Peak Inn, Sherpa and he owns the place we stayed at the first night."

"Maybe that's how they found us so quickly."

Harris nodded.

"Then there are these." She picked up one of the pile of papers. "All invoices for weird stuff, medical supplies."

"The drugs?"

Harris took one of the clear bottles out of her pocket and squinted at the tiny writing, then flicked back through the paper.

"Yes, and then there's one for harbour services."

"What are harbour services?" Fisher said, glancing over.

"It's not specific."

"What about the boxes of workwear, underwear and sanitary towels?" he said, and she quickly picked out a sheet of paper and nodded before pulling out the next.

"Four pallets of medication. Was it in that room you found?"

"Yeah, could easily have been four boxes."

"Boxes? How big?"

"About the size of a shoe box," he said, glancing over to see her shaking her head, eyes scanning the invoice again.

"Four pallets. That would be near six hundred shoeboxes," Harris said, still scanning the page. "And it was only delivered three days ago."

"Does it have a delivery address?"

"No. The space where it goes is blank."

"That's odd. Isn't it?"

"Another one for medication." She pulled out a second bottle, nodding as she spoke. "Fifty bottles of Flunitrazepam."

"What's that?"

Harris picked up the iPad and tapped the name into Google.

"Rohypnol."

"The date rape drug?"

"Yes."

As she spoke, a memory tugged from the back of his mind.

A car horn sounded, blasting with an urgency as he realised he'd closed his eyes. Shooting his lids wide, he swerved back to the left side of the road, an oncoming white van fishtailing as it recovered from its evasive manoeuvre.

Harris looked at him and raised her eyebrows.

"He fucking drugged us."

Harris stared out to the road as Fisher continued to speak.

"On the Friday night, he bought us a round of drinks. He fucking drugged us." Hitting his palm on the steering wheel again, his voice rose. "Why didn't we realise? We all felt sick in the morning. Alan was throwing up all over the place."

"Stop it. Stop beating yourself up," Harris said.

He sat up in his seat, surprised at the authority in her voice.

"Why would you realise? You were a group of friends having a drink."

His fist hit the wheel again, then corrected as the car swerved to the left.

"They went through our stuff. They went through *Susie's* stuff. They fucking drugged us so they could go through her bag." Breathing heavily, he sensed the warmth of Harris's hand on his shoulder and felt himself calm.

"And Rihanna's," she said, as she saw his breath slow.

"How do you..." He stopped himself mid-sentence. "Her bag went missing, but she got it back. Untouched in the toilet."

Harris nodded.

"And they seemed to get drunk so quickly, and Charlie couldn't stay awake to check Rihanna had gotten home safely. We should tell her. Reassure her she couldn't have helped."

"Take your own advice," Harris said, still watching the road.

"Why go through their stuff?"

"They're keeping them alive. I think they're checking there's nothing wrong with them, making sure they're not drug dependant, like with insulin or asthma or something."

Fisher nodded. He wanted to pull over; he felt the emotion boiling inside him. He needed a release. They had so much of the gruesome picture, but they still didn't know where to find them.

"Rihanna leaves her drugs at home. They wouldn't know," he said with ragged breath.

Harris nodded again.

Fisher remembered the medication he'd found and looked sharply in her direction.

"But I found these," he dropped the packets of pills from his coat pocket on her lap.

"Contraceptives. You can see the prescription label on the side," she said, as she pointed at the over-printed sticker.

"Time to call the police?" he asked after a few seconds thought.

Harris shook her head without hesitation.

"We're still nowhere. We only know where they've been. We don't know where they are now. We've only got this far because we're not the police. If we stop breaking laws then it slows to a snail's pace. Warrants, judges, suspect's rights, they take time."

Fisher let the silence build. She had a point. The police hadn't helped so far.

He saw her head twitch before he caught sight of a flickering blue light coming towards them at pace; the bulk of the fire engine screamed past them in what seemed like no time. He watched as it disappeared from the rear-view mirror.

Coming to a T-junction, he signalled right.

Harris stared at him with her brow furrowed. "Where you headed?" she said, as he pulled in the direction away from Bangor and their hotel.

"My secret agent spidey-senses are tingling," he said.

Her cheeks dimpled with laughter. "Let's get this right. You've been masquerading as an agent for three days now and you think you can spot a tail?"

Fisher nodded with a cheeky smile. "White BMW Three Series, two cars back."

Harris didn't lean forward for a look in the mirror, just carried on reading through the invoices.

"Two hundred times fifty milligram bottles of Pentobarbital, two hundred litres of saline preparation and IV bags, sold by Pharmaline Ltd."

"It's all gibberish to me," he said, flicking his eyes back to the rear-view mirror.

"I'll check what the Pentobarbital is but the saline bag is for an intravenous drip. Keeps you hydrated when you can't drink." She moved the invoice to the bottom of the pile and scanned the next one. "Five times Abbott Free Go XL400, sold by Sensuer Medical Ltd. Again, no delivery address."

Fisher excitedly interrupted. "That's the company my mate works for. He might be able to help."

Harris continued to read the next invoice. "Harbour services for Holyhead port. There's a statement showing a service provided once a month." She paused and scanned the page. "Second Monday of every month."

"That's today," he said, glancing in her direction. "We need to get to Holyhead."

"Swap over at those traffic lights," she said, pointing to an approaching junction.

***

In the passenger seat and with Harris driving, Fisher pulled the thin layer of plastic covering the touch screen of the last unused phone. As it finished booting, he tapped in a number from memory. After four rings, his friend's cautious voice came over the speaker.

"Hello?"

"Hi, mate," Fisher replied.

"James, fuck me. We've been trying to get hold of you for the last two days. Where are you? This isn't your number. Any news on Susie?"

Fisher interrupted the spray of questions. "Sorry, no time. All I can say is I'm fine, there's no news on Susie and it's great to hear your voice, but I need to ask you a question. And a favour," he added quickly. "It's a massive favour and you gotta trust me on this."

"Shoot," Andrew replied with barely a pause.

"Can you tell me what an Abbott Free Go XL400 is?" Fisher said, reading from the invoice in his hand. He sensed in Harris's twitch of her head that she'd heard Andrew's laughter down the phone.

"Well, that has to be the last thing I thought you'd ever say to me. It's an intravenous pump. In fact, it's a battery-powered ultra-portable intravenous pump. The XL400 designation means it delivers a very low dose of medication over a very long time. Can be up to thirty days on one charge."

Fisher could hear the pride in his voice as he showed off his intimate knowledge.

"Thanks, mate. Can you find out where a shipment of these was delivered in the last few days?"

"I suppose," he replied, drawing out the word as he thought. "We don't sell many. They're very specialist. And expensive."

Fisher could hear the desperation in his friend's voice as he tried to figure a reason for the obscure request.

"I *will* tell you what's going on, just not today."

"I know," Andrew replied. "Have you got any more info that can help?"

"I've got the invoice in front of me," Fisher said, and dictated the details down the line.

"Should be okay. I know all the girls in finance."

Fisher couldn't help but laugh. "And now for the favour."

"Okay," Andrew replied, making no attempt to hide his curiosity.

"I need it tonight."

The line went silent for a moment and Fisher took the opportunity to lean forward, sitting back as he saw the white BMW still in the short procession of cars behind them.

"Well, it's a good job I'm a collector of phone numbers then, isn't it?" He said goodbye and hung up the call.

Within ten minutes, the phone came alive.

"You got a pen?" Andrew said, then didn't wait before reciting the address.

"Even for you that was quick," Fisher replied, as he scribbled on the back of the invoice.

"Just a few calls," Andrew replied, laughing.

Fisher could hear the twist in his voice and knew there was more to his tone.

"What have you done?"

"Nothing," Andrew replied, the smile obvious. "But you've got three dates when you're back."

"Thanks, I think." Fisher was about to sign off when his friend spoke again.

"Whatever you're doing," he paused, "be careful." Then he clicked off the call.

Fisher looked down at the address and breathed a sigh. It felt great to hear from Andrew as a warm rush swam through his body. To be so trusted by someone, to have so much faith. He already knew he had his back and looked forward to chewing this all over with him, beers in their hands.

"One Sanctuary, Holyhead, LL65 1AR," he said, finally taking in the scribble with his fingers tapping the postcode into the car's Sat Nav.

"Bingo," he said, pointing at the map on the tiny screen. "Change of course." As he spoke the last word, his voice cracked again.

Harris looked over and saw his hand trembling. With the light almost gone, his body pressed against the seat as the car accelerated as hard as the Fiesta could.

Weaving through the quiet roads, the car stopped hard at a junction; Holyhead and Bangor to the left and an unpronounceable town signposted right.

Harris flicked the indicator to the right as the tyres kissed the white line. A couple of cars passed across their path and with a heavy rev of the engine, they took off sharply to the left, her head twitching back and forth to the rear-view mirror.

"Hate to say it, but you were right," she said, her voice calm as she pushed the accelerator, pulling the cars in front towards them.

32

Fisher turned in his seat and through a haze of bright headlights he saw the white of a car only a short length behind; the shark fin phone aerial told him what he'd feared. The BMW.

Squinting through the brightness to catch a glimpse of the driver, he could only see a silhouette before he heard Harris push the revs up on the engine.

Turning back, they'd caught up with the traffic ahead.

Harris knocked down the gear, the engine screaming as the car shot forward again, his body swinging wide as they swerved out into the outside lane and passed cars in quick succession. Still headlights bathed their interior, the tail matching their speed and manoeuvre.

"What now?" Fisher near screamed.

"Can't let him get in front of us," she said, her voice calm until she seemed to hesitate.

"No. I've got to stop him. He could have anything planned." Fisher tilted in his seat and watched as the BMW hovered arms-length from their bumper.

"He's not trying to overtake and he's moving around back there."

"Get your gun out," she snapped.

Fisher fumbled in his coat pocket and pulled out the gun, checked the chamber and ran his thumb over the safety.

"Hold on," Harris said with an urgency in her voice.

He clenched his left hand around the door handle just as Harris dabbed the brakes. The sudden loss of momentum jolted him forward, the interior darkening as the BMW's headlights went below their rear window.

Harris stared at the rear mirror as Fisher turned in his seat, both seeing the figure's outstretched arm but neither heard the shot, just the crack and spray of hundreds of cubes of glass as the rear windscreen shattered.

Her attention fixed back on the road while Fisher remained locked in a stare with the thick-necked black man, one fat hand on the steering wheel, the other pointing the gun.

Harris pushed the car on and with the wind whistling at their backs, the man disappeared behind the haze of brightness. As the gap grew to the length of four cars, she shouted over the din.

"Grab something."

With barely enough time to react, she slammed her foot against the brake pedal, leaving her foot hard to the floor.

Fisher lurched forward, his seatbelt biting into his shoulder, forcing the gun to fly from his grasp as the BMW slammed into the back of their car to the cartoonish soundtrack of grinding metal.

A calm descended as both cars stopped.

Blinking away his daze in the darkness, the only light came from the flashing warnings on the dashboard as he scoured the footwell. To his side, Harris shook her head, her fingers fumbling at the ignition just as the engine came back to life.

He pulled his seatbelt loose from his chest, his breath painful as he leant forward to grab at the gun spotted by his left foot.

Stamping at the accelerator, unclear harsh words under her breath, the tyres screeched, metal complained and scraped at their backs until with a snap of plastic, the car jerked forward and they were soon back to full speed.

Fisher risked a look behind him, the pain already beginning to ease, and saw no sign of movement.

Harris slowed the car to a sensible speed.

He craned his neck at the damage, the boot lid twisted out of shape and bent upward. He dared not think what it would look like from the outside.

Without warning, Fisher's window exploded. He sat stock-still, frozen into the seat. He'd felt the bullet pass close to his head and heard Harris screaming an order but he couldn't process the words.

She hit him in the shoulder, the pain bolting him around to see the smashed headlights and the crumpled bonnet of the BMW back on their tail.

Pulling up the gun, Fisher clicked off the safety and without pause, loosed off a round through the back window.

The wind forced in his face, the blasts screamed in his ears, the muzzle flash blinded him with every shot. The thirteenth round smashed through the shattered grill, crashing against the engine block, causing the spark which ignited the hot fuel spraying over the engine. Still rushing forward, the BMW was engulfed in flames.

Fisher watched, his empty weapon still pointed to the slowing car as the explosion came, shrapnel flying in every direction and pain searing his face.

For a moment he stared at his hand marked in blood as the second explosion ripped through the air; the car a speck in the distance when the third explosion lit up the horizon.

33

Wind screamed through the missing windows as they drove, Fisher silently grateful Harris had chosen the quiet local road running parallel to the Expressway.

"Think I might have lost the deposit," Fisher shouted, forcing a laugh.

Her dimples remained hidden, her concentration unflinching as she stared cold and firm at the road ahead.

He glanced at the Sat Nav, showing ten miles from the address he'd tapped in and a further ten from Holyhead. As he looked up, Harris pulled into a lay-by and brought the car to a stop.

Without a word she took a deep breath, pulled open the door and he followed.

Even by torchlight they could see the hideous extent of the damage. The plastic trim around the bottom of the boot had been left behind. Where the bumper should have been, buckled metal stared back, the paint worn away in great swathes to reveal past the white primer.

The high-up rear lights had avoided the collision, only to be peppered and cracked with shrapnel from the first explosion. The worst saw a great knife of metal stuck from where a bright brake light had once been. The boot lid had been forced upward and bent at an obtuse angle, gaping an opening, leaving the aluminium case moments from spilling.

Harris pulled open the mangled boot lid and Fisher caught the case from tumbling to the Tarmac. With the rest of the boot emptied and placed on the back seat, she opened the portfolio and stuffed unseen articles into her jacket pockets.

Back in the car, she handed him a green box of ammunition and she swapped the tiny Beretta for the black of the Glock.

As he refilled each round, Harris left the car again. He half-watched her survey the nooks and crannies and edges of the car with her torch.

With the Browning full, she re-joined him with the frustration of a fruitless search clear in her expression. He turned to see her staring back, her fingers pointing to her cheek. He touched his own and a needle of pain shot across his flesh, the aftermath of a glancing blow evident as he pulled down the visor mirror.

With no time to linger, Fisher spotted a great wedge of jagged plastic embedded in the dashboard.

Soon back on the move, neither tried to beat the chaotic wind. The first words spoken came from the Sat Nav, announcing a turn a few moments ahead.

After the turn, the car's frame complained as they limped along the potholed road. The Sat Nav announced with clarity they had reached their destination.

Harris stopped the car. They were in the middle of darkness, their limited vision only picking out shades of countryside surrounding.

With headlights full in front, they scoured the horizon at a crawl.

After another mile, the hedge-lined track swept to the right. As they took the turn, a seven-foot chain link fence loomed in the headlights with a tall gate blocking their path. A mud-smeared sign hung in the centre, bold black letters said *Private Property, Keep Out* on the once-white background.

Harris idled the car up to the gate, its beams catching a distant gothic outline, the ground between them a weed-covered expanse.

With a jerk of her wrist, the lights went dark. A draft of air filled the car as she cracked the door and stepped out.

Fisher followed, his survey darting around, listening to the snap of crickets and the gentle stir of the wind.

The building shadowed against the shine from a half moon and with no lights to tell them otherwise, they seemed to be the first visitors in some years.

"Have we got the right place?" Fisher whispered at Harris's side.

She replied with the twist of her torch, the beam highlighting a fresh deep rut to the side of the road.

He nodded even though she wasn't looking.

She'd stepped forward to the gates, the brightness concentrating on a chain wrapped around the gate, shining back from the large padlock.

"Looks like no one's home," Fisher said under his breath.

"Why are you whispering?" she replied, without turning his way.

"Just feels like a place you should." He caught a glimpse of her smile.

"This is the place," she said, and opened the car door, switching the lights back on with a twist of her wrist. She moved back to the padlock and pulled at the thick chain wrapped around the two halves of the gate, then moved around to the back of the car, pulled the mangled boot lid before reappearing with a length of bright orange rope.

"Should do the job," she said, pulling it tight in her hands then kneeling in front of the car, a finger popping a plastic cap in the front bumper. After screwing the towing eye into the threaded hole, she tied off the rope and wrapped it around the lock with a knot that made Fisher wish he'd been to Scouts more than twice.

"Jump in," she said, as she slid into the driver's seat.

The speedo showed twenty-five as the rope went tight and the gates sheared off their hinges, jumping towards them, pulled by the tension.

As Fisher opened his eyes, she had slowed the car, the gates dragging to a halt. With a slash of the rope, together they hefted the mangled poles and chain-link to the side and were soon beyond the gnarled fence line.

The tyres trampled weeds, some taller than the car, freeing the headlights in bursts to bounce from the grey stone of the building.

As the last of the towering plant life flattened, the building seemed to have grown taller. Its long three storeys bright and shadowed at the same time in the headlights, a clock tower rising another two high, dominating its centre, looming over an oval double wooden doorway.

The clock had no hands and all but the white of the nine o'clock segment had long since been smashed. The walls were sandstone bricks, worn smooth against the elements, with large wooden windows each with six smaller panes, jagged fingers of glass were the only remains in the spaces between. Most of the dark grey slate still sat on the roof, its flatness punctuated with tall chimneys, some still straight.

The Fiesta complained with each wide pothole, the chassis creaking as she steered around the worst, guiding them to the left of the wide building. Tiny shapes darted, flashing in their path, jumping this way and that before the true shape of the building became clear when they rounded its corner.

So far, the building had looked like the flat line of a Tee, but now they could see a single storey block jut out from the centre, seemingly backwards into the expanse of the night. The turning headlights caught the final edge, revealing another curiosity which took a few seconds to register in Fisher's head.

The roof ran a continuous grey, neatly tucking into the angle they'd first seen. The dark sandstone lines were the same, but that couldn't be said for the glass in the modern white plastic frames.

The Fiesta carried around the building, the burden on the frame never easing. As they came around the base of the single storey line, they saw the rows of shipping containers lined up along this new side of its length.

Harris slowed the car, soon rolling to a stop, and Fisher stared out before looking at her, turning quickly back to the set of uPVC doors in the side of the building, its bright white nearly hidden between two rusty containers.

Harris killed the lights and they stepped out in unison.

The air had chilled since they were at the gate, wind gusting across their path as they walked together with care through the thick weeds at their feet.

Arriving first at the window, he could find no view inside, just the black of heavy drapes. Still side by side, they crept around the building, with each step their night vision improving and the clicks and creaks of nature seeming to settle.

Around the front, shattered glass crunched under their feet, rubble scattering until they climbed up the jagged stone steps.

In the moon shadow of the clock tower, they pushed against the wooden double doors, but they'd long dropped on their decayed hinges, the wood sunken deep into cracks in the stone.

Fisher moved to a nearby window, picked a slice of fallen slate from his feet and cleared the shards around the frame. The rotten dividers crumbled at his touch and he boosted himself up on his hands, turning onto the cold stone window ledge where he took a deep breath and shuffled his legs over.

34

Hovering on the sill, Fisher let his legs dangle into the darkness as his eyes began to adjust. With the first shapes beginning to form, he took his weight on his arms and shoulders and landed hard, his legs unsteady as his feet twisted on the loose ground. Sweeping the unseen rubble to the side, he barely heard Harris touchdown behind him.

The view lit in a dim cone, the beam flickering as shadows danced on the walls, seeing for the first time the thick carpet of debris. Brick, dark charred wood and sheets of distorted plaster lay crumbled everywhere he could see in the limited angle.

Washed-out packaging mingled among the sea of disorder with discarded bottles and crushed cans of strong cider at every turn. A snap came from behind with the beam doubling in brightness, sparkling the dust as it swirled silently from the long rotten ceiling.

Fisher's survey followed the bright beam as it scanned the wide reception. No furniture remained, just a wooden staircase rising halfway to the ceiling, the rest toppled at its feet.

Where plaster still held a loose grip to walls, graffiti covered every surface, the once-vivid colours now pastel. Doors were found on three points of the compass. White paint peeled from most, except for the door to the east piled high with drifted rubbish.

The torch beam hovered at the northern doors, then picked out a path, rubble pushed either side leading to the west. Fisher pointed in the dark to the west doors and with a nod of the torch, they picked their way forward.

Edging closer, he saw the door to the left barely hung on the bottom hinge with the top pulled from the frame, sagging towards them. Fisher pushed through the right with a weightless ease that made him take notice. He thought he saw Harris nod in the shadow as he turned to see her follow.

They were in a corridor running along a narrow west wing into the distance, the torch beam dissipating before it could cast on the far reaches. The floor had been swept to the left for several paces, piled up against the walls and ceilings left to shed.

The torch scanned up to the ceiling, highlighting wooden battens exposed in patches like the ribcage of a rotting skeleton, between which a yellow string of lamps ran from the door to where the floor had been cleared. He turned and guided the warmth of Harris's hand, following its yellow path to a rough hole smashed in the wall behind them.

She let go as he took the torch, directing the beam to the right and the long row of rooms off the corridor. Most were missing their doors, the wood long gone or lay on the floor. Some still hung loosely in place. The nearest two stood upright and closed.

Fisher crept to the first and found it unlocked; the windows inside were boarded up with rough, paint-splattered chipboard. He could almost smell the stench from the pub.

Harris woke him from his pause with her hand on his shoulder, pointing his arm and the torch down to the floor and the covering of scattered empty boxes. Even without brushing away the fine spray of dust, he could see brands recognised from the invoices.

The second room was a mirror image, except the boxes were sealed and neatly stacked in order, still shrink-wrapped to wooden pallets. With a sweep of his hand, he wiped a film of flaked paint and pulled at the plastic, grabbing and unfolding a neat delivery note. Under the focus of the torch they huddled to read, accounting in their heads, totting up half the quantity of the invoiced goods.

Back in the wide reception, Fisher took up the route of the yellow cable as it burst from the wall, winding its way around the ceiling and following whatever substance remained before disappearing through a hole cut with hammer blows above the north wing doors. He jolted as Harris coughed and he felt the dryness of his throat as he breathed in the dust.

Slowing his breath with his hand pressed on the double doors, he searched for the cable as he pushed through, following it down the wall to his left by the torch beam. Pausing his breath, he listened to the unmistakable whine of rotor blades somewhere in the distance.

"Helicopter?" he said without turning. "Because of the crash," he reassured himself under his breath.

The torch flickered and faded in brightness. Handing it backward, he heard the clap of metal against her palm. The brightness redoubled for a flash and he saw where the cables ended before darkness covered them again.

Putting his hands forward, he touched the hard plastic of the yellow transformer. Letting his fingers follow its smooth curves, he felt the angled shape of a rocker switch. As he pushed it home, he paused, catching that sound again, a deep hum of air, but took comfort in its growing distance.

The whine must have distracted his senses as when the lights flickered on the smell of stale urine and decay took him by surprise. Pulling his hand from his eyes, he blinked away the last of the brightness, marvelling at the vast scale of the bright room.

Fisher wasn't surprised by the rows of rusty-framed beds lining the walls, or the mattresses, thin and stained, sat on each, or the browned rails hanging to the ceiling above each bed with no sign of the curtains that had once hung.

The walls had been scraped and painted, but the texture of flake still more than evident under the thin layer. He caught a tiny hint of the paint somewhere mingled with the stench in the air and drew a slow, deep breath as his gaze fell on the double doors at the end of the room, their surface bright and new.

Side by side they walked between the beds. Fisher tried not to shudder as he saw each new detail. The blood-soaked cotton wads spread at the floor. The metal restraints at the head and foot of the beds. The bright sharps boxes full, theirs contents edging out.

In the far corner sat an old sofa and overstuffed chair. The thin television they faced couldn't have been more out of place. Pizza boxes, beer bottles and the shine of aluminium covered the surrounding floor.

Walking over, Fisher pulled at a greasy box, finding the crust still supple between his fingers.

Side by side they moved, stopping only as they stood at the double doors. Fisher turned to face Harris and she turned to him, their hands pushing at the wood and they passed through into the darkness.

Part Two

The Present

35

Fisher watched, inhaling wafts of bitter steam from the porcelain pot between them.

"Now you know everything," he said, closing his eyes, his head sinking at a right angle as he listened to the coffee pour in the two white mugs.

Dawson remained as quiet as he had throughout the long hours of narration.

"Now you know why I've got to go. We were so close."

As he spoke, Fisher felt Dawson's sudden unease and he straightened up, widening his eyes with the question hanging on the thick lines of Dawson's brow, almost twitching at hearing his bass voice. It had been so long.

"But the girl on the slab?"

Fisher's eyes closed, his head lolling forward.

"Rihanna Summers," he said, opening his eyes, watching as Dawson's expression relaxed. "Susie's still out there. We were too late for Rihanna, but we still have a chance. She's somewhere in the middle of the ocean, heading to who knows where and for who knows what. I've got to find her. Please tell me you understand?"

He watched as Dawson stared back into his desperate eyes, a wave of panic rising at the thought of him not understanding, even though he'd bared it all.

"Barbados," Dawson said.

Fisher blinked wildly, his head shaking from side to side at the sudden word. It meant nothing to him.

"Barbados?" Fisher repeated.

Dawson nodded, his expression still blank. "We haven't been idle, Mr Fisher. That ship you saw, it was the third time in port. Every second Monday it took on four containers."

Fisher continued to shake his head. "You've got to let me go," he said, as his fingers grasped at the table's edge.

"Just a bit longer. I've got so many questions," Dawson said. "We've heard stories. We had intelligence. Cold War stuff really, patchy at best."

For the first time, Fisher caught the smallest change; the soft glint of moisture in Dawson's eyes.

"Can you imagine what a force you could be for our side?"

"Side?" Fisher said, his face screwed up, the word rattling out of place.

"Her Majesty. Britain. The Allies, call it what you like."

Fisher thought he saw the slightest upturn in the corner of Dawson's mouth.

"The good side."

Sitting back, a sudden anger rose from inside Fisher. "Have I just arrived in a comic book? I'm fucking serious." His fist banged on the table. "I've been hiding away for years because I didn't want this day to come, but when Susie disappeared, I couldn't do nothing. Now I've told you everything and I'm leaving." The legs of the chair scraped against the tiled floor as he stood.

Dawson didn't flinch. "Think of all the people you could help. Together we can make a real difference."

"You don't get it, do you? Did you listen to what I've been telling you?"

Dawson narrowed his eyes but still didn't speak.

"The consequences, god damn it. When I was a stupid, twenty-one-year-old, I told a nightclub bouncer my family were rich just to get into a club. Two days later, my parents were kidnapped and held for a ransom we could never pay." Fisher rubbed his temples with the palms of his hands.

"They sent my mum's finger to me in a box." He looked down at his feet. "Their bodies were so unrecognisable they had to be identified by DNA."

Fisher paused to slow his words.

"The guy with Susie's phone, I told him he was safe. He thought he was unbreakable and was murdered the same day. When you found us, I was scared for my life. I told Harris your men were going to shoot. She must have known they were on her side but still she raised her gun. Those last few days are littered with more examples than the last twenty-five years, and you want me to come and do it for a living?"

"We'll help you find your friend," Dawson said, looking up at Fisher.

The breath sucked from Fisher's lungs and he rested his hand on the table to steady himself.

"We can take care of all the consequences. We'll work out a way. It's you who doesn't understand. You're too special to waste hiding away."

Dawson stood and walked to the door, then turned back.

"I'm afraid fate has ambition for you."

***

Her head throbbed as she cracked open sore eyes, but catching a tiny ray of light, she clamped them shut.

She couldn't think.

She couldn't remember.

The throbbing died down as she took a deep breath.

With a blocked nose, air only came when she sucked through a loose gap in her mouth.

She remembered nothing.

She couldn't remember where she was.

She couldn't remember why she lay on her back.

She hated laying on her back.

She hated laying on her back on a cold, wet mattress.

Her arms wouldn't move.

Her hand wouldn't move.

A tiled room flashed into her thoughts as she slipped out of the moment.

36

Still standing, Fisher flinched as the door opened and Dawson strode in with a hint of what could have been a smile. In his hand he held a rectangular black box, which he placed on the table as he sat opposite.

Fisher recognised the phone Harris had left behind in her car as he retook his seat at Dawson's request.

"We have over a hundred mathematical geniuses and five supercomputers on the payroll. They spend their day forecasting. That is all they do. We tell them what's happening in the world, they crunch the numbers and tell us the probability of what will come next. We tell them our options and they calculate what is likely and unlikely to happen. They tell us the consequences. We're already doing this and we can do it for you, too."

He pointed to the device on the table. "With this communicator, you'll have access to them twenty-four hours a day. Like predicting the weather, they don't always get it right, but we know what's likely to happen and we can help train you to analyse the course of action you want to take."

"If I'm not hurried then I can do this myself. It's just when I panic, like when there's a gun trained at me. I," Fisher stuttered, "I can't think."

"We can train you to think. Did you see Agent Harris fluster?"

Fisher shook his head and took a deep breath.

"Here's the deal. We'll help you find Susie. We'll train you, give you an agent, money, logistics, whatever you need. All I ask in return is you think about coming to work for us." Dawson paused, staring back at Fisher's lack of reaction before speaking again. "I need to be clear. We don't make this offer lightly. Someone high up is putting their balls on the line for you."

"Why?" Fisher replied, leaning forward in his seat.

"Because of what you can do. Agent Harris has corroborated your story, she's given a personal recommendation. That goes a long way, believe me."

Fisher's eyes shot wide and leant forward. She's alive.

"How is she?" he asked, trying to calm his voice.

"I'll take you to see her."

"She's here?"

Dawson nodded and Fisher leant back, staring at the phone. Harris was alive and they were going to help him find Susie. For now, he didn't care about the rest.

He took a deep breath and stared at Dawson.

"You got a deal."

***

Time passed.

Her head still hurt.

Something brushed against her face, but she didn't care.

Something took the weight of her body and she drifted through the air before landing propped against the cold.

Her eyes wouldn't open.

She could feel her entire body but couldn't move an inch.

She heard voices, muffled and woollen against her ears. She made out the odd word. English she thought, but still couldn't understand the flow.

They were upset. They were men. A spark of fight filled her nerves. She heard swearing, the voice right in her face. She'd wet herself and they were having to clean up.

Her trousers were off and her pulse began to pound.

She screamed. Her mouth didn't move and no sound came out.

Her feet hurt, her face sore and she could feel herself drifting to one side.

She fell to the floor and her head smacked hard. An angry voice boomed far away and she was in the air with a sharp scratch in her buttock.

She stopped caring as water washed over her, pushing away the pain.

37

Fisher watched for a reaction. If there was any change between the thick lines and the dark leather, he certainly couldn't tell.

"Follow me," Dawson said, as he picked up the phone and walked through the door Fisher hadn't noticed had been left open.

As Dawson disappeared, Fisher stood for a moment and looked around the blank room.

"No going back," he whispered and let himself be led through the drab corridor he'd travelled many times, the walls alien without the flank of armed agents with their faces hidden behind masks.

Reaching a break in the corridor, a left turn would take him to the bare quarters he'd spent so much of his time stewing in. His muscles moved to turn but he watched as Dawson led on, only stopping as he reached a door to their right, pulling out his bulky phone and pushing it against a low-profile white box attached to the wall at his shoulder height.

Fisher caught up, watching as a tiny LED on the bottom edge lit green, its flash accompanying a clunk of mechanics echoing from the wall and the door swung away.

He followed into a concrete staircase with steps running down, the walls blank and unfinished with no windows or paint or any such thing. Their footsteps echoed down three floors before Dawson used his phone to unlock huge steel doors as the floor levelled out.

Light burst from the other side as the metal parted; a heavy rumble ran up their feet as the doors slid to each side. Squinting, Fisher saw to a reception. There were no words to describe it as such but the tall, wide white counter and two smile-less square-shouldered men in black suits gave him all he needed.

They were underground but somehow natural light shined from above, bouncing against the tall smoked glass wall wrapping in a semi-circle around the room.

Taking first steps behind Dawson, he took note of doors either side of the counter. Both were unmarked and shadowed with movement somewhere behind.

As they approached the counter, the right guard gave a respectful nod in Dawson's direction. The other didn't flinch, his attention remaining fixed below the high counter.

As Fisher followed a step behind, he caught sight of four fierce short-barrelled machine guns resting on their stocks in a glass-fronted cabinet at the guard's backs. The shock felt less than it should have; he'd had so many pointed at him in the last few days.

"Can you sign our friend in please?" Dawson said. "Visitor's badge for now."

"Yes, sir," the same guard replied with a military sharpness, handing over a clipboard covered with a single printed form.

Leaning on the counter Fisher added his details before handing it back.

"Please look into the camera," the guard replied, pointing to a small black box hung on the wall at head height.

Fisher glanced at the box and a flash bulb ignited the room from a location he couldn't spot.

A few seconds later, the guard handed over a rectangle of white plastic strung on a black lanyard. The card had Fisher's photo and the word Visitor in bold red letters that seemed to shimmer across its entire length. The characters 'F9' sat large and dark in the right-hand corner.

With the pass hanging around his neck, the glass doors to their left opened and he followed Dawson along the pristine white corridor.

A step ahead, Dawson used his phone to access doors, the traffic of suits and lab coats lessening with each until their journey became lonely.

Still he hadn't spoken. At the final door, Dawson straddled the threshold as he held the wood open and swept his hand to beckon him in.

Fisher felt a foreboding, a sudden fear it could be a cell or some lab where his world would quickly crumble. Instead, as he hesitated, he saw a wide room with a large oval table at its centre, more than twenty chairs circling its edge, and two people. The sight of someone he recognised sent butterflies shooting from his stomach.

With a bowed head, she poured over papers, but turned towards him, a smile blooming, those dimples as deep as ever. Harris looked more beautiful than the crystal-clear image in his head, and alive, despite his worst fears from watching her laying unconscious while they dragged him from her side with her name screaming from his lips.

Soaking up her smile, he crossed into the room and kept his gaze fixed as if afraid she would disappear should he turn. Wearing the same grey trouser suit and white blouse, with her strawberry blonde hair tied behind her head, it seemed as if they had never left each other's side.

They were, in the snap of a moment, back in the investigation and it felt amazing. A mumble of words from his side and the other person, a guy he only saw through his peripheral vision, stood and closed the door to leave them alone.

Fisher couldn't speak, but her smile grew with each silent moment.

"Sorry," he finally managed. "Sorry."

"No lasting damage," she said, brushing off the comment with a shake of her head.

"I thought you were dead. They wouldn't tell me."

"I'm sorry you had to go through that."

"I saw you go down."

"Things are not always as they seem. I'll show you later," she replied. "But I've got a beautiful bruise."

"I'm sorry," he replied, his gaze still fixed on her.

"Stop apologising."

"Sorry," he said, smiling as he realised. "Listened to any good quiet music recently?"

They both laughed, the dimples deepened.

His smile fell from his lips as he spoke. "Why didn't you tell them?"

"They needed to hear it from you. From the beginning."

Fisher didn't speak straight away, then dipped his head in a shallow nod.

"Thank you," he said.

***

Her first thought was the nausea.

Her second was the spin of the room.

Her third came seconds later as she was thrown in the air and hit the floor hard, crashing down against her left hip.

Her fourth was gratitude; the sliver of consciousness growing wider. She couldn't feel pain.

Like a computer booting, her senses were slowly kicking in one by one.

She tried to force her eyes open, managing a tiny slit.

She saw the darkness all around, smelt the vomit and the petrol fumes.

She felt a low rumble, constant since she'd woken, now stopped.

The room slowed around her.

She lay in silence.

Time passed; she didn't know how quickly.

Her vision exploded with brightness and she vomited.

The light disappeared as a shadow loomed. She knew it wasn't happy, but she didn't care. The wave of warmth washed that all away.

38

Fisher turned as he heard the swish of the door behind him. Dawson came through with someone who could well have been the other guy from before, balancing two white jugs and a leaning tower of mugs on a tray.

"I've told Clark you have agreed to let us help you find your friend," Dawson said, his open palm gesturing to the seats.

Fisher stayed standing, blinking at the sudden interruption.

"Sorry, where are my manners?" Dawson said, nodding to the guy who'd placed the tray on the table. "This is Mr Clark."

Neither tall or short, Clark looked somewhere in his mid-twenties; with round, thick-framed glasses and a white short-sleeved shirt, he wouldn't have looked out of place alongside Fisher on his old university course.

"He is Agent Harris's Field Analyst," Dawson continued. "And provides support here at the Operations Centre. They make a very effective team."

Clark offered his palm in Fisher's direction and they briefly shook hands.

"I've assigned them both to the investigation," Dawson added, as he pushed a mug of what smelt like coffee towards Fisher. "Sit, please."

Fisher chose a seat, leaving a single space between him and Harris as Dawson spoke again.

"As I said, Mr Fisher, you have the full resources of the agency at your disposal. Mr Clark, please arrange a communicator and hook-up for Mr Fisher."

Clark nodded as Dawson picked up his cup.

"I'll let you get on with it, ladies and gentlemen," Dawson said before leaving with a mug in hand.

Clark sat two seats to Fisher's side as Harris shuffled her chair closer to the table.

"Okay, let's pick this up where we left off," she said, looking between the two of them in a manner seeming to disregard the last four days.

"Shall I?" Clark said, swapping glances between them.

Fisher watched Harris nod and he turned to Clark without responding, trying to switch his mind back to where they'd left off.

"Three months ago, the group began kidnapping non-locals fitting a certain profile from locations around North Wales."

Images of the two women fitting the profile flashed into Fisher's mind. Susie as she stepped from the car, remembering his surprise at her hair dyed bottle blonde. Her face full of pleasure at seeing her friends as she bounded into their arms. The girl he'd never known who stood in summer, her hand offered to the horse with a smile beaming with excitement of her life ahead. The image replaced with the coldness of her body in torch light.

"Evidence strongly suggests they were held in Llanberis for a period of time before moving them to Holyhead for transport out of the country."

Fisher nodded slowly, taking a deep breath, attempting to maintain his focus on the words and not on the women the words were about.

"That's what we know. What are the gaps?" Clark said, looking between the pair.

"Where do they go?" Harris said, her words filled with the reverence Fisher had expected. "I mean specifically?"

Clark scribbled a note. "Why on a ship? Why in ISO containers?" he added.

"Easier to hide?" Fisher suggested.

"Yes. Saves the attention of immigration," Clark nodded in his direction. "Oversight on freight by sea is minute compared to air. They wouldn't need a big operation to get them through."

"But how do they survive in a shipping container?" Harris asked.

"We assume they need to?" Clark said.

Fisher felt his breath catch and he shot a look to Harris. She put her palm out towards him and glared back at Clark.

"Evidence points to their welfare being taken care of," she quickly said, turning back to Fisher. "You saw it yourself."

Fisher relaxed and let his lungs fill.

"They'd have to be modified, or otherwise have their own supply of air," Clark said, making another scribble. "One of the drugs you found, Pentobarbital, is used for medically inducing a coma. Having them out cold would make them much more manageable for the journey. There would be a few issues to overcome though."

"Like?" Harris said, raising her eyebrows.

"The drugs would need to be continuously administered. They'd need to manage sustenance, deal with bodily functions etc," Clark said, counting off the points with his fingers.

Both Harris and Fisher's eyes lit up as he spoke.

Harris spoke first. "The medical kit from Abbot. That'd do the trick with the drugs," she said, looking to Fisher as he nodded.

"Dangerous though," he said. "If something goes wrong, would they have someone to help?" He could see from Harris's expression she didn't know for sure, but he wouldn't like her guess. "They'd need to be hooked up to a catheter, IV saline and nutrition," he added.

"Remember this is the third time they've done it, so they must be getting it right," Clark added, for the first time seeming to understand the need for reassurance.

"It makes sense," Fisher said.

"And we know where, roughly," Harris added.

"Seems an odd place though. I was expecting the Middle East or Far East or Russia," Fisher said.

Clark took his turn to nod.

"How long's the journey from Holyhead to Barbados?" Harris said.

Clark scribbled on his pad. "About ten days on average," he replied.

"And I've been here for four days?"

"Six," said Harris, watching as Fisher's eyes darted open.

"They'll be in the middle of the Atlantic by now. We haven't got long," he said, fidgeting forward in his seat.

"Stay with the process," Clark said. "It works."

"So who are they?" said Harris.

"Does it matter? We just need to get her back," Fisher said, raising his voice.

"I know you're worried about Susie, but we're worried about them all," Clark said. "Those on this ship and those who are already over there."

Fisher moved back into the crease of his seat, a blanket of guilt wrapping around him as he began to think about the women in the container with Susie. The women in the two ships which had left twice before. The woman whose belongings he'd rifled through on the top floor of the pub.

"Sorry," he said as he looked down at the table.

"It's okay. Just stay with it," Clark said, flicking his gaze back to Harris as she spoke.

"We know about Tristan Tomkin-Smythe. He's our only link to a suspect."

"His thugs, the guys at the pub, on the trail. They were from the Caribbean," Fisher said.

Clark reached under the desk and pulled out a wireless keyboard. Resting it on the table, he tapped at the keys.

The lights dimmed and an image appeared on the wall in front of them. Fisher watched Clark as he opened an application and typed in Tristan's full name into a search box at the top of the screen. Clark asked for a description and tapped the words as Fisher dictated.

"Has someone searched the pub for clues?" Fisher asked as Clark finished typing, his gaze fixed on the rotating hourglass.

“Burnt to the ground. They found remains of one body with fatal gunshot wounds, a few spent shells, that's all,” Harris said, as the hourglass was replaced by a database record filled with text. Each of them concentrated on the information.

Tristan Tomkin-Smythe, son of Rupert Tomkin and Felicia Smythe. Rupert Tomkin had been British High Commissioner in Barbados for ten years. The screen changed to a picture of a head and shoulders shot of an older gentleman; above a caption read 'Rupert Tomkin'.

“We’ve got an extensive file on this gentleman. Remember him?” Clark said, looking at Harris.

She smiled back with narrowed eyes in reply. “I guessed a connection when I first heard his surname,” she said.

Clark turned to Fisher. “He was quietly removed from office when two prostitutes were found at his Government residence when his family were away.” Clark switched the view back to Tristan, then clicked a tab and an image filled the screen.

“We've already sent out a request for both their detentions, but we…” Harris said as Fisher interrupted whilst shaking his head.

“Sorry, guys, who’s that?”

Both turned and looked at him.

“Tristan,” Clark said, after checking back at the screen.

“It’s not,” Fisher replied with a shake of his head.

***

On her back, her eyes wouldn't open and limbs wouldn't move.

Despite the shivering, she couldn’t feel the cold.

She had no idea where she was and couldn’t decide if the place was silent or her ears were paralysed along with the rest of her body. An image of the tiled bathroom floated into her mind. The picture crystal clear. She remembered speaking to someone, James, she knew now.

Oh James, where's my knight in shining armour when I need him?

Her hearing worked, an electronic beep, but her thoughts drifted before she could be pleased.

***

"What do you mean it's not him?" Harris said, turning wide-eyed towards Fisher.

"It's not him," he replied with a shrug. "There's a resemblance. I'll give you that, but the bone structure's all wrong."

"How many times have you seen him in the flesh, Mr Fisher?" Clark said.

Fisher could tell he was trying to keep his disbelief hidden. "Only the once," he replied, and could almost hear Clark's sigh as he settled back into his seat.

"So how can you be sure?" said Harris, lowering her brow.

"I'll show you," he said, motioning for the keyboard and mouse in front of Clark. "Do you mind?"

"By all means," Clark replied, pushing over the controls.

With a tap of the mouse and a flurry of keys, the contents of Fisher's cloud account projected on the wall. Hundreds of folders filled with tiny photos took up the display.

The cursor hovered on the last folder, named after a date two weeks ago. As he clicked, the icon images of Snowdon and his friends at play populated the wall. Fisher moved the mouse to the right and the images slid to the left at speed. The campsite. The climb. The group photo, their faces full of achievement at the peak. The miles of rolling hills.

The dash of photos stopped at the last, its darkened scape filling the screen. Fisher to the left of the shot, his arm around Susie at the front of the pub. He couldn't help but linger on her smile, a wave of emotion welling up until he caught a brightness in the background, another face inadvertently caught in the shot.

Zooming in, Susie's smile filled the screen and he panned left, scrolling up over her shoulder towards the pub entrance and the other clear face. Those features struck forever, frozen mid-step. The man in the Arun jumper.

"That's him," Fisher said, clearing his throat. He heard the clatter of Clark's pen as it dropped to the floor and he turned to see him staring open mouthed at Harris.

Fisher followed his look and saw his expression mirrored. "What is it?" he said into the silence, but neither offered any answer.

Moments seeming like minutes passed until Clark reached over, grabbing the keyboard and mouse, almost falling backwards as he pushed out of his chair, saving the image as he stood.

"Are you coming?" he said with insistence, still looking at Harris.

She looked awkward and barely able to stand, her eyes wide, but she followed without question as if Fisher wasn't in the room.

39

Fisher sat alone for what seemed like an age and could feel his state of mind slipping back to the previous days. The constant watch of the door, the insecurities roaming around his head.

He blinked as the door opened and the pair were back, composed and expressionless, sitting down in turn. Fisher didn't hide his screwed expression as it swapped between them.

Clark was the first to speak. "Sorry, Mr Fisher," he said, surprising him with a chirp in his voice.

Fisher looked to Harris, expecting to see the same turnaround, but instead saw the tiredness in her eyes as she smiled away his concern.

"So where were we?" Clark picked back up, his fingers pressing three keys to unlock the screen.

"What just happened?" Fisher said, both eyebrows raised.

Clark glanced towards Harris and he caught her shrug as he spoke.

"Best not to ask," he said.

"So we're just glossing over that you both just had a meltdown?" Fisher said, leaning forward and swapping glances between the pair.

"We'd have to lie," Harris added, her smile somehow melting most of his concern. "We know how. We know where, but we still don't know why."

"I'm afraid we can hazard a good guess, but you're not going to like it," Clark said, the skin around his eyes tightening.

"It's fine," Fisher said, shaking his head. The new discussion taking his mind from where he had wanted to focus. "We're going to get her back before she gets there."

"White slave trade," Clark said, letting the words hang in the air. "You just have to look at the victim's profiles."

"Slaves?" Fisher added with a grimace.

"They'll be used or sold as sex slaves."

Fisher let out a sigh as he moved back in his chair. He'd already guessed as much but still felt his insides tighten as he took in the words.

"We leave no one behind," Clark added to nods around the room.

***

A flicker of a conversation filled her head.

They were interrupted.

She remembered her quiet words with James.

It grew clear in her mind, the clearest for days. Then the memory wasn't there. Gone.

She knew it was important but why, she didn't know.

She remembered Gwynn and she felt her chest tighten. She knew he was the monster.

Movement interrupted her new terror. Then a sound. The click of a button. An electronic beep.

She didn't care anymore and relaxed to sleep.

40

Clark left the room after excusing himself and Fisher turned to Harris, hoping for some comfort. Instead, he watched as she stared to nowhere, a vacuum of expression on her face.

Moments later, she spoke, the words low and full of emotion. "He'll pay for this," she said, and must have sensed his stare as she turned to meet his gaze, her face lighting. "For Susie. For Rihanna. For every single one of them."

Fisher bowed his head and joined her in the silence. He thought of Susie's parents. The conversation had stuck in his mind. He'd sat opposite, her mother broken with tears as he spoke about his ideas.

His thoughts drifted to Rihanna and then to the conversation with *her* mother. Her journey had come to an end, the worst that could have been feared. He looked from the floor.

"Mrs Summers?" he said in a low voice.

Harris gave a shallow nod. "I spoke to her."

"What did you say?"

"The truth. One version anyway. She asked me to thank you."

"For what?"

"For finding her."

Fisher's mind reeled around the words. A thank you for finding her dead daughter. Why?

The door opened, pulling him back from the black hole of failure.

"She was dead before we started looking."

Fisher smiled as she exercised her knack of knowing what to say.

Behind Clark, a thick set man strode through the door, his tan suit tense across shoulders and skin rounding at his neck as the shirt collar dug tight against a sun-leathered complexion. Along with the grey shine of his crew cut, deep lines traced middle age around his face.

"This is Mr Miller," Clark motioned with his palm.

Fisher tried not to stare, catching sight of a missing little finger on Miller's giant offered right hand.

"Mr Fisher," he said, surprising him with a tone that didn't reverberate his chest. "Military Liaison." His muscular bulk dwarfed the chair as he sat near the door.

"Mr Miller is going to present his plan to rescue the abductees," Clark said, turning back towards him.

Fisher sat straight, turning a keen ear as Miller puffed out his chest and spoke.

"This is a straightforward assignment. The Rashana has been located in the Atlantic. My team have already met with a rapid vessel in the region and are on an intercept bearing. Contact will be at night, where we'll take out the crew, secure the abductees, tag the containers and take the ship to port to see where they transport the cargo. Shooting fish in a barrel," he said with triumph in his voice as if he had already completed the mission.

"Thank you, Mr…" Clark begun but Fisher cut him off.

"Then what?" he said, much to Miller's surprise.

"We'll work with the local authorities to raid the final destination, securing the perpetrators and any further victims," Miller replied, his tone matter of fact. "We train for this type of operation all the time," he added, turning back to Clark.

"I hope you don't think I'm being rude, but..." Fisher said.

Miller turned back; his eyes tightened as Fisher spoke.

"I have some questions."

Miller's expression relaxed and he looked on with amusement.

"What happens if the crew are involved in the crime?"

"They'll get their dues," Miller quickly replied.

Clark fidgeted in his chair.

"What if the crew are supposed to provide a signal announcing their safe arrival?"

"We have ways of extracting compliance," he said, holding up his four-fingered hand. "I've been on both sides of the table."

"With the best will in the world, you can't be sure."

Miller didn't reply; instead he stared at Fisher, his face reddening as Fisher spoke again.

"What if they open the containers before they get to where the others are being held? Maybe they open the containers and find there's nothing inside? What if the local authorities are in on it at some level?"

Clark spoke before Miller had a chance. "That last one is a real possibility, I'm afraid," he said, his attention on Miller's scarlet face.

"Okay. We'll handle the inland raid ourselves," Miller replied, pushing out his chest.

Clark shook his head. "Foreign Office won't authorise action on sovereign soil, not without permission, and we wouldn't get it."

Miller took a deep breath before letting his shirt buttons relax. "You've clearly got your own solution, so let's hear it, Mr Fisher."

Fisher nodded. "We assault the ship," he said, his hand gesturing to Miller as he spoke. "Then replace the crew with our guys, rescue the women, and sail to Barbados. Meanwhile, we seal all but one of the containers up, leaving one modified so it can only be opened from the inside, where we secure an assault team. At the destination we wait, bursting out at an opportune moment and raid the place with the advantage of surprise. No permission to seek. No chance for corruption."

The room stayed silent. Fisher looked at Miller staring him down. He looked to Clark and saw the first gleam of a smile. He turned to Harris and watched her beam in his direction.

"I'm impressed, Mr Fisher," Miller finally said, breaking his trance, then poked a finger in the air. "There are a few little problems with your plan, but I like the idea of the assault team in the container. What's your background?"

Fisher saw Clark subtly shake his head and Miller cut himself off with another question.

"How do you propose we can be certain to get the signal from a hostile crew?"

"That's why I'm going to be there," Fisher replied, but the two men were already shaking their heads in unison.

***

The climb. She remembered the climb. She remembered the satisfaction as the cold, crisp air bit at the back of her throat. She remembered the warmth, her arms stretched around her friends as they posed.

She remembered Andrew and James, their faces lit with delight as she pulled up in the car. She remembered George's grumpy scowl as he peered bleary-eyed out of his bedroom window, her hand still forced down on the horn.

She remembered sitting in the crook of her broken sofa, her lines laid across her lap as she watched the world go by her window, fuzzy dialogue running over and over as she tried to make it stick.

She remembered the frustration.

She remembered tidying the flat, her head thick with cotton wool, the vinegar waft of stale alcohol as she grasped wine bottles and plastic glasses into black liners.

She remembered the party, her flat full of friends.

She remembered the message from James. 'Can't make it, something's come up x.'

She remembered the worry. Was he slipping backwards?

She remembered she had planned to talk to him, but now he wasn't coming.

She remembered the morning, her head sore from expensive measures of vodka.

She remembered the queue, the bouncers. She remembered being friends with people she'd only just met.

She remembered the man lying beside her.

She remembered talking about the experiment. That was it. He wanted to know more about James. She'd lied to her friend. She didn't want to tell him she'd let him down. She didn't want to tell him she'd been picked up in a club, had a one-night stand then told him about her closest friend.

She couldn't remember telling him.

She couldn't remember if he already knew. She hadn't told anyone since she'd first put two and two together weeks after they'd become friends. It was easy then, his constant feature. But now all he felt was guilt.

Oh James, she called out silently. It was such a bad time, losing his parents.

She knew he'd been close to the edge. She knew of his lone struggle, but they wouldn't let him. She and Andrew talked with him for hours and hours. They were with him, silently, just being around, keeping him from spiralling.

They knew how close he had come.

The beep came. She stopped caring.

41

"You're not coming," Miller said, his head still shaking from side to side. "I'm told you've not had a day of training. There's six months of hell before we'll even let you pass wind on the outside of these walls, Mr Fisher."

Fisher sat in silence, holding back any reaction.

Clark spoke. "Mr Fisher, you've done a great job so far, but I'm afraid it's time to let us take it from here. I'll get your programme organised and you can start training tomorrow."

Fisher didn't react.

"You're still welcome to sit in on the planning."

He still didn't reply, just stared back.

"Great," Clark said when he didn't get a refusal, and rummaged through the papers in front of him before turning to Harris. "Is there anything you need to close off before you leave?"

"Leave?" Fisher said, flicking his attention to Harris.

"Agent Harris will be accompanying the team," he said, looking down at his notes.

"You just finished telling me it's a military operation. Why do you need to take Harris?" Fisher said, his voice urgent.

"I'm sorry, Mr Fisher. I'm not being rude but we have an operation to plan," Clark said, whilst looking down at the papers.

Fisher stood and moved to the door. "That's not the deal."

As the door opened with a twist of the handle, Fisher hesitated, half expecting it to be locked. After hoping they hadn't seen his pause, he walked out into the corridor.

With his heart pounding hard in his chest, he looked left then right at each of the bright white corridors. They were a mirror of each other, with no hint where to start his search.

To his right he spotted a man turn from a door in the distance, his blue suit striking against the stark form of the corridor.

As he saw Fisher striding towards him, the smartly dressed guy flicked his gaze to the pass around Fisher's neck. Opening his mouth on a pause, his psyche ingrained with politeness as he shook the outthrust hand.

"I'm authorised," Fisher confirmed and the stranger's expression relaxed. "Can you tell me where Mr Dawson is?"

Without hesitation the stranger replied. "He's just stepped into the gents. I'm sure he won't be a moment."

Fisher spotted the small white sign jutting from the wall further down the stark white corridor. He turned and strode in the direction.

All but one of the grey stalls were empty. He waited until the lock slid, the door opening on Dawson's face void of surprise.

"Deal's off, Mr Dawson."

"Think again," Dawson replied, his gentle voice pulling at a long-atrophied memory.

"Then I'm going."

Dawson shook his head. "It just wouldn't be safe."

"I'm going."

Dawson took a step back into the stall. "This is not the way to start your career," he replied, showing his palms.

Fisher took a step forward.

"What's the point in resisting?"

***

Her mind jarred against her muscle's inaction as the memory floated vividly in her head.

He wanted her to observe James, record information. She wasn't told why and was too out of it to ask.

But why James, if not for what he could do?

She'd let him down, but she couldn't remember how.

She couldn't remember betraying him.

She couldn't remember putting him in danger.

A wave of panic flushed across her. If it wasn't going to be her, then who would step in to replace her?

Was it James who ultimately needed rescuing?

42

Dawson followed as Fisher walked into the conference room, a fixed stare set across his face.

"He goes with you," Dawson said to Miller's immediate reaction.

"Sir," he protested, pulling himself up in his seat.

"That's an order." Dawson cut him off with his palm in the air.

As Miller sank back, he eyed Fisher with suspicion.

Fisher turned to Harris, prepared for the disappointment in her expression, but could see none. No surprise or shock, just a minute nod in his direction. A nod he soon doubted he'd seen.

As quick as he'd delivered his instruction, Dawson turned, leaving Fisher to retake his seat, stealing himself for the outrage.

Miller didn't disappoint. "I don't know what kind of bullshit this is but all I need is an inch of a reason, you understand?"

"I understand," Fisher replied to the thick, pointed finger jabbing in his direction. "I'll leave you on the boat when I've got Susie."

"Ship, Mr Fisher," Miller replied through gritted teeth.

Clark shuffled his papers once more, his only reaction before they began discussing the arrangements.

Harris explained without detail, that Fisher would be able to extract any information from the crew, assuring Miller he could trust in Fisher's ability to get his task done.

Miller seemed to soften as Harris spoke, her words carrying more weight than he thought would have been possible.

Miller stated his two conditions. Pass a strict medical and be able to handle a firearm.

Harris gave Fisher no chance to reply, assuring Miller there would be no problem with either.

Miller left to make arrangements, including organising for HMS Westminster, currently on anti-drug patrol in the Caribbean, to head to Barbados with an apparent fault. A little part of Britain for them to escape to.

The three remained and discussed the detail.

It wasn't long before someone knocked at the door and in came a plump, thirty-something woman with brunette hair tied back in a ponytail, wearing a lab coat and pushing a two-level metal trolley as Clark jumped to hold the door.

Fisher looked intrigued at the two crisp white boxes, one the size of a shoebox, the other much smaller. He sat upright in his chair as he saw surgical gloves and a wire-form pistol, a tiny glass cartridge in place of the stock.

"Mr Fisher," Clark said, stirring him out of his wonder. "Miss White here is going to fit you for your communications platform."

Fisher gave a wary smile.

Miss White returned with a curt nod and pulled the gloves onto her chubby, pale hands.

"Let's leave them to it," Clark said, looking at Harris.

Fisher watched on, wide-eyed, as she straightened out the gloves, desperately trying to guess why her hands needed to be protected.

"Quick tutorial," she said with full formality as she picked up the larger of the two boxes. The box slurped air as she pulled off the lid. Angling the contents towards him and pushing it in his direction, the light caught the rectangular communicator he'd grown to recognise.

Standing over him, she held the box out. "Take it," she said with a curt command. She didn't try and hide her frustration as his fingers hesitated above the device.

"It won't bite," she said, which failed to provide him any reassurance, but still he put his fingers into the cut-outs of the foam and cupped the cold metal, which felt lighter than he'd expected but had the sturdy feeling of an iPhone.

As he turned it in his hands, the screen lit up and the small white Apple logo appeared on the dark screen. After a few seconds, he saw a message pop up.

Identity verified.

"This is the iComm5B Universal and it's just synchronised with your identity. From now on, only an employee in your section and with your clearance or greater will be able to use it, except for emergency calls," she said.

He battled with his inner geek, his sensible side winning out to stifle the smile and hold his excitement behind his lips.

Miss White eyed him with suspicion, seemingly sensing his restraint. She continued speaking as she stared.

"It may look like an Apple device from the outside and it works like an Apple device, but there are many more things going on behind that veneer. We call it a Universal Platform." She slowed her voice down as if he'd aged seventy years. "In lay-men's terms it means along with a vast array of embedded functionality, it has the ability to connect to a multitude of other task-specific devices."

"Like those in the V32?" Fisher interrupted.

"Yes," she said, snapping her gaze back to the phone. "It would take too long to describe all of these functions, but Clark will be able to train you as you go along, but in brief." She took a deep breath. "It has an ultra-wide band sensor array, from radio waves through to gamma radiation. It's also a communication device, with access to all digital communications platforms, including military frequencies and SkyNet5."

Fisher thought better of interrupting to ask.

"It has a high-resolution camera which includes a gain multiplying CCD and image intensifier. That's night vision to you. Now this is very important. Running through the circuitry there is a thin layer of stable plastic explosive that can be remotely detonated to render the device useless and untraceable. If you lose the platform or determine that it has, or is about to be compromised, inform Clark. We will take care of the rest. But beware," she paused.

He watched her left eyebrow raise as she continued.

"There is a recent trend of agents using this function to take out certain..." she paused as she seemed to choose her words. "Obstacles. Don't do that," she said, shaking her head.

"Have you fixed the battery life?"

She nodded, a smirk in the corner of her mouth. "It's been fixed for years. The manufacturers hold back progress to keep recurring business. It will last a week of continuous use on one charge."

He nodded, unsurprised as his finger slid around the icons, most of which would look at home on the phone he'd owned for the last few years.

"To get to the advanced features, just push the home button till it clicks twice."

Without hesitation, Fisher pushed the round home button. It felt just like his iPhone, and like if it had been, nothing interesting happened.

"Harder," she said.

He pressed again and felt the button click beneath his thumb, then pushed a little harder still. The button responded with a second click, the image switching to second home screen that he hadn't been able to see, despite swiping left and right.

The screen filled with a multitude of new coloured icons. Sensors, a night vision camera and a tracker mingled with others whose names were jumbles of letters he didn't understand. He couldn't help but smile.

"We're not done yet. We need to install the cranial interface," she said as she pulled open the smaller box.

Fisher watched wide-eyed as her hand went to the wiry handgun. His stare fixed on the box. He took in a gulp of air, the tip of the barrel sliding into the smaller packaging.

"This is the handsfree audio interface and allows limited handsfree control, some of which is still experimental."

"Now that is cool," he said, forgetting to hold back.

"Yes, it is. It will allow you to make and receive calls and set up some actions after you have trained it to your patterns. To start you simply update it with a simple but obscure thought. That thought will tell the device you are going to issue a handsfree command, then you issue the command."

"Uh, how do I issue a command?" Fisher said, interrupting, his eyebrows raised.

"You think it," she replied.

"Think it?"

"As I say, it is still somewhat experimental. Remember first to choose an activation command. I know someone who has set his obscure thought as eating mud, but it should be personal to you," she said, bringing the grip of the gun out from the packaging. He saw small claws at the muzzle gripping a plastic black capsule. Fisher tried to follow her as she walked behind him.

"Look forward," she snapped. "And I'd keep still if I were you. You don't want me to miss."

Tensing, he felt a sharp pain behind the back of his left ear, his hand shooting to the source where he felt a small bulge. As he continued to explore, it disappeared.

"How does that feel? Any pain?"

Fisher paused for a moment then shook his head.

"Now, try calling someone using the handset. The interface will auto adjust the volume depending on the ambient noise, but it will need to balance itself the first time."

Fisher blinked away a slight blur to his vision then selected the call icon; a long contacts list opened on the screen, each name unrecognisable. Out of curiosity he scrolled to H and there she was. Simply Harris.

He laughed to himself and pressed to dial. The ringing tone burst into his ears, but as it quickly decreased in volume, he realised he wasn't quite hearing with his ears.

"It's working then," Harris said as she answered the call.

The door opened. Harris and Miller walked in.

***

The smell had gone. The air clean and fresh.

She still lay on her back, light leaking through her closed eyelids.

She forced them open, but quickly squinted closed as the brightness rained from a high, domed ceiling.

She moved her head from side to side, surprised as the muscles complied.

Relaxing her eyes, she saw blurred beds, a feeling of relief washed over her.

She was in a hospital.

She'd been saved.

43

As Harris sat, Miss White and the trolley disappeared out of the door before Fisher had a chance to thank her.

"Efficient woman," Fisher said.

Harris nodded, smiling as she rubbed behind her left ear.

Fisher turned, expecting to see Miller rubbing his own, but instead paused on his scowl in his direction.

"We deploy in three hours," Miller said, moving to tower over him. "You okay with heights?"

"I think," Fisher replied with wide, questioning eyes. He expected some sort of compassion to match the words, but there was none in Miller's tone. Still, knowing he'd never had a problem staring down from a tall peak or looking out to a city from a high floor of a tower block, it didn't concern him until he saw a slight smile raise in the corner of Miller's mouth.

"You're green as they come, but remember you asked for the ride," he said, without hiding his amusement.

Fisher gave a shallow nod, hanging on the words while a dread built in his stomach.

"The only way we can join up with HMS Daring without slowing down the interception is by a pond splash," Miller said, his smile widening.

Fisher turned to Harris, his eyebrows raised as the new weight lifted from his shoulders.

"Oh, a seaplane?" he said with a deep out breath.

Harris shook her head and the weight piled back.

"It's military lingo for jumping out of a Hercules and parachuting into the Atlantic."

Fisher's eyes widened further. "Is that safe?" he blurted, the words fuelling Miller's mood.

"Relatively," Miller said.

Fisher cursed under his breath at his pause for effect.

"We'll land in their path and they'll pick us up as they head past. It's best way to save time."

"I've never jumped out of a plane before. Is there really time to learn?"

"Don't worry, you'll jump with me, in tandem," Miller replied, coughing a chuckle into his fist.

"Um." Fisher tried to the fight through the mist clouding his thoughts. "Can't I jump with Harris?" he said, looking with a longing in her direction.

"She's not certified," said Miller in quick reply.

"You'll be fine," Harris said, holding her palms in his direction.

"You can always back out," Miller said, a single eyebrow raised.

Fisher gulped down a breath. "I'm coming."

"Okay," Miller said, his face straightening. "Between now and nineteen hundred get up to speed on how not to die when we jump and pay a visit to the medical centre, but first I want to see you shoot. Harris tells me you have some skill."

Fisher shrugged.

"Well, I want to see for myself. Let's go."

Together they filed out, following as Miller led them down sterile corridors with a pace telling Fisher he knew them well. Down three levels, the sparse traffic of lab coats and suits turned to military fatigues and service dress as they arrived at the first labelled door he'd seen since his arrival.

The quartermaster's station resembled a supermarket, the shelves stocked with backpacks, webbing, ropes and survival equipment. Each unpriced item in one of three dark colours, camo, black or sand, except for a stack of brightly coloured ammunition boxes he recognised from Harris's kit.

To his left, in front of a wall of brown boxes, a soldier identifiable by his brown and green fatigues, stood by the entrance to a mesh cage holding enough weaponry to stage a coup in an African nation.

Inside were a library of weapons on bookshelves, repurposed with assault rifles sat on their stocks and sniper rifles in a myriad of lengths, each weapon strung with a number on cardboard tags tied around the trigger guard.

Looking closer, Fisher saw each weapon was unique; similar weapons stood next to each other, but being a variation on the next. A different shade. An extra attachment mounted on the rails. A shorter barrel or a foldable stock.

Miller stepped across Fisher's view and handed the attendant a written note, snapping him to attention before disappearing out of the room.

Fisher watched as Harris scanned the shelves at his side, while Miller began to pick, handing Fisher what appeared to be a black well-starched vest. The quartermaster came back through the door and placed a dark plastic crate at Miller's feet.

"The remainder will be at the assembly point as requested, sir," he said in a well-rehearsed beat before moving back to his position.

Miller filled the crate with his own selection and without words they headed out of the door. Turning an abrupt left and passing two doors either side, they soon arrived in a small changing room where Miller set the box on a wooden bench.

"Put it on," he said, pointing to the vest.

As Fisher undid the fold, he found the material stiff, but soon had it over his head. He could barely notice its weight as it sat on his shoulders.

"It's an ultra-thin ballistic vest. Won't stop the momentum but will stop the penetration."

Fisher looked at Harris, a wisp of a smile on his face. She raised her eyebrows in his direction. "Don't laugh, it's what saved my life," she said, then cautiously looked to Miller.

Fisher's smile dropped as he saw Miller watching him, his hand drawing something from the box.

"This is serious, Mr Fisher," he said in a low voice and with a single smooth movement, a thick-bladed knife appeared at his hand and he took a step forward.

Fisher felt the pressure in his ribs like a punch and looked down with alarm to see the point of the blade pushing hard against his chest.

"I get the idea," he said, his hands high in the air.

Still Miller held the pressure.

"Miller," Harris snapped at his side.

The relief came in an instant as the knife slid into the top of the man's boot.

"Enough fooling around. Let's see if you can handle this," Miller said, moving to the side to reveal a copy of Harris's Glock alongside spare clips, a box of rounds and a shoulder holster. "Follow me," he said, before Fisher had time to fully take in what he was looking at whilst bundling up the items into his arms.

Harris took the gun from the top of the pile.

Butterflies building in his stomach, he followed her as she held the door on the other side of the room. Thick glass blocks ran along the complete length of the new corridor, the other side of which stood a stark concrete firing range. Six lanes disappeared into the distance with empty metal hangers waiting for ill-fated targets at their starting positions.

The metal of a lock clicked and Fisher turned to Miller who had his phone in his hand, opening a door a few paces in front. As it swung open, he could smell the chemical exhaust, reminding him of the day he'd pumped bullets into the tree.

With ear defenders issued as he stepped through, he watched Harris set up a target, imagining the scowl on the unseen face of the dark silhouetted torso as she placed it in the hanging clips before sending it off down the range.

As it arrived at the twenty-metre line, Harris stepped back and rested against the far wall.

"It's all yours," said Miller, pointing to the Glock Harris had placed on a table beside the firing position marked with white paint.

Fisher stepped up to the dusty marker and picked up the Glock in his right hand.

Fumbling at first, he pulled back the slide and confirmed only air filled the chamber. Pushing the catch beneath the trigger guard, he released the magazine and placed it on the table with his gaze roaming the black composite for the safety.

"You'll be a long time," Harris said as she turned to Miller. "He's only used the L9 before."

Miller nodded and shouted over. "There's no manual safety. Just pull the trigger back all the way."

Fisher looked back with a bunched expression.

"The safety's internal," Harris added, still leaning against the wall.

Fisher nodded away his questions and turned back down range. The weapon felt lighter than the gun he'd targeted at the tree, but it still had the same feeling of precision as his fingers tightened around the grip.

As the seventeenth smooth round pushed against its spring, he slid the clip home and chambered the first. Pointing down the range, he turned his head to Miller and saw the nod of approval.

Fisher let his breathing rest, taking his time, drawing his eye along the centre of the gun and the middle of the black-headed target. The featureless face momentarily took on a quiff of brown hair and an arrogant sneer as the gun kicked back.

The bullet buzzed the targets hair. Pleased with the result, he fired again, punching a neat hole through the indistinguishable right eye. Eight rounds followed, then seven more. Fisher's smiled stretched his mouth when he saw the target's head reduced to a web of black paper.

Checking the weapon, he laid it to rest and turned for his dressing down.

"Not bad," Miller said. "How many times have you shot before?"

"My second," Fisher said, trying to hide the surprise at Miller's softened tone.

Miller nodded, his light eyebrows raised. "Have you ever had an eye dominance test?"

"A what test?" Fisher replied, moving his head to the side.

"Okay," Miller said, moving to the back of the room whilst holding his palm out for Fisher to stay. "Point your finger at my right eye," he said.

Fisher did as asked.

"You're right eye dominant. We'll train that out of you in the next few months, but for now just close your left eye when you shoot and always aim for the centre mass," he said, pushing out his enormous chest. "There's more to hit and you'll likely put a man down." Miller held his palm open to the range.

Fisher stepped up, reloaded the clip and ran over Miller's advice. Seventeen rounds went clean through the torso before he looked back.

Miller nodded again as he stepped forward, clipping a fresh silhouette. With the ill-fated page arriving at the thirty metres line, Miller spoke as he walked to the door.

"Find me in the gym when you're out of ammo."

Fisher took his time and continued to practice, stopping as he watched another target emerge in his peripheral vision. Its form travelled up to the sixty-metre marker, almost halfway down the range and he watched as Harris showed him how it should be done.

With the last of the brass sprayed across the concrete, Fisher worked his mouth to ease the ache of his constant smile. A tone rang in his head. He turned to Harris as she walked to his side.

"You'll get used to it," she said as she pointed to his pocket.

He pulled out the phone and saw an icon showing he had mail. Someone he didn't know told him he was licensed to carry a concealed pistol, attaching a document detailing the terms and conditions. He'd read it later.

Harris led them the way they'd arrived, refilling their ammunition and handing him a cloth bag filled from the guarded shelves.

"So when do I get a V32?" he said, still grinning as they walked the lonely corridors.

"Six months. If you still want it by then," she said, with no sign of a smile.

"I thought this was my training?" he replied.

Her dimples came out strong. "Months of pain, that's your training."

Fisher didn't know what to reply; he wasn't sure if it could be that hard. Maybe she was preparing him so he found it easier when it did really start. He felt like asking her what it involved but thought better of it, instead letting her lead him around the complex in silence.

Eventually they arrived to the smell of stale sweat, dusty plastic and the squeak of rubber against a varnished floor. Through open double doors they saw Miller standing next to a crash mat, drinking from a mug and talking to a tall man with long Gaulish features who wore white shorts and a t-shirt rimmed with a red line.

Beside them a group of enthusiastic men in black shorts and white tees played a hard-knocking game of five-a-side football. Seeing them approach, Miller beckoned them over as he laughed with the man next to him, both their smiles dropping as they arrived.

"This is Sergeant Belgard," Miller said, pronouncing the name with a French flair.

Fisher nodded in Belgard's direction but got no response as Miller continued to speak.

"He'll brief you on what to expect when we jump from the sky. Oh, and good news, I checked the weather. Looks like it's going to be a good day for it." Miller smiled at Belgard before heading towards the doors.

The Frenchman's accent matched his features as he took pleasure in explaining the dangers of a water landing in tandem, his tone growing higher as he explained with excitement they would have to separate and free fall for the last few seconds of the jump.

He turned to Fisher, telling him not to worry; Miller would do everything for him. The lifejacket would inflate on impact and the beacon would activate. The words had been chosen for maximum effect at Miller's command, Fisher had no doubt.

Harris tried to settle his obvious nerves as she took him on another epic journey, ending in a well-equipped medical centre. After a short stay, the medical tests showed an elevated blood pressure, which the medics dismissed as nerves when he mentioned he'd just been informed he'd have to jump out of a plane for the first time.

After being collected by Harris, they sat down to a simple meal in the facility's stark mess room. Conversation turned to their last day together, with Fisher keen to know how they'd been found.

With Harris reminding him to eat, she told how Clark had realised early on something wasn't right. He took it upon himself to trace them to the airport. Dogged hard work filled in the blanks with the car companies, then he let the ANPR system do the rest. Tracing them to Birmingham airport, he guessed their plan to change cars and it only took a few hours to get the details of the second.

With a few more hits from the cameras on the way up to Snowdon, then on to the Express Way, CCTV picked them up at the port, but his breakthrough came when they hired the Enterprise car. Unbeknown to Harris, all Enterprise cars are fitted with trackers. Clark hacked into their system and when the electronics registered the car crash, they moved in with a team who were already on standby.

His efficiency had surprised even her.

With the meal over almost as soon as it had started, she led them to the accommodation rooms buried deeper in the complex. Leaving him to shower and change, Fisher lingered by the open doorway until she disappeared out of view.

***

She tried sitting, desperate for a better view. Still her muscles ignored the urgency. Blood pounded at her temples but despite the frustration she could see her vision clearing with each passing moment. She blinked and for the first time saw marks on the high ceiling, then the stains on the bumps of the not-quite-right walls. Her head turned to the side and she saw the old beds and began to question the rusting restraints hanging loose at their sides.

She looked along the blue cloth clinging to the contours of her body, her blood cooling at the sight of leather bracelets clamping her wrists to the bed.

A door opened at the other end of the room and a voiceless thought jumped into her head. What's he doing here?

An electronic beep signalled beside her.

Panic rushed through her veins, she screamed without noise. She wasn't ready.

Still her muscles relaxed, her blood warmed and she slipped back away.

44

Fresh from the shower, Fisher heard a knock at the door and with a towel wrapped around his waist, he opened it to Harris. Dressed from head to toe in black, her head turning back from down the corridor, she dropped a black rucksack at his feet.

Losing himself in her hazel eyes, a cold stream of air sent a shiver along his back and he blinked out of his stare. Harris looked him up and down, dipping her eyebrows.

"I'll be back in ten minutes, put some clothes on," she said with her mouth in a smile as she headed down the corridor. Fisher stood and watched her slender figure disappear from view.

Closing the door, he emptied the contents of the rucksack on to the bed. Out fell a masculine equivalent of what she wore. The shoes were the right size, as were the trousers, shirt and thick black jacket made from tough material dotted with hundreds of pockets. In the side compartment he picked out underwear, deodorant, shaving equipment, a toothbrush and spearmint paste.

Dressed in his new clothes, he glimpsed the shoulder holster and the Glock sitting in front of the TV. After taking a few minutes figuring out how the holster worked around his shoulders, the handgun rested snug under his left armpit.

Standing in front of the mirror and in a rare moment of vanity, he looked over himself, fixing on the thin dark line now he'd removed the bandage.

He'd love Andrew to see him now. Swearing under his breath, he realised he hadn't spoken to his best friend for days. Grabbing his communicator, Fisher dialled Andrew's number from memory. A recorded welsh voice came on the line warning the call was insecure. Andrew's voice came after, followed by the tone of his voicemail.

"I'm a shit mate, but I'm okay. Sorry for not calling. Will call you when I can but I'm okay. Don't try ringing me back, I've lost my phone."

He breathed a sigh of relief, pleased not to have to lie and answer the obvious questions. There'd be time for a full debrief over a beer when this was all over. He stood in front of the mirror; a smile bloomed. Just two weeks ago he was a tree surgeon going nowhere by choice, but now look what he was doing.

A pang of guilt cut short his reflection. Susie was still in grave danger. Now wasn't the time to enjoy himself. Now was the time to listen to his hosts. To help them find her and make everything alright again.

Harris returned sooner than he'd expected and together they climbed five flights of stairs to find Miller and one other, a carbon copy in bulk and stature, his expression austere as his mouth ground on gum. They were waiting by the exit, both dressed the same as him, with four enormous kit bags by their feet.

"You're here," Miller said with impatience as they came through the doors, then threw one of the heavy bags at Fisher. The other guy carried the two by his feet.

Peering into the early evening sky, it wasn't lost on him that he'd stood at these doors so many times already and half expected a hoard of arms to drag him back.

The increasing whine of engines caught his attention. He followed the others around the cold concrete, finding the source, a grey Merlin helicopter sitting a short walk away. Its bulk nestled on a tarmac hard standing with the blades slow, but speeding more with each rotation.

He followed Miller through the side door and into its dark belly, an airman in a green flight suit stowing his bag and ushered him to a seat along the fuselage.

Miller handed Fisher a headset he'd grabbed from behind his head. As he clasped the seat buckle, he felt a flip in his stomach as the aircraft lifted. The headphones came to life with voice.

"Short hop over to St Athen to pick up the Hercules, then it's over to Gibraltar for a drink before the drag to rendezvous with Daring," Miller rattled out. It took Fisher a few moments until he understood the words.

"How long?" Fisher said into the boomed microphone at his mouth.

"Ten hours," Miller replied, flashing his flattened palm out in front of him twice. "Or thereabouts, depends how much progress Daring makes. This is Mr Bayne," Miller continued, pointing two fingers out at the soldier sat opposite. "He'll be the engineering specialist overseeing the modifications to the containers." Bayne grunted a greeting, his expression turned from stern to contemptuous while still rolling gum in his mouth.

Fisher looked around the cabin, desperate to talk to Harris but didn't want to let the others hear. Instead he gazed at the scenery running below the windows, watching the bleak hazel scrub of the moors turn green, neat hedges zipping past as the land ordered into cultivation.

Scattered houses became estates, before turning back to rolling grass once more until the flash of a wide motorway with pin-prick cars tracking like ants on drugs.

The ground grew closer. The engine tones relaxed. The image from the window swung as they turned and he caught first sight of a long runway with huge aircraft dotted to its side. A second turn and he caught the unmistakable hulk of a Hercules transport looming outside an even greater grey hanger.

The rear ramp sat open consuming a trail of uniforms busy conveying boxes, while others huddled around two aluminium cargo crates, pushing up the incline in slow motion. No sooner had their craft settled on its wheels than the side door pulled open from the outside and the crewman dropped their bags on the tarmac.

Fisher followed the single file to the Hercules, listening as their feet clanked on the metal ramp to join the containers now mounted in the centre, their bulk strapped down to a central track in the belly of the giant aircraft. The four turboprop engines were already turning, thundering heat and noise around the fuselage to be their home for the next ten hours.

Seeing the canvas webbing seats, he threw away any thought of comfort on the journey, selecting a space a few paces along from Harris, with Miller and Bayne opposite. Sitting, he closed his eyes at the sight of the two tightly packed parachutes which would soon carry their fragile forms through the air. A necessity, he tried to reason to no one but himself.

Hearing footsteps up the ramp, he watched two RAF crewmen nod to Miller and with one hand on a large red button, the ramp rose high, sealing them from the outside.

One of the crewmen motioned in their direction to grab their headsets from behind. With Harris already wearing a pair, he fumbled his own into place and listened to a safety briefing he thought perhaps a little too late, his attention on the engines already increasing in pitch and the bumps in the ground coming up through the wheels.

He watched the two soldiers opposite, their eyes closed, the only movement the slow roll of Bayne's jaw. With the aircraft tilting upward, he felt the familiar leap in his stomach when the ground no longer exerted its force.

Slouching back in his seat the drone of the engines became his new focus. He turned to his side and Harris, serene with her eyes shut and closed his own letting the hypnotic hum send him off to sleep.

A firm tap to the arm and he woke with a start to see a crewman stood above him shouting.

"Just while we land."

A few moments later he felt the bounce of the wheels as they pushed against the tarmac. Coming to a stop, they sat with the engines pounding, until with no warning, rolled, pitching up and climbing back to the air. He pictured the solid ground of Gibraltar, their last for some time, he hoped. Surveying the cabin, he closed his eyes as the parachutes came back into view.

***

Fisher smelt the tang of mint over the fumes and oil and heard the ever-present drone of the engines before the pain in his chin. The sensation sharpened him out of his half dream and opening his eyes, Bayne's face filled his view.

The soldier held a left-handed finger over his mouth, sending waves of slow minty breath over his face. Fisher couldn't see the knife in his right, but he could feel the tip under his chin.

Bayne smiled, his weathered teeth on show, along with the fleeting white of gum. Fisher's survey darted first to Harris's feet motionless beside him, then to Miller's closed eyes, his head up straight as if he were staring straight in his direction.

"It's just you and me," Bayne said, his voice barely cutting through. "I've been told to keep an eye on you. You're not meant to be here little boy. All of us work well as a team. Trouble only comes from the outside. Are you trouble?"

Bayne loosened the knife to let him reply. Fisher's mind raced and he didn't know what to say, couldn't believe what was happening. These guys were meant to be on the same side and he sat stunned, everything fixed in fear until a fresh wave of mint washed over his face.

"'Cos if you're trouble then we might as well end this here. A little accident mid-air, over the sea." Bayne lifted his eyebrows and cocked his head to the right. "Sorry sir, he just fell out the back! You understand?"

Fisher gently nodded.

"So are you trouble?"

Fisher sat still, a sudden thought coming to him. Was this guy for real or could it be a test? His adrenaline rose as a sudden confidence cleared his mind. He made a decision in a split second, lifted his head and with both hands shoved the knife to the side, his forehead smashing against the bridge of Bayne's nose.

45

"Wakey wakey," came a deep voice over the headset as turbulence shunted him forward. This time he hadn't been sleeping. At first the headache had kept him awake, then the fear of another encounter. He opened his eyes to find Miller staring at him with his head in the same position as when he'd slept.

"I've never seen a rookie so calm before a first jump," he said laughing. If only he knew, Fisher said to himself and stood, his feet unsteady as they rocked to the side. He risked a look at Bayne and saw a strip of white tape on his nose.

He hadn't been dreaming!

To his left Harris pulled on a black dry suit, tight over her clothes.

"We jump in forty minutes, get your suit on," the same voice said in his ear. "Anything you don't want to get wet, pack into these dry bags," Miller said, pointing to bright orange sacks on the floor next to Harris.

Fisher leant forward and took the suit out of the heavy holdall and laid it on the floor, stripped off his shoes and jacket, then threw his impersonal possessions, the gun and the phone into the bag. His gaze caught Harris, her lithe body slipping gracefully into the rubber, pausing on every tight and defined curve. She looked up and he turned away hoping she hadn't noticed.

Staring at his suit, he sat back on the canvas seat and after twenty minutes of graceless battle he pulled the zip high at the back. Bayne glanced over and threw a plastic bottle on the canvas next to him. Talcum powder. Fisher mouthed a sarcastic thank you. Bayne returned with a half-hearted salute. Miller walked over, swaying this way and that and helped Fisher with his harness and life jacket.

"Don't mind Bayne, just a bit of banter."

With the dry bag tied to his ankle, Miller pulled at straps, everything tightening around him. When fully trussed,

Miller headed away as the headset crackled with static until a voice sent his pulse sky high.

"Tee minus ten minutes to target."

The aircraft jumped to the side, pushing Fisher back into his seat. The motion lulled and Harris shuffled over, pulled his headset to the side and shouted in his ear.

"Don't know about you but I'm bricking it."

"I wasn't till you said that," he lied, not doubting her line had been for his benefit. Still they both laughed, shouting conversation about how they'd slept until the voice came back.

"Tee minus two minutes."

The two aircrew fussed over the crates, heading backwards and forwards across the fuselage, their movements used to the flurries of turbulence. The main lights went out and three caged lamps bathed them in red as they burnt bright along the cramped interior. Miller walked up and strapped a jumping helmet to Fisher's head before connecting his front harness to Fisher's back, all the while Bayne checked over Harris's kit.

They each clipped a short cord to a runner in the ceiling. The red lights flashed once and the ramp began to whine open. As the metal parted the wind kicked up and screamed despite their ear protection, sucking air out of his lungs as the dark rolling clouds came into view. Lightning flashed across the opening. Miller's voice shouted in his ear.

"See. A good day."

"Target in nine. Eight. Seven. Six," said a different voice shouting over the wind. The crewmen moved behind the first crate while the aircraft pitched up, Miller grabbing Fisher around the waist. "Five. Four. Three. Two. One. Target."

Red changed to green and the two crewmen heaved the bound crates along the runners, Fisher's alarmed gaze following as their short tethers tightened, the crate dropping into the frenzied air. The chute shot out, air gathering under the silk, catching, billowing open and slowing to a float. He watched the box spiral down before he saw the chaos of the ocean.

The second crate broke his wide-eyed trance as it rushed past to join its companion. Green turned to red and he breathed a sigh of relief. They'd have to find another way. There was no chance they could jump in this storm.

He tried to twist but Miller pushed him forward towards the open end of the plane. Hadn't he seen outside? His head screamed as he struggled against his tight harness. The lights were red. The conditions awful. They wouldn't survive this jump, but Miller still pushed him along, ignoring his useless complaint. A crewman grabbed the headset from his head and it dawned on him as he looked down the ramp and the violent white water. In one last effort he turned his head just as the lights turned green.

"Go, Go, Go," came Miller's scream in his ear and they edged forward, rain lashing his face.

46

They were out. Nothing Fisher could do would change that.

Squeezing his eyes shut, he bit down to stifle a scream. Nausea washed over him along with the rain and wind. He opened his eyes, took a wet breath, but despite the battering rain the terror soon subsided.

He felt weightless as he hurtled towards the ground. Wind gusting in his face, he took his first look at the ocean just as the last of the crates disappeared to be engulfed by a huge wave.

Panic lapped as Miller tapped his shoulder. He tucked his arms in tight to his chest. Just before a jolt pulled him by the straps, the parachute flying from Miller's back. The wind almost instantly died back.

With astounding contrast, a calm settled over their travel until the wind gusted water into his face. His nerves eased as they glided towards the sea. A huge wall of air caught him in the face and sucked the breath from his lungs. Choking, they started to spin, their speed quickly building.

Miller behind him shook, kicking out his legs to regain control of the collapsed chute. Fisher closed his eyes, images of his body flashed before him, washed out and blue on a faraway beach. Susie spoke. He couldn't hear what she said but he knew he had to survive. Opening his eyes, he straightened his legs, tucked his arms back to his sides and took a deep breath. Miller hit him in the back and he accelerated towards the waves separated from his surrogate at a speed he knew he couldn't survive.

It felt like an age before the water engulfed him, longer still before he stopped his breathless descent. Desperate for air, suspended and motionless in the water, he prayed to a god he didn't believe in. He knew nobody listened and he couldn't wait. Kicking his arms and legs and with a loud pop, the vest inflated. Finally breaking the surface, he sucked in a wave of salty water. Waves crashed over his head as he threw up his lungs, pushed his head back and gasped for breath.

Control came as he learnt the motion of the waves, bobbing up and down, saltwater stinging his eyes. With the wind and waves pushing him from side to side he saw nothing but dark water around him.

He leant himself back and looked to the skies, no sign of the aircraft or the others. He was alone in the middle of the Atlantic, convinced Miller had drowned, Harris and Bayne hadn't followed their suicide jump.

He bobbed alone in the middle of the Atlantic.

47

As the waves crashed around him, he tried to turn. Fighting the bulk of his life vest, his head hit against something solid, a great pressure pulling on the harness at his back. Before he knew it two pairs of hands grabbed him up, throwing him down into a rubber boat.

"Nice day for it sir," shouted a man in fatigues, a Royal Marine by his shoulder badges as another threw Miller beside him. Fisher lay dazed, elation coursing through his veins. The rain had calmed and the waves seemed to still, like the gods had given up after failing in their claim.

Fisher sat up, the boat already speeding to two black torsos bobbing in the water. He blinked twice seeing Harris smiling and Bayne still chewing through his scowl. All safe in the RIB, a hand pointed to the warship, the sun breaking through as the clouds melted away across the horizon.

He stared intently at the ship which looked like nothing he'd ever seen before. Her tall, pyramid like mast, its base as wide as the deck, ran through the centre, protruding high into the air with a giant rotating globe on top. HMS Daring looked as if from a science fiction movie, its sleek triangular lines cutting through the water towards them.

They stopped halfway down the side of Daring's length, their engine slowing as a crane swung from somewhere high on the enclosed deck. Four hooks bore down, carrying them with graceful motion to a hangar in the side of the ship. With a hum of pneumatics, they pulled in, coming to rest with sailors busying around them.

Miller slung his bag over his shoulder and jumped from the boat, nodding backwards as Bayne followed. Fisher and Harris climbed on to the deck and were met by two fatigue-clad soldiers with few determining features. Fisher looked for unit insignia but could see only blank shoulders. The left of the two spoke, his voice curt and deep as he offered out two small white towels.

"Welcome to HMS Daring. Please follow me and we'll get you settled in."

***

Every few hours, or days or weeks, she would rise from a deep, unnatural sleep. Her senses slowly coming back, along with the power to think. Each time she would reach an understanding, then nothingness came again. Each time was the same and different. The fear. The panic. The memories dribbling in. Now time for the frustration, realising she'd gone through this so many times before. Then came the beep.

It was time again. The same and different. Her brain active, her memory clear and she pushed herself not to panic. She'd realised she wasn't in hospital, instead somewhere held against her will. Then came the voices loud to her delicate ears. Two different men and she understood their speak.

"Are you sure?"

"Let me have a look."

"Shit."

"So we're one short."

"And no time to send a hunting party."

"Shit."

Another voice broke in, commanding and further away to her right.

"We'll deal with her when we get back, shove her in there."

If she could open her eyes, she knew who she'd be looking at.

48

Water still dripping from their suits, Fisher trailed Harris as she followed the two silent men leading them through wide open bulkhead doors and corridors he thought too cavernous for a naval vessel.

Clean metal ducts criss-crossed above their heads, pipes snaking between brightly coloured cables tracking their path along the walls, as ranks walked past going about their own business. Down they headed through open hatches, arriving soon at a small canteen bare of sailors, just a lone guy in chef's whites stood behind a scant servery chopping with enthusiasm. The talkative guide spoke for the second time.

"Take a seat. You'll be collected after you've had food." He nodded to the chef and both their escorts turned and left.

Fisher let out a long sigh as he remained standing.

"What's up?" said Harris, pulling out her clothes from the dry bag.

"I thought I was going to die out there."

"Yeah. Thrilling though," she said beaming towards him.

"Now what?"

"We wait," she said, laughter bubbling across her face.

"Oh."

"Get used to it, it's not all jumping out of planes and shooting bad guys."

"They could have at least given us a tour."

"Don't feel too bad. It's their billion-pound new baby. Ninety percent of it's still classified," she said, moving towards the toilet marked with a black stick in a skirt. As she left the chef brought over a tray stacked high with sandwiches.

Fisher sat and started on the stack. After an hour the same escorts returned, guiding them to an empty two-bunk room, where they did as ordered and dropped off their gear, following again through the maze of corridors in silence and arriving at a nondescript open hatch.

Inside the low-ceilinged room rows of seats faced toward a projected crest. A bare arm and a hand thrusting into a cresset of fire. Around the grey walls were naval photographs hung beside paintings and portraits, many of which were of the Queen. All but two of the seats were filled.

Over thirty navy blue shirted men and women sat quietly talking amongst themselves. On the first row were three men in camouflage fatigues and two male naval officers stood with Miller facing them from the front.

The escorts ushered Fisher and Harris to the spare seats, three rows from the front, then walked away without any word. The room hushed as one officer, his shoulders decorated with a row of bars, spoke. His pronunciation clean and precise. His voice deep and compelling.

"For the benefit of our two guests," he said with a short nod in their direction. "I am Lieutenant Commander Angus Lower, Executive Officer of HMS Daring and I'd like to welcome all of you to today's command briefing for Operation Salve. The briefing will form two parts, after a basic brief I will be asking most of you to leave. Apart from our two guests, if you need to remain then you would have already been informed."

"This is a three-phase operation. Phase one will begin when we get to within ten nautical miles of target Alpha. There we will shadow, fully silent, until the second phase. There will be a go window of four hours before we move to the second phase. At which point we will move up to one nautical mile and launch the two RIBs, with Daring continuing to shadow at distance until phase two is complete. In the third phase we will come along side Alpha where we expect to take up to thirty guests."

"The helo will be on standby for a one-minute launch during phases two and three. We have made preparations that a large number of the guests will require medical supervision, with all first aid and medical staff to be at readiness. The troop accommodation has been cleared for this purpose. Preparations have also been made for a number of detentions.

We will be alongside the target for around twelve hours and then return to Blighty. Risk to Daring is minimal; risk to offshore teams is reasonable. Sub Lieutenant Chambers will now run through the meteorology."

A young uniformed woman sitting in the front row jumped up from her seat and stood next to the projector image. She clicked a remote control in her hand and the screen came to life with a weather map showing no land.

Fisher dissected the basics of the complex information, the storm which had tracked up from Central America was already a hundred miles away and the skies would be clear for the operation. The female officer sat back down and the officer who stood next to the XO ordered the first wave of people to leave.

Left with only seven others in the room, three naval officers and one black clad soldier dotted around the seats, Miller took over and delivered the details, including timings and boarding procedures.

He explained without mentioning names his two guests were to stay back with three operatives in the secondary launch but would board when secure. Mr Smith, Miller motioning to Fisher, would interrogate the crew and the rest of the team would set about the containers.

As the briefing concluded Miller led them back through the ship, down into the bowels of the vessel where they found his team in two of the six-berth crew compartments. Miller called them forward and without salute, they lined up in no hurry in the corridor.

"Let me introduce you to the cream of the British Military," Miller announced. Fisher wasn't sure if he'd been joking as he watched the ramshackle bunch with beards and mismatched dress resembling convicts, not the starched and well presented sailors he'd seen across the ship. Still with pride clear in his voice, Miller introduced each of them by nickname as if randomly choosing the words. Miller lingered over three of his men, Lucky, Boots and Biggy, those were to be on the second launch with Fisher and Harris.

Biggy was the squad leader, a well built, stocky man, his afro hair tight to his scalp the only tidy part of him, his dark, exposed forearms covered in tattoos that cut off at the cuff. He stepped forward and held out a huge paw, smiled and spoke in a deep welsh accent Fisher wasn't expecting.

"Mr Bayne tells me you're a man not to mess with."

Fisher smiled as he tried his best to return the firm shake.

Next came Lucky, tall and wiry, a thick white scar running from his right eye to the top of his ear. A clue to his nickname, Fisher was sure. With deep-tanned skin, Boots had a face mottled with dark freckles, a bushy ginger beard sprouted on his face and long, thick eyebrows grew unchecked.

Miller again introduced Fisher as Mr Smith, but Harris apparently needed no introduction and hugged most of the team, banter free flowing as she moved around the room. The introductions over, Biggy chatted with Harris about someone he didn't know who couldn't make it because his wife had just given birth, all the while Fisher followed behind until they reached their bunk. As Biggy retreated, he advised Fisher to sleep if he could.

"You don't know when you'll next get the chance."

"Were they SAS?" Fisher asked as he settled on to the bottom bunk.

"SBS," Harris said. Fisher didn't reply. "Boat. It stands for Boat," Harris said, filling the silence.

"They seemed a bit," he said hesitating as he struggled to find the word. "Normal. I would have thought special soldiers would have been different somehow."

"Call them soldiers again and you'll soon see how normal they are."

***

She'd been moved. She knew straight away.

Her memory had come back quickly this time. The place was dark and her breath reflected back at her. A slow rumble of vibration hung around, along with the sensation of rhythmic movement making her eyelids heavy.

She tried moving. Still her muscles felt weak and refused to comply.

She remembered the voices talking about her. The halo of brunette. They were going to do something different so she wouldn't go to waste. But it had to be done quick.

She was travelling, she was sure of that. Maybe this was her chance. Maybe there were people around outside. Maybe they would hear her. She opened her mouth and screamed, but no noise came out.

She started to cry, tears rolled down her face, tickling her skin as they slid to her ears.

She drew in deep breaths and took comfort she still could.

She'd been awake for a long time, at least it felt that way. Her mind felt amazing, so clear.

She remembered the last night she was free. Her friends. She went to the bathroom, attacked from behind, something over her face. She fought. Fell. Hit her nose on the floor. The blackness. The conversation with James. Why hadn't she just told him? She had to break free, she had to get out of this box.

The tide rolled in and she melted away.

49

Sleep didn't come. Fisher tried to relax but no matter how hard he willed, how hard he wanted his thoughts to go away, he could only lay waiting. Waiting and thinking. Hanging around. Doing nothing.

Harris had told him the saying in the military. Hurry up and wait. How true it seemed in his first outing.

The last twenty-four hours had been another whirlwind. A lifetime away from two weeks ago and his normal life. Now his uniqueness was known to more than his friends. A live firearm rested beside him and he could kill if the situation wanted. He partnered with a beautiful agent, or spy, or call her what you like. He might be falling bad.

He'd jumped out of a plane and it wasn't on fire and would land if he just stayed on board. He was about to witness a Special Forces takedown and was hours from being reunited with Susie. For the first time in months, no years, he corrected in his head, he was happy. Scared too. He was scared of Susie being hurt, apprehensive of the operation.

Fisher smiled. Despite everything, excitement rushed through his veins. With a dark chapter in his life about to close, a whole new story opening before him, he didn't know what it would bring but he couldn't sit still at the thought.

Glad to have his self-indulgence interrupted, their call came sooner than he'd expected in the form of a figure clad from head to toe in black, his welsh accent cutting through the silence.

"It's time boys and girls," he said from behind black warpaint, slinging a thin black life vest and helmet at each of them in turn. Fisher pulled the life saver over his jacket, watching Biggy beckoning him forward with his fingers thick with black before scraping the darkness across Fisher's face and flinging the open container in Harris's direction.

Each resembling shadows, Biggy led them for their final journey through the ship and to the darkness of the RIB hanger. The thick roller shutters were open, but the only source of light came from the quarter moon and its reflection on the calm ocean. Service men guided them to their seats among the other dark figures, before retreating as Biggy took his place in front with an assault rifle slung across his chest.

Weapons cocked around them as motors began to hum, near-silent hydraulics whined as the RIB lifted from its rest, stopping with precision in mid-air. Without longer than a second's pause, they were thrust out beyond the dimensions of its mother.

A light breeze whispered across their blacked out faces as they swayed side to side above the sea. The hum came again, this time quieter still and they lowered at pace, touching down in the Atlantic with barely a splash. Lucky and Boots unclipped the hoist links in a single fluid motion, the cables rising home as the outboard engine fired up. Still the near silence persisted from where he sat.

Fisher drew a deep breath as they moved off.

Passing Daring's bow, he watched a shadow of the second RIB on their starboard as it mirrored their speed, cutting through the calm dark waters. Turning to face ahead he caught first sight of the Rashana, its bow shining like a beacon on the horizon.

Holding tight to handles the two boats approached in unison, the target growing with every moment. Individual lights soon became clear around the ship and it wasn't long before he recognised its shape from the port.

They'd been so close.

Excitement, fear, anticipation charged through his veins. Life pumping around his body, his jaw ached from his clenching teeth, his fingers stiff from his grip.

With an unseen signal both RIBs slowed. Fisher's boat more than the other as it swung left to let the assault boat lead. They were close now. He could feel the thick rumble of her engines in his chest, her dense exhaust a welcome assault on his senses. The three blacked out warriors lifted their assault rifles towards the deck, ready to cover their comrades impending action as the pilot held the course straight.

Fisher saw the first line of containers washed with orange light on the deck. He wanted to reach out but couldn't keep his gaze from the assault craft as it swung into the ship's wake.

Each second they gained on the target, the rough water parting by silent power as they crept along the bright red hull. His survey switched to the deck as each pair of eyes scoured for movement with the RIBs matching pace.

He watched a crewman in the lead boat shoulder his rifle, grabbing the bottom rebar welded to the hull. The time had come and one by one six shadows climbed into danger. With the last man clamped to the ship, their pilot killed his engine, their craft drifting silently along the length and into the shadows.

Fisher turned back and they'd each disappeared. He held his breath with a sudden foreboding in his gut.

50

Shots didn't ring out and too quickly in Fisher's mind, by some unseen signal their pilot moved the RIB below the steel rungs, Biggy shouting in Fisher's direction.

"Up you go lad," he said pointing up the sheer side. Surprising himself, Fisher sprung to his feet and grabbing the cold rungs, pulled up the convex curve of metal before latching on to a black-gloved hand reaching from above. The roll of Bayne's chin greeted him as he scrambled to the deck.

"All secure sir," he said with a barely visible black plaster on his nose confirming the identity. "Six crewmen accounted for and detained. Ship's log confirms but we're undertaking a thorough search as we speak." Fisher gave a nod, his gaze settling on the rusting steel containers as he took a step forward.

"The bridge sir," Bayne said pointing him along the deck with an open hand. Fisher knew with reluctance he had a job to do before he could take Susie in his arms. There were others who needed his help.

Hearing footsteps rise up from the water, Bayne led him along the length of the deck. Fisher's hand reached out, brushing his fingers against each container as he passed until he climbed the metal steps to the bridge.

He heard, then felt in his chest, the engine's speed lessen. On the bridge Miller stood beside two operators with their weapons pointed to six black crewmen kneeling on the floor in a semicircle. Each man's hands were bound behind their backs with white quick-close tie-wraps. Sweat poured from their brows.

"Who's in charge?" Fisher said in the direction of the terrified captives. Miller let his assault rifle down on its straps and picked up the oldest man by his shoulders, pulling him to his feet. Fisher walked along the short bridge, Miller guiding the crewman to follow. They headed through a rusted steel door and into a nearby corridor, pulling off his black gloves he turned to face the captive.

"Release the cuffs."

Miller complied without question. The captive's arms dropped to his sides. Fisher grabbed his left, pulled up the sleeve of the thin shirt and clasped his hand around his sweaty wrist, staring into his eyes. He could feel deep fear radiating towards him.

"You can trust me," Fisher said in a soft low voice. The captain gave a slow nod, but didn't speak. "I'm here to help you," Fisher continued. "How many crew?"

"Seven," the captain replied in a deep Bajan voice. Miller flinched at the words and touched his neck whilst speaking quietly into his radio.

"What is your cargo?"

"Cars."

Fisher released his grip.

"Who owns the cargo?"

"Don't know his name."

"Who collects them?"

"I call them on the shortwave and unload, just like any other."

"We're not going to let you deliver the cargo," Fisher said then paused. "We want you to help us. Are you going to help us?" Fisher asked, his hand back around his wrist.

"Yeah man."

"Tell this man what you have to say," Fisher said pointing at Miller. The guy nodded and his fearful expression lifted. Fisher could wait no longer, his job here was done and he ran back through the bridge. As he got to the door, Bayne barred his way and for the first time he noticed the heavy engine din coming from his back despite the ship just gently rolling in the water.

"Wait here, there's one more crew unaccounted for."

Fisher stepped around him.

"These guys are harmless," he said, rattling down the wrong metal stairs.

Bursting through the open hatch and into the cramped engine room the drone of the idling engine surrounded him.

Realising his mistake but not understanding where he'd gone wrong, he slowed and slipped to the greasy floor. A bullet pinged off the left engine block and ricocheted around the steel room. The fall had saved his life.

As he lay flat on his back with a sharp pain in his neck slowly subsiding, he lifted his head to see a young black face with wide white eyes peering around a bulkhead, locked with a stare straight at him.

A gun rose up from somewhere at the scared guy's side and Fisher's feet slipped in the grease as he tried to gain traction by grabbing at the metal of the hot engine, his skin near burning as he barely managed to pull himself up. A second shot rattled the room and footsteps clattered against the steps behind him.

"Stay there," Fisher shouted. "I'm okay." The footsteps stopped with a third shot ringing off to echo throughout. Fisher finally gained grip and lunged forward, trying to wedge himself to a gap in the heavy equipment. His back faced out and he struggled to turn as another shot came near, the closest yet.

Eventually he twisted around, squeezing in the tight hole with the bulkhead to one side, the hot engine to the other. Sweat poured from him as he fumbled for his gun.

"We're not going to hurt you," Fisher shouted above the din. No reply came. Fisher had managed to turn himself around but the only way he could reach his gun would expose his arm out of the steel hiding place. Remembering what sat on the deck, he gained a sudden focus. Susie needed him.

Pushing his arm forward and under his jacket, shots rang off in quick succession. With his hand on the Glock, Fisher rolled forward, but with his foot out in front he struggled for traction. As he slid across the floor he turned to his right, pushing the gun out in front and pulled the trigger.

Through a blur he caught those eyes, narrowed and white against the black face, the circular end of a barrel just below. As a shot rang out Fisher returned with two, his shoulder crashing against a wall. Movement caught in his vision to the left, a boot landing to the floor, another launching to jump over him. Two silenced thuds announced the rush was over and a huge hand stretched out to help him to his feet.

"They're opening them up," the Welsh voice said. Fisher slipped up the stairs without more than a nod.

51

Breathless, Fisher found Harris standing next to Lucky wielding a large pair of bolt croppers.

"Where've you been?" she said looking at his grease-soaked clothes.

"Let's do this," he replied shooting a look to the thick padlocks of the container. The bridge mounted lights burst on, illuminating the deck as it chattered with the boots of sailors climbing aboard behind him.

The container's heavy steel doors were secured with four vertical bars running over the top of the container to its base. Each bar levered at a right angle at waist height. Each lever tied with a lock to a container door. With a glance in Harris's direction, Lucky stepped forward putting the sharp jaws around the nearest padlock. The first lock clattered to the floor in one swift motion. The rest followed shortly after.

Two sailors stepped forward, pulling levers in unison and the bars released their hold on the door. Fisher's breathing grew shallow, the moment finally here. Light flooded the inside of the first half of the container, salty air giving way to a heavy, stale odour.

So many times he'd try to picture the scene, but still nothing had prepared him for the two camp beds low to the floor with two young blonde women in blue overalls lying on thin plastic mattresses.

His hand went to his mouth at the sight of the large IV bags sagging nearly empty as they hung from hooks welded to steel, a clear tube disappearing inside their utilitarian clothing. On the floor lay bags full of deep orange liquid and an intravenous pump, the brand soon recognised with its tube snaking up to a bared arm.

A figure pushed past as Fisher stood fixed to the spot and examined the first woman on the right. A sudden remembrance flushed through his mind and he stepped into the container, staring at each of the expressionless faces. Neither were his Susie, but they were someone else's.

They'd talked before about the other woman caught up in whatever this was, but still he couldn't help but focus on the one he knew. For the first time he felt a deep guilt for those thoughts. They'd been unreal and easy to overlook. Until now. More real than ever, their lives were worth as much as Susie's. There were other James Fishers out there. Other people who would not rest until they found the ones they loved.

Collecting himself, Fisher lingered over the girl unconscious on the left, watching for the slow rise and fall of her chest. He pushed his hand out behind him and Harris placed a torch in his hand. Susie wasn't in either of the other beds, but his disappointment didn't last long, quickly calling the medic forward. With her skin almost translucent and her bones more defined, number four looked in danger even before he saw the empty IV bag and the pool of liquid on the floor.

Fisher picked his way out of the busy container as the medics checked for immediate risks before they could figure out the safe way to bring them out of their current state. The fresh sea air gave a relief to his senses and he stood at the edge of the deck. Taking deep breaths Fisher caught sight of the running lights of Daring as she made progress towards them.

Grabbing the cutters from Lucky who stood at the doors of the container, horror radiating from his face he moved to the second container questioning the decision not to tell everyone what to expect. The padlocks from the second container fell in quick succession. As the doors creaked open, Fisher scanned the contents, four more unrecognised, blank-faced women, but at least all were breathing.

A sailor rushed past him as he left for the next. Four more locks down and he took a step back as the doors swung open. The putrid smell screamed for attention. Harris, at his shoulder, bellowed for assistance and wrapping his arm around his nose and mouth, Fisher headed in, but the thick odour still came close to overtaking him.

Gagging, the first two girls looked barely alive. The third was dead and had been for a long time. Fisher hovered, staring at the remains of vomit around her nose and mouth. Despite not being Susie, his sorrow manifested in a deep pain in his stomach. Her neighbour was close to the edge and he could barely see an occasional shallow breath. The medics piled in, their torches zipping around the faces. Holding two corners of the bed, he helped lift her out into the fresh air.

Gagging as he carried, barely managing to keep the vomit down, Fisher's feet shuffled along the metal floor. Lowering her weight, as the salty air hit his lungs he threw up on the deck, others around him following suit.

She wasn't in the third container either. The four women were safe, at least they didn't look the worst.

Barely composing himself he stood by the fourth. He didn't want to open it. He knew this would be Susie's and there was a good chance she could be dead, but in that moment, there was still hope. Before he looked, she was either dead or alive, a fifty-fifty chance. When he opened the container, it would be certain. As if understanding his reluctance, Harris pulled the bolt cutters out of his hand and snipped off the locks.

Together they pulled open the doors and took a tentative breath. Decay didn't hit their senses. Stale air the only change and hope welled as he stepped inside.

Two young women lay in the front pair of beds, both looked alive and strong. He rushed his survey forward with the torch and saw two empty beds, two pumps, two full IV bags but neither were connected. He checked the two faces again, pausing carefully over each before stepping back into the night with a slow shake of his head.

Rihanna was dead. She didn't need her bed.

The other should have been Susie's. He'd been too late.

52

"She's not on the ship," Clark said as Fisher answered the incoming call.

"How do you…"

Clark cut him off.

"He took a private flight from Anglesey airport to Barbados, the day we picked you up."

"And?"

"Manifest shows only one passenger," Clark said, but Fisher didn't let him finish.

"How does that help?"

"And a corpse," Clark said. Fisher shivered, his stomach cramping. "She's in the coffin. She's alive, I mean," Clark hurriedly said. "They must have wanted her quickly for some reason."

Fisher looked out into the ocean as he ran his thoughts back and forth over the words.

"What? How do you know?"

"Why take a dead body? They left the Summers girl on the slab."

Fisher paused, staring back out to sea, a weight lifting from his shoulders.

"Can we trace it?" he said quickly.

"It comes back as one of his holding companies," Clark said and hung up the call.

Fisher stood at the edge of the deck staring into the dark horizon, a void in the pit of his stomach.

How many times was this going to happen? Blind alleys. Hope dashed.

The Rashana swayed as he watched the might of Daring nearly with them. He stared at the ship, now brightly lit up from fore to aft. HMS Daring, a mighty symbol of a British power. Adventurous Courage, the meaning of the name.

Now was the time for his courage.

He had to carry on.

He had to keep going. Keep searching and travel with the team. To Barbados.

He felt Miller come up behind him.

"I'm sorry she wasn't here," he said, his voice softer than he'd heard before. Fisher ignored him. "What you did to the Captain earlier," he said then paused. "It was amazing. I've seen some funky shit in my time, but that takes the biscuit."

Fisher didn't react. He heard the scrape of Miller's feet as he turned to leave.

"I'm coming with you," Fisher said still staring out across the ocean. Miller stood still.

"I thought you'd say that. I think it's a bad idea," he paused again. "But I'm going to allow it. I've seen what you can do, so I guess there's no point objecting."

Fisher nodded.

"But remember, I'm in charge. I'm here to keep everyone safe, if you jeopardise the men then I will not pause for a microsecond before putting you down.

A familiar voice came from behind Miller.

"Don't worry, I'll look after him." It was Harris.

"Anyone else?" Miller said holding his hands in the air as he walked off.

53

Two hundred metres of flat sea separated the two ships as Daring came along side. The deck of the Rashana swarmed with more uniforms ferried over, mixing with the black clad soldiers fussing around the containers.

Fisher joined a huddle, keen to help and listened to the medical team agreeing to withdraw the drugs and let the women wake up over the next few hours so they could be thoroughly assessed. The Merlin would soon be launching to transfer them over in their sedated state.

Orders were soon shouted and radioed across the water and as Fisher watched, brightly coloured helmets busied around the aircraft on Daring's flight deck at her rear. With their safety checks completed, each hurried back and forth, releasing straps securing the Merlin to the deck. The rotors soon wound up to full speed and with a hand signal from a yellow helmet, it lifted into the air.

Within a minute the downdraft battered the deck of the Rashana. Fisher held his arm over his eyes as the helicopter perched across three containers, then he joined a chain of sailors as they pulled black kit bags and stretchers out of her loading doors.

Within five minutes the four sickest women were stretchered aboard and in the air, officially rescued. Four more trips and the rest of the women and the medics followed, the fifth trip reserved for the female corpse, treated with the same care as those who still had their lives.

The last took the body bag pulled from the engine room, rested on the floor with the remaining kit. The captain had explained through tearing eyes the boy had been so afraid of pirates.

Activity shifted, operators splitting kit bags to carry the gear to unseen locations while Miller and Bayne busied themselves around the contents of the crates dropped on deck.

For the next hour sailors documented the scene, detailing everything found in each of the containers. As each was photographed the contents were removed, placed in large plastic see-through bags and carried off to Daring.

Engineers followed behind, welding the doors shut, expert hands angling blowtorches to keep the appearance as normal as possible. They'd chosen the last container as their home for the onward journey and hands set about cleaning while others rigged cameras on each top corner.

Tiny holes for cables were drilled through the thin steel skin and miniature cameras fitted with fisheye lenses giving a one-hundred-and-eighty-degree field of vision. Breather holes were drilled around the roof and welders rigged the doors to be openable only from the inside.

Oxygen cylinders were loaded and a fridge-sized carbon dioxide scrubber, designed for submarines and spacecraft, was pushed into the corner to provide extra relief. Along with a thin, sound-deadening carpet, a fold up table and twin laptops were added.

Miller had planned for a team of six in the container, but with Fisher and Harris they would be pushing the upper limits of survivability. He made it clear their eventual exit may not be a purely strategic decision.

Together they inspected the finished work illuminated by the deck lights. Miller still complained about the lack of an emergency escape hatch but the engineers couldn't make it work in time. The Rashana's crew were temporarily released from their handcuffs and moved onto a waiting RIB for transfer over to Daring.

As the first signs of morning grew on the horizon, the time came to continue their journey alone. RIBs took the last of the navy personnel, except those staying as the new crew. Fisher heard news of a positive prognosis of the girls, all of which were now awake and suffering from dehydration and malnourishment, but nothing seemingly life threatening.

Harris joined him at the edge of the deck and they watched Daring slowly peel away before it disappeared from the horizon as the sun took its place.

Ten men to rely on, not a hundred and sixty. Four days to fill before he could dream of an end to the nightmare adventure.

As the four-man Royal Navy crew guided the vessel towards their objective, Fisher kept busy. He'd train with Harris, trying in vain to keep up with their special forces escorts. Hours running the short deck. Up and down the clanking metal steps. Down to the engine room, turning to run up to the bridge. Raising and lowering anything heavy they could find, fuel containers and engine spares in the most part. Pausing relentless in the press-up position, weights bearing down on their backs, then sit-ups with an elephant's weight on their chests.

Fisher marvelled at the capability of the human body, but soon settling for his own lesser pace, a mean effort, nonetheless.

When they weren't training their bodies Harris would show him more dimensions to the communicator. He learnt how to carry out basic thought commands and she trained him how to track team members, programming his phone to be able to locate her implant and the transponders each of the team carried around their necks.

In the evening they would all sit together, chowing on their ration packs. He'd listen intently to their stories of war and conflicts he hadn't even heard of and tales of misadventure he struggled to believe.

Over the next four days he got to know the team. Although Miller was the officer and the senior on the operation, Biggy ran the men and the respect they held for him couldn't be clearer.

His short stature wasn't the only reason for his nickname, at five foot eleven the comparison could only have been to his fellow squad-mates. He could always be found in the middle of conversations, whether serious or light-hearted, he gave his fair share to the others.

Boots, a sniper specialist, was tall and thin, packed with plenty of muscle. Hailing from the North East of England, judging by his accent, in the rare times he spoke his words were usually thought-provoking or profound. Fisher guessed his role gave him plenty of time to think and reflect while covering his buddy's backs or poised to perform a pinpoint strike.

Lucky was the squad medic and practical joker. All of the squad liked a laugh but from what he'd seen so far, Lucky was in the middle of a joke, either the source of the setup or being paid back for some earlier prank. Bayne, Fisher already knew, the engineering and technical specialist, he would be in charge of the surveillance while they were in the container. He hadn't talked much since the Hercules and Fisher wasn't about to change that.

The last of the group was Hotwire. He started his career in the Fleet Air Arm, which was an unusual route of entry into the Special Boat Service, but his flying skills had come in handy on a mission a few years ago.

In desperate need he stole a light helicopter, helping them out of some sticky situation or other. People said he had a chopper stashed somewhere in South America and planned to pick it up when he left the service.

***

Waking with a start, Fisher heard gunfire cracking on the deck above. He startled to the empty bunks around him and jumped out of bed.

Pulling the Glock out of the holster still strapped around his shoulder, he pushed open the wooden door, crashing it against the ship's superstructure. Running up the stairs he burst into the bright sunshine where shots lit the air right above him. Through the outer door he turned upwards to see Harris, Biggy and Hotwire stood on the roof of the bridge, handguns out in front, firing at blue barrels, their makeshift targets set out on the stern.

Panting away the panic, he pushed the Glock back into its holster as he tried to recover his breath and hide the alarm carried on his face.

Harris caught sight of him and beckoned him up the steps on the side of the bridge. Before he climbed, he rubbed his eyes, they'd been on board two days now and his body ached from relentless training.

Dragging himself up the steps he caught sight of the arsenal of weapons laid out across the wide faded roof. As he looked along the line-up of assault rifles and handguns, Biggy spotted him, shouting over with an assault rifle in his hands.

"Did we wake you?" he said wearing a smile. Fisher shrugged, did a complete turn marvelling at the calm, featureless ocean. He flinched as Biggy popped off five rounds in quick succession, watching the new holes appear in tight formation.

"Want a go?" Hotwire called. A smile replaced Fisher's sleep weary frown and he pulled out his Glock. He peered down the range, chose his target, aimed for the centre section and reeled off six rounds. Pausing, he admired the scatter pattern he'd created in the blue plastic.

"Not bad," Hotwire said at his shoulder. "Give me the gun."

Fisher handed it over and Hotwire released the clip. Placing it on the deck he bent at the knees, scattering the remaining rounds on the hot steel roof. He pulled a box of rounds from his combat trouser pocket, then refilled the clip with a random sequence of live and blank shells. Handing back the weapon by the barrel, he kept hold of the clip.

"You've got a slight flinch when you fire. Aim at your target," Hotwire said pointing down range. Fisher pointed the unloaded Glock at the same barrel. Hotwire's hand appeared from the right of Fisher's vision, placing a silver coin on the top of the slide.

"Try to keep it there as you pull the trigger back," he said. Fisher applied pressure and the coin clattered to the roof. Hotwire replaced it and after a few more attempts he learnt to pull the trigger straight and level to stop the coin falling. Hotwire handed the clip back and Fisher pushed it home.

"First one's blank. Now try to stop anticipating when the gun will go off," Hotwire said over his shoulder. Fisher felt himself tense each time he pulled the trigger, his body readying itself for the loud explosion and the force of the recoil. The blanks had all the noise and drama but with hardly any recoil, the anti-climax helped his body to relax and his targeting became tighter.

"Of course, in real situations you only have microseconds to aim. It needs to be an instinctive reaction, muscle memory and for that you'll need weeks of training. But we can still have some fun," said Hotwire, as he handed over one of the machine guns they'd used to clear the Rashana.

Fisher holstered his empty Glock and carefully took the large black killing machine, handling it like a baby. Hotwire explained the weapon was a carbine, the Heckler & Koch HK53, and gave him a crash course on its use, pointing his finger at components on his mirror image weapon in his hands.

After the five-minute tutorial he passed him a full magazine as Harris moved and sat as far behind him as possible, pushing her fingers in her ears.

Following Hotwire's guidance, Fisher pushed the magazine home, set the rotary selector above the grip to fully automatic, pushed the cocking handle down with the palm of his hand and rested the stock into his shoulder.

He pointed the lethal weapon down the range, lined up the two sights, took a deep breath and gently squeezed the trigger. As the trigger reached halfway two rounds reeled off in quick succession. The recoil felt lighter than he'd expect. Pulling the trigger again, all fury exploded from the muzzle, spent cartridges showering out of the side, pinging as they hit the steel floor. The magazine emptied in seconds. His smile made his face ache.

"Fun, isn't she!" Hotwire said as he handed over another magazine.

***

In the quiet time Fisher tried to condition his mind. He knew he had to stop thinking about Susie. He had to stop thinking the worst, or best, could be around the corner, resolving to take every knock back, every blind alley, as part of the journey.

He cared for her, he craved to see her, to know she was okay. He loved her. He already knew before she disappeared, but now he knew how deeply he felt for her. Not a sexual love. He didn't fancy her. He didn't want to marry her. He cared for her, like he thought he would love a sister.

Often his thoughts would turn to Harris. With her, pure animalistic drive took over. The perfect woman. Her body and what it could do. Her brilliance and how much she cared, but he couldn't make a move yet, if ever. He couldn't do anything to get in the way of the hunt.

But maybe when this was all over, maybe he would really find out how she felt. Maybe.

But now it was time.

The waiting was up. Again.

54

With the coast looming on the horizon, Miller declared the time for wandering the deck had ended and ordered the squad single file into the dreary light of the container.

With three hours of sailing until the main port in Bridgetown, they performed their final drills and checked their kit one last time before pulling the container's heavy left door closed, leaving the right slightly ajar.

They travelled like this for two hours, Fisher longing for the freedom of the deck to stretch his legs. Sitting in one spot in the slowly drifting heat had already taken its toll on his aching muscles.

A knock echoed on the side of the metal container, the signal from the crew he'd dreaded and time to say goodbye to the wisp of air. He watched as the crack of sunlight disappeared to nothing, the dim light of laptop screens, their brightness turned to a minimum, the only remaining source fighting away the complete blackness.

Fisher turned to the screens, his only other choices were to close his eyes or stare at the washed-out features of his fellow passengers. Instead he stared at the live satellite view, their vessel a wedge shape just visible in the centre of the image transmitted thousands of miles from a borrowed US surveillance asset.

Finding if he didn't blink, he could just about make out their slow progress. The round twin images on the other screen were almost as unmoving, the calm waters and distant coast barely changing as he tried to remain still, tried to think of anything but those doors opening in a hail of bullets.

Mostly he thought of the growing heat, watched as Bayne would wipe down the laptop screens to prevent the condensation killing their advantage. Averting his eyes, one by one each of the team stripped to their bare chests, Harris showing no hesitation as she stripped to her bra. He tried not to stare, tried not to look out of the corner of his eye. Tried not to peer at her beauty in the pale illumination.

A low hum came from the back of the container as the scrubber kicked into life to clean the air of the killer exhaust. He turned back to the distorted image through the fisheye lense. His heart began to pound at the sight of the stretched-out port.

Within twenty minutes they were stationary dockside, lolling gently side to side. The image to port followed stacks of containers rising and falling. To starboard, a mammoth rusting vessel did the same. Fisher could feel the tension in their hiding place, each of them steeling themselves for the sensation of the crane lifting them to the dock, a process each man and woman knew had not been designed with live cargo in mind.

An hour of searing heat passed before the thump of clamps reverberated around the hollow container. Fisher grabbed at one of the hooks welded to the metal skin and watched Harris turn side to side, her gaze catching on his and she shuffled up to share his hold. The others grabbing at what they could.

The container raced upward, the sensation in their stomach at first much like an express elevator until they zipped to the left, swaying side to side at a halt mid-air. He tensed and felt her hand tighten in anticipation of the drop, the crash to the hard dock floor, but the landing felt lighter than he'd expected and he gave silent thanks to the unseen operator's care.

Eight pairs of eyes scanned the fisheye images, each glad to see they were safely on the dockside and seemingly anonymous among hundreds waiting for collection. The clamps released with no delay, thirty seconds later another container landed with a crash on top of them.

Two more consecutive clatters and they knew they were at the bottom of a pile. Fisher eyed the satellite screen, the image speckled with static. Adrenaline subsiding.

The hours passed and he found sleep impossible, the heat barely tempered with the containers sheltering them from above. He slipped in and out of waking dreams, unable to tell one minute from another. The doors pushed open and she was there, pushed open again and danger loomed large in the shape of a giant tiger.

He tried to shake the visions, instead stared in Harris's direction. Her eyes were closed, her face serene as she rested her head against the steel wall. He flinched as he heard her talk, despite being sure her mouth hadn't moved.

"Don't say anything," she said again, the voice loud and clear. No-one around them flinched, as if she'd said nothing at all. A thought occurred to him. The stress had been too much. He wasn't suited for this line of work. First hallucinations and now he was hearing voices in his head.

He remembered the implant as she spoke again.

"I'm using the communicator to talk. It's mind control, kind of freaks you out I know. It's a direct link, point to point, radius of about two hundred metres," she stirred and they made eye contact. A knowing smile on her face in the dim light. "I was going to trick you, but it's too hot to play games. Now be careful when you try this, once you've used your activation thought you need to watch what you think. Your mind might betray some inner emotion. With practice that'll improve." She smiled, turned and closed her eyes.

Oh shit, look away, he thought, knowing the thoughts running around his mind every time he saw her delicately lit, curvaceous body. Stop, he said almost out loud. He tried to turn his thoughts to the mundane. He thought of running, his feet pounding the pavement. He thought of his friends back home. He thought of Susie. He said his activation command in silence.

"How's that?" he said without moving his lips. "What a stupid thing to say," he thought and pressed his finger to his mouth. "Oops."

"Well done," she said.

"Fuckin' A." The thought slipped out and Harris laughed across the link.

"Now all you need to do," she said but he couldn't hold himself back and interrupted.

"Your tits are amazing. Shit, sorry."

"Don't worry, and thank you," she said. "All you need to do is practice thinking what you want to send. Mentally visualise pushing them down a phone line, then try doing the same but pushing the thoughts you don't want to send into a brick wall. If you keep pushing most of your thoughts to the brick wall, with practice only those thoughts you want to will be transmitted."

Like a recovering Tourettes sufferer he spent the next few minutes practising, his conversation punctuated with random swearing. Then he stopped. Bayne shuffled in his seat and all eyes were on the CCTV images, their ears tuning to the rise of voices outside.

Soon no one could fail to hear the chatter, each gaze fixed on the screens and the two Caribbean men, one plump, one thin, both wearing customs uniform topped with hi-vis waistcoats. They walked along the corridor between the stacks of containers. Over the shoulder of the plump guy he carried a set of bolt croppers and at each container they stopped to examine a clipboard carried at the thin officer's side.

The pair soon stood outside their doors with a dread filling Fisher's thought. In none of the scenarios racing through Fisher's head could he imagine they wouldn't be able to feel the humidity and stench of the eight bodies festering in the steel box. The bigger man lifted the mechanical jaws up. Hotwire had his gun levelled as the jaws wrapped around the fake lock.

55

"Wait," came the high voice of the thin official as he held his palm in the air, his eyes darting over at his clipboard. The padlock rattled against the thin steel as the pincer released its grip.

After several missed breaths he tucked the clipboard under his scrawny arm, a hand rummaging in his trouser pocket. Fisher drew in towards the screen, watching as he pulled out a crumple of paper. All eyes scanned the creases, the short guy flicking between it and the printed declaration stuck to the side of the container.

"It's on the list," he said shaking his head. The big guy stepped back with an intake of breath, then rotated and they swapped glances, holding each other's attention for what seemed like an age before turning and moving onto the neighbour.

Fisher swapped a look with Harris and she replied with a shallow nod. They knew something. The tension dissipated and Hotwire's stance relaxed, the assault rifle's muzzle dipping towards the floor.

"Hey," came a distant call from the other side of the metal. Muscles tightened in an instant, eyes scanning the screens as a small green van rushed in from the left of the frame. They watched three guys unfold from the cab. Two wore the same uniform, the third, who was at least a foot taller, wore a shirt and tie underneath his bright yellow vest.

Plump and thin came back from the right, the scrap of paper hurriedly jammed into a pocket as they meandered to the newcomers. Fisher sat only a few feet away as the shirt and tie ordered plump to crop the locks on their container. All were surprised when thin put up a valiant defence, claiming it had already been searched and cleared, but his objections were cast aside with a sweep of a hand.

Hotwire snapped his weapon upright, Lucky joining by his side. Biggy stepped up but instead of setting his own stance, he placed his hand on Lucky's barrel, pushing it towards the floor. His left hand drew a three-sided rectangle in the air then pushed his palm out flat. Fisher watched as both relaxed at the unreadable signal.

The locks fell one by one and the two uniforms strained at the clamps in vain, joined reluctantly with thin and plump, but still the clamps held firm. The shirt and tie grunted and pulled them back, eyeing the seals of the container. Fisher shot an alarmed look at Biggy. Hotwire and Bayne had their rifles aimed.

The next few moments happened in a blur; Harris turned to the screen pulling on her shirt. She scanned left and right, the rest of the operators pushed to the door, Biggy following behind.

Fisher watched as they didn't stop. Hotwire pulled the catch, fresh air and blinding light streamed into the container. He watched them on the screen, only hearing their footsteps as they swarmed the wide-eyed officials, grabbing their throats and covering mouths, each soon overwhelmed and down on the hot tarmac.

Following Harris, they were bundled into the back of the van as she pulled open the unlocked doors, the suspension bouncing with each sudden addition. Fisher watched as she looked at the camera, her mouth silently forming his name.

Shielding his eyes, he met her at the back of the van where Biggy and Miller were quiet in discussion, thick handled knives held to each of the captive's throats.

"We can't let them go, they'll give us up in a second," Biggy whispered.

"We can't take them with us. There's no room and not enough air," Miller said.

"We can't kill them, well maybe these two," Biggy said, his knife pressing harder at the throat of the plump one whose eyes flinched with tears. Harris tapped Biggy on the leg as he stooped.

"Leave it with us," she said, much to Biggy's surprise. "This is where he earns his passage."

Without delay or complaint, the operators withdrew the knives one by one and backed out of the van, disappearing around the side. Biggy was last out, Harris took his rifle and pointed it into the darkness.

"You know what to do," she said to Fisher, not taking her eyes or aim from the trembling captives.

***

Fisher stepped back into the darkness of the container and watched the van disappear out of view. Harris came back within a few moments more. With the door sealed, he breathed the last remnants of the fresh air and slowly felt himself relax, only for his heart rate to spike with a clash of metal reverberating through the box. He turned to the screen to see the top container flying out of sight.

Thirty seconds later the crane's arm returned, a loud metal thud and the clamps located and lifted the next two, one after another until their home sat alone on the tarmac.

Another thirty seconds and they were gently placed on the back of an articulated flatbed truck, the landing gratefully cushioned by the trailer's suspension. The front cameras pointed at the back of the cab and the rear cameras to the brown doors of another container. They were blind and it would soon be time for the action to begin. Time to find if Fisher had succeeded with the captain.

They lurched forward, the roads smooth as they dressed and packed their gear away in black rucksacks. Biggy pushed out energy bars, making signs for everyone to eat.

The roads soon began to deteriorate, up and down potholes, thrown left and right with sharp corners. As they juddered along Bayne tried in vain to track their position by the grainy satellite image. After twenty minutes and a quick right turn, the lorry slowed as it bounced over deep ruts, jarring the passengers inside. Just as his nausea began to peak, the truck stopped, shuddering into reverse.

A few seconds later and the noise of the engine increased in pitch and they caught first signs of the driver, a short, grey afroed man in blue dirty overalls as he appeared between the cab and the container. Operating long ball-topped levers, the rear container slowly slid away from the cab and for the first time he realised they'd arrived, their destination slowly coming into view.

To the front there wasn't much to see, just an expanse of green countryside surrounded by cut grass, bushes and trees that were much like at home, but the plants were slightly different, bigger and just a touch alien to him.

In the rear view they could see two containers already unloaded through giant doors, sat on a packed mud floor in a tall, red painted wooden barn.

Fisher counted at least two men watching the process from inside.

They wore farmer's dungarees, their edges slightly shabby, like the building, but he saw no visible weapons. Biggy lifted his hand in his peripheral vision. Fisher turned and saw no smile, just his thumb pushed out in front of him, pointing to the ground.

No sooner had the first container landed on the hard-packed mud, the driver scrambled with opposite of Caribbean pace to the back of the trailer, pushing the ramps vertical.

The engine note changed as they jolted forward and back, sliding through another set of doors and dropping without grace. Light cut from the screen and the barn doors folded closed, the truck already in the distance with the last crack of light. As the image rebalanced, Fisher saw no sign of the spectators.

Biggy took short and considered steps to the back, his hand twisting at a large red valve just visible. His fingers pushed at a button to its right. The silence Fisher thought he'd been hearing, deepened further.

His chest tightened, his breath drew in. He knew the psychology but there was no telling his body. Fisher turned back to the exaggerated view from the cameras and the cavernous interior of the barn. The long, dark beams running across the vaulted ceiling and the windows the length of the wall, their glass thick with years of grime.

All at once, eight pairs of eyes spotted movement on the left of the video feed. Each pair saw the same jumble of figures two containers along and as their voices began to carry through the steel, a loud clash of metal confirmed their struggle with the doors impossible to open with blows alone.

Voices raised further, the frustration clear in the language which seemed to be almost English. As a single voice rose clear from the crowd, the others faltered and the flurry of activity stopped. They watched as the figures moved closer, crowding the next container. The hammer blows came again.

Now closing on their immediate steel neighbour, Fisher counted three distinct figures in the circular camera image. Out of the corner of his eye he saw Boots hold three fingers in the air. The locks fell to the floor and hands reached around separate clasps, swapping to try the others as they failed in turn, their frustration clear in their angered demeanour.

Hands held up in the air, the voices turned to argument. Still it was difficult to make out all but the occasional word recognisable as English through the rapid delivery and deep accent. The voices abruptly died and they walked the way they'd come, quickly disappearing from view.

Biggy looked around each of his men in turn, then to Harris, all nodding a reply to the unspoken question. He stepped to the doors, Harris guiding Fisher to the back of the container. The team silently stepped forward, weapons ready for mortal combat.

Hotwire stood next to Biggy with a hand in the air and five fingers splayed out, barely visible in the low light. A flash of light came from the laptop. A barn door slammed to their left. Biggy nodded; Hotwire counted down silently on his fingers.

Four.

Three.

Two.

Biggy's hand went to the lever.

One.

Zero.

As he pulled the level up the team surged forward, bumping together as the door stayed firm.

Recovering quickly, the crew slid back giving Hotwire space as he held the lever. Biggy shoulder-barged the door with his bulk, but it didn't move.

They were trapped.

56

The team shuffled noiseless, further back into the darkness as Bayne leant forward, angling his head at each face of the lever.

Fisher looked to the laptop. Using the trackpad, he zoomed in on the picture of the door until it loomed large in the extremity of the fisheye lens. Pointing to the screen with Harris peering over his shoulder, he saw no reason for the failure of the lock. Fisher quietly called to Bayne.

"Wriggle the lever up and down."

Bayne did as asked, but Fisher saw no movement on the live feed. With a few steps he stood at the doors, lowering to his shoulder and squinting to peer through the tiny gap at the bottom of the tall steel doors.

Along its length he could see a slit of light leaking from the other side. He crawled along the width inspecting every inch, Bayne moving out of the way as he cut across his path. At the far end he saw the problem. One of the large bolts had slipped out of place by a tiny fraction, enough to jam the container door shut.

"Do we have tools, something flat?" Fisher said quietly in the darkness. Bayne produced a knife and handed it over and Fisher fed it into the gap, but as he pushed the tip it just wedged tight.

"Anything thinner?" he whispered, but nothing came forward.

Jumping to his feet, he peered around the interior, at the stark contents and what each held in their hands. Nothing caught his eye until he saw the table. Moving up to the simple chipboard, he offloaded the two laptops to the floor, mindful of the cables disappearing off to each camera. Straining in the reduced light, he examined the table whilst still holding the knife in his hand.

An idea struck him and he rolled the table on its side and felt around the edge in the low light. Finding what he needed he jabbed the combat knife in between the layers of the tabletop, working it backwards and forwards. After a few moments he handed the knife to Harris, put his fingers either side of the gap he'd made, then pulled the stiff laminate from the chipboard underneath. With a fist size piece snapped off, he knelt back by the door.

By this time Bayne had figured out his plan and stood ready with the handle, while Fisher slid the thin but rigid laminate, pushing it easily through the crack under the door. After a quick action of his wrist he nodded to Bayne. The lever went up and light spilt in as the door eased open, bathing them in a welcome waft of fresh air.

With a wide smile Bayne nodded in his direction and gently thumped him on the arm. As they stood smiling, relieved at no longer being trapped in the metal hell, a click came from the other end of the container. All eyes shot on Hotwire as his left hand frantically pointed at the laptop screen, the other beckoning the door towards them. Staring at the screen, they realised they were not alone.

Bayne quietly pulled the door tight as they watched a lone native amble towards them with his hands in his jeans pocket. Slowly walking from the other end of the barn, he peered at each of the metal doors in turn, his feet absently kicking a plume of dust from the ground.

Breath seemed to stop in the container as the figure wandered around the side of their container where the front camera's picked him up for the first time.

His heart pounding, Fisher watched intently as the guy walked absent-minded around the barn, his own gaze flitting toward the dirty windows and the faint green on the other side.

Fisher's impatience grew. Every passing second could mean the return of the other men. He could talk this single guy around, but an angry mob would mean spilt blood and no one wanted that. He formed a plan in a flash but with no time to talk it over, the rest of the team staring at the laptop screen, Fisher lifted the lever and quietly pushed open the oiled door to flood light across the interior.

A quick glance back and their shocked expressions confirmed it was the last thing the team had expected as they turned to him, weapons pointing in his direction. Fisher pushed his finger to his mouth as they stared back. Biggy stepped forward, but Harris put her hand up to stop him. She'd understood.

Pushing the door up behind, he drew in a deep fresh breath trying to make as little noise as possible. Taking a second to bathe in the pure air, he let the comparative coolness of the Caribbean day suck away his fatigue.

The moment passed and taking care with each step, he turned around the side of the container before stopping and listening. With no movement apparent he leant around the metal side and saw the guy still staring out of the window, getting a good look at his wiry frame and grey flecks in his tight short hair. He looked more like a farmer than a money-hungry mercenary.

Fisher stepped forward, treading the hard-packed mud as if made of tin foil, taking one step slowly forward, then another. Fisher hadn't heard any sound but still his target turned towards him, his eyes wide open and flitting right then left, then back at Fisher before freezing still.

Taking his chance, Fisher lurched forward bent at the waist and arms reaching out in a pincer. The guy stood frozen, his eyes growing impossibly wide, fixed to the spot with indecision as Fisher ran at him. It took until Fisher's right shoulder smashed square in his stomach, taking him to the ground before he gave a reaction. Both were down in the dirt, their breath pushed outward as they hit.

The guy woke from his fright, sending punches at Fisher's face, but his fists were too close to get any real power behind the attack. Fisher tried to grab at the flailing arms but the fists kept flying. Pushing his head tight to the guys chest, he held his hands on the guy's frightened face.

"You trust me," he blurted out. "I'm not trying to hurt you." The blows weakening as the words processed, eventually stopping as his will to fight dwindled.

Still laying on top, Fisher felt the guy's muscles relax and as he began to squirm, he rolled off into the dirt. Picking himself up, Fisher watched the familiar confusion and offered his hand out, pulling the guy from the floor before brushing himself down with his palms.

He couldn't help but laugh and felt the tension fall.

"Sorry about that," Fisher said. "I thought you were someone else." The guy's eyes were still wide. The confusion still present. "I'm a friend of Tristan's. Just out for a wander," Fisher continued. As he spoke his face relaxed from their tension. "Sorry fella, what's your name?"

"Gus," came the deep accented voice. Fisher stuck out his hand.

"Pleased to meet you Gus," he said shaking the extended palm. "Tristan asked me to do a security review."

"Oh," Gus replied, his arms slouching to his side.

"How many guys have you got?" Fisher asked, taking a step towards him.

"Ah, twenty including myself."

"Weapons?"

Gus nodded.

"We got AKs and Hi-powers."

"Are you expecting a war?"

"Always," Gus replied.

Fisher contemplated his next question, but before he could speak, he heard the creak of a wooden door and looked to the side to see light spilling from the other end of the barn. His attention flicked over.

Two of the others had returned, one holding the rubbered handles of a rusty wheelbarrow, in its bucket sat a bright blue oxyacetylene gas canister. Their gazes met and he let go of the handles, the barrow legs thudding against the baked ground, the cylinder crashing to the thin metal of the barrow.

"Who the fuck is he?" the guy shouted at Gus.

"He's with Mr Sir. Doing a security review," Gus casually shouted back. Fisher smiled in their direction. They stared wide-eyed and walked towards him.

"Are you fucking stupid?" he said and turned to Fisher. "Who the fuck are you?" His yellowed eyes were wide, his mouth scowling. A few steps forward and he reached around to his back and pulled out a handgun, pointing it at Fisher's head.

"I wouldn't do that," Fisher said, his empty hands out in front. The other guy pulled out an identical weapon as they held their position. Fisher turned to see Gus's face full of confusion.

"But, but," he stammered, then grabbed his head as though he had a terrible ache.

"What you done to him?" the other guy sneered and began to march forward waving the gun like a baton to an angry tune.

57

Fisher blinked as air coughed at his back. The two men fell to the floor, their bodies thudding into the dust. Turning, he watched blood pool around Gus's head, a sudden guilt biting. He stared at his round blank features. He'd been naive, but not innocent in all this.

Movement drew his attention and he turned to see Biggy, Boots and Miller still peering down the sights of their silenced HKs.

Before the thick crimson could reach his foot, he moved away, watching Biggy whisper orders and the men peeling off to the four corners as they appeared from around the container with their heads raised and mouths wide sucking in deep breaths.

Fisher watched the corpses confirmed and disarmed, Miller exaggerating the show of each weapon's brass filled chamber, much like Harris had before.

Startled by a touch at his shoulder, he turned to see Harris.

"You okay?" she said, her voice soft and quiet.

"Yeah, I'm fine," he said trying to hide the lie.

"You were brave," she said, her eyebrows raised. He knew she probably thought something else but couldn't bring herself to say.

"And stupid," Biggy added interrupting. "But the primary intel could be worth it."

"Makes up for the satellite going to shit," Bayne added at his side.

Fisher smiled to himself, then waited for the questions which didn't come. No one asked why Gus had been so willing and before he could think about it anymore, Biggy beckoned him back over to Gus's limp body. Doing as told, Fisher dragged the corpse towards the container by the shoulders.

Harris watched at the far window. Bayne followed Fisher and began busying himself inside the container, ripping at cables, meticulously piling every scrap of evidence into his rucksack, leaving Fisher to wonder how he would fit the oxygen cylinder and fridge sized scrubber into the same bag. His train of thought fell away as he saw the plastic rectangle of green dough in Bayne's hand.

Ten minutes later and with the dead sealed away, Fisher helped to kick up dust, covering the patches of black soaked earth as he listened to Miller and Biggy quietly review the tactical situation.

Observations around the building, and the still grainy real-time satellite image, confirmed the entrance road came in from the north, the doors they were loaded through faced out to the east. Both aspects had nothing but wild land for miles and with sea to the south, they were right on the coast in the middle of nowhere. Perfect operational territory.

To the west sat a large house, a three-storey colonial palace with grassland stretching between it and their location. A well-worn path ran between the two. They had an hour before the sun would retreat and they would kick off the assault, storming the house at twilight.

A force of seventeen lightly armed, poorly trained locals had been accounted for so far, none of which would be a match for their training and the advantage of surprise.

Harris and Fisher were ordered to wait in the barn for when the most dangerous phase of the operation had been completed. Fisher willingly butted in with agreement. He had no plans to be shot.

The last hour of light passed swiftly, during which time they made their final preparations. Packing up their gear, they were careful not to leave any evidence of their existence, knowing full well their presence on the island broke numerous international conventions.

The time soon came for the group to separate and Fisher stood next to Harris, his gaze fixed as the shadowy figures left the barn one by one, fading out of sight across the grassland. For the first time in five days they were alone and the building felt very empty.

Seemingly unconcerned, Harris fiddled with her phone rather than watching the team head out to danger. Fisher couldn't understand how she could keep so calm. Unlike her, nervous energy filled him to the brim. Despite his best efforts trying not to think about it, he felt so close to Susie.

Surely she must be here this time?

The light had faded quickly and they sat in the dust with silence between them and their backs against the wall away from the sticky blood-soaked floor. Harris moved her head sharply to the side sending Fisher's thoughts looking for the reason why. Had she heard something?

Straining to hear, he only caught the incessant call of insects, the likes of which he'd only heard before in films. He turned his head but could barely make out her beautiful features. Without warning he felt her warm hand on his upper leg, sending a bolt of electricity up through his groin. Not wanting to move, not wanting her to either, he tried to keep still.

His concentration fell apart, thinking only of her hand on his leg. Her long slender arm. Her athletic upper body. Her ample breasts. He tried to stop thinking, this wasn't the time and certainly not the place. The task seemed almost impossible until he heard the radio chattering on the other side of the thin barn wall.

58

Harris had heard the chatter too, her hand leaping from Fisher's leg and he turned, only barely making out her outline.

He heard her stand, the dirt scraping under her shoes. He did the same and a hand clamped around his wrist, gently guiding him along the wall and in between the metal containers. There they waited. The radio chatter soon passed but he heard what could be footsteps.

A minute later they confirmed they hadn't been hearing ghosts as a loud creak came from the barn door. A loud slam followed as it shut. Light and shadow pranced around the corrugated roof and they waited breathless, watching the dance move closer. It passed by with no pause, soon fading to nothing.

They listened intently to the footsteps on the dirt floor as the newcomer continued their journey to the right. The last of the light stopped moving, the ceiling brightly spotted in one place. Fisher reached out to the darkness in front to communicate with Harris, but he couldn't find her at arm's reach.

Something scraping on the dirt floor distracting his search, the sound of tiny stones dragging along a wooden board. Then came a dull thud, like a heavy sack being dumped on the floor. He wanted to call out to her. He wanted to know the plan he knew she would have already formed, but it was too late, he couldn't raise even a whisper for fear of drawing the visitor nearer.

Stifled to inaction, all Fisher could do was to watch the light grow brighter across his path.

Remembering the gun at his side, Fisher's fingers fumbled for the Glock as he stared at the narrow source of light passing the edge of the corner, the bright beam dazzling his vision as it turned in his direction. With his hand still struggling to get purchase, his heart sank at what would come next. The beam flashed from his eyes and he caught the shadow of her slender features.

"You got to see this," Harris said, beckoning him out of the darkness. His feet fixed to the spot, his breath racing in and out as he tried to catch up with what had just happened. With the light from the torch beam back in the main room he looked to his side, somehow expecting she would be by his shoulder. "Fisher," Harris called with an insistent whisper.

Taking a deep breath, he stepped forward and into the vast main space of the barn. To his right, stray light shone on a motionless mound slumped to the floor and as the torch beam caught, he saw a man huddled in the recovery position.

Next to the body stood a wooden crate full of fat yellowing bananas, the grey of a Browning Hi Power pistol contrasting as it sat on top. Fisher's gaze caught a thick sheet of plywood, which he ignored in favour of the large expanse of darkness to its side.

Harris passed over the torch and set about binding the man's arms and legs with his own shoelaces and while she dragged his weight behind the nearest container, Fisher stepped toward the darkness. The torch probed forward as the ground dropped away at his feet.

"What is it?" she said returning for the crate.

"Don't know?" Fisher replied staring down at light catching on the grey of stone deep in the partially covered hole. Without warning the torch blinked out. Fisher hit at its side to no effect and he jumped as Harris spoke close to his ear.

"What's wrong with it?" she said. He turned to see her face glow in the dim light of her phone's screen.

"It's done," he replied then looked back as her eyes widened. He knew to be quiet and watched her tap at the screen and as a smile raised in the corner of her mouth, she turned the phone around in her hand.

Fisher recognised the dark screen of the tracking app she'd briefly shown him back on the Rashana. Concentric circles grew from the centre, pinging their green dots as they rose from the middle of the screen.

He expected to see the blues of the team but instead three red dots blinked bright as the circles passed over, their positions jumping closer to theirs with every second. They were outside of the barn and he knew where Harris would usher him before he felt her hands on his shoulder.

Their hands gripped the edge of the heavy board and together they dragged it further to the side. Fisher could barely make out the dimensions of the hole, let alone the motion of her hands as she silently beckoned him into the darkness.

Still he went down on his behind, his legs dangling into the void below sending tiny stones and dirt showering down. He peered in, but it made little difference and felt the nudge of Harris at his back. He shuffled forward, trying to remember where he'd seen the stone floor and if it had covered the entire width of the hole.

With a second nudge and the sound of radio chatter growing near, he let himself drop with his heart in his mouth, his legs jarring as they hit the ground after what seemed like a long fall.

Barely getting his bearings, he felt the wood of the crate as Harris passed it down then lowering to his side without giving even a puff of air as she landed. Resting the crate beside his feet, he raised his hands and found he'd only dropped to the height of his shoulders. Together, they man-handled the thick wooden cover back over the hole where they found true darkness.

Fumbling with his phone, his torch app activated shortly before Harris's at his side. Blinking at the bright contrast the two beams scoured to get a feel for what they'd just dropped in to.

They stood on stone covering half the size of the opening, with their feet a twitch away from the first of many galvanised metal descending steps. Between the checker plate treaded steps he saw a long rotten predecessor, its wood crumbling back to earth. Spinning the torchlight, he examined the grey stone walls of a passageway which appeared to have been roughly carved out of the bedrock, decades, or longer ago.

The beam swept over an old metal light-switch mounted on steel conduit running along the left side of the wall. Following the conduit, he passed the beam over a caged glass bulkhead light a few steps below then counted one more evenly spaced lamp before the horizon of his light ended.

Sweeping the torch to the right he watched the steps disappear down into the unknown. He daren't touch the light-switch for fear of what else would illuminate, and where. Above his head hung a pulley wheel fixed into the ceiling, its metal worn silver but slick with clean grey grease.

Fisher angled the torch in Harris's direction and they stood listening, each silently debating their next course. They had to leave their promised post, but should they hide and hope for the best or explore what had been gifted to them?

Harris checked the sensor on her phone and watching over her shoulder he couldn't see any sign of the red dots above, but her head shook and Fisher guessed she didn't trust the screen. Stone walls could block any signal.

Sudden voices above gave the answer. With the decision clear to both, they turned, treading carefully as they headed down into the darkness. Shadows danced along the walls, their beams scouring every nook and cranny with their feet light footing each step.

Flicking his attention constantly upwards, he almost hit his head on the regularly spaced pulley wheels so many times as his gaze returned to watch the caged bulkheads clinging to the walls. The voices behind grew quieter with each step of what Fisher thought could be an endless descent.

A hundred steps saw the last of the metal and together they stopped as their feet landed on dusty, well-trodden stone. They waited, straining to hear but nothing came back except for the occasional drip of water from somewhere their phone torches couldn't penetrate. Walking on, passing two coils of bright red rope, the ends tied to form a sling, they slowed their pace further still.

Fisher could feel the temperature cool and the first wafts of an oaky tang filled the air. Not long after they found darkened casks of rum, neatly stacked two barrels high along the side of the corridor. As the corridor continued case after case of wines from all over the world rose high up the curved walls. European, Australian, African and American labels stood next to great curls and long drops of meat hung in a line above their heads as the corridor widened.

Without warning Fisher pushed his hand over the torch, fumbling the light off and Harris followed suit. He'd heard something, a noise he couldn't place. He tried to still his breath and listened again, stepping close to Harris, their elbows touching. Still only hearing his shallow breath, he waited, apprehensive in the darkness until another not so pleasant smell drifted their way. As he tried to picture the source, he caught another sound, but what made the noise he still couldn't tell.

Repeating his attempts to force his breath to slow, he waited for Harris's instruction, but instead remembered Miss White's austere lecture about the phone. Nearly bursting with laughter, he unlocked the screen, double pressed the home button and selected the night vision camera.

After a short pause the screen came alive with light, then blinked back to darkness. He pushed the phone out in front of him, but the screen remained stubbornly blank. About to growl in frustration, he felt a hand on his and Harris took the phone.

While angling the screen in his direction, she selected the menu and a list of options appeared. Passive mode showed a small white tick. She moved her delicate finger to Active mode and handed it back. The screen lit with a dull white as he pointed the lens towards the ground shining back with an eerie green as he pushed it out in front. He watched a green wall curve to black in the distance.

Shuffling forward, intent on the screen, squinting for any detail, the sound came again. The same as before, but this time he knew it was a whisper for sure.

Turning his phone towards Harris, the screen lit with her beauty in negative and he watched as she gave an exaggerated nod. She'd heard it too and he reached inside his jacket. Harris did the same and they edged forward with their guns out in front.

The whispering grew with each step, a woman's faint voice gently reverberating. A distinct second joined the low call. His feet crunched on a loose grain of gravel, the noise echoing like the loudest of horns. The voices stopped and he watched the nothingness of the corridor widen out in front of him.

His pace quickened and Harris's finger appeared as a black line on the screen. He watched as she switched the mode to Infrared and the picture changed again. Beacons of white light crowded horizontally across the screen, the ghostly light disrupted with dark vertical lines and he stopped, trying to decipher the meaning.

The glowing light moved and he stared at the screen. The heat moved again, growing taller, rising from the floor. Realisation came just as he heard a woman's timid voice in the darkness.

"Is there someone there?"

59

Fisher leapt into action, spinning on the spot, his fingers tapping at the screen until he could see the round of the wall switch a few paces back. Reaching out, probing with his fingers, he watched the screen and pushed at the metal. The room lit with an orange glow and turning, an involuntary sharp breath pulled into his lungs.

The dim light revealed a cavern stretching as wide as the barn and out just as deep. At the edges, rusting steel bars rose from the cold floor up to the hard stone ceiling more than double his height.

Ahead, the walls pulled in and an orange lit corridor disappeared around a corner. Only then did he catch the first signs of movement. Having almost forgotten the words he'd heard, he took a few steps forward with Harris matching his pace.

White shapes huddled in the corner of the cage to his right. More movement came at the edge of his vision and he turned left, catching more bundles of white. The images shuffled backward in his mind when he saw a woman standing, her hair almost snow white with one hand clasped around a steel bar, the other shielding her eyes from the dull light.

"Oh my god," Fisher said, his stare fixed forward.

"Help us," came her faint voice in reply. Her hand moved to reveal her stunning pale beauty. As Fisher stepped forward, he could see her full length white dress, the material so thin he could make out her shadow beneath its layers even in the poor light. Still walking, he scanned left and right, eyes widening with horror as bundles of material began to stir and frightened eyes peered back cautiously in his direction.

With each step Fisher could feel his heart pound deeper, every aspect of his body pulling down in the sorrow and despair of the room. His legs grew heavy and his breathing laboured. Harris touched his arm.

"Find a way to let them out. I'll cover the exits." Fisher watched as if in a dream, her right hand outstretched and finger pointed towards the corridor ahead. With her words he felt the weight lift and sprang into action, holstering his gun as he ran towards the closest of the standing women.

She backed away as he neared.

"It's okay, we're here to help you," Fisher said, keeping his voice low as he held out his palms. "How do we get them out?" Fisher said screwing his face up as he peered at the lock.

No one replied. She wasn't giddy with excitement, instead he could see the mistrust in her distant expression. A sob came from somewhere in the room and her expression seemed to relax.

"There's a box where you came in," her soft voice said with a pitiful cry, curling and echoing at his back. "It's all right. He's not one of them," she said looking past him. The cry died to nothing when Fisher turned, already jogging back to where they had come in.

With his head bobbing side to side to take in where each woman now stood and held themselves up against the bars. All were a near mirror of the next. Blonde. Classically beautiful. Hollywood's modern picture of perfection.

A wooden grocer's box he hadn't noticed on the way in stood beside the opening, its sides battered with age and the branding long faded to a smudge of colour. Flipping the box over, he found a large bunch of aged keys, each length and dimension identical. Gripping them tight in a fist, he rushed back and took a deep breath as he pulled up. He couldn't help but marvel at her beauty close up.

Finding it hard to break his gaze, he stood transfixed on her face. Tight lines of young, fresh skin ran unblemished by make-up. Her eyes were a striking blue, piercing somewhere deep inside him. Feeling the dig of the metal in his palm, he uncurled his fingers and began to fumble, rattling inside the steel lock key by key.

"What's your name?" he asked, his voice hoarse against a dry throat.

"Melissa, people call me Mel," she replied, her sound barely heard.

Fisher fumbled the bunch and the keys fell to the floor, its echo startling breath from around the room.

"I'm Fisher. Nice to meet you. How long have you been down here?" he said trying the fourth key.

"I'm not sure," she said, her voice now a whisper. Metal clanked against the lock and he barely could hear her as she spoke again. "I've been counting my meals. I guess about a month or more. I'm not sure," she said, her voice growing louder. "Some were here before me." The fifth key worked in the lock and Mel stepped back as the door swung with a loud whine towards her.

With the door fully open she sprang forward and he took a pace back as arms wrapped around him. Feeling her warmth, he heard excitement growing in the room and her overwhelming sense of joy as she hugged him tight.

His emotions built and he felt himself struggling to fight back a tear, her gratitude coming close to overwhelming him. Somehow, he managed to gently prise away her arms, but still she followed as he moved to the next cell, forgetting which key he'd used and began trying them all.

"Do you know why?" Fisher said looking back behind him. The murmur of voices stopped. Mel's face pointed to the dirt floor.

"We're sold."

"Not anymore," he quickly replied and behind him the chatter built even louder than before.

"They paraded us around, showing us off. We have to dance or do…" she stopped abruptly. "Do other things." She paused again as Fisher rattled through the keys. "We don't all come back down."

Fisher drew in a deep breath, not daring himself to think on her words, his mind struggling to stay focused when he heard the echo of his name in a voice he hadn't heard in such a long time.

60

"James?" the voice came again. Fisher looked up open mouthed, not daring to believe his ears.

But there she stood, draped in flowing white, a brunette halo of roots running from the top of her once blonde hair.

"Is it you?" she said blinking two cells down from where he stood. Fisher gasped at her blackened right eye and her bottom lip cut wide. He grabbed at the bars as he stumbled forward, his head so light.

"Susie?" he whispered, still not believing, fumbling through the keys with a renewed fever as he arrived at the barred gate. Her hands grabbed at his jacket, pulling him towards her, clinging through the bars, tight in an embrace. With tears in his eyes he pulled away knowing there would be a right time. Letting the water run down his face he sobbed with laughter, the keys jangling until the lock clicked wide. Barely letting the bars swing wide enough, she raced through the gap to clamp herself around him and squeeze the air from his lungs.

"I don't believe it, am I awake? You're okay," she said, disbelief in her voice as she fought with her emotions.

"I'm fine. I didn't dare to hope, but you, your face, what happened?"

"Just a scratch. I'm not like the others," she said peering timidly around the dark room.

He held her tight and they wept without holding back.

"I'll keep you safe," he said softly as she sobbed on his shoulder, turning her as they stood.

"They took someone else," he barely heard her say. "I wasn't good enough. They took someone else in my place."

Fisher held her close.

"I knew you'd look for me, but I never thought you'd find me."

As they embraced, he opened his eyes and saw the longing in the other pairs spread across the cave. He also saw the fear they'd get left behind.

Prising himself from Susie, he turned to see Mel stood watching, a wide smile on her sodden face, then to Harris with no tears, but the glimpse of a warm smile which turned flat with a nod and he understood the meaning. They had to get a move on.

Unlocking each cell, the women joined the procession behind him, Susie then Mel, walking in his wake as one by one he set them free. Having no choice but to accept each embrace until he could pull them off and move to the next, stopping only when the last of the locks opened.

Susie grabbed him again, turning him towards her and staring straight into his eyes with a seriousness that stopped his attempts to peel her away.

"I have to tell you," she said, her voice shaking with fear.

"What is it?" he replied, holding her by the shoulders.

"They know."

"Who knows what?" he replied raising his brow.

"They're coming to get you," she replied. Fisher gave a chuckle and kissed her on the forehead.

"It's okay. They found me. Everything's okay," he pointed to Harris and turned to look at the women clustered around him. He'd released eight frightened women in total. They'd been so right about the profile. Nine beautiful women, one more of a girl. Closer to sixteen than twenty. He grabbed Susie's hand and moved to where Harris stood guard. Like sheep they followed.

"We can't go the way we came. Our best bet is to move forward," Fisher said, leaning in to Harris.

"I agree," she said. "Upstairs should be clear by now." As she finished her sentence a loud clatter of metal echoed from the corridor ahead, nine pairs of eyes locking onto Fisher. In turn he stared at Harris wide-eyed. Each stood still, transfixed, listening for what was coming towards them.

The pound of speeding footsteps and the pant of heavy breath.

61

Fisher saw no panic in Harris's eyes as she ushered the crowd back. Fisher took the direction and corralled the terrified women through the chamber, heading back into the first corridor.

Looking over his shoulder he watched Harris remain, standing to the side of the opening with her Glock in her right, her left groping in her pocket. He turned and waved the women further around the corridor.

In the warm glow he watched the women huddling at his front. Susie's arms outstretched, groping for him. The others, white-faced, their eyes screaming with terror, their breath shallow and speeding.

He let Susie hug him tight whilst pushing his fingers to his lips in a vain attempt to prevent a catastrophic scream. Peeling Susie off for the second time, he turned, listening with intent. Above the din of breath, he heard the steps loud and fast and a collective gasp let out as a deep Bajan voice blurted.

"What de…?"

The sound of something metallic rattled to the dirt floor and with barely time for it to echo the sound replaced with a flurry of activity.

Turning to the women, he held his palms out, pulled out the body-warm Glock and stepped around the corner. Hugging the wall, he rounded to see a man, afro hair tight to his scalp, laying prone facing the floor clawing at a ligature wrapped around his neck with Harris on his back straining at the wooden ends of the wire rope. Fisher watched as his bulky hands dropped and the slow moment of death came, his fight flickering out.

He stared at Harris. Her determined expression. Knuckles white with effort with one last tug before dropping his face into the dust.

She released the cord and flexed her hands, looked up and saw Fisher stood watching. Her face replied without pride or elation as though she expected to be judged. Fisher walked slowly up to her. As she stood, he pulled her to an embrace. At first, she flinched against his touch, then gripped for a brief moment until they parted.

Without discussion, each grabbed a leg and dragged the hefty man across the dirt and into the nearest cell. Harris picked up the AK, released the magazine and threw the machine gun after him, stuffing the rounded metal into her jacket pocket.

Light footsteps echoed into the chamber, Susie the first to reach him and grab his arm. He watched the women's eyes as they darted around, one or two smiled as they saw the black mound in the cell. Mel came from the back and leant into Fisher. With her voice so quiet he could hardly hear.

"I heard something along the corridor behind," she said, her head flicking back from where she'd come. Fisher nodded and pulled his hand to her back, hurrying them forward towards where Harris stood with the dull bulkheads gently lighting their way forward.

It wasn't long before they came to a set of stairs just like the first. Harris lead the way into the eerie orange glow while Fisher hung back, counting each lamb as they followed. Susie clung to him as he lingered, their ears pricked for any sign from behind.

One by one they followed up the steps and found there were fewer than had led them down to the terrible place. Their short journey ended on a landing, their progress stopped by a large metal door covered in battered white paint flaking to the floor.

Fisher arrived to find Harris peering through the keyhole, its surround reinforced with a plate of riveted metal. He redrew his Glock and motioned the girls flat against the cool stone wall, but instead of trying the handle, Harris pulled him aside, his interest growing as for the first time he saw something alien in her face.

Concern.

She leant near. So close he could feel her breath on his ear.

"There's something I need to tell you before we go through that door," she whispered. Fisher kept quiet despite his instinct. "You've found Susie. Your priority is to keep these women safe."

He squinted and gave a shallow nod.

"Whatever happens you need to get these women away. You understand?"

Fisher turned his head, his lips nearly touching hers. They lingered for a second before she pulled back.

"What have you got planned?"

"Nothing," she replied, but her words did nothing to convince him." I need to find where the others are and the paper trail."

"Tell me," he insisted, knowing she wasn't telling him everything. "You know I don't need to ask."

She smiled and drew a deep breath, as if she knew the exact words he would use.

"He's a dangerous man. I'm here to make sure I finish him properly this time."

Fisher tipped his head to the side. "This time?" he said, leaning closer, but she kept quiet. He put his hands on her upper arms and leant in towards her. She nodded and started to speak.

"You're not alone. He can do things too. Somehow, he can control pain. He used to work for us, until he killed my mentor. We all thought he was dead." She paused to swallow and looked back down the corridor. "I thought I'd killed him. When we saw the photo on the wall, I knew I'd failed. So you get out of here and keep these women safe."

Fisher paused, contemplating her words. *He can do things too* stuck in his mind. He took her hand and gently squeezed, then turning to the door he saw nine faces smiling weakly in his direction.

Before his cheeks could blush, he turned back to the door and tried the handle. Fisher looked back at Harris as the handle turned. Without pause, she beckoned to him to open the door and as it swung wide she burst through, leading with her left shoulder and the Glock out in her right. Fisher jumped through to follow in her wake.

Bright with spotlights pointed the length of the wall to their right, their entry into the windowless room startled no defence.

"Clear," she called in a stage-whisper.

Painted crisp white with a sofa wrapped around two of the walls, a bar with a huge range of drinks took up the last. Along from the bar the wall filled with ropes, chains and studded leather leashes, each hung from hooks and arranged by descending size.

All around monotone photographs basked against the white, each with the same theme. Blonde Caucasian women in their prime. Clothes non-existent. Faces pained in posed erotica. Set in the far corner of the room, a short set of carpeted steps rose to lead up with a highly polished banister to the next floor and the shine of a dark wooden door.

"This is where they made us dance," Mel said, her voice quiet. He turned to see the girls had followed behind, each of their faces pointed to the floor.

"It's like a cattle auction," Susie added grabbing at Fisher's arm.

He turned to Mel to say something, but his attention caught by another wooden door at her back.

"What's through there?" Fisher said flicking his head towards it. Each woman shook her head, but the youngest took a step forward.

"Outside," she said. Fisher walked up to the door, closing the steel entrance to the dungeon and rattled the new handle. His survey shot around the room as he found it locked, but paused when he caught Harris heading up the steps. "The key is somewhere back there," the girl said, pointing to the bar before blending back into the crowd of white.

Rattling through the junk behind the bar he soon found a key, its size and shape looking right. He tested it in the lock. A perfect fit. He turned it anti-clockwise, the mechanism operating and he waved the women away from the arc of the opening. Out of the corner of his eye he saw Harris crouch, with his hand still holding the handle he waited for the all clear. As if she'd heard something, her eyes went wide and she frantically shooed them away with a flurry of her hands.

Fisher wretched open the door, gun out in front. He took a step through and fresh sea air wafted across his face. Despite the darkness he soon made out the white of waves crashing on the moonlit beach, sand only a short step away. Seeing no obvious trap left and right, he ushered the women out one by one.

"Run to the beach and keep going," he shouted. Harris stood bent at the waist, Glock out in front. "Let's go," he called.

"I'll be there in a minute."

Fisher turned on his heels and grabbed Susie's arm, following the barefoot race across the sand, counting up to nine as he checked each.

Five minutes of puffing and with aching legs from running in the sand, they huddled on the ground and he counted each exhausted puff of white.

"Where's Harris?" he said, twitching his head this way and that. Susie shook hers with wide eyes. Fisher snatched back to the house in the distance. Bathed in shadow, he could see no one in the bright of the sand running in their direction. He turned back to Susie and the panic on her face. She knew his plan before he did.

"Don't leave me," she cried. Fisher grabbed her by the shoulders.

"You're safe, I need to help her. She's the reason we found you."

"She told you to stay with us."

A battle raged in his head. He had to help but he had to protect Susie. He had to protect all of them. He had to protect Harris. He watched as the women sat down on the beach, their eyes darting as they huddled close.

"You love her, don't you?" Susie said, her face settling to stare at the ground.

"I think so."

Looking up she showed no surprise. Without warning his head racked with pain. A feeling different to anything he'd felt before. Somehow, he knew it wasn't his pain. Pushing his palms to his temples, the feeling subsided, leaving him weakened with dread icing his veins.

"Go," Susie shouted, pointing at the house.

62

Gunfire crackled, light flashing across the top floor windows as Fisher's feet slipped in the sand with the house growing in his vision at a frustrating pace. Calves burning, he arrived back at the door and with a quick glance across the beach, he burst back into the room where he'd last seen her.

Giving up his attempt to raise Harris on his phone, Fisher's gaze flinched at each difference. The open door from where she'd joined the battle. Bullet holes strafing across and the spray of blood pulling the breath from Fisher's lungs. Stumbling forward, his gaze caught on round brass embedded in the wall. Four shots had ripped through the wood and smashed into the clean white.

Gunfire rattled the air, but barely heard by Fisher's cotton-wooled ears as he trudged forward, lifting his feet one step, then the next with his hand grabbing tight to the banister. Forcing himself to keep steady breath, he crested the stairs. With sound rushing close, his muscles tested, energy surging when he saw a black guy slumped at the foot of the corridor's far door.

The air cracked again, this time at a distance but still he stooped as it rang, only standing tall when the air stilled once more. Pulling at his Glock he crept along the wood panelled corridor with his shoulder tight against the wall. He daren't look at the body as he stepped over and into a darkened kitchen the size of his entire flat, but the remains of the great battle took his mind from the comparison.

Bullet holes riddled each surface. Cupboard doors and windows smashed through. Crockery spayed in pieces, joining the great litter of spent cartridges across the streaked, tiled floor. And those smells. Copper and cordite. One inevitable with the other.

The house stood quiet, not even the creak of floorboards stirred the silence. Until with each of his steps the crunch of debris seemed to call out for him to be found. Without realising, he followed a line of blood which ended abruptly with another calming intake of breath. He took a long step over the dead mercenary, his head at a right angle against the wall, Fisher's gaze lingering too long on the yellow of the eyes which seemed to stare back into his soul.

Out of the kitchen he sped into a grand hallway, his feet sending hollow brass casings pinging across the floor. He turned upward to follow the dark panelled walls as they rose up the stairs spiralling high around the edge. One storey, then two more after.

Fisher pulled himself tight against the wall, his feet at the bottom of the stairs as combat flared unseen but not unheard. Too many options raced through his thoughts, to go this way or that, he had no idea. Three more doors stood on this floor alone. Another three on each of the floors above, plus more which were hidden from his vantage.

A stern voice seemed to call in his mind and he remembered the communicator. Double pressing the home button the screen came alive. Concentric circles pulling out from the centre. Dots, red, green and blue pinged all over the screen.

With a quick count, nodding to himself as each of the six blue dots moved however slowly in groups of two. He took the moment to recover his breath, counted eight hostiles in red, their pulsing lights spread and disorganised across the area, then he focused on the single green. The glowing green of Harris. The light sat stationary. A red beacon nearly purpling with intensity beside it.

Gunfire exploded above; the two nearest reds simultaneously vanished. Fisher raced up the steps, abandoning all hope of stealth. One floor up he stood in front of the door staring down at the screen. She was on the other side and he pushed the phone into his pocket, checked down the sight of his Glock and slowly turned the handle.

63

With the gun pushed ahead, Fisher yanked the door wide, forcing his survey around the room then repeating again in vain.

The bedroom stood empty, with the only sign of life being a single shaded bedside lamp glowing to the right of the dark wooden bed dressed as if ready to be slept in.

With the Glock in his right and the communicator in his left, Fisher couldn't understand how the dot appeared in front of him on the screen.

Twisting and turning whilst watching the view move confirmed the device worked. He had the right location. He stared at her green dot, its brightness so close to his, he knew he should be able to reach out and touch her.

Looking up again, he checked he hadn't missed anything when a creak of dry wood came from above, the realisation hitting him with alarm. The screen showed two dimensions. Above stood the third.

With his heart thumping from the run up the stairs, he stood outside a door identical to the one below, even down to the bright shine of the brass handle where hands had polished better than any cleaning routine.

Wrapping his fingers around the metal, a muffled deep voice startled him. A voice from beyond the door.

"Come in," the voice repeated. Catching the sound much more clearly this time, he recognised it in an instant, despite having only heard it once before.

Fisher pushed the door with the barrel of his Glock and standing in the room he saw the man he knew only as Tristan. The door had opened onto a wide bedroom, the same, for all intents, as the one below. A four poster on the far wall, dark furniture lining the flowered wallpaper.

Tristan stood tall, his left hand clamped, fingernails biting into Harris's neck as she knelt facing towards Fisher. In his right he held Harris's Glock jammed at her temple. Neither the scene or the split in the side of her forehead gave him the greatest shock, it was her blank expression and the tears drying down her face overwhelmingly pleading for him to leave. At her knees he caught sight of the green circled screen of her phone. His green dot joining hers, washing away the blur of the red.

Tristan wore a long sleeve shirt with the top two buttons undone. The collars leafed wide either side and the arms rolled in neat folds past the elbow. His hair matched when they'd met in a whole different climate, thick strands quiffed high in manicured perfection. His expression was the only clear difference. The smug, deceitful curl of his lip replaced with a manic wide smile showing his perfect whites. His eyes reddened around the edges with effort.

Fisher stretched out his gun towards Tristan's chest.

"Shoot me and she dies too," came Tristan's harried voice still taking care to maintain his crisp English accent. Frozen in indecision, Fisher looked knowing the moment had passed to use surprise if there ever had been one. He felt his arms weaken, his head became light, beginning to sway to the side, he blurted out.

"You evil mother fucker." The words seemed to recharge his strength.

"Evil?" Tristan replied, his voice dripping with fake surprise. "Just trying to make a living. Capitalism, supply and demand. If it wasn't me then it would be someone else, and all that bullshit. You should give it a try." Fisher watched Tristan's grip around her neck tighten, kicking at the back of her ankles. "Stand up bitch," he said, keeping his eyes fixed on Fisher as he in turn watched Harris and her pained expression rise to obscure his face.

"Get me a chopper and she lives," Tristan said, despite being behind his shield he could hear the smile in his voice. Fisher nearly let a shot ring out, aiming for a thin sliver of arm swaying in and out.

"You're not leaving this room alive," Fisher shouted.

Harris flicked her stare to the floor.

"If we don't do this soon then I'm taking her with me. I hope you had enough time to get to know our dear Carrie." Tristan pulled her backward as the second door flung open, Biggy and Miller bursting in with their rifles levelled at Harris's torso.

As he jumped Fisher caught a glimpse of his face, his eyes wide and intense. He watched Tristan's arm muscles tense and Harris let out a blood curdling cry, he could almost see the electricity streaking through her body.

All he could do was watch. He flicked his eyes to Biggy, who shook his head in reply. Twitching around the room, desperate to see something he'd missed, something that could turn the tide in their favour.

For the first time he noticed the glass doors to the balcony and looked back to Biggy who shook his head again. Anger built and his blood felt like it boiled as it coursed through his veins when he settled back on Harris. Although the pain had stopped, she sobbed, bloody tears rolling down her face.

His thoughts flashed to Susie, but she was safe. They'd come all this way and they'd saved her. He'd succeeded in his self-imposed mission and along the way he'd found someone special. Now Tristan was about to wipe her out before they had a chance to find out what could be between them. With his gun wavering, Fisher could feel his own pain building. Tears of frustration rolled down his face.

"Take the shot," Harris shouted without moving her lips. "Take the shot. He'll do it again. He'll take Susie again."

Fisher felt something inside him erupt.

"Noooooooo," he screamed at the top of his voice, the sound reverberating as he felt an invisible energy pulse from his fingers in a wave across the room. "Drop your weapon," he screamed slowly with his face contorted.

Tristan's gun hand dropped to his side leaving a deep red mark on Harris's face. Miller and Biggy, powerless too, let their weapons relax. Tristan let go of her throat and she pushed herself forward, falling to the floor, gasping for air on all fours. Each were spectators as Fisher stepped forward, his gun hand pushing out in front.

Tristan's gun hand twitched. Fisher pulled the trigger clean, straight and all the way home. The bullet hit the centre mass, the force smashing Tristan's body into the wall behind, but as he fell backwards his gun came level, the muzzle lighting up to smash a round into Fisher's stomach.

Two thumps of air came from his right. He watched two holes appear in Tristan's forehead, his expression full of confusion as his view tilted upward, further and further until he felt a great pain across the back of his head and everything went dark.

64

"James."

The muffled word came as a surprise from the darkness.

"James," the soft voice said again, her words crystal clear in the warmth of the room as dull colours slowly came into form.

Her heartfelt call repeated and Fisher opened his eyes to see Harris leant over, her face only a breath from his. She's going to kiss me, he thought, excitement running through him as his vision cleared.

"No. I'm not."

He watched her mouth, the words in silence and he blinked, pulling himself up against Biggy's outstretched arm.

"He'll be fine," Harris said, not holding back her laughter, drawing away as he rose.

Rubbing the back of his head, he stood, pulling down the vest which had been folded up to uncover his unmarked stomach which hurt like hell.

The pain fell away as he saw Tristan's body and he drank in the image of the wound in his chest, two bloodless holes, high on his face.

He turned to Miller and Biggy; both replied with relaxed salutes in unison.

"Job done," said Biggy. "The bus is waiting outside."

"And look what I found," Harris said, waving a leather-bound book in her hand. "It's a list of transactions. Codes for names. It should give us enough to get our teeth into so we can trace the rest of the women."

Her expression so filled with joy, Fisher couldn't help but wonder if the pain he'd seen in her face had all been in his imagination.

Miller herded them out of the room. With Fisher's head still foggy, his nostrils filled with the unmistakable smell of cordite as they walked back through the house.

The four squad mates joined their exit procession with a few flesh injuries amongst them, but nothing more.

Tramping across the sand, Fisher caught sight of a beached white catamaran, men in combat fatigues herding them aboard.

Susie stood in a low doorway waving.

Taking short steps to board, he turned back to the house.

"No prisoners?" he said to no one in particular.

"Swimmer canoeists don't stand the embuggerance of prisoners," a Marine announced proudly.

The engines revved, Biggy and Hotwire pushed the boat off the beach, jumping on at the last minute and they sailed off the sand towards the waiting destroyer somewhere out in the ocean.

Fisher watched the house halo on the horizon, a thick plume of smoke rising into the night sky.

65

Fisher sat opposite Harris, each on an overstuffed leather sofa, their bodies moulding into the comfort. A squat table rose between them. On its top stood a crystal glass pitcher, near empty of a red concoction beside two half-filled glasses.

Together they waited in the basement lounge of the British High Commission in Bridgetown, showered and changed after disembarking HMS Westminster with the sunlight streaming on their backs over the horizon.

With her wound cleaned and held together with butterfly stitches, her hair hung loose around the shoulders of her crisp white blouse.

"Thank you," she said, as she took a sip of her drink with her feet curled underneath her.

"And thank you," he replied, raising his glass.

She stood, moving the pitcher around the table and sat next to him.

"The boys are looking forward to working with you," she said, then paused, the silence anything but uncomfortable. "Did you know you could do that before?"

"Do what? Rescue beautiful maidens?" he quickly replied with a smile.

Harris shot him a playful look, raising her eyebrows.

It was his turn to pause. "No. Never been able to project like that. Don't know if I could do it again," he said, then went quiet for a moment. "But I want to find out on my own terms."

"You can trust me," she replied, her gaze never leaving his.

"I know."

With her head moving slowly closer, he could feel his pulse pounding across his body. Staring into her hazel eyes, she looked back unflinching.

Her breath fell gently on his face, their lips touched and the door flew open.

Susie burst through the doorway, her face sleep-drowsy and they both pulled away, resting against the ends of the sofa.

"It's time to go," she said, oblivious to the interruption and disappearing as quickly as she had come.

They lingered, exchanging grins, then grabbed their diplomatic passports and left the room.

66

Fisher stared at the lumbering hulk of the 777's wing through the triple paned glass, cool air brushing across his face. He looked to his phone, his finger tapping on Andrew's number as he swirled ice in a short glass of clear liquid.

Taking a sip, he gritted his teeth as the vodka bit at the back of his throat.

"Fucker," Andrew's sleep hardened voice came back against his ear.

Fisher couldn't help but laugh.

"Sorry, mate, did I wake you?" he said, with his laughter growing in volume.

"You're on your way home," he replied, no question in his voice.

"How did you…?"

"Susie's dad's been spreading the news. You weren't mentioned but I guessed you'd be following."

"I'll tell you all about it over a beer."

"Too right you will and you're in luck. Alan's organised a party. We've all gotta be there, like it or not, he said. You should get a text soon."

"You won't get any complaint from me. Get some sleep and I'll see you this afternoon when you pick me up from Heathrow, Terminal 3. Flight BA3154," Fisher said, hanging up before Andrew could process.

He laughed to himself, thinking of Andrew's reaction. Throwing back the vodka, he stared out through the window to the white clouds below. One last party, then the hard work would really start.

The bed in first class gave him the best sleep he'd had in an age, only opening his eyes as the descent announcement drifted over the speakers.

On landing, the three of them were herded off the plane by the cabin director and taken to the airport's VIP lounge to be met by two tall suits whom Harris seemed to be very familiar with.

Susie reluctantly let herself be taken home by her parents as Fisher promised he would come and see her as soon as he could.

As he left her drifting to Arrivals, he held back, not wanting to be spotted by her small crowd; not ready for the questions he didn't know how he could answer.

With Susie gone, one of the agents produced an attaché case, ripping away the yellow diplomatic seals and opening it to reveal their side arms.

As Harris checked her weapon, Fisher saw a familiar grey Merlin landing a short way over the tarmac.

"We head to the Breacons in ten minutes. Dawson wants to know your answer," Harris said, her voice soft, but back to business.

"Tell him it's a yes, but I can't start till tomorrow. Got a party to go to," Fisher replied, a grin beaming. "You can come if you want." He saw the hesitation in her thoughts, but the shake of her head showed which side of her won over.

The suit-clad agent prompted him to take his weapon.

"You take it for now," Fisher said, turning to Harris.

"No. You're a valuable asset, Fisher, and not just to us."

After a moment of hesitation, he took the weapon, inspected the empty chamber, pulled back the slide and placed it in his holster. Arrangements were made; he would meet back in the terminal at the same time tomorrow.

As he turned to leave, he paused. He should invite her again. Give her another chance. They could let their hair down together.

Fisher looked back to speak, but she'd already started walking to the airfield.

He turned back and headed out into the arrivals lounge with his head down until he heard a loud expletive break the hum of the concourse.

Andrew beamed as he stood leaning, almost toppling the flimsy barrier. They exchanged a firm handshake before it turned to a hug normally reserved for when they'd been drinking.

Neither stopped chatting as they walked to the car park; James paused, opening the car door with his gaze turning skyward as he caught sight of the Merlin rising into the air.

He should have called out to her the second time, but he'd be seeing her tomorrow, picking up from where they'd left off. Butterflies bubbled in his stomach as his thoughts turned to the adventures to come.

On the short drive, James settled back in the car seat, happy for Andrew's non-stop narrative of everything that had been going on whilst he'd been away. All the while he knew Andrew was dying to ask, but gave James as much space as he needed.

"So what shall we do till seven?" Andrew asked as he squeezed the car into a space outside James's flat.

"Six. Alan's text told me the party's at six."

"Oh, okay. What shall we do till six?"

"You can help me pack. I'm going away for a little while, new job. I'll tell you all about it when we crack the beers."

His flat was as he'd left it. The smashed phone sat on the table and he didn't touch the symbol of his old life; instead, he spent most of the time in silence, taking in Andrew's stories and before he knew it, the time to head to the party came.

Andrew explained Alan had rented a new flat just down the road as he'd finally managed to get a manager's job at the local supermarket.

James took comfort that everyone's lives were the same and hoped Susie would be able to settle back into normality.

Still with the one-sided chatter, they walked the ten minutes to the new flat, already planning for a cab ride home with the amount of alcohol they were planning to drink.

James knocked on the door at the new address and Alan quickly greeted them, sweeping his curly hair from his forehead. His eyes widened and cheeks bunched in surprise as he saw Andrew and James standing on the doorstep, but before they could ask, he relaxed with a handshake as they stepped in through the front door.

"Just moved in," Alan stuttered, pointing to the front room, empty aside from two white plastic garden chairs. "Getting the rest of my stuff at the weekend."

James looked at Andrew and both laughed.

"Don't be nervous. It's only us," Andrew said, shaking his head as he spoke, but before he could speak, Alan disappeared and came back with two warm beers.

"You not having one?" Andrew asked. "Is it a fucking party or what?"

"More on its way," Alan replied, chewing his lip.

Fisher's phone rang in his head and he picked out the handset so as not to confuse the others.

"Fisher, it's Clark."

"Hi, Clark. Don't worry, I'll be there in the morning."

"Sorry to bother you, but we've picked up three rather suspicious men coming to the building."

"How do you...," he stopped mid-sentence; his mouth gaped as he heard a heavy knock at the door.

Alan turned, walking to the short hallway.

"I suggest you leave via the back," came Clark's voice.

Fisher didn't understand. How did they know someone was at the door? Were they watching him? What the hell? Was he not allowed to have a night off before he started?

"Are you okay?" Andrew asked as he saw the pained expression on James's face.

"It's nothing," he replied, but his mouth fell wide as three very large men wearing black woollen hats stepped from the hall, their confused expressions alternating between James and Andrew.

Alan ran in from behind with his hand outstretched, pointing in James's direction.

"Him," was all Alan said before the three men pulled down ski masks and pushed their hands into leather gloves. "Don't let him touch you," Alan shouted.

By now, Fisher had filled in the blanks.

As he reached for his gun, another insistent knock pounded at the door. Two of the masked men pulled pistols, the third grasped a long thin baton as they edged towards him.

At their backs, three loud gunshots burst, light pouring in from the hallway.

Guns levelled in James's direction. Andrew jumped in their path and Fisher pushed him to the side. A loud crack rang off from somewhere in the room, the noise dulling his hearing.

Andrew went down, falling to a heap with his arms at an unnatural angle.

A sudden shot of electricity ravaged through Fisher's body, spasming his head to the side and forcing him to watch as Harris fired off a volley.

His vision slowed and he felt himself falling, watching two of the men smash backwards to the wall, the third ripping at his mask and launching towards Harris.

Fisher's head smashed against something hard, sending him spinning in the opposite direction.

With darkness racing in from the edge of his vision he saw his best friend's blank expression.

Fisher's eyes startled wide to a bullet hole in the centre of Andrew's forehead.

To be continued.......

Liked what you read?

Please leave a review on the platform you used for the purchase or **Goodreads.com**. Honest reviews are difficult to come by and are so important to indie authors like me.

FREE BOOK

If you enjoyed the first in the James Fisher series and want to read more about Agent Carrie Harris, why not check out OPERATION DAWN WOLF for FREE. All you have to do is join my mailing list at www.gjstevens.com

Operation Dawn Wolf is a spy-thriller following Recruit Harris as she endeavours to survive the near-impossible Special Operations selection process. If you like high-stakes thrills, strong female heroes, and action-packed adventures, then you won't be able to put down GJ Stevens' intriguing novel.

Other Books by
GJ Stevens

Post-apocalyptic Thrillers

IN THE END – Out Now
BEFORE THE END – Out Now
AFTER THE END - November 2020

SURVIVOR – Your Guide to Surviving the Apocalypse – Out Now

Action Adventure Thrillers

James Fisher Series

Fate's Ambition – Out Now
Their Right to Vengeance - 2020
Book 3 (TBC) - 2021

Carrie Harris Series

Operation Dawn Wolf – Out Now
Lesson Learned (TBC) - 2020
From The Dead (TBC) - 2021

Printed in Poland
by Amazon Fulfillment
Poland Sp. z o.o., Wrocław

52996248R00214